A Queen's Rebel

First published in eBook and paperback 2024

•

© Sam Burnell 2024

•

The right of Sam Burnell to be identified as the author of this work has been asserted by her in accordance with the Copyright, Designs and Patents Act 1988.

All rights reserved. No part of this publication may be reproduced, stored in or introduced into a retrieval system, or transmitted, in any form, or by any means (electronic, mechanical, photocopying, recording or otherwise) without the prior written permission of the writer. Any person who does any unauthorised act in relation to this publication may be liable to criminal prosecution and civil claims for damages.

Sam Burnell

Thank you for respecting the hard work of this author.

***Please note, this book is written in British English, so some spellings will vary from US English.***

A Queen's Rebel

Sam Burnell

**For All My Children**

*Jules*
*Saffron Syxx Rozi*
*Savannah Skye Juliet Storm*
*Spyke Gabriel Reuban*

A Queen's Rebel

## *Character List*
### *The English Court*

*William Cecil – Secretary of State*
*Somer – Crown Servant*

### *Fitzwarren Household*
*Catherine Fitzwarren – wife of Jack*
*Elizabeth (Lizbet) Fitzwarren – Wife of Richard*
### *Knights of St John*
*Emilio de Nevarra – Nephew of Philip of Spain*
*Sebastian – Monk of the Order*
### *Other Characters*
*Master Threadmill – Jack's Lawyer*
*Myles Devereux – a London Merchant*
*Andrew Forrester – Steward at Cumnor Place*
*Alphonso – Part of the Italian Embassy*

Sam Burnell

## Contents

| | |
|---|---|
| CHAPTER ONE | 8 |
| CHAPTER TWO | 12 |
| CHAPTER FOUR | 28 |
| CHAPTER FIVE | 37 |
| CHAPTER SIX | 45 |
| CHAPTER SEVEN | 57 |
| CHAPTER EIGHT | 70 |
| CHAPTER NINE | 81 |
| CHAPTER TEN | 91 |
| CHAPTER ELEVEN | 104 |
| CHAPTER TWELVE | 113 |
| CHAPTER THIRTEEN | 131 |
| CHAPTER FOURTEEN | 137 |
| CHAPTER FIFTEEN | 141 |
| CHAPTER SIXTEEN | 153 |
| CHAPTER SEVENTEEN | 161 |
| CHAPTER EIGHTEEN | 167 |
| CHAPTER NINETEEN | 174 |
| CHAPTER TWENTY | 187 |
| CHAPTER TWENTY-ONE | 202 |
| CHAPTER TWENTY-TWO | 209 |
| CHAPTER TWENTY-THREE | 218 |

A Queen's Rebel

CHAPTER TWENTY-FOUR ................................. 229
CHAPTER TWENTY-FIVE ................................. 237
CHAPTER TWENTY-SIX ................................... 245
CHAPTER TWENTY-SEVEN ............................. 251
CHAPTER TWENTY-EIGHT ............................... 257
CHAPTER TWENTY-NINE ................................. 266
CHAPTER THIRTY ............................................. 269
CHAPTER THIRTY-ONE ................................... 278
CHAPTER THIRTY-TWO ................................... 287
CHAPTER THIRTY-THREE ................................ 295
CHAPTER THIRTY-FOUR .................................. 302
CHAPTER THIRTY-FIVE ................................... 305

## CHAPTER ONE

On his knees he stared down at the body.

The silence around him thick and suffocating. His hand still gripped the knife, its blade slick with the red evidence of its work. The gash across the throat of the man before him—a second unhappy mouth etched deep into the flesh—the cut deliberate, clean, and precise. A cruel reminder of the finality of death. The blood had ceased to pour from the veins, pooling beneath the body like a quiet, dark reflection, an eerily serene pond spreading across the floorboards. He regarded the corpse with a curious mixture of annoyance and contempt.

The body, once full of life, now lay in an artful final arrangement. An arm outstretched, fingers delicately curled, as if still reaching for something that had escaped its grasp. The face, though twisted in the last moments of life, still bore a horrified expression—eyes wide, locked in disbelief and terror. But soon, that would soften and slacken as the muscles in his face gave way to the stillness of death, leaving behind nothing but the quiet serenity of the inevitable. His eyes lingered on the body, his breath steady, his thoughts wandering, but only for a moment.

The guards, summoned in haste, tumbled through the unlocked door, their boots steps immediately faltering on the boards. Men at the rear banging into their comrades as they drew to a sudden halt. Haste wasn't needed - the man kneeling on the floor was making no bid to escape, and those few first moments of discovery were theirs alone to savour. What they had found wasn't just a grim discovery but a moment frozen in time.

A virgin scene.

# A Queen's Rebel

The heavy scent was an unmistakable one, smothering that of aged wood, dust, and cold hearth ash. Tinged with the smell of iron from the forge, the metallic smell was raw, over-powering and at the same time repulsive and intoxicating. Evoking fascination and unease in those gazing at the macabre.

None of them dared to speak immediately. They were transfixed, as if the very air had thickened around them, like statues in the face of a grotesque masterpiece. The body on the floor—beautiful in its stillness—seemed to have become something other than just a man. It was now part of the room, part of the atmosphere, part of something larger that none of them could quite grasp. The six men who had entered the room approached cautiously, eyes wide, alert and silently delighting in what they had found. As if frozen, the scene before them, statue-like, was there to be admired in all its gory finery. So recent was the death that they knew the murdered man's breath lingered still in the air.

Not one man drew a blade.

There was no need.

And in respect for the deceased soul that had so recently been released, when they did speak it was with hushed tones.

A guard cleared his throat, the noise loud in the stillness, he spoke the words that broke the silence. "Rise, sir," he commanded, as if that might somehow change what had already transpired.

The spell broke, the statue dissolved as they watched. The man reached and pulled a cloak over the body obscuring from their view the tortured eyes, and they were disappointed that their inquisitive gazes could no longer feast upon the violation.

Expelling a long breath that set the dust motes dancing in the shafts of light that lay across the corpse the murderer rose smoothly, his eyes still lingering on the body.

# Sam Burnell

No one moved.

So tranquil was the scene, the guard could find within himself no sharp word of command or order, he felt as if he was intruding, as if they had burst in upon lovers, the discovery of murder should not be so.

But it was.

This was not a scene of murder but instead one of sacrifice. It was wrong. Where were the sharp movements, shouts, pleas, the wail of the dying, the objections of those about to be arrested? Where?

The guard, feeling the weight of the moment, spoke softly but firmly. "You'll need to come with us."

They took him to the Beauchamp Tower, which caused him to smile as he was led up the narrow stairs. The guards did not pressure him inside, and neither did he make any attempt to flee, but walked before them as they bid. A guard opened the door, the keys a noisy and uncoordinated jangle, at odds with everything they had witnessed, he looked up apologetically at the prisoner and held the lose keys close to still their noise when the door was locked.

The man let out a long breath and surveyed his new accommodation. A table, a chair, a candlestick, a window, paned with glass and closed, walls decorated with the graffiti of the damned and a bed. Names, final words and even pleas were cut into the stone walls, some old and darkened with age, but many fresher, their lines clean and the outlines of the letters fresh and bright.

Peeling off the ruined doublet he dumped the blood sodden garment on the top of the table, sighed when he observed that so much blood had soaked through to stain his shirt, and shaking his head reclined on the bed.

A Queen's Rebel

Pulling his boots off and taking a moment to arrange the pillow he wondered if sleep would be too much of a request.

After all, it had been a long day.

## CHAPTER TWO
### THREE MONTHS AGO

When the steward appeared in the doorway, Lizbet's hands were sticky with dough. His expression was a mixture of discomfort and unease. His usual self-assurance seemed to have deserted him, replaced by something that made Lizbet instantly wary.

"Lizbet, there are men... from the Order of St. John," he began hesitantly, "asking for your husband. And Lord Fitzwarren."

Lizbet frowned, pausing in her work. The Order of St. John? Knights? Her pulse quickened as she wiped her hands on her apron. "Knights?"

The steward shifted his weight. "They're in the Lord's room. I told them both were absent, but they refused to accept that as an answer. I told them Lady Catherine was at the market, so they are asking for you."

Lizbet's stomach tightened, apprehension mingling with irritation. Knights from the Order of St. John asking for Richard and Jack? What could they possibly want here? She glanced down at her flour-dusted dress, briefly considering whether to change, but dismissed the thought. What would it matter?

Snatching a damp cloth, she wiped her hands with quick, frustrated strokes. "This will not be pleasant whether I'm dressed for the occasion or not," she muttered.

Straightening her shoulders and taking a deep breath, she marched toward the Lord's room, the steward trailing behind her like a shadow.

When she opened the door, the sight that greeted her made her breath catch in her throat. Three men stood inside, their presence filling the

# A Queen's Rebel

room with an oppressive air. They were tall, broad, and imposing, their gold-trimmed cloaks and polished boots a display of wealth and power. One of them turned at her entrance, his sharp eyes boring into her as if assessing her worth.

"I am Elizabeth Fitzwarren," she began, forcing her voice to remain steady. "My husband, Richard, as you have already—"

Her words faltered. Next to one of the knights stood a woman holding a small child. Lizbet froze, her gaze locking onto the boy. His dark curls framed a round, cherubic face, and the familiarity of his features sent a jolt through her chest.

"Dear God," she whispered, her voice barely audible.

The knight who had turned to face her inclined his head with an air of impatience. "I am Señor Fabrizio Montella, and as you can see, your son has travelled with us from Malta. I am here to speak with your husband. Where is he?"

Lizbet's heart pounded as she stared at the child. Her son. Angelo. She hadn't thought of him as more than an abstract idea for years, and now here he was, in the flesh, staring back at her with wide, uncertain eyes.

"My husband is not here," she managed, her voice tight. "We received word that Lord Fitzwarren and his brother are in Scotland."

Montella's brow furrowed. "Scotland? Why?"

"The Queen's army is deployed there," Lizbet said automatically, though her focus was still on the boy.

"He is part of the Queen's force?" Montella pressed.

"I—I don't know," she stammered, her voice faltering. The boy squirmed in the nurse's arms, reaching toward the ground.

Montella turned to his men and barked orders in Italian. "We are getting nothing from this woman.

We will go to the court. Send word immediately if he returns," he added curtly to Lizbet before sweeping from the room, his men following in a swirl of cloaks and commanding presence.

The room seemed to deflate when they were gone, the silence stretching out uncomfortably.

The nurse, awkward and flustered, attempted a curtsy before setting Angelo down. "Go, Angelo," she said softly in Italian, urging him toward Lizbet. "Go to your lady mother."

Angelo hesitated, his thumb slipping into his mouth as he regarded Lizbet with cautious curiosity. He took two small steps forward but stopped abruptly. His small face crumpled, and with a loud wail, he turned and hurled himself back into the nurse's skirts, clutching them desperately.

"Angelo, Angelo," the nurse murmured, crouching to soothe him. Her voice was gentle, and her words were a string of apologies in Italian. "It has been a long journey," she explained, looking up at Lizbet with a strained smile.

Lizbet, swallowing the lump in her throat, forced herself to focus on something practical. "Is he hungry?" she asked her voice tight but kind. "Come with me to the kitchens. Let's find you both something to eat."

The nurse relieved, nodded and scooped Angelo up into her arms. Lizbet led the way, her mind racing.

That night, long after the house had gone quiet, Lizbet sat alone by the fire, her hands trembling in her lap. Angelo's arrival had shaken her to her core. She had expected to feel something—maternal instinct, relief, even joy—but all she felt was guilt.

She hadn't wanted him here. She hadn't wanted to face him, to see Andrew Kineer's face stamped onto a boy she was supposed to love. Angelo's rounded cheeks, his bright eyes, and even

# A Queen's Rebel

his defiant little pout were all echoes of a man she despised.

And yet, he was innocent. A child. Her child.

Tears welled in her eyes, spilling over onto her cheeks. She hadn't cried when she left him in Malta, nor when she boarded the ship to England and closed the door on that chapter of her life. But now, confronted with Angelo's presence, the weight of her rejection crushed her.

Richard and Jack were gone, and Catherine—snide, superior Catherine—laughed when she returned and found out Angelo had arrived. Lizbet had no one to turn to, no one to confide in. Her loneliness was suffocating, and her guilt only made it worse.

She knew she would have to accept Angelo and find a way to bridge the chasm between them. He was hers, whether she liked it or not. But how? How could she love him when every glance at his face reminded her of the man who had caused her so much pain? What would Richard and Jack think when they saw him? Saw that the shadow of Andrew Kineer still followed them.

By morning, Lizbet had pushed aside her feelings of guilt and grief, focusing instead on the practicalities of Angelo's arrival. The boy needed clothes suitable for England's damp and chilly weather, proper shoes to replace the soft leather slippers he had arrived in, and, perhaps most importantly, he needed to learn English.

Maria Bianchi, Angelo's nurse, and the boy spoke only Italian. Lizbet, fluent in the language, found herself mediating between them and the household staff. It was a small satisfaction to her that Catherine, for all her sharp wit and condescension, would not have been able to manage this task.

Catherine's French was passable, but Italian? Not a word.

As Lizbet dressed for the day, she considered her plan. Angelo's first lesson would begin immediately with English words for the world around him. If nothing else, it would give her a reason to spend time with him, to start the slow, uncertain process of building a bond.

The boy was seated at the table in the kitchen, his chubby fingers poking at a slice of bread and honey. At the same time, Maria hovered beside him, her hands fluttering nervously. Lizbet entered, greeted Maria with a polite nod, and took a seat across from Angelo.

"Buongiorno, Angelo," Lizbet said gently.

He looked up at her, his dark eyes curious but cautious. "Buongiorno," he replied, his voice small but clear.

Lizbet offered a smile. "Inglese, Angelo. 'Good morning.'"

Angelo frowned, his thumb edging toward his mouth.

"Good," Lizbet repeated slowly, pointing to herself, then the room, "morning."

Maria muttered something under her breath in Italian, clearly uneasy with Lizbet's intervention. Angelo hesitated, glancing between the two women.

"Good morning," he said finally, the words thick and awkward on his tongue.

Lizbet's smile widened. "Bravo, Angelo!" She clapped her hands softly, and the boy's cheeks flushed with a shy smile.

Later that day, Lizbet took Angelo to Master Drew the tailor. The trip was an adventure for the boy, who had never seen an English town before. He clung to Maria's hand, his small fingers clutching hers tightly as they walked through the streets, but his grip loosened as his curiosity grew.

The small bell over the tailor's door tinkled as Lizbet stepped inside. Maria and Angelo followed

# A Queen's Rebel

behind. The nurse's expression was wary as her eyes darted around the unfamiliar space. The shop was tidy but bustling. Bolts of fabric were stacked high on shelves, and the musty scent of wool filled the air.

Master Drew, a stout man with a shock of silver-streaked hair and sharp eyes that missed nothing, was bent over a client, measuring a length of dark blue fabric against his shoulders. His apprentice stood at the ready, holding chalk and pins, though he appeared more nervous than helpful.

The tailor glanced up at the sound of the bell, his eyes landing on Lizbet. Recognition flashed across his face, followed quickly by delight. He straightened abruptly, abandoning his client mid-measurement.

"Lady Fitzwarren!" he exclaimed, his voice carrying through the shop. "It's been far too long! How fares your husband?"

The client, a well-dressed merchant, turned, his mouth open to protest the interruption, but Drew was already waving him off. "Thomas, see to this gentleman," he instructed his apprentice briskly, thrusting the fabric into the boy's hands. "Ensure it's a perfect fit."

Thomas blinked, wide-eyed, as he fumbled to take over while Drew bustled toward Lizbet, his arms spread wide.

"My lady, it is an honour as always!" he said, bowing deeply. "To what do I owe this pleasure? And who is this fine young gentleman?" His eyes landed on Angelo, who was half-hiding behind Lizbet's skirts but peeking out with wide, curious eyes.

Lizbet smiled politely, tilting her head in acknowledgement. "Master Drew, this is Angelo. He has recently arrived from Italy and needs proper English attire."

Drew's sharp eyes sparkled at the mention of business. "Ah, Master Angelo! Welcome to England, young sir!" He crouched slightly, putting himself at Angelo's eye level. "I'll wager you'll be the finest-dressed lad in all of London when we're done here, won't you?"

Angelo's thumb found its way to his mouth, and he stared solemnly at the tailor, saying nothing.

"He's a little shy," Lizbet explained, glancing down at the boy.

"Quite understandable," Drew said, rising with a knowing nod. "A new place, new people—it can be overwhelming for one so young. But no matter!"

He clapped his hands briskly, summoning the apprentice, who darted over with a measuring tape. "William! Clear the station at the back and fetch the finest bolts of fabric we have—nothing but the best for Lady Fitzwarren's young gentleman."

Lizbet stepped forward, smoothing his unruly curls. "He will need several sets of clothes," she began, her tone calm but businesslike.

Drew's smile widened, practically splitting his round face, and he asked. "Several sets? And linen and hose?"

"Of course," Lizbet confirmed.

"And the....style, if I can ask?" Drew asked hesitantly.

"He is my son, Master Drew, so please dress him accordingly," Lizbet said.

"My lady, you honour me! We'll see to it immediately. William, where are you!" Drew barked.

"Yes, Master Drew!" the apprentice squeaked, rushing to obey.

Drew turned back to Lizbet and gestured toward a plush chair near the fitting area. "Please, make yourself comfortable, my lady. And Master Angelo, if you'd be so kind as to let me take your measurements? It won't take but a moment."

Angelo glanced up at Maria, his small face uncertain. She crouched beside him, her voice gentle. "It's alright, Angelo."

The boy hesitated, then nodded slowly, allowing Drew to take his hand and lead him to the fitting platform. Maria hovered nearby, her worry etched on

# A Queen's Rebel

her face as she watched Angelo submit to the measuring tape.

Drew worked quickly but carefully, jotting down Angelo's measurements in his notebook. "What a fine lad you have, my lady," he said, glancing over his shoulder at Lizbet. "He'll cut quite the figure in proper English attire, I assure you."

Lizbet smiled faintly, watching as Angelo tilted his head curiously at the tape stretched across his shoulders. Drew's chatter seemed to put the boy at ease, and by the time the tailor had finished, Angelo was even smiling faintly.

Drew clapped his hands again, summoning his apprentice. "Thomas, fetch the charcoal grey and forest green wool."

Lizbet rose from her seat, smoothing her skirts. "Thank you, Master Drew. I trust you'll have everything ready soon?"

"Of course, my lady," Drew said with a bow. "It will be my utmost priority. And can I suggest you make a visit two shops along to Master Rhymes, he is an esteemed cobbler."

As they prepared to leave, Drew knelt once more to Angelo. "Master Angelo, you'll be quite the gentleman when you return to collect your new wardrobe. And perhaps, next time, you'll let me teach you a little English, eh?"

Angelo tilted his head, clearly not understanding, but Lizbet translated, and the boy nodded shyly.

Lizbet inclined her head toward Drew. "Thank you, Master Drew."

Drew, beaming, opened the door for them, bowing deeply as they stepped out into the busy street and headed towards the cobblers.

As they walked away, Angelo slipped his small hand into Lizbet's, glancing up at her with a shy smile. Lizbet felt a lump rise in her throat, her heart softening toward the boy. It wasn't love—not yet—but it was a start.

## CHAPTER THREE
## TWO MONTHS AGO

Richard arrived at the Fitzwarren house. Catherine would be happy to find out that her husband, Jack, was back in London, but she wasn't going to be too pleased when she found out he was injured and currently in the care of the Order of St John—particularly when one of their more enigmatic members, Emilio de Nevarra was also in London.

They met in the room that had once been occupied by his father. Apart from the removal of the bed and the old man's chair, it hadn't changed much. A small fire burnt in the hearth, and Richard took one of the fireside seats while he waited. Though well-lit by the morning sun streaming through the windows, the room felt colder than it should have; despite the fire, a quiet tension seemed to hang in the air. His feet crossed at the ankles, and resting back in the chair, his dark eyes met those of the woman staring back at him from the painting on the wall. Jack had lost weight over the last few weeks as they'd journeyed back to London; his cheeks were hollowed, and his similarity to the woman on the wall was even more striking than usual.

The door opened. Catherine appeared in the frame, her expression unreadable. Richard rose smoothly from the chair and smiled, stepping towards her. Her eyes had already run over him; her gaze had missed nothing. His clothes were travel-stained, and his boots lacked polish.

"Where's Jack?" Her voice was nervous and high-pitched, and her hands suddenly fastened into the fabric of her dress. The still-open door behind her had been forgotten.

"He's in London, and he's well," Richard reassured quickly. He took her hand in his and drew her into the room before pushing the heavy door closed. "You are looking well."

"Why is Jack not here?" Catherine's feet were planted firmly on the floor, and she didn't move any further into the room.

"Sit, please, and I will tell you," Richard said.

Panic widened her eyes, and Richard spoke quickly, his tone light and humorous. "Do not fear for him. Jack is as hearty and whole as when you last saw him, only just a little fried around the edges."

"What do you mean?" Catherine said.

"I cannot, in all conscience, converse with a pregnant woman who is standing in a draught near the door. Will you please sit down," Richard said; this time, he took her arm in his, and she allowed him to lead her to the chairs near the fire.

Catherine lowered herself into the chair with a motion peculiar to pregnant women, and when she was seated, Richard sat opposite.

"Tell me," Catherine said without preamble.

"We have just arrived back in London. I could not send a message, and I arrived here before any other stray news could reach your door. Jack will be well, he broke an arm and suffered some burns ..."

"What happened to him?" Catherine's voice was explosive in comparison to Richard's calm, reasoned tone.

"War is what happened, the viciousness of men's actions. Jack was caught in the midst of it. He will be home soon," Richard couldn't help but notice how tired she looked, her shoulders heavy as if weighed down by more than just the pregnancy. "He has a broken arm and several broken ribs. I am assured he will be home with you again very soon."

She raised an eyebrow at his words. "Where is he?"

"Catherine, Jack needed the best care he could get. The Order has one of the finest hospitals in the

# A Queen's Rebel

city, and I assure you, Jack is in good hands. I would not have left him there had I thought otherwise," Richard said.

Catherine's eyes narrowed. "He is with the Order and no doubt Emilio de Nevarra," she said, her voice tight. "I see. That explains a great deal."

Richard leaned forward slightly. "He is there for only a few days, no more, and then he will return home to you." Richard lied smoothly.

Catherine's expression hardened, her lips pressing into a thin line. "I don't trust him, Richard. I've seen the way he looks at Jack – and so have you. I knew he'd followed him to Scotland, I have my sources as well, and now they are back he is still keeping Jack close."

Richard felt a sudden pang of discomfort. He'd not realised she knew that De Nevarra had been with Jack in Scotland, and Catherine had clearly had several months to consider and resent that fact. Still, he couldn't help but feel sympathy for her. She was pregnant and alone most of the time while Jack was away.

"I understand your feelings," Richard said carefully, "The Order's reputation is built on its dedication to healing and care, and I am sure you'd want the best for Jack."

She shifted uncomfortably in her seat, her fingers brushing lightly over her belly as though seeking comfort. "And what of me, Richard? What am I supposed to do while my husband is in that hospital? You think I haven't seen the way Emilio looks at him like he's some kind of prize to be won? I don't trust him."

Richard stood and moved toward her, his expression softening. He could see the strain in her face, the worry etched into the lines of her forehead. He placed a hand gently on her shoulder, trying to offer her reassurance. "Catherine, Jack will be back soon. De Nevarra is not in London either. I'll personally make sure we get him home as soon as possible. He's been asking for you, and when I leave here, I will be taking him news that his wife and his child are safe."

Catherine didn't speak for a long while, her gaze distant. Finally, she exhaled sharply as though giving in to the exhaustion of the conversation. "I suppose I'll have to take your word for it."

She finally gave him a small, reluctant smile, though it was strained. "Thank you, Richard. I've been so afraid these past few months. I just want Jack home and this child to have a father."

"I, too, want that to be the case, and Jack also."

Richard left shortly afterwards, wondering exactly how many lies he'd just told, at least three. Jack hadn't regained consciousness, Emilio was most definitely in London and at his brother's side, and Jack hadn't been coherent for long enough to ask for a drink, let alone enquire about his wife's health.

Richard found Lizbet at the Fitzwarren house out in the garden, her skirts pulled up from the damp grass, her arm in mid-swing as she pitched a stick into the air. The dog, an eager and muscular beast, shot forward with a bound before halting abruptly, its head whipping back toward its mistress as if questioning her silent command.

Lizbet's voice rang out, clear and firm, as she sent the dog after the stick. "Go."

Richard let his presence be known with a wry smile. "It's not just marlinspikes you can pitch well."

The sound of his voice cut through the air. Lizbet froze, her expression hardening, and the dog turned sharply, claws tearing at the grass as it hurtled back toward her side. The animal's ears flattened, lips pulling back to reveal sharp, glistening teeth, and a deep, guttural growl rumbled from its chest.

# A Queen's Rebel

Richard stopped dead, his hands raising in a placating gesture. "I see Devereux followed my instructions. What is he called?"

Lizbet made no immediate move to answer. The dog positioned itself before her like a sentinel, its body taut with readiness. Its growl deepened, and Richard's smile faltered under the beast's steady glare.

"Lizbet," Richard said softly, his tone measured, "I mean you no harm."

Her hand finally went to the dog's collar, gripping it tightly as she issued a firm command. "Cease Loki."

The dog's growl subsided into a low rumble, but its eyes never left Richard as it lowered its stance, clearly still ready to act. Lizbet straightened, brushing stray hair from her face, her gaze fixed warily on the man before her.

Richard lowered his hands and spoke gently. "I am pleased to see you well."

She nodded but said nothing, her knuckles still white against the dog's collar.

"The last time we met," Richard continued, his voice tight with discomfort, "circumstances were not so... favorable."

Lizbet flushed at his words, but still, she remained silent. Her fingers twitched against the collar as though seeking strength from the beast beneath her hand.

Richard hesitated, his hands clasped behind his back. The pause felt weighty for a man usually so composed and sure of himself. Finally, he spoke. "It's about Jack."

Lizbet's breath caught. "Jack? What—what's happened? Is he—?"

"He's alive," Richard said quickly, his tone firm.

She exhaled shakily, relief mingled with fresh worry. "Injured? How bad

Richard moved to sit across from her, leaning forward, his elbows on his knees. "There was an incident. A plan went... astray. Jack was caught in the blast of an explosion."

Lizbet's hand flew to her mouth. "An explosion? Oh, God, Richard..."

"A broken arm and few cracked ribs," Richard lied. "He's at the Order's hospital."

Lizbet nodded, though she could hardly process what he was saying. "He's in London now?"

"Yes," Richard said. "He's in good hands and should be home very soon. I came only to assure myself of your well-being and to ask if there is anything I might do to improve it."

For a moment, Lizbet seemed lost for words, her mouth opening and closing as though testing the weight of a response. Finally, she shook her head. "No."

He hesitated. "I hear Catherine has not extended you the welcome we would wish."

"She is unhappy that I am here," Lizbet admitted quietly, her voice tinged with weariness.

Richard's jaw tightened. "If it would help, I can remedy that."

Lizbet nodded again, this time more mechanically, her eyes flickering between Richard and the dog.

Another silence fell between them, brittle and taut. Then Richard's gaze softened. "Angelo?"

The single word hovered between them, charged with meaning. Lizbet's flush deepened, and she looked away. "He is well," she said simply.

Richard exhaled, relief flickering briefly across his face. "I had word he had arrived from Malta."

But whatever further conversation might have followed died before it could begin. Richard straightened, bowing slightly as though the formality might lessen the tension in the air. "I will see to your comfort."

# A Queen's Rebel

And then he was gone, his footsteps retreating through the garden. Lizbet stood there for a long moment, staring at the spot where Richard had disappeared. The stick lay forgotten in the grass, and the dog nudged her leg, sensing her turmoil but unsure of its cause.

Lizbet, still holding the dogs collar, found herself alone. A few words, such a brittle exchange and it was done.

## CHAPTER FOUR

Jack's thoughts swirled, sluggish and disconnected, like fragments of a dream he couldn't quite piece together. He stared at the low ceiling above him, its beams rough and uneven, and the realization struck him again—he wasn't on the ship. The endless groan of timbers and the constant rocking of the waves were gone. Instead, there was stillness, an unfamiliar calm that felt oddly oppressive.

Had it been days? Weeks? He couldn't tell. His head throbbed faintly, a dull, insistent pressure behind his temples. The memory of the ship felt distant now, like a story someone else had told him. Something had changed, and it felt like that change had happened long ago, yet his body still carried the disorienting sensation of being unmoored.

The room came into sharper focus as his vision steadied. Small. Quiet. The glow of the fire to his left filled the space with a steady warmth that contrasted sharply with the deep ache in his bones. He turned his head slightly, wincing at the effort, and took in the scene. A small table beside the fire held a lamp, its yellow glow casting soft shadows across the walls. Next to it sat a sturdy brown jug and two wooden cups, their simple, utilitarian shapes oddly comforting.

His throat burned with dryness, and Jack swallowed reflexively. The sensation was sharp and raw, as though he'd been breathing ash. His gaze latched onto the jug with the desperation of a man crawling through a desert spotting water. Slowly, he tried to push himself up, but his chest rebelled against the effort, the tightness there clamping down like a vice.

## A Queen's Rebel

Pain exploded from his shoulder blade and rippled down his back, sharp and unforgiving. He sucked in a breath—more a gasp than anything—and fell back against the pillows, his body trembling from the exertion. The faint sound of his own voice surprised him.

"Sweet Jesus," he croaked, his voice a dry rasp, cracked and weak. It sounded foreign like it belonged to someone else.

The voice that answered was gentle yet tinged with relief. "Lord preserve you, I've been waiting days to hear you speak."

Jack turned his head slightly, his sluggish mind taking a moment to locate the source of the voice. A monk, robed and rotund, rounded the end of the bed, moving into Jack's line of sight. He slopped liquid from jug to cup and brought it to Jack. His hair was silvered at the temples, and his hands moved with the steady precision of someone accustomed to care.

"You'll be wanting a drink," the man said, moving toward the table with measured steps.

Jack tried to nod, but even that tiny movement sent a twinge of pain through his neck. He blinked hard, fighting the disorienting haze that clung to him. His mind felt like a labyrinth, each thought tangled and uncertain. He didn't recognize the man and didn't know where he was, but the promise of a drink was enough for now.

"Hold my arm with your good one, that's right, and I'll lift you up."

Jack's right hand gripped the offered hand, and he raised himself slowly from the bed. The cup was applied to his lips, and cool ale flooded his dry mouth, banishing the hard, dry feeling that had lain there. He tried to take in another mouthful before he'd swallowed the first, and the liquid ran from his lips. The motion sent another ripple of discomfort through Jack's body, but he bit back the groan, threatening to escape. The cup was pressed to his lips, and the first sip was almost overwhelming. The water slid down his throat, soothing the raw ache there, though his muscles protested against swallowing.

"Steady, just a little at a time," the monk advised, "There's more pouring down your chin than you're swallowing. I've plenty more, no need to go about it like a hound in a desert."

The cup was removed from his lips, a cloth applied to his wet face, and the wooden rim brought back to his mouth. This time, he drank slower. A pillow was tucked behind his back, and the supporting hand was removed, and he found himself propped up. Applying his tongue to wet his lips, eyes closed, he rested back against the pillows.

"I'll set the table here, next to you, and the cup is full. Can you reach it?" The monk adjusted the small table next to the bed with quiet efficiency, his movements deliberate as he ensured the cup of water was within easy reach. He leaned down slightly, peering into Jack's face with a mixture of concern and satisfaction.

Jack blinked, the effort of focusing on the monk's face requiring more energy than he expected. He extended his right hand slowly, every motion dragging against a tide of stiffness and discomfort, and gave a faint nod.

"Good," the monk said with a small smile. "I'll return soon. Brother de Nevarra wished to be informed the moment you woke."

Jack watched through heavy-lidded eyes as the monk exited the room, the faint sound of the door closing leaving an eerie quiet behind. For a moment, he stared at the jug on the table, the polished surface of the wood glinting in the flickering candlelight.

Swallowing against the dryness in his throat, he raised his right hand to rub at his face. His fingertips brushed against his jawline, finding nothing but the faint rasp of a day's stubble. He frowned. He couldn't remember shaving. Instinctively, he tried to move his left arm, but pain lashed through him like a white-hot brand, forcing him to abandon the effort immediately. His breath caught in his throat, and he let his arm fall limply back onto the blankets.

Broken ribs. His mind clung to that fragment of memory. His ribs and, perhaps, his arm—yes, he had injured them both. But how? And why?

And where was he?

The room's unfamiliarity unsettled him, yet at the same time, there was something faintly familiar about its modest warmth. The fire crackled softly in the hearth, its light painting the walls in dancing patterns. He couldn't place it, but he felt sure he had been here for some time. The monk had spoken to him with a familiarity that suggested days, perhaps even weeks.

The door swung open suddenly, jarring Jack from his sluggish thoughts. His head turned slowly, and his gaze settled on a figure entering the room—a face he recognized immediately, wearing a broad grin that carried genuine relief.

"I told them to inform me the moment you woke. Trust you to drag me from my bed in the middle of the night!" Emilio said, his tone teasing but warm.

"Middle of the night?" Jack echoed weakly, his voice cracked and uncertain.

"Indeed! They've not even rung the bells for Lauds yet," Emilio replied, scooping up a chair from the side of the room and planting it by the small table. He dropped into it with easy grace, his movements betraying none of the fatigue his dishevelled appearance suggested.

Jack studied him through half-lidded eyes. Emilio was dressed hastily, his shirt untucked and his doublet hanging open, its buttons undone. His fingers were bare, missing their usual assortment of rings, and his hair was a tousled mess. Jack noticed that Emilio's boots were not fully buckled, and the leather straps were dangling loose. He had clearly been roused from sleep, but there was no irritation in his demeanour.

Questions churned in Jack's mind, colliding with one another in a disorganized jumble. He tried to speak, but all that came out was a ragged string of incomplete words.

"What... where..."

Emilio leaned forward, his smile fading slightly as concern softened his features. "You can't remember?"

Jack shook his head, frustration mingling with fear as he struggled to piece together what had happened. His memory felt fragmented, like shattered glass, each piece reflecting a different, disjointed image.

The panic must have shown on his face because Emilio's hand came to rest on his forearm, firm and reassuring. "Jack, all is well. You had an accident, but you'll recover. You're safe now."

Jack's eyes drifted to his immobile left arm, wrapped tightly in bandages and resting against his side.

"It's bandaged," Emilio explained quickly. "That's why you can't move it. You need to let it heal."

"What... happened?" Jack managed, his brow furrowing as he tried to dredge up memories from the murky depths of his mind.

Emilio leaned back in the chair, his boots propped on the edge of the bed. "You, my reckless friend, tried to blow yourself into the afterlife," he said, a hint of amusement creeping into his voice.

Jack's face remained blank, and Emilio elaborated. "You set a fuse—far too short, by necessity—and were caught in the blast. Do you remember now?"

The fuse.

Jack's mind latched onto the word, and memories began to flood back like a key turning in a lock. The dark night, the short fuse pinned down with a broken ring, Emilio's voice shouting his name in panic, the icy slap of seawater, and the rough hands hauling him onto the deck of the *Luciana*.

Jack's unfocused gaze sharpened as he lifted his eyes to Emilio's face. "Where... am I?"

"In London, Jacques," Emilio said gently. "At the Order's hospital. Richard went to Berwick and secured the services of an apothecary. He came with us to London and gave you herbs—henbane, I think, or opium—to ease the pain. The monks have been tending to you ever since."

"Opium?" Jack repeated, his voice tinged with alarm.

Emilio leaned forward, his hand gripping Jack's arm reassuringly. "They know what they're doing, Jack. It was only enough to keep you still, to let you rest. You're awake now, and they won't give you any more. I'll make certain of that."

Jack's gaze wandered around the room, his thoughts still hazy. "I feel like I've broken a few ribs."

Emilio shook his head. "Several, so I am told, and the explosion burned the skin on your back and your arm—that's the pain you feel."

Jack's brows knitted together. "Burned?"

"It could have been much worse," Emilio said, his tone lightening. "The seawater, I'm told, saved you from the worst of it. The monks tell me you'll have scars, but they'll fade. And, be honest, you've already got a few of those."

Jack managed a weak smile. "That's a relief."

Emilio laughed, the sound warm and genuine. "Was that an attempt at humor?"

The conversation tapered off as fatigue pulled Jack back into sleep. When he woke again, the monk had returned, a calm presence beside him. He explained that Brother de Nevarra had been summoned to court and sent his apologies for not being there. Jack closed his eyes again, the pieces of his memory slowly coming together as sleep claimed him again.

Jack's body twitched violently under the sheets as the nightmare pulled him deeper into its clutches. The warmth of the room faded into the cold, unrelenting darkness of the sea. His breath came in ragged gasps, his arms flailing weakly as though still gripping the oars. The bed seemed to pitch beneath him like the boat, and the sound of Emilio's panicked voice echoed through his mind, mixing with the hissing roar of fire igniting black powder.

The memory played out in sharp, unforgiving detail, a dagger twisting deeper into his chest each moment. The boat rocked beneath him, Emilio's voice was strained but commanding, the cold barrel of black powder spilling its deadly contents. Trembling and wet, Jack's hands struggled to hold the fuse steady. He could feel the weight of the kegs around him, smell the acrid tang of powder in the air, and see the faint light of the Luciana disappearing into the darkness.

The fuse burned brighter, shorter, mocking him. Jack struck the embers in the glass box, coaxing the flame, his heartbeat roaring in his ears. He couldn't fail—couldn't afford to.

He dropped over the side of the boat into icy water, the cold searing his lungs as he gasped for breath. The world tilted; the shock of the sea enveloped him. He swam hard, every stroke a desperate battle against the freezing waves. In the nightmare, the sea wasn't just cold—it was alive, pulling him back toward the fire, the explosion, the chaos. The water's weight dragged at his limbs as if punishing him for his choices.

And then he heard Emilio.

The sound cut through the nightmare like a blade. Emilio's voice was not one of calm this time,

# A Queen's Rebel

but of terror. Jack turned in the water, the burning taste of salt choking him. He couldn't see Emilio. He couldn't find him. The barrel he'd clung to was gone, lost in the swirling darkness. Panic surged, his thrashing as he fought against the current.

"Emilio!" Jack shouted, his voice hoarse, the cold seizing his throat.

There was no answer. Just the roar of waves and the distant thunder of the explosion. Fire lit up the night sky, illuminating the sea in a blinding orange flash. Jack's heart seized—had Emilio been too close? Had he miscalculated? He dove beneath the surface, arms straining as he clawed through the murky depths, searching, always searching.

"Emilio!" Jack's voice cracked, fear clawing at him. The water felt endless, suffocating. He couldn't breathe. He couldn't see. He—

"Jack!" A firm hand gripped his shoulder, shaking him. "Wake up. You're safe. Jack. I'm here."

The nightmare's grip began to loosen, Emilio's voice anchoring him. Jack surfaced, gasping, his eyes snapping open. His body trembled violently, slick with sweat. The room's warmth, the soft glow of the lamp, and the solid presence of Emilio at his side brought him hurtling back to reality.

Jack blinked, disoriented. Emilio knelt beside him, his hand still on Jack's shoulder, his face etched with concern.

"You're not in the water, Jacques," Emilio said, his voice low and soothing. "You're here. You're safe."

Jack stared at him, the nightmare still clawing at the edges of his mind. "You—" His voice faltered, his throat dry and hoarse. "I thought—"

"I'm here," Emilio interrupted gently. "You didn't lose me."

Jack exhaled shakily, his chest heaving as he tried to calm himself. Emilio's hand didn't move, steadying him. The weight of it and its warmth felt like a lifeline.

"I... I couldn't find you," Jack murmured, his voice raw, his eyes wet. "In the water. I thought you—"

"I'm right here," Emilio reassured him. His dark eyes were intense, filled with something Jack couldn't quite name but that he knew was raw. "You didn't lose me then You're not that lucky."

Jack's gaze flickered away, shame and gratitude warring within him.

"You need rest," Emilio said after a moment, his voice softening. "The nightmare is over. I will stay as long as you need me."

Jack nodded faintly, his body sagging against the mattress.

"Thank you," Jack whispered.

Emilio's expression softened, a flicker of something tender crossing his face. He squeezed Jack's shoulder before leaning back in the chair, leaving Jack with the lingering warmth of his touch.

The room fell silent again, save for the crackle of the fire. Jack closed his eyes, the nightmare fading, but its echoes were still whispering in his mind. He didn't know what terrified him more: the memory of the sea or the depth of Emilio's gaze. Both threatened to pull him under.

## CHAPTER FIVE

Alphonso dropped into the chair, the weight of the day pressing heavily upon his shoulders. A scowl marred his features as he stared into the ornate mirror before him, his daze lingering on the twisted lines around his eyes and the pockmarks that scarred his cheeks. The room around him was dimly lit by the flickering glow of a few candles, casting soft shadows on the tapestries that lined the walls. His attention flickered to the young boy standing nervously beside him, a tray laden with pots, brushes, and powders in his hands.

"Master, do you wish...?" The boy hesitated, the question unfinished as he looked at Alphonso, waiting for the order.

Alphonso sighed, leaning back further into the chair, his eyes fluttering closed as he spoke, "Yes, get on with it."

The boy moved forward, his steps tentative as he took the first brush, dipping it into a pot of clear paste meant to cover Alphonso's face. The coldness of the brush on his skin sent a jolt through him, his body tensing. A small hiss of discomfort escaped his lips, but he said nothing, allowing the boy to continue. The brush swept across his cheek, but Alphonso's patience quickly began to fray. He felt the liquid chilling him, and without a second thought, his right hand shot out. He gave the boy a hard clip around the back of his head, making him drop the brush.

"Warm it, you fool," Alphonso growled, his voice tinged with anger.

The boy, wide-eyed and startled, scrambled to retrieve the fallen brush. Alphonso didn't even spare him a glance as he wiped his face roughly with the cloth he had snatched from the nearby table.

A smooth and steady voice from the doorway broke the quiet of the room. "Aspettare fuori," the voice said, the words rolling out in perfectly clipped Italian.

The boy's movements faltered for a second, and then, without a word, he rushed for the door, slipping through it and disappearing into the hall. Alphonso's jaw tightened.

Alphonso stood quickly, smoothing his doublet. His mind raced, but his eyes—eyes that had long ago perfected the art of hiding emotion—slowly turned toward the figure standing in the doorway. Tall, lean, and sharp-eyed, Emilio had changed little in the time since their last meeting. He had the same dark gaze and cold composure, though now there was a distance between them—a chasm that Alphonso couldn't ignore.

"My Prince, I had no idea you were back," Alphonso said, bowing his head.

Emilio's gaze was unreadable as he stepped further into the room, his boots silent on the wooden floor. He did not immediately reply to Alphonso's words, choosing to observe the scene before him, his expression unreadable. The silence stretched between them. Emilio's voice finally broke the tension, but it was not warm, not with the familiarity of the man he once was. It was business-like, cold.

"You've let your temper get the better of you again, Alphonso," Emilio remarked, his tone clipped and condescending. "Still the same as always. Impulsive. Reckless."

"Emilio," Alphonso purred, rising with a fluid motion.

Emilio ignored the remark, his gaze sweeping the room. The tapestries on the walls, the gilded mirrors catching the flicker of the firelight—it was all so deliberately opulent, just like its owner. The air was thick with the cloying scent of rosewater and something subtler, more intimate, that turned Emilio's stomach.

"You think I don't know what you did?" Emilio said, his voice low and threatening. His boots echoed sharply on the floor as he stepped closer.

Alphonso arched a brow, his lips twitching into a faint pout. "You'll have to be more specific, caro," he replied, his tone infuriatingly calm. "I do many things."

"You sent the barrel from the deck of Lucianna towards Jack," Emilio said, stopping just short of Alphonso. His hands were clenched at his sides, the tension in his shoulders barely held in check. "You tried to murder him."

Alphonso sighed dramatically, tilting his head as though Emilio's accusations were nothing more than tiresome theatrics. "Murder?" he echoed, his voice light. "The barrel missed, there was no harm done. A mere inconvenience."

"A mere inconvenience?" Emilio's voice rose, sharp as a blade. He stepped closer, the anger in his eyes blazing. "He could have died, Alphonso!"

"But he didn't," Alphonso countered, his voice softening as he stepped closer. His fingers reached out, brushing against Emilio's sleeve. "You made me jealous, I could not help myself. You know how I am."

Emilio froze, his jaw tightening as Alphonso's hand lingered. The Italian's touch was light, almost coaxing, but it sent a wave of revulsion through him. He didn't pull away. Not yet.

"Jealous!" Emilio said, his tone flat, his expression hard.

Alphonso's pout deepened, his dark eyes glistening as he turned his head slightly, the firelight catching the smooth curve of his jaw. "You wounded me, Emilio," he murmured. "It was jealousy. You've always been mine. Can you blame me for wanting to keep you safe from someone who would take you away from me?"

Emilio's lips twitched, almost a sneer, but he quickly masked it with a neutral expression. "You think trying to murder him keeps me safe?"

"He's nothing, Emilio!" Alphonso said suddenly, his voice breaking into a plea. He moved closer, his hand sliding down to clasp Emilio's wrist. "He doesn't see you, not the way I do. He doesn't understand you. But I do. I always have."

Emilio didn't answer. He allowed Alphonso to take his other hand, the Italian's thumbs rubbing small circles over his skin in what he must have thought was a soothing gesture. The touch sent a ripple of distaste crawling over Emilio's skin, but he kept his face impassive.

"You've always forgiven me, caro," Alphonso said softly, his voice dropping to a conspiratorial murmur. "I know you will again. We're too much a part of each other to let this ruin what we have."

For a moment, Emilio let the silence hang between them, allowing Alphonso's hope to swell. Then he gave a small, measured nod, his expression carefully neutral. "You're right," he said at last, his voice low.

Alphonso's smile returned, slow and satisfied. He stepped closer, his hands sliding up to rest on Emilio's shoulders. "Ah, caro," he murmured, tilting his head as he leaned in, his lips brushing Emilio's cheek.

The kiss lingered a moment too long, the cloying scent of Alphonso's rosewater filling Emilio's nostrils. He forced himself not to flinch, though his muscles tensed involuntarily. When Alphonso pulled back, his smile was triumphant, his gaze glittering with satisfaction.

Even as Alphonso's lips brushed against his, as the warmth of Alphonso's body pressed close, Emilio's mind screamed at him to pull away, to hurl the man to the floor. And yet, his arms betrayed him, tightening reflexively, refusing to break the contact. The kiss lingered uncomfortably long, the seconds stretching into what felt like an eternity. When they finally parted, Emilio inhaled sharply, his chest rising and falling in uneven breaths, though it had nothing to do with desire.

Alphonso pulled back, a satisfied gleam lighting his dark eyes, his expression filled with triumph. He smiled, self-assured, and spoke with the false humility Emilio had come to expect. "My prince," Alphonso murmured, his voice soft with practised contrition. "Forgive me."

Emilio hesitated, his jaw tight, forcing himself to meet Alphonso's gaze. The words burned as he uttered them. "I forgive you."

The transformation in Alphonso was immediate, like a hound who had just reclaimed its master's affection after a scolding. He sprang back, delight spreading across his face, his entire demeanour shifting to something almost childlike in its eagerness.

"I sent messages to the Order's offices, to anyone who might know where you were!" Alphonso mewed, his words spilling over themselves. "I was desperate for news. Those barbarians locked me on that wretched ship, Emilio. Alone. I had no word of you, nothing! I begged for information and prayed fervently. The last time I saw you, they were hauling you from the sea. I feared the worst, feared... But it wasn't true. The Lord heard my pleas and delivered you back to me."

"Quite," Emilio replied, his voice measured, his features carefully neutral. He stepped backwards creating a buffer of space between them. "You're staying with the Ambassador?"

"Of course," Alphonso replied, his tone shifting to something playfully coquettish. He moved toward Emilio again, his hand reaching out to rest lightly on Emilio's arm. "The Ambassador welcomed me back warmly. I am ever so grateful, but any duties he gives me will not occupy all of my time. I have plenty of hours to devote to more... personal concerns."

"I've been away on business for the Order," Emilio said, turning abruptly to break the contact and forcing Alphonso to relinquish his hold. "I only just returned to London."

Emilio glanced toward the window, the faint light filtering through and catching on the delicate glasswork. His mind churned beneath his calm exterior. He could not let Alphonso suspect the depths of his disdain. Not yet. For now, he needed Alphonso close, if only to watch him. To contain him. But as Alphonso spoke again, his words filled with shallow charm, Emilio's thoughts drifted. The man's presence, his cloying touches, the lingering trace of his kiss—it all felt like poison.

The room was dim, the only light coming from the low embers of the fire in the hearth and the flicker of a single candle on the bedside table. Jack lay in the narrow bed, his breath coming in sharp gasps, his head tossing against the sweat-dampened pillow. His voice, hoarse and strained, broke the stillness of the night.

"No—Emilio!" His arm jerked upward, the bandages on his burned skin pulling taut as if he were trying to fend off an unseen attacker.

Brother Anselm and two others were already by his side, one gripping Jack's shoulders while the others tried to restrain his flailing arms. Jack's cries grew louder, more frantic.

"Hold him still! He's going to tear open the burns!" Brother Anselm barked.

Jack's strength, fueled by the nightmare's fury, was startling. His eyes snapped open, wild and

# A Queen's Rebel

unfocused, his mind trapped in the fiery chaos of his dream.

"The fuse! Light the fuse!" he gasped, his words incoherent to those who didn't know the horrors playing out behind his eyes.

With a sharp motion, his arm broke free from the monk's grasp, the force causing him to twist violently on the bed. The movement tore at the newly healing skin on his back, blood seeping through the linen bandages.

"Brother Anselm, he's going to hurt himself more!" one of the younger monks cried, panic in his voice.

When Emilio returned the next day, it was to find the room unnervingly still. Jack lay motionless, his face pale, his lips slack, and his eyelids fluttering faintly as though caught in some half-waking dream. Emilio's heart clenched at the sight.

"What's wrong with him?" Emilio demanded, his voice sharp as he turned to Brother Anselm, who stood by the door with a sombre expression.

"The nightmares," Anselm said, sighing heavily. "They've grown worse. Last night, we had to hold him down. He tore the healing skin and reopened the sores. There was no other choice but to give him laudanum."

"You drugged him," Emilio said flatly, his tone laced with accusation.

"It was that or watch him undo weeks of healing," Anselm replied, though there was a flicker of defensiveness in his voice.

Emilio's jaw tightened as he moved to Jack's side. He sat on the edge of the bed, his hand brushing lightly against Jack's. The skin was cool to the touch, and Jack didn't stir. His chest rose and fell in shallow, even breaths, but there was no other sign of life.

"I will be here. Every night. Do not give him this again," Emilio said quietly, then to Anslem. "If he so much as stirs, send for me."

The bell had just rung for Lauds when they knocked on his door, Emilio followed Anslem back to Jack's room and bid him leave them. Sitting close, he tightened his grip on Jack's hand and leaned close, his voice low and steady.

"Jacques, listen to me," he murmured. "It's a dream. You're safe now. I'm here."

Jack's head turned slightly, his lips parting as a faint sound escaped him, but the tension in his body didn't ease. Emilio moved closer, his other hand pressing gently against Jack's shoulder to keep him grounded.

"You're not in the water. There's no fire, no powder. Just me, Jacques. Just me," Emilio's voice was firm and commanding.

Jack fought against the dream. Then, slowly, his breathing began to steady. His fingers twitched in Emilio's grasp, the faintest sign of awareness.

"Emilio?" The word was barely audible, cracked and fragile, but it was enough to make Emilio's throat tighten.

"I'm here," Emilio said softly. "I'll always be here."

Jack's eyes fluttered open briefly, unfocused and glassy, but they found Emilio's face. A faint smile ghosted across his lips before sleep claimed him again—this time, a quieter, more peaceful rest.

## CHAPTER SIX
## A MONTH AGO

The door creaked softly as Catherine stepped into the room, her hands resting lightly on the swell of her pregnancy. The sight of Jack, propped up against pillows with a blanket draped across his lap, brought a mix of emotions that flickered across her face—relief, concern, and a shadow of apprehension. The fire in the hearth cast a warm glow across the room, but it couldn't fully mask the pallor of his skin or the tightness in his jaw.

"Jack," she said softly, her voice barely above a whisper. Her smile was warm but tinged with worry, her joy at seeing him overcoming the initial shock of his appearance. She closed the door behind her, her movements careful and deliberate.

Jack's eyes fluttered open at the sound of her voice, and for a moment, he seemed disoriented. Then recognition softened his expression, and a faint smile tugged at his lips. "Catherine," he rasped, his voice carrying the faint hoarseness of exhaustion. "You've no idea how much I've missed you. Come in. I promise I'm not as bad as I look."

Catherine chuckled softly, though the sound was more out of relief than amusement. She moved toward him, her hands instinctively reaching out as if to steady herself. "You look better than I feared," she lied, though her eyes betrayed her unease. "But you should have told me. Richard said only that you'd broken ribs."

Jack grimaced, shifting slightly under the blanket. "Richard was sparing you the worst of it. I told him not to worry you."

Her gaze drifted to his left arm, swathe bandages and lying motionless at his side. The burns on his shoulders and upper chest were visible where the blanket had slipped down, red and raw even in the dim light. Her breath caught in her throat. "Jack," she murmured, "how did this happen?"

He hesitated, his fingers tightening slightly around the edge of the blanket. "An accident," he said finally. "Nothing heroic, I assure you. Just poor judgment and a bit of bad timing."

Catherine's brow furrowed, but she chose not to press further. She perched carefully on the edge of the bed, her hand finding his. "I'm just glad you're home."

Jack gave her hand a gentle squeeze, his smile more genuine this time. "So am I. And you—how are you? How is the child?"

Her hand drifted to her belly, her smile widening despite her concern. "We're both well. Impatient, though."

Jack's face lit up, the exhaustion momentarily forgotten. "I can't wait," he said, his voice tinged with wonder. "To hold my child. I've been thinking about it constantly."

Catherine's eyes glistened with unshed tears. "You'll make a wonderful father, Jack."

"And you'll be an incredible mother," he replied, his voice soft but filled with conviction.

For a moment, the room was silent save for the crackling of the fire. Catherine stroked his hand absently, her thumb tracing over the ridges of his knuckles. "Rest now," she said finally, her voice firm but kind. "No more heroics for a while."

Jack laughed, the sound weak but genuine. "Agreed. Though you'll have to remind me of that when I'm feeling better."

"I will," she said, leaning forward to kiss his forehead. "And you'll listen to me for once."

"As always," he murmured, his eyes already beginning to close.

# A Queen's Rebel

Catherine rose slowly, careful of her balance, and adjusted the blanket around him. She lingered for a moment, watching him as his breathing evened out. Then she turned and left the room, her steps soft and measured, her heart lighter than it had been in days. For weeks, her worry over Jack had been an unrelenting weight, growing heavier with each passing day. When Richard had first told her Jack was in the Order's hospital, she had been seized with panic, imagining the worst. Richard's reassurances, brief and vague as they were, had done little to soothe her. Broken ribs, he had said. That was all. Nothing more. But Catherine had learned long ago to read between the lines of Richard Fitzwarren's measured words.

She had imagined every possible scenario. Was Jack lying in agony, unable to breathe? Was his life slipping away even as she waited helplessly for news? Every knock at the door had sent a chill down her spine, every silence stretched unbearably long, and every whispered conversation in the house had seemed to carry the weight of unspoken fears.

And then, finally, the day had come when they brought him home. Relief had flooded through her, so powerful it had nearly brought her to her knees. But as they carried him upstairs, and she caught her first glimpse of his pale face and the bandages swathing his arm and shoulders, the relief had mingled with a fresh wave of worry. He looked so fragile, his strength—so much a part of the man she loved—seemed like a distant memory.

And the burns. Catherine's throat tightened at the memory. Richard hadn't said a word about those, and when she saw the angry, raw marks on Jack's skin, she had to fight to keep her composure. She'd wanted to cry out, to demand why she hadn't been told, but what good would that have done? Jack was here now. He was alive. That was what mattered.

Still, the fear lingered at the edges of her thoughts. Would he recover fully? Would he ever be the same? The weight of those questions pressed against her chest, but she forced herself to push them aside. Jack was strong. He was resilient. If anyone could come back from this, it was him.

As she reached the bottom of the stairs, Catherine paused, her hand resting on her belly. The child stirred within her, a soft, insistent reminder of the future they were building together. Jack had spoken with such tenderness about meeting their child, and that memory brought a small, bittersweet smile to her lips. She couldn't let her worries overshadow the joy that was coming. Jack needed her to be strong, just as he had always been strong for her.

Jack was home. He was alive. And no matter how uncertain the road ahead, they would walk it together.

A week later, Jack sat slouched in the chair by the fire in his London home, staring into the flames as they flickered and danced. The familiar warmth of the room was a comfort, but the restlessness building in him gnawed at his patience. After weeks confined to the hospital of the Order, it was a relief to be home, but the novelty of new surroundings was wearing thin. He craved movement, freedom, something beyond these four walls.

A sharp knock at the door jolted him from his reverie. Jack straightened in his seat, irritation flashing across his face. "Enter?" he called.

The door creaked open, and his steward entered, his demeanor composed but faintly uneasy. "My Lord, a gentleman has arrived to see you. He says he is expected."

Jack's brow furrowed. "Expected? By whom?"

# A Queen's Rebel

Before the steward could respond, the answer stepped into view. The man who entered the room was clad in the unmistakable black habit of the Order of St. John, the white cross stark against his chest. He had the bearing of someone used to command: tall, broad-shouldered, his face weathered by time and experience. A neatly trimmed beard streaked with gray framed his strong jaw, and his piercing eyes seemed to assess Jack in an instant, cool and deliberate.

"I am Brother Sebastian," he announced, his voice a deep and measured baritone. He stepped forward and extended a sealed letter. "I bring word from Brother de Nevarra."

Jack took the letter, his jaw tightening as his irritation grew. Breaking the seal, he unfolded the parchment and scanned the contents. Emilio's familiar handwriting greeted him, its tone unyielding:

*Jack,*
*Brother Sebastian is one of the Order's finest—dedicated, capable, and maddeningly stubborn. He will ensure your safety and well-being, and, knowing you as I do, I refuse to take no for an answer.*
—Emilio

Jack let out a sharp sigh, folding the letter with deliberate care and setting it on the table as though that simple act could contain his rising frustration. "So," he said, fixing Sebastian with a flat stare, "Emilio thinks I need a nurse."

Sebastian remained impassive, his hands clasped loosely in front of him. His presence was calm but unyielding, like an immovable stone in the middle of a turbulent stream. "Brother de Nevarra has entrusted me with your care," he said, his voice steady and deliberate. "It is my duty to fulfill that trust."

Jack leaned back in his chair, rubbing his temples. The ache in his shoulder flared as he shifted, and he resisted the urge to wince. "Let me guess," he said, his tone sharp. "You've come all this way because he ordered it, and you've no intention of leaving."

Sebastian nodded slightly, as if conceding the point. "Brother de Nevarra made it clear that your well-being is paramount. I do not question my instructions, my Lord. Brother Anselm will see to your daily needs, and I will attend to everything else."

Jack's brow furrowed, his irritation deepening. "Everything else?" he echoed skeptically. "If you're here to manage my spiritual needs, you might as well save yourself the trouble and leave."

For the first time, Sebastian's composure softened into the faintest hint of a smile, subtle but undeniably present. "There is more to a man's mind than his reverence for God," he said evenly. "Though I am at your service should you wish to discuss that as well."

Jack snorted, shaking his head. "More to my mind, is there?" His voice was laced with dry humor.

"Brother de Nevarra has confidence in my abilities," Sebastian replied, his tone as steady as ever. "As I have in yours. But this is not about whether you believe you need assistance. It is about ensuring your recovery."

Jack stood abruptly, though the sudden movement sent a jolt of pain searing through his shoulder. He caught himself against the edge of the chair, clenching his jaw. "Recovery? I'm not dying. I don't need half the bloody Order stationed at my house."

Sebastian took a deliberate step closer, his presence as calm and unshaken as the tide. "Respectfully, my Lord, your opinion on the matter is noted but irrelevant. The Order has deemed this necessary, and I will not waver in my duty."

# A Queen's Rebel

Jack stared at him, momentarily struck silent by the monk's quiet but immovable authority. There was no room for debate, no plea for understanding—only an unassailable resolve that left Jack feeling oddly outmaneuvered in his own home.

"You don't strike me as the sort who takes no for an answer," Jack muttered, his frustration giving way to reluctant amusement.

"I am not," Sebastian replied simply, the faint smile returning to his face.

Jack exhaled sharply, shaking his head as he sank back into the chair. "Fine. You're here now, so I suppose I'm stuck with you."

Sebastian inclined his head, the faint smile lingering as if he were humorously aware of the victory. "It seems we are both stuck, my Lord."

Jack couldn't help but let out a short laugh, his irritation dimming. "God help me. Emilio sent the most stubborn monk he could find."

Sebastian's smile deepened ever so slightly. "It would seem he chose well."

Within a few days of Richard's visit Lizbet had been rehoused. Angelo and his nurse moved with her, and Lizbet found herself surrounded by an efficient household, and Froggy Tate who also seemed to have received instructions from Richard. It was easier, that she could not deny. The house stood proudly on the banks of the Thames. Constructed of sturdy brick and dark, exposed timbers, its gabled roof rising sharply against the sky. Tall, mullioned windows glittered in the sunlight, their tiny diamond panes set in intricate lead patterns that reflected the ever-changing moods of the river below. A small dock extended into the water, complete with mooring posts, a flat-bottomed skiff tethered and bobbing gently with the tide.

The house had come with a message

"This is yours, and yours alone. No man can take if from you. In the following days my lawyer will call and finalise the documents to transfer to you the title."

Lizbet had paused before the doorway, taking in the imposing structure that now belonged to her. It was larger than she had expected, larger than she needed, but its size spoke of opportunity, of a new beginning far removed from the turmoil she had left behind. The merchant and his family who had vacated it had done so in haste, their wealth and aspirations now bound for Holland, leaving behind much of their furniture.

Standing looking down from the paned window of her new bedroom she was hit suddenly by what had happened. Richard too had clutched at the practicalities of the situation, it was all superficial, he'd felt compelled to do something, and he had, swiftly and efficiently – exactly the same way as she had dealt with Angelo. The knowledge seemed to create within her a cold hole. This would be it. He'd reunited her with her son, provided for them both, given her an income she could never had even dreamed of – and left. His work was done, his conscience clear. No doubt from time to time he would check that his provisions were still adequate, but nothing more. There simply was no need. Lizbet turned from the window, her foot caught on the edge of a rug and she stumbled forward. Without realising it, with no warning, she had arrived at the end of a road. Whatever happened from now would be by her own design alone.

Lizbet's dealings with Angelo continued to be based around practicalities. He was well housed with a room for his nurse, he had food, clothing sufficient for English weather, a servant had been provided from the Fitzwarren household expressly to serve

# A Queen's Rebel

Maria, who had also been provided with clothing more suited to a northern climate. He had a crib, there were wooden toys, the rooms were warm, the fire baskets always full, his linen was washed and changed, in every respect he was most suitably catered for.

Lizbet, whose Italian was the best in the house, found Maria likeable and, more importantly, devoted to Angelo. He had, she assured herself, no need of a mother, that role was already adequately filled, and Lizbet had no desire to remove Maria. He was three and there was no need yet to consider a tutor for the boy, but it was Maria's desperate desire that he be raised in the catholic faith, so far there had been three conversations on the subject, all of them ending with tears on the part of Maria.

Lizbet cared little, she had said as much, but she had said that there was a danger, and it was not the faith of England. On the final occasion she had relented. Who would care if a small boy and an Italian nurse practiced the old faith out of sight behind closed doors? Who would know? And so she had patted Maria on the arm and the woman had soon after set up a small shrine to the lady in her room.

As the fire crackled softly in the hearth, Lizbet wiped her tears, her gaze fixed on the flickering flames. She felt raw and uncertain, burdened by the weight of a motherhood she hadn't sought and a child she didn't know how to love. But Angelo was here, a part of her life now, and she could no longer run from him. No matter how much it hurt, she would have to try.

Steeling herself, Lizbet took a deep breath and stepped toward Angelo's room. His high, unrestrained laughter spilled through the door, mingling with the warm, lilting sound of Maria singing a familiar Italian melody. Lizbet paused, her hand on the latch, the sound both comforting and alien. For a moment, she hesitated. It had been easier to leave Angelo in Maria's care, to let the devoted nurse fill the role of mother. But Lizbet knew it couldn't continue. Angelo was her son. If she couldn't feel the bond naturally, she would have to build it.

Pushing the door open, she stepped inside. Angelo sat on the floor, clutching a wooden horse, his curls gleaming in the firelight. Maria, startled by Lizbet's entrance, began to rise from her seat, her sewing forgotten in her lap.

Maria hesitated. "Madonna, he has been playing all morning. Perhaps he is tired."

"Then I'll read to him," Lizbet replied, her tone sharper than intended. "Leave us."

Maria's uncertainty was evident, but she obeyed, gathering her sewing and retreating from the room with a reluctant glance at the child. Angelo looked up at Lizbet with wide, curious eyes, his toy horse clutched tightly in his small hands.

"Angelo," Lizbet began, her voice softening as she knelt beside him. "Would you like to hear a story?"

He nodded cautiously, his thumb creeping toward his mouth. Lizbet drew a small, worn book from her pocket, its leather cover warm from her hand. "This is the story of St. George and the dragon. Do you know it?"

Angelo shook his head, his curiosity overcoming his reserve as he edged closer. Lizbet opened the book and began to read, stumbling over Italian words she tried to translate. Her voice felt awkward, unpracticed, but Angelo didn't seem to notice. He leaned against her knee, his small fingers tracing the colorful illustrations of knights and castles.

When she read of the dragon's roar and St. George raising his sword, Angelo gasped in delight, tilting his head back to look up at her. Lizbet smiled faintly, though the ache in her chest remained. She held him close, but a part of her still felt like an observer, watching from a distance and waiting for the connection to feel real.

Over the following weeks, Lizbet forced herself more fully into Angelo's life. She hired Master Wright, a gentle tutor with a calm demeanor and a knack for engaging young minds. Lizbet sat in on their lessons, using the opportunity to teach Angelo English. The process was slow, but Angelo's bright eagerness made it easier. His childish mispronunciations drew rare laughter from Lizbet, and she found herself correcting him with more patience than she expected.

"Chair," she said one afternoon, pointing to the object in question.

"Chera," Angelo repeated, his brow furrowed.

"No, chair," Lizbet enunciated, drawing out the word.

"Chair," he said again, his face lighting up when she nodded. "Chair! Chair, Mama!"

Lizbet froze, the word striking her with unexpected force. Mama. It came so naturally from him, as though he had always called her that. She nodded slowly, unable to speak, and patted his head, a lump rising in her throat.

In the evenings, Lizbet read to Angelo by the fire, choosing English tales like *Robin Hood*. Angelo would act out the scenes with his wooden toys, mimicking battles with bows and arrows. Lizbet played along, though her enthusiasm often felt forced. Still, she praised his efforts, encouraging him to repeat the stories back to her in English.

Maria sometimes watched from the doorway, her expression a mix of relief and quiet approval. Lizbet didn't ask for her thoughts, but the nurse's presence was steady, and Lizbet found herself relying on her more than she cared to admit.

The bond between Angelo and Loki, Lizbet's loyal hound, formed almost instantly. Loki, a large and exuberant dog had offered her comfort during her loneliest moments. Now, it seemed the mischievous hound had found a new partner.

"Loki, stay," Lizbet commanded one afternoon as Angelo darted across the room with a wooden horse. But the dog ignored her, bounding after the boy with his tail wagging furiously.

Maria, folding linens in the corner, gasped in horror. "Signora, the dog is too large, too wild! He could hurt the boy!"

Lizbet glanced at the pair. Angelo had dropped to his knees, wrapping his arms around Loki's neck as the hound licked his face, eliciting a delighted squeal. "Maria, look at them. He's perfectly gentle."

Maria shook her head, crossing herself. "Madonna, protect us. He is an animal, Signora!"

"And he's good company for Angelo," Lizbet quipped with a wry smile.

Maria muttered a prayer under her breath, but her protests were half-hearted.

Wherever Angelo went, Loki followed. The dog sat dutifully by Angelo's chair during lessons, sprawled at his feet during meals, and curled up beside him at night. Lizbet often found the boy asleep by the fire, his small hand tangled in Loki's fur. The sight brought a warmth to her heart she hadn't anticipated.

Late one evening, Lizbet tucked Angelo into bed, smoothing his curls as he murmured softly in Italian to Loki, who had settled himself on the rug beside the crib. Lizbet stood for a moment, watching the two of them, before whispering, "Goodnight, Angelo. And goodnight, Loki."

As she turned to leave, she felt a flicker of peace, fragile but real. Perhaps, she thought, this was how love grew—slowly, in small, unexpected moments.

## CHAPTER SEVEN

The guards stood to attention, stepping aside as Richard followed Cecil into his bustling outer office. The space was brightly lit and alive with activity. Four scribes with ink-stained fingers worked diligently at their desks, heads bowed, quills scratching across the parchment. They didn't so much as glance up when Cecil entered, too engrossed in their tasks and knowing better than to cast their eyes over anything that was their master's business.

The room was crammed with as many desks as it could reasonably hold, leaving only a narrow passage leading to Cecil's private office. A series of wooden trays hung precariously along one wall, some overflowing with documents, others haphazardly stuffed with jars of pens, inkpots, and the occasional stick of sealing wax. Amid the administrative chaos, two guards stood at attention by Cecil's office door, their presence taking up valuable floor space.

The keyholder, stationed to the left, moved swiftly at the sight of his master, stooping to unlock the heavy wooden door set into the arch of grey Norman stone. As the door creaked open, Cecil gestured for Richard to enter.

"Must you really drag me in here?" Richard muttered, irritation lacing his words as the door closed firmly behind him.

Inside Cecil's private domain, a sense of controlled order replaced the chaos of the outer office. A dark iron chandelier hung from the ceiling, suspended on thick chains. Its many candles burned steadily, casting a bright but uneven light over the desk below. Richard noted the chandelier hung so low that Cecil would have to rise with care to avoid catching his head on its metal arms.

The walls, entirely windowless, were packed with shelves groaning under the weight of documents Cecil kept from prying eyes. Tall, floor-mounted oil lamps stood at intervals, their flames shielded by glass, casting a steady orange glow illuminating the shelves and contents. Shadows danced across the papers, giving the room an oppressive air as though the weight of state secrets hung as heavily as the clutter of parchment and leather bindings.

Cecil moved to his desk without a word. The faint scrape of his chair against the stone floor was the only sound as Richard surveyed the space, his dissatisfaction plain on his face. He didn't take the seat opposite Cecil but stood, arms folded, regarding the statesman with a cold gaze.

Cecil smiled. "And how are the Fitzwarren brood faring? I hear your brother is soon to have a child that rather places an obstacle between you and any inheritance – very sad."

"You are correctly informed. However, I do not view that as an obstacle," Richard said, failing to keep a trace of sourness from his voice.

Cecil sat back in his chair. "Have you found another way to secure yourself a fortune? Do tell?"

Richard did not reply.

"We both know we stand on opposite sides of a very fine line, and if you have been offended, I have not the time, nor the will, to debate it," Cecil said bluntly.

"If time is so precious, why have you summoned me?" Richard replied acidly.

"I want you to investigate a death," Cecil said, both his palms lightly tapping the desk.

"A death. Any particular one?" Richard replied.

# A Queen's Rebel

"This one," Cecil picked up a sheet of curled paper and held it towards Richard. The Coroner is John Pudsey. Start there."

Frowning, Richard stepped forward, took the page, and scanned the text.

*Inquisition as indenture held at Cumnor in the aforesaid county Oxfordshire on 9 September in the second year of the reign of the most dread Lady Elizabeth, by the grace of God queen of England, France, and Ireland, defender of the faith, etc., before John Pudsey, gent, a coroner of the said lady queen in the aforesaid county, on inspection of the body of Lady Amy Dudley.....*

Richard raised his eyes from the report, and when he met Cecil's, he saw that the man was smiling. "You want me to investigate the death of Robert Dudley's wife?"

Cecil's smile spread. "I do indeed. I know you are a thorough man and resourceful."

"Is there a specific conclusion you wish to draw from this?" Richard said, his tone still annoyed.

"It is not a matter of what I want. It is a matter of the truth," Cecil said, grinning, "Enjoy the wine. It's not often Dudley comes in useful, but on this occasion, he has excelled himself. Find him guilty and .... Well, we both know how well that will be accepted, and find him not guilty, and the very fact that you investigated this dreadful event will sour her Majesties favour."

"Even though you have requested that I investigate?" Richard replied.

"Don't be naïve, Fitzwarren. It is not I who have requested that this matter be investigated most thoroughly, not at all," Cecil said, settling a satisfied smile onto his lips.

"The queen," Richard replied bluntly.

"Indeed, Her Majesty wishes for the world to know that her Robin is free of guilt," Cecil said.

Richard planted his hands on the edge of the desk and leaned towards Cecil. "This is your doing. You've persuaded her that open review is the only way to clear Dudley's name of the rumour of murder – and she is willing because you've hinted that should a marriage ever be brokered, his name would need to be cleared. Haven't you?"

Cecil leaned back in his chair. "A matter of perfection, don't you agree?"

"Dudley likes you not at all, and with good reason and any lingering affection the queen feels for you, I imagine, will be fully expunged by the time this sordid matter is concluded. Find him guilty, and you'll hang – if you are lucky. If you find him not guilty, you'll still be the foul tool that raised questions against poor Robin. Her majesties displeasure will need to land somewhere when you present your inevitable conclusions. This investigation is a matter of due process; doubts have been raised against the legitimacy of the Coroner's court verdict, and the matter must be investigated. And who better to handle the filthy task than your already soiled hands."

Richard stood back up and folded his hands across his chest. "There is, I have to admit, a certain acidic beauty in your plan."

"That you recognise it heartens me even further," Cecil said with evident satisfaction. "Now go on, off you go."

Cecil shooed Richard towards the door.

Richard had no choice – and Cecil knew it.


If a day could be accounted for in terms of the weather, then today, in England, it was a good day, despite Cecil's attempt to sour it. The sky above the

# A Queen's Rebel

gardens was sapphire blue, with faint wisps of white silky ephemeral clouds decorating it but not obscuring the sun's rays. Two magpies, in their black and white court livery, hopped on the grass some way distant and, from behind the finely trimmed box hedge came the sound of laughter and the stray notes from an idly played lute. and above in an oak tree, a robin trilled as he patrolled his territory.

The queen, seated on the middle of an alabaster bench thoughtfully strewn with brightly coloured cushions, her skirts arrayed with precision by her ladies, was listening to Robert Dudley read to her from where he was seated at her feet on yet more cushions.

Richard Fitzwarren was watching and, at the same time, not watching.

"You were, so I've heard, friends once," a voice Richard recognised said in his ear. It was Alphonso, who had come to stand behind him.

"And once, she was not a queen," Richard replied, not bothering to turn around.

"She mistreats you, does she not?" Alphonso rounded the end of the wall and sidled up next to Richard. "It is hot, and look, Dudley lies there in his shirt, does it not bother you that your queen leaves you to cook like a pig on a spit in the sun?"

"What an eloquent image," Richard replied dryly.

"And rumour also whispers that Dudley has no liking for you," Alphonso continued as he hitched himself up on the wall next to Richard, crossing his legs artfully. "I hear you are now left to chase only old men and fools?"

Richard knew he was referring to the recent arrests of Fletcher and Dalton for subversion of the sumptuary laws, a poor task set him by Cecil. "And why would a man not revel in easy work? After all, as you pointed out, it's hot."

"As hot as the fires of hell?" Alphonso said, "I am sure you pray that your queen has made the right choice when she upset Rome."

"Rome was upset long ago and by her father, if you recall," Richard said, his voice bored.

"Ah," Alphonso tapped his nose. "But remember, poor Queen Mary, God rest her magnificence, returned this heathen isle to the true faith."

Richard was already tiring of the conversation; every encounter with the Italian was a poor war of words; Richard could rarely be bothered to mount an attack and would rather let the Italian blunder through his ranks and leave believing he was the victor. However, today was hot, Dudley was irritating him, and so Richard folded his arms and regarded Alphonso with a cool gaze, rather than answering the question he asked. "Where is De Nevarra? Lost him again have you?"

A sudden and quickly hidden scowl blighted the falsely youthful face, quickly hidden behind a broad smile. Alphonso waved his hand airily. "He is here, and have no fear; he will find me soon enough."

Richard, his gaze resting critically on Alphonso's face, examined the false exterior of powder and paint. It was artfully done; from a distance, he had the exquisite outline of Michelangelo's David, smooth and perfect. But youth was long gone, his cheeks were scarred with pockmarks, and the creases around his eyes and mouth were just a little too deep. His life lacked hard physical activity, and whilst that might have saved him from the occasional scar, it had allowed his body to soften. Alphonso had, it was fair to say, little left to offer.

Alphonso's eyes narrowed, and his mouth pressed into a thin, hard line under Fitzwarren's scrutiny. "What?"

# A Queen's Rebel

"You're older than Emilio, the thought had never occurred to me before," Richard said simply, wondering if Alphonso's exterior would crack.

Alphonso dropped from the wall abruptly putting a little distance between them.

"That's better, the façade does not fare well any longer under close scrutiny. But, if the candles and the lamps are out, then I suppose he would not notice, although your skin does appear to be a little slack ..." Richard had reached forward and ran a finger over the back of Alphonso's hand.

Alphonso retracted it as if the touch had burnt, colour from his skin pressing through the paste on his face. He didn't speak again but turned on his heel and left. Richard, a satisfied smile on his face, watched him go. Feral and self-serving, the Italian wound his way like a cat through the scattered courtiers in the garden, seeking out a new admirer.

He knew he should have dealt with Alphonso better. But unfortunately the Italian was right, it was too hot, he could feel the sweat beneath his clothing pool and then run down his spine, and Dudley .... then there was Dudley.

A man who would be king.

That thought was not a comfortable one. Edward Courtney had also walked down that path, and it led to his demise. Would Dudley make the same mistake? Indeed, could he?

Richard took a step to his left, where more shade was offered. Behind him, he heard the sound of gravel biting into boot soles, the noise coming towards him.

"Is this as good as summer gets on this miserable island?" The voice, when he heard it, was one he welcomed. The clipped, irreverent Italian belonged to Emilio De Nevarra.

"He went that way," Richard said without looking around, pointing to a gap in the box hedge Alphonso had disappeared through earlier.

Emilio ignored his comment and said instead. "I heard you have been charged with another odious task. How hard you must work to upset your masters."

Even Richard was surprised by the speed with which the task Cecil had set him had spread. "It's a challenge I aspire to rise to."

Emilio gave a small laugh. "If anyone could be weighed by regret, it has to be Dudley. I would imagine he curses himself daily for placing himself in the position of being unable to marry your queen."

"No doubt he does," Richard replied coolly.

"Then perhaps that is why your queen favours him so well, the simple fact that he cannot wed her; he can be everything else – friend, confidant, but he can never possess her."

"A feeling not unknown to yourself," Richard replied.

Emilio leaned his head towards Richard. "You are becoming tedious."

"I lack amusement; I shall take it where I can," Richard replied, then changed the subject and said, "You should visit him. He's insufferably bored, driving his wife to distraction and the servants to seek new positions."

The pause before Emilio replied was overly long. "It would not be ....wise at the moment, and I have ensured he is in good hands."

"Too busy watching someone else?" Richard ventured.

Emilio looked at Richard directly. It seemed for a moment that he would say more, but instead, with a casual wave of his hand, he said, "Do you not sometimes feel the gallows trap tremble beneath your feet?"

"So seriously put, are you concerned, now, for my wellbeing?" Richard asked, amused.

"Perhaps. Dudley dislikes you already; after all, you were instrumental in the execution of his father and brother," Emilio said.

# A Queen's Rebel

"I think many would argue that the Earl's own actions were pivotal in bringing down the axe," Richard replied.

"I am sure they were, but there are few who survive to attach blame to. Your Queen Mary has gone, and only you are left, and it must twist in Dudley's stomach to see you at court," Emilio replied.

Richard was sure Emilio's assessment was accurate, but instead, he said. "It is all a matter of weight."

"Weight?" Emilio questioned, his brow furrowed.

"Weight and its distribution," Richard said, leaning his head towards Emilio. "At the moment, I have a few allies supporting the door from beneath."

Emilio raised an eyebrow. "Let us hope they do not turn their backs on you. Otherwise, the fall could be rather sudden."

"Speaking of sudden falls. You know why the barrel fell from the Lucianna into the skiff breaking Froggy's arm?" Richard's voice was serious.

The Italian tapped his heavily ringed fingers along the top of the wall. It was a long moment before he gave his answer. "I know."

There was a silence between them. Emilio broke it eventually. "The barrel was freed from the deck, the lashing's cut through with a knife, and the barrel hefted over the side and dropped. It missed its target. It was to have landed on Jack."

"Was that the first time?" Richard asked.

"I believe so," Emilio replied. "If it was just Jack, if it had been solely that alone he would be dead already."

"Italian politics?" Richard said, his face grimly set.

Emilio shook his head slowly. "Worse. Family politics. Ambition and greed wrapped in silk, wielded like a blade. Alphonso is here for more than jealousy or petty revenge. He has a purpose—a spy's purpose."

Richard straightened. "Who is he working for?"

"That is the question, isn't it?" Emilio said, a faint bitterness creeping into his tone. "He moves within Elizabeth's court, his charm disarming, his presence innocuous. But he's not here by chance. He has been sent to gather intelligence, and until I know who controls him, I cannot act against him."

"Why not cut him loose now and deal with the consequences later?" Richard asked bluntly. "You're no stranger to taking risks."

Emilio's gaze turned sharp, his usual coolness giving way to a flicker of frustration. "Because Alphonso's leash is longer than it appears. If I act without understanding the hand that holds it, I risk bringing the wrath of an entire faction—perhaps even one within the Order itself—down on us all. The repercussions could destabilize more than you or I can anticipate."

Richard tilted his head, studying him. "And you're just going to let him continue?"

"I am watching," Emilio said firmly. "Alphonso is not clever enough to orchestrate this alone. He's a tool, a charming blade sent to slip between ribs and spill secrets. But whose blade? That is the puzzle. And until I solve it, he remains untouchable."

"I imagine that's difficult for you," Richard said bitterly.

Emilio allowed a faint smile, though it lacked any warmth. "I am a knight of the Order, Fitzwarren. Patience is a weapon I've learned to wield. But even weapons can dull with time."

There was a pause, heavy and thoughtful, as the two men regarded each other. Finally, Richard broke the silence. "And if you find out who he's working for?"

Emilio's voice dropped, his tone laced with quiet resolve. "Then Alphonso will learn the full extent of my anger."

For the first time, Richard felt a flicker of something resembling pity for Emilio. The Italian was

# A Queen's Rebel

ensnared in a web of alliances and betrayals, unable to move freely without risking everything. But the feeling was fleeting, Richard knew better than to linger on sentiment.

When Emilio turned to leave Richard watched him go. The intrigue surrounding Alphonso might have been Emilio's burden, but the weight of Dudley's investigation loomed large in Richard's mind. It did not even feel that long ago that he'd been involved in the death of Dudley's father. He had been present, and the final words, nay, speech the man had delivered before the axe fell, had been a long one. Richard could recall the three scribes employed to transcribe his final words busily scratching away on their parchments at their portable desks. He had ensured that there were enough so that every word was recorded, and above them, he had a tent erected to deselect the elements should it rain. This was not an occasion on which he wished the ink to run. The day before the execution the scribes had assembled, and he had taken to the scaffold himself and read aloud some lines to ensure they could hear. The distance had been judged too far, and the desks and tent had been moved much closer to the wooden structure.

Nothing had been left to chance.

Nothing. Or so he had thought.

The scribes hadn't really been needed; they were there simply to ensure that there could be no doubt as to what was in those final words—after all, he'd written them himself and checked them against the transcripts. The Duke had done a good job under the circumstances, and there had been very little variation in his delivery from the one Richard had written for him.

His speech had begun with the traditional narrative.

Sam Burnell

*Good people, all you that be here present to see me die. Though my death be odious and horrible to the flesh, yet I pray you judge the best in God's works, for he doth all for the best. And as for me, I am a wretched sinner ... "*

And then the crux of the matter, the statement that was to ensure that his son, Robert Dudley, kept his head. It was the price of retaining, if not his life, then his lineage.

*And one thing more good people I have to say unto you, which I am chiefly moved to do for discharge of my conscience; that is to warn you and exhort you to beware of these seditious preachers, and teachers of new doctrine, which pretend to preach God's word, but in very deed they preach their own fancies. Remember the manyfold plagues that this realm hath been touched with all since we dissevered ourselves from the catholic church of Christ. Have we not had war, famine, pestilence, the death of our king, rebellion, sedition among ourselves, conspiracies?*

Then, annoyingly, he'd finished with a statement of his own,

*And yet this act Wherefore I die, was not altogether of me (as it is thought) but I was procured and induced thereunto by others. I was I say induced thereunto by others ....*

Richard recalled his annoyance at the time – procured and induced by others! The queen was not going to be happy – and she hadn't been. The Duke was being executed as the perpetrator of the plot to subvert the primogeniture of the monarchy, and then he'd alluded to being a mere tool in a grander scheme! As he'd spoken those words 'procured and induced thereunto by others," the Duke's steady gaze had found Richard standing near the scribe's tent, his expression mutinous.

That final transgression by the Duke had cost Richard some time on his knees on the cold flags outside Mary's private chambers, where she had bid him consider his errors, blaming him entirely for the Duke's variation on the agreed speech. Richard supposed it was a fairly lenient penalty in comparison to what the Duke had received.

Robert Dudley, Richard mused, should be grateful to him. His knees had taken the brunt of Mary's anger, and more of the Earl's children had not been called to answer for his crimes. Richard unwisely reminded Her Majesty that the Earl had delivered the speech she had requested and confirmed that England should unite behind the Catholic faith and that all manner of ills that had blighted England were due to the abandonment of Rome. His rash reminder that she had got what she wanted from the Earl, if he remembered correctly, had cost him another two hours on the flagged floor.

## CHAPTER EIGHT

The door to the Angel swung open with a creak, and Richard Fitzwarren stepped inside, greeted by Nathanial. The clatter of London's chaos outside was muffled as the door closed behind him. The familiar warmth and scent of incense and spices wrapped around him like a blanket, offering a brief reprieve. He sighed, rubbing his face, and made his way through the narrow hallway to Nonny's rooms.

Nonny released him and stepped back, her perfume still trapping him in its hold. "Why so serious?

"Is it that obvious?" Richard said without humour.

Nonny her head slightly to one side nodded. "I am afraid it is," she said, her voice warm, but sharp with curiosity.

Richard moved toward the chair by the hearth, it was filled with silken cushions and Nonny watched with a raised eyebrow as he ejected them to the floor before seating himself. He closed his eyes for a moment, inhaling the heavy, familiar scent of the room—spiced wood, dried flowers, and the indulgent perfume of incense.

"Well, now you have made my furnishings homeless, are you going to tell me what 'as happened?" Nonny seated herself opposite him and folded her hands in her lap, regarding him with a serious stare.

"Have you got all night?" Richard replied wearily.

"For you, of course, I 'ave," Nonny smiled.

Richard groaned and leaned back in the chair, examining the ceiling for a moment before returning

# A Queen's Rebel

his gaze to Nonny. "My life is currently becoming a liturgy of lies."

Nonny frowned. A foot extended from beneath her voluminous skirts, clad in neat red leather, and it connected sharply with his shin. "You know exactly what that was for!"

Richard reached down to rub his shin and avoided her sharp gaze. "I suppose ...."

Nonny cut him off. "You can suppose what you like but do not bring less than yourself to me in the future. Feeling sorry for yourself, what shame is this?"

Richard raised his eyes to meet hers, his own a little shocked. "I forget myself, madam."

Nonny did not reply but continued to regard him with a cool stare.

"With my shield, or preferably on it, is the phrase that I believe you are thinking," Richard said.

"Luckily for you, I am not from Sparta but Saint-Brieuc," Nonny replied curtly, her annoyance with him still persisting.

"And does that make a difference?" Richard asked, then added, "I would wager the women of Saint-Brieuc are just as formidable."

"Do not waste your charm on me, Richard, I will not be won over so easily," Nonny said.

The silence hung in the air between them. When she felt he had suffered enough, she said. "You were in Scotland, I 'ere," Nonny said

"I was," Richard replied.

Nonny smiled. "So, what 'ave you brought me?"

Her words were forgiveness, and he allowed himself a small smile. Reaching inside his doublet, he removed a soft leather pouch and handed it to her.

Nonny accepted it, her pale ringed hands tugging at the gold cord that held it tight, then she shook out into her palm an exquisite pendant, the gold heavily linked chain slithering between her fingers. Crafted into the shape of a heart, the central ruby tugged in the candlelight in the room, seeming to send it back to the eye tenfold. It was surrounded by emeralds, which, in turn, were surrounded by an elegant and intricate weave of gold threads.

Nonny held it up before her by the chain, the pendant turning on the end, emitting a rich red light. "It is delightful." Nonny dropped the pendant and chain back out of sight into the black leather pouch. "And much better than the trinkets Devereux has brought.

It was Richard's turn to raise an eyebrow. "And why does he want to win your favour?"

"He didn't; he wished to sell them. I have not yet decided whether to buy them or not," Nonny said. She reached towards the floor and lifted a bag. The contents jangled, and the noise was clamorous and slightly unpleasant.

Richard took it from where she held it towards him. Lowering it to the floor, he pulled open the strings. Dipping his hands into the bag, he brought out a gold cherub. "Really?"

"Indeed, what worth have they? What can I do with that? When he is next here, he can take his ugly church trinkets back with him."

Richard had in his hand a crucifix. The style was old, the proportions clumsy, the body was made of wood, and it was overlayed with a thin gold veneer held in place with gold wire. It was old, and the wire had snapped in several areas; with the tension released, the creased gold foil had begun to peel from the wood. Richard returned it to the bag and lifted out a silver chalice. It was poorly made, and the base looked like it belonged to a candlestick originally. He dropped it back into the bag and drew the cords tight, he lifted it from the floor and was about to swing it back towards Nonny when he changed his mind and said instead. "You have, I assume, no intention of paying for these?"

Nonny's reply was simply a look of revulsion aimed at the bag.

# A Queen's Rebel

"Would you mind if I returned them to the owner?" Richard said.

"You would be doing me a favour. The longer they are here, the more the foolish man will believe I am interested in his tinkers' goods," Nonny said, waving her hand towards the bag.

"Now, tell me, what has brought you to my door this time without a smile on your face?" Nonny asked.

"It is, madam, a matter of murder," Richard said bluntly.

Nonny rolled her eyes. "Ever the dramatic. Whose?"

"Dudley's wife, Amy. I am to investigate the findings of the coroner's court and make a pronouncement as to whether I believe them to be correct or whether foul play was involved," Richard said dryly.

"Oh dear," Nonny said, "that will be very problematic."

"I'm glad you think so. Simply investigating the issue is going to make me unpopular enough, and if I find she was murdered then ...." Richard paused. "That can never, of course, be the outcome."

Nonny shook her head. "Of course you must confirm that the poor lady fell and that it was an accident," She leaned towards him, her eyes twinkling. But would it not be interesting if you knew it was otherwise? Indeed, would it not be even more interesting if you held proof that it was otherwise?"

"The thought had occurred to me," Richard replied.

"Well, I am sure you can twist it to your cause if you want to," Nonny said, then asked, "Tell me, how fares your brother? I do miss him."

"What is he? A bloody celebrated seer. It seems everyone misses him!" Richard exclaimed.

"He is good company, and when he sings he reminds me of my poor Giovani," Nonny said smiling.

"How so? Could he make the dogs cover their ears as well?" Richard said.

"You're jealous. When you lend your voice to song it sounds like an injured deer. Don't try and interrupt and deny it. I've heard the evidence with my own ears on more than one occasion when you've been drunk," Nonny said.

Richard laughed. "It's true I cannot deny it. Jack is back at the Fitzwarren house in London. He broke quite a few ribs, and the burn on his back is still healing, but he's mending well. De Nevarra has one of the monks of the order there who is limiting his freedom, and very soon I fear they will come to blows."

"Well then, take him with you," Nonny said.

"What? Take Jack to Oxford?" Richard replied.

"Indeed. Why not," Nonny said.

Richard opened his mouth to object, stopped himself and nodding slowly, said. "Why not indeed."


Richard knocked on the door to Jack's room, hesitated momentarily, and then pushed it open. "You look like you've just been informed of your funeral arrangements. What's the matter now?"

"Emilio's meddling again. This time, he's outdone himself."

Richard raised a brow, intrigued. "Meddling, how?"

"He's sent me a monk."

Richard stilled, then turned fully toward him, his curiosity clearly piqued. "A monk? For what purpose? Your spiritual salvation?"

Jack's laugh was short and dry. "Hardly. Emilio claims Brother Sebastian is to ensure my 'well-being.'"

# A Queen's Rebel

Richard's lips twitched, the beginnings of a smile tugging at the corners. "A nursemaid, then. How considerate of him."

Jack leaned forward, resting his forearms on his knees, his tone laden with sarcasm. "Oh, he's more than a nursemaid. Picture a stone wall in black robes, adorned with a large white cross, and a voice so authoritative it could command armies. That's Brother Sebastian."

Richard, unable to suppress his amusement, chuckled. "He sounds delightful. What's the issue? Perhaps a bit of discipline would do you good."

"Discipline?" Jack's scoff was louder than intended. "This man speaks as if God himself handed him the authority to correct me. Every word is laced with this maddening quiet disapproval, though he's far too polite to voice it outright."

Richard turned, leaning against a coffer, his grin widening. "You mean to tell me a man of the cloth is outmanoeuvring you with a few well-placed glances and subtle words?"

Jack's lips twitched, but he wasn't about to concede the point. "It's not the glances. It's the lectures. If I hear one more veiled sermon about the virtues of patience, I shall lose mine."

Richard laughed outright at that, the sound filling the room and warming the air. "So, the fiery Italian has appointed himself your keeper, and you've been saddled with a monk who dares to question your ways. I fail to see the tragedy here, Jack."

Jack leaned back in his chair. "The tragedy is that he doesn't question me outright. No, he wraps it all up in this air of practised calm, as if he's waiting for me to realise the error of my ways on my own."

"Perhaps he's not wrong."

Jack's eyes narrowed. "Don't side with him."

Richard tilted his head. "Would I dare!"

Jack snorted, the firelight catching in his eyes. "You're insufferable."

"And you're predictable." Richard's grin softened. "I have a story that will take your mind from your irritating monk."

Jack's eyes narrowed, fixed upon the bottle in Richard's hand as if just noticing it for the first time. "You're drunk?"

"Not yet, but give me an hour, and if God has mercy, I will be," Richard replied.

"Am I going to prefer to be in a similar state after the revelation you are about to make?" Jack asked.

Richard grinned. "Remember you told me to not keep my woes to myself. Well, brother, I am here with woes aplenty for us both. Are there any cups?"

Jack pointed towards a small table near the fire, regretted his impulsive movement and grimaced, as he watched Richard fill two cups and then turn back. He gave one to Jack, and hooking a stool with his foot, drew it towards Jack and seated himself.

"Go on," Jack said.

Richard raised his cup. "To ..... to tranquillity."

"If you say so," Jack replied dryly.

"I wish I were a rabbit. If I were, Jack, I'd spend my efforts burrowing a hole so far underground that no one would ever find me," Richard replied.

Jack accepted his brother's cup and settled back in the chair. "Go on, entertain me. The day thus far has been dull."

"Where to start?" Richard let out a long breath, his eyes on the floor between his boots. "Cecil ...."

"That bastard ...."

"God's bones! Jack! Do you want to let me tell this story or not?" Richard said, meeting his brother's eyes.

Jack's reply was an apologetic smile.

"That bastard Cecil has given me a death to investigate," Richard said, then waving an arm in the air and said dramatically, "Was it an accident or, more damned likely, was it murder?"

Jack opened his mouth to say something, instantly thought better of it and closed it.

"Well done," Richard replied, taking a sip from the cup. "A woman is found at the bottom of the stairs, her neck broken. Did she fall, or was she pushed? There are no witnesses, it seems, to the poor ladies' fall; the house was empty of servants, and no one heard her cry out or even heard the noise of her descent. Silently, she left the world. I often wondered if the ear does not witness a sound, then does the sound actually exist?"

"What?" Jack blurted.

"If, for example, this cup falls from a table while there is no one in the room to hear the clatter it makes on the wooden floor, does that noise exist? I always thought that ...."

"You are drunk! I don't give a damn about your wandering thoughts, get back to the woman you were telling me about," Jack said.

"Ah yes, sorry. So she was found dead. But the question is, was it murder? The coroner and the appointed jury thought not, but the question remains, and 'that bastard,' as you refer to him, would like me to review the facts," Richard replied dryly.

"Why?" Jack said, confusion in his voice. "Who was she?"

"Now that is the question, who was she, indeed," Richard reached inside his doublet found the report he had been given by Cecil and slung it into Jack's lap.

Jack abandoned his cup on the side table and drew the paper towards him, flattening the sheet with one hand. "You could, on occasion, just tell me."

"It's more entertaining this way," Richard said, smiling and emptying his cup.

"Who for?" Jack said, then turned his attention to the report.

Richard watched him read, waiting until the moment his brother reached the fourth line.

Jack looked up, shock on his face.

"Exactly! That is why I wish to become a rabbit," Richard said filling his cup badly and slopping a quantity over the rim to land on the floor.

"My God! Does the queen know?" Jack spluttered.

Richard shrugged. "Emilio knew within the hour of Cecil appointing me to the task, so we can assume she does."

"But why? The coroner's report says it was an accident," Jack said, sounding confused.

"Why? Because no one, and I mean no one, perhaps with the single exception of the queen herself, believes it," Richard flung his arm wide.

"That's true, but how is this going to help?" Jack said, cinfused.

"Simply this. Dudley's wife's death is a blight on the reputation of her favourite, not something she can countenance, and Cecil (the bastard), has convinced her that a reinvestigation of the facts will go some way to confirming that this was an accident and that the queen is taking seriously the allegations against her Master of the Horse. The queen believes that a second investigation will still the rumours and exonerate him from any wrongdoing which would make him a suitable marriage prospect, should she wish," Richard explained.

Jack shook his head. "No-one is going to believe it, they are still going to think he had her killed so he could marry the queen."

"True, but Cecil, the bastard, can be persuasive and right now, the queen would like Robert Dudley not to be suspected of foul play," Richard said.

"What are you going to do? If you investigate this and find that the coroner's verdict was correct then it'll make no difference unless you find some new fact that they overlooked, and if you find it was murder .... Well, then the queen is going to be wildly unhappy," Jack said, then realising the enormity of the problem said, "You've got to prove Dudley is innocent, compellingly so, or you are damned."

"Absolutely," Richard said, a slight slur now blighting his speech.

"And there is no chance of you being able to turn down this task?" Jack asked.

"None whatsoever. Cecil is going to sit back and watch me light my own pyre and laugh while I do. Unless I can dig a rabbit hole deep enough to take everyone with me, I don't have a choice," Richard replied.

"We could leave England. I've no care for this country," Jack said quickly, "The Lucianna is still in London."

"And Catherine, she's near her time. You can't drag her onboard the Lucianna now," Richard replied. There are too many fates in my hands. If I thought I could scoop all of them up and carry them safely, Jack, I would. But it would be like trying to hold water; some would trickle from my grasp and be lost."

Jack swallowed hard. "We shall tread this road together."

"I need to go to Oxford; you can't come with me," Richard said, raising his head from his hands.

"It's not far, and if I don't get out of here soon then there will be another death to investigate, and the cause will be boredom," Jack said grinning.

"You can't ride," Richard smiled evilly, "We'd need to put you in a litter, it'd take days to get you there."

"I'll ride," Jack said through gritted teeth. "I'll not arrive anywhere like a damned priest."

Richard was examining the floor again thoughtfully as if the answer he needed were there. "It would be a slow journey, but if you are sure."

"That's not what I expected you to say! Thank you," Jack said, genuinely shocked. "I thought you'd stagger from here, find the first horse you came to, and spur it to Oxford without me."

"I rather think, on this occasion, I would appreciate your company," then, with an evil grin, Richard added. "I'll arrange for a litter to accompany us, just as a precaution.

Jack threw his empty cup towards his brother, who snatched it out of the air.

## CHAPTER NINE

The White Hart Tavern sat in a bustling corner of London, its whitewashed walls streaked with grime but still gleaming faintly in the golden haze of the setting sun. The air was thick with the warmth of a hot summer evening, the kind that left a cloying stickiness on the skin and made the streets smell of baked stone and sweat. The sounds of laughter, clinking tankards, and a lute playing a lively tune spilt out from the open windows and carried on the heavy, warm breeze.

Richard Fitzwarren strode toward the tavern with his cloak casually thrown over one arm, his hat in hand, and the weighty pouch of gold beneath it. His step was purposeful, and his dark eyes scanned the crowd loitering outside. Merchants haggled, sailors shared bawdy stories, and a few dogs dozed lazily in the shade of the timbered building. Richard paid them no mind. His business lay upstairs.

Matthew, Myles' man, saw him the moment he entered and nodded towards the stairs. It was a silent message that Devereux was in his rooms above the tavern. Richard took the stairs two at a time and let himself into the outer room; the door to Myle's private room stood open, and Richard stepped inside. He abandoned his cloak, hat and the bag on the enormous four-poster bed that dominated the room. Rumour had it that Myles had taken the monstrosity in payment for a debt and then refused to part with it. His eyes landed upon the hilt of a sword resting against one of the bedposts.

Wrapping his hand around it, he lifted the weapon with practised ease, turning it to catch the light.

"And what do we have here…" he murmured, inspecting the blade.

"You saw it the moment you stepped through the door," Myles Devereux said, his tone tinged with amusement. Despite his nonchalance, there was a hint of satisfaction as he watched Fitzwarren examine the sword.

Richard snorted softly. "Hard to miss when you've left it on display like this." He ran his thumb along the guard, tracing the familiar design. "That's Norfolk's coat of arms."

"You're correct," Myles replied. "I'll gift it to Matthew in time. He has his eye on it."

"I'm sure he does. It's a fine piece," Richard said, turning the blade slowly. His fingers brushed against the runnel, smudged with dark, crusted stains. His expression hardened. "But it's filthy. You should take better care of it. Whose blood is this?"

"No one you'd know," Myles said, his tone casual, though satisfaction flickered in his eyes. "But he's no longer a problem."

"I can see that," Richard replied dryly. He angled the blade, his attention narrowing on the faint smear where the blood had pooled. His mind worked quickly, details falling into place like puzzle pieces. "The blade went in here—about this deep. He was wearing leather, wasn't he? Taller than you by a good foot, I'd wager. And he met his end…" Richard's gaze shifted to the floor. "Right there. Just in front of where you're standing now."

Myles stiffened slightly, his amusement waning. "Any more guesses you care to make?" he asked, his voice sharper now.

Richard didn't look up, still absorbed with the weapon. "Not guesses," he corrected. "The blood ran quickly down the runnel before the blade was pulled free, so the strike must have been upwards. The

# A Queen's Rebel

blade was withdrawn before the blood reached the hilt." He pointed the tip toward the floor. "It was then turned point down, and that's when you got this second stain here." He tapped the blade against a faint brown mark near the foot of the bed. "Your carpet, Myles, has been rather poorly cleaned."

Myles' jaw tightened. "Very good," he said sarcastically, clapping his hands with exaggerated slowness.

Richard raised a hand to silence him. "I'm not done." He pointed to another faint mark on the floor. "The blade went right through him, leaving a stain where he landed—on his back, I'd say."

Myles narrowed his eyes. "And how, pray, do you know that?"

Richard looked at him sharply, a wolfish grin tugging at the corner of his lips. "Simple. He had to be within striking distance, and there's no space for him to have fallen forward. And, though I admit this is a guess, I doubt even you would drive a blade through a man's back."

Myles's expression soured, but Richard pressed on, brandishing the sword lightly in his direction. "He was also a fool. And slow-witted."

"That's quite a claim," Myles snapped, his temper flaring. "How can you possibly know that?"

Richard shrugged, his tone maddeningly casual. "Easily. He wasn't similarly armed. There's not enough room in this chamber for proper swordplay. He was too close to you when you struck, meaning you took him by surprise. My guess," he smiled, turning the blade again in his hand, "The sword was already resting here by the bedpost. You had the advantage of reach, and he didn't."

"Meaning?" Myles prompted, his voice tight.

"Meaning," Richard said, lowering the blade but letting his words cut instead, "he never stood a chance. And neither will you if you don't clean your damned sword."

Richard Fitzwarren turned the sword in his hand, the weight of it familiar, the bloodied runnel a silent storyteller. His gaze flicked to Myles, who lingered by the desk, watching him with wary eyes.

"You struck before he could lay a hand on you," Richard began, his tone measured but sharp. "A direct thrust like this—" he raised the blade, angling it slightly "—would have been deflected easily by anyone with even a shred of skill. Which means your man wasn't trained. Few are, truthfully."

With that, Richard pivoted the blade, extending the hilt toward Myles.

Myles hesitated. His hand hovered, his eyes flicking from the sword to Richard's unreadable expression. At last, he gripped the leather-bound hilt and lifted the weapon, holding it level.

Richard studied him, his sharp eyes tracking every subtle movement. "One of the first lessons," he said, his voice low, deliberate, "is how to disarm your opponent. A man without a weapon is far easier to kill than one holding it."

The action was swift, too quick for Myles to anticipate. Pain shot through his wrist as Richard's hand struck with precision, knocking the sword free from his grip. The weapon clattered, the quillons rattling against a coffer lid before the blade snagged awkwardly in the carpet.

"What the Devil was that for?" Myles snarled, retreating a step and clutching his wrist.

Richard feigned innocence, his brow arching slightly. "Sorry?"

"Sorry?" Myles spat, his face a mix of anger and humiliation. "You nearly broke my bloody wrist!"

Richard stooped to retrieve the fallen sword, his movements unhurried, calm. He propped it back against the bedpost with a shrug. "You bested a half-wit, Myles. Don't delude yourself into thinking you can wield this against anyone who's ever had proper training."

# A Queen's Rebel

Myles's temper flared, his cheeks reddening. "A lesson? You arrogant cur!"

"It's been said," Richard replied smoothly, his tone maddeningly composed. "But hear me out. Nearly every man who knows how to use a sword had one thrust into his hand before he lost his milk teeth. It's instinct for them. Don't think you can match that overnight—or at all."

Myles rounded the desk, placing the solid oak barrier between them, his glare unwavering.

"Settle your temper, Myles," Richard said, dropping into a nearby chair. "You know I'm right."

"You could have just told me," Myles snapped, though the heat in his voice had dulled slightly. "Words would have been sufficient."

"You forget, Myles. I know you too well." Richard glanced at Amica, Myles' cat, as if sharing a private joke. "Your master," he said to the cat, "is hot-tempered at best and stubborn beyond belief at the worst."

"That's harsh," Myles muttered, though he didn't deny it.

"But true," Richard replied smoothly. His tone sharpened as his dark eyes locked on Myles. "And Andrew would have my head if I didn't deliver an adequate warning."

"Now that was unfair," Myles shot back, his frustration flaring anew.

"Perhaps," Richard said, his attention drifting back to Amica. "But the warning has been delivered, and I owe it to your brother's memory to give it, blunt though it may have been."

Myles cursed under his breath but circled the desk and dropped into the chair opposite Richard.

"Let not arrogance and ignorance be your undoing," Richard said, his voice low and cutting.

Myles crossed his arms, a sulky edge to his expression. "I could surprise you, Fitzwarren. Maybe I'll learn to wield one."

Richard's smile deepened, though it didn't reach his eyes. "As I said, most men with skill began before they could spell their own names. It's a little late, Myles. And I'd hate for you to meet a man as good as my brother."

"Or you," Myles said.

"Obviously," Richard said, then after a short pause Richard retrieved a small pouch from inside his doublet and held it towards Myles. "And now for a change of subject."

Myles leaned towards his guest and took it, releasing the strings he peered inside. "I see you have been to the Angel."

"They are not to Nonny's taste, she asked me to return then, however I have a question, how many church trinkets do you have left?"

"The gold had a value, and most of it is gone. Not that I got a fraction of what it was worth from you, " Myles Devereux grumbled.

"You got a good price, better than Mya the Jew would have given you, and let's not forget that you did stamp the reverse of all the coins with the wrong die, a mistake if you remember that I had to answer for," Richard said sternly.

Myles draped a leg over the arm of the chair and regarded Richard with a cool stare. "I am but poor stuff when compared to yourself, a simple man who tries to do his best. You should have noticed."

"I'll accept that. I should have; you are right," Richard said; the cat on Devereux's knee abandoned its owner and strutted across the carpet before jumping soundlessly onto Richard's lap.

"Traitor," Myles said, fixing the cat with a cold stare.

"Your cat is like its owner, eager to annoy," Richard replied, grinning.

"So, what do you want?" Myles changed the subject, his eyes still resting on his cat lying on her back, purring, eyes closed.

# A Queen's Rebel

"You happened upon quite a hoard, and not all of it was easy to trade in. There were reliquaries and other items. Do you still have them?" Richard asked.

Myles smiled. "Why?"

"Because I would like to buy them, maybe all, depending on how much you have?"

Half an hour later, Myles Devereux, holding an oil lamp in his hand, entered a stable behind his Tavern, the White Hart. When Richard was inside, he closed the door and dropped a bolt in place.

"Interesting, not many stables bolt from the inside," Richard observed.

"This one does, and with very good reason," Myles set the lamp down on the floor.

There was little to see; the floor was swept clean of old bedding. The door was solid and new, and the walls had two small shelves, one on either side, where unlit lamps were sat—also unusual for a stable. Richard watched as Myles lifted each one down and lit it from the one he had brought before setting them back on their shelves. When he had finished, the small empty room was bathed in light.

Myles lifted the lamp and handed it to Richard, "Step back against the stable door and hold this."

Richard obliged, and as he watched, Myles Devereux found two disguised handles beneath the planking of the back wall. Pulling on them hard, the whole wall section tilted forward until it lay upon the stone flags. Myles took the lamp from Richard and walked into the small room that had been hidden at the back of the stable.

It was filled with an untidy array of boxes, folded altar plates, and a coffer crammed with silverware.

Myles, seeing Richard's eyes rest on the silver, said, "It's poor quality, and so I've left it to last; it's not worth much."

"Maybe not to you," Richard lifted out a chained thurible.

"These are the items we dare not sell," Myles pointed towards the wooden objects.

"What were you going to do with them?" Richard asked.

Myles shrugged. "It's well-seasoned wood. I thought I'd have it fed into my fire over the winter."

Richard lifted a box from the floor. It was wooden, with an intricate pattern on the top, there had been jewels in the corners and these were now missing. Lifting the lid Richard looked inside.

Myles, looking over his shoulder, said. "Some poor bastard's finger. That's the most popular item I've found. Finger bones, a few rusted nails, some teeth, splintered wood, shards of pottery crusted with dried flecks of blood and stained rags are the items you'll find in here."

"And you've checked them all?" Richard replied.

"Of course, there was a finger very much like that, and upon it was this," Myles extended his right hand towards Richard, "Have you seen a finer ruby?"

"You should be careful, that looks like a bishop's ring," Richard said, selecting another box.

Myles twisted his hand, his eyes still on the gem. "I think you are mistaken, Fitzwarren. It looks like my ring."

Richard ignored him and lifted another lid. The treasure was inside an iron nail, square-headed, rusted, and stained.

"Now, these did intrigue me," Myles prodded the nail in the box with a finger before stooping and lifting a silver chalice from the floor, its contents rattling as he did so. "Look at these? They're long, short, broad, and narrow, and this one is so small I don't suppose it would be strong enough to hold a mouse up with."

Myles sifted his hand through the collection of nails and lifted one from the chalice. It was vicious-looking, and from its colouring, it was bronze. It was about seven inches long, with a square profile and a large flat head. The head bore the marks from a hammer, and the point was bent. "This would be a more likely candidate."

Richard twisted his face as he examined it. "Are you sure? Would they nail up their criminals with bronze nails? Iron would be cheaper."

"Fair point, like this, then, but iron," Myles said, discarding the nail and then dumping the chalice back noisily where he had found it.

"Then the altars. They, too, have been a trove of gifts," Myles picked one up.

It was a portable altar. The two sides folded out, and then a central section came forward to support it and provide a base for a crucifix or chalice. The wood had been split apart where it would have formed a base, and the bottom section pulled away.

"Each one was like an oyster to you, wasn't it," Richard observed dryly, his fingers running over the damage.

"It was mostly rubbish, the odd gem, but in the main fragments of bones and scraps of cloth a botcher wouldn't even bother with," Myles said, "I should not have been surprised that there was little of worth. All require a relic to be included; that is the unwritten lore of the catholic faith, but it would be a sin to break it open and gaze upon it, so they can include any scrap they like from the rubbish heap."

Richard shook his head. "You are a cynic, Devereux. They could, but often the relic is provided by the man who commissioned the piece and to them, it would have some worth."

"True, and in those instances, I did find a few items of worth," Myles leaned towards Richard and said with an evil smile, "And as you say, I do like a surprise."

Richard stood back and surveyed the remains of the hoard. "Very well, so the only question that remains is how much?"

"Which ones do you want?" Myles said, his eyes straying back to admire the ruby on his hand.

"All of it," Richard replied, grinning.

## CHAPTER TEN

Jack sighed deeply, his patience wearing thin. He gestured toward the door, towering over the servant who was nervously wringing her hands. "I'll not have my wife hiding from me," he said firmly. "Step aside."

"But, My Lord, she insisted," the maid stammered, her cheeks reddening. "She said it's not … seemly for you to see her in her state."

Jack groaned and pinched the bridge of his nose. "Seemly? We're married! What nonsense. Is she alone?"

"She's with Mistress Turner, My Lord," the maid answered, her eyes fixed firmly on the floor.

"Good," Jack muttered. He stepped closer to the door and knocked firmly. "Catherine? It's me."

A muffled response came through the heavy wooden door. "You're speaking to me now, Jack."

"Not like this," he called back, exasperated, resting his forehead against the door. "Let me in."

"Absolutely not!" Catherine's voice carried both a smile and a note of finality. "I told Mary it wouldn't be proper. My confinement started yesterday, I did tell you."

Jack laughed softly, shaking his head. "Proper? We've shared a bed, Catherine. I've seen you more improperly than any man alive."

A gasp and a snicker from the other side of the door made Jack grin. He could imagine Mistress Turner's scandalised look.

"Jack Fitzwarren, have you no shame?" she replied, though amusement laced her tone.

"Not when it comes to you," Jack retorted. "I'll settle for speaking through the door if I must, but I need your blessing."

"Blessing for what?" Catherine's curiosity piqued.

"For Oxford," Jack said, straightening up. "Richard is heading there on some business, and he's asked me to join him. I promise to be gone no more than two weeks."

A pause followed, and Jack held his breath. He heard hushed whispers on the other side of the door, no doubt Catherine consulting Mistress Turner. Finally, her voice returned soft and affectionate. "You have my blessing, Jack. The babe is not due for a month. Go to Oxford and relieve your boredom before you drive us all mad, pacing the halls."

Jack grinned. "You noticed that, did you?"

"I'm with child, Jack, not blind," Catherine teased. "But I'll miss you. You'll write to me?"

"Every day if it pleases you," Jack promised, his voice warm. "I'll leave you in peace before Mistress Turner brands me a tyrant. Take care of yourself."

"I will," Catherine replied, her voice soft.

With a spring in his step, Jack turned away from the door, his earlier exasperation forgotten. He was halfway down the corridor when he muttered, "Now, where's that damn brother of mine?"

Jack found Richard lounging in the study, a goblet of wine in hand and an amused expression on his face as Jack strode in.

"You look pleased with yourself," Richard said. "Managed to sweet-talk your way through a locked door, did you?"

"Not exactly," Jack replied, collapsing into a chair. "But I have her blessing."

Richard raised his goblet in a mock salute. "Well done. Now the question remains: can you keep up with me for a few weeks in Oxford?"

Jack grinned. "I'm more concerned about whether Oxford can keep up with us."

## A Queen's Rebel

Richard's sharp eyes swept over his brother as he lounged in the chair across from him. Jack was still the same figure he'd always been, his frame betraying no signs of a life indulged in excess or comfort. But Richard's practised gaze didn't miss the subtle details that others might overlook—the hollowness in Jack's cheeks, the sallow pallor to his skin that hadn't been there before, the slight hesitation in his movements as if his body were not entirely his ally.

"You look like a ghost, Jack," Richard remarked, his tone wry but edged with concern.

Jack rolled his eyes and waved a dismissive hand. "Don't, Richard. I've had enough coddling from Catherine to last me a lifetime."

"Coddling?" Richard arched an eyebrow, leaning back in his chair with the casual grace of a man who noticed everything. "I'd wager she's more likely to knock sense into that thick skull of yours than coddle you."

Jack managed a faint grin. "Perhaps, but it's all in good faith."

Richard's expression softened, but his scrutiny lingered. The illness that had clung to Jack months ago had left its marks, faint but undeniable. His movements lacked the brisk confidence that once defined him, and his laughter—though still frequent—was quieter, as if restrained by some invisible tether. The broken ribs had knitted, and the burns were mostly healed, so he had been told, but weakness still lingered.

"The journey may do you some good," Richard said finally, his tone lighter, though his gaze remained searching. "A week in Oxford, away from Catherine's watchful eye and these stifling walls. Fresh air, a bit of intrigue."

Jack raised an eyebrow. "Fresh air? Oxford? You must be thinking of some other place entirely."

Richard allowed a ghost of a smile to curve his lips. "Perhaps. But it's better than sitting here, letting yourself fade into the background."

Jack shifted in his seat, brushing off Richard's scrutiny with a casualness that didn't quite convince him. "I'm fine, Richard."

Richard leaned forward, his elbows resting on his knees as he studied his brother. "Fine, perhaps. But not yourself. Oxford will remind you who you are—if the journey doesn't first."

Jack tilted his head, his grin returning in earnest this time. "Careful, Richard, or I'll start to think you're concerned about me."

The following morning, Sebastian woke Jack earlier than he would have liked. The monk had different ideas about how the day was going to start. "Your muscles need to remember how to move before you can wield a weapon properly."

Jack rolled his eyes, wincing as the motion tugged at his shoulder. "I think my muscles have remembered quite enough, thank you. I've been walking around the house just fine."

Sebastian straightened, his calm demeanour unshaken. "Walking and fighting are two very different things, my Lord. The strength required to hold a sword steady, to parry, to thrust—it does not come from gentle walks along the corridors."

"What do you want me to do?" Jack said resignedly.

"Raise your left arm, hold it out …. Not like that, straight, yes, better," Sebastian said. "Now straighten it."

"I can't, you know that," Jack said a little sullenly.

"No, I don't. Why do you think you can't straighten it?" Sebastian asked.

There was a dark flicker of fury for a second in Jack's eyes. "Because I've been cooked like a rabbit in a pot, if you remember, and my skin will not let me move as I used to."

Sebastian nodded. "That is partly true."

"Why only partly," Jack shot back, lowering his arm.

"Please keep your arm out straight. That's good. Now flex it a little more at the elbow, there. " Sebastian put his hands on Jack's arm, forcing it straighter.

"Damn you, don't it'll ...."

"It'll what, hurt?" Sebastian said, releasing Jack's arm. "You can lower your arm for a moment. It hurts here, Jack," Sebastian leaned forward and tapped Jack's temple. "Now raise your arm again, close your eyes and think about what I said when you push your muscles to straighten it ... that's right, maybe a little more. Clench your fist, and roll your arm to the left and then the right. Good." Sebastian's thick hands guided Jack through the motions.

After another ten minutes Jack had sweat on his brow, and he had to admit the pain he was feeling was that of unused muscles and not the searing pain he'd suffered when the burns had cracked and peeled.

Sebastian smiled and lifted an empty water jug from the table. "Hold this h, arms fully extended, and keep it steady."

Jack obeyed, gripping the jug tightly and holding it out in front of him. "This is easy."

Sebastian didn't respond, simply stepping back and watching. After a minute, Jack's arms began to tremble, the strain of holding the weight growing steadily worse.

"Still easy?" Sebastian asked, raising an eyebrow.

Jack gritted his teeth. "Absolutely."

"Good," Sebastian said with an almost imperceptible smile. "Now raise it above your head and hold it there."

Jack groaned but complied, the muscles in his shoulders and arms burning as he struggled to keep the jug aloft. After another minute, he lowered it with a gasp, nearly dropping it.

"I suppose you think this is helpful," Jack muttered, rolling his shoulders to ease the ache.

"It is," Sebastian replied, unbothered. "You're rebuilding your strength, which you'll need if you're to regain your skill with a blade."

By the time they finished, Jack was thoroughly exhausted.

"I don't think I've ever worked this hard without a sword in my hand," Jack said, half-laughing, half-complaining.

Sebastian gave a rare smile. "Then imagine how much harder it will be when the swords return."

Jack groaned, leaning back against the wall. "God help me. You're relentless."

"I am," Sebastian said with a small bow. "And you'll thank me for it. We'll continue tomorrow, my Lord. Rest well."

Jack watched him leave, shaking his head. Despite his aching muscles, he couldn't help but feel a flicker of gratitude. But still, he was looking forward to the short visit to Oxford, and he had no intention of taking Sebastian with him. Maybe when he returned, he'd listen to the monk.

Jack went off searching for his brother and was directed towards the stables after a few dead ends.

Richard, seated on a half barrel, a coffer before him, was restoring the shine to Church silver. A slow process; on top of the coffer were two silver chalices he had completed, their radiance restored, but to his right, a box held many more dull and dirty items awaiting the pressure of cloth and paste.

The door rattled as someone on the outside tried to lift the latch on the stable door. "Richard? Are you in there?" It was Jack's voice, the latch rattled again.

Richard hesitated. He could ignore him.

"I was told you were here, what are you doing?" Jack said, a boot, this time kicking at the bottom of the door. "I can see the light round the side of the door."

Sighing, Richard rose and removed the pg holding the door closed. Jack let himself in. "Secure it behind you if you would."

"And what requires such secrecy," Jack said, turning back and surveying the inside of the tack room. Pulling a closed box across the floor, he set it next to the coffer and sat opposite his brother. Jack was never one to stand if he could sit.

"Well, now you are here, you can help; it should take less time with the two of us," Richard said and flung a cloth towards his brother.

Jack caught it mid-air and looked around the room. "Less time to do what?"

"Clean, polish, and organise dear brother," Richard said, an arm swinging around the room.

Jack's gaze rested on a silver cup Richard had been polishing and then ran to a box filled with the same, their surfaces dull and tarnished.

"Exactly, there is a lot to get through," Richard said.

Jack leaned forward and plucked one from the box. It was a squat silver chalice. The rim on the outside had a dozen or so square indents, all empty, where once gems had rested. "Why?"

"You are nothing more than a bag of questions, are you? Polish, and I will provide answers. Fair?" Richard said, nudging a pot of paste towards Jack that sat between them on the top of the coffer.

Jack lifted the pot, dipped his cloth into it, and began to apply it to the silver. "This is poor stuff?

Where did you get it? It's too coarse for silver. It'll mark it."

"Not just a bag of questions, it seems there is space in there for plenty of complaint as well," Richard grumbled.

"I'd not use this on my horse's tack, never mind these ornaments," Jack said, pushing the pot back towards Richard, "It's not been ground finely enough."

Richard prodded the earthenware pot with his finger, sending it back towards Jack. "It was all I could get, and a few scratches won't, on this occasion, matter, it is the overall presentation of the items that I am aiming for."

Jack lifted the pot again and dipped a finger in, shaking his head. "It's the pumice that's not been ground fine enough. Christ you can even see bits of shell in this."

Jack rose, the pot in his hand.

"Where are you going?"

"To fix this!" Jack said, lifting the bar from inside the door and disappearing, leaving Richard alone.

Jack returned ten minutes later. The paste was now in a pestle. Jack dipped his fingers in and rubbed some between his thumb and forefinger. "Better?"

Richard dabbed some on to his cloth and swirled it on the surface of a plate. "Better," he admitted grudgingly.

"You might have been forced to clean your horse's tack as a lad, but I was the poor bastard who had to make that paste," Jack said, tugging his seat closer and taking up his cloth and the silverware again.

"I said it's better," Richard said again.

"I don't suppose you even know what's in it?" Jack continued to scoff as he massaged the silver with the cloth, the brilliance of the metal beginning to emerge as he rubbed.

# A Queen's Rebel

"Of course I do," Richard replied inadvisedly.

"Go on then, what's in it?" Jack said, continuing to work on the chalice.

"Pumice," Richard replied quickly.

Jack looked up. "You only know that because I told you it wasn't ground fine enough. What else?"

Richard lifted the pot to his nose and sniffed tentatively.

"Ha! You don't know," Jack sounded delighted.

"Alright, there's pumice ...."

"You've said that," Jack interrupted.

"Will you let me finish! There's pumice and egg shells ...."

"Yes."

"And also, piss," Richard added.

Jack laughed, a tear leaking from one corner of his eye.

"What's so funny! There's piss in everything that leaks past the door of an apothecary's," Richard said, annoyed.

"If this had piss in it then it would take the shine rather than restore it. Just admit it, you haven't got a clue," Jack said, still chuckling, satisfied with the shine on the chalice, he set it next to the others Richard had completed and selected another from the pile.

"Alright, I admit it, you sainted bloody martyr, I haven't a clue. And I don't need to, either," Richard replied.

"Why's that then?" Jack said, holding a goblet at arm's length and examining his work.

"I've got you," Richard said, an evil smile on his face.

Jack ignoring the comment, said instead. "Come on then, tell me why we are busying our evening indulging in women's work without so much as a glass of wine to slake our thirsts."

Richard reached down toward the floor, smiling he produced a jug and slopped wine into two of the vessels that had already been cleaned.

"I've just cleaned those!" Jack exclaimed.

"All part of the plan, my dear brother. I wish these to look cared for, and, at the same time, in use; the odd wine stain will add a certain amount of authenticity," Richard said, raising a chalice and toasting his brother.

Jack took a sip and grimaced. "I swear they sour the wine."

"It's probably all the grit and shit you failed to clean from the inside. Mine tastes fine," Richard said happily.

Jack emptied the chalice, holding it forward for a refill. "So, why are we doing this?"

Richard tipped the wine jug. "Well, I need to create a plot, and these are going to be the props for that plot. The substance that will give form to what otherwise would be mere words."

When Richard had finished outlining his use for the church trappings, Jack had a grim look on his face. "You are an evil bastard, but you know that, don't you?"

"If there was another way …." Richard said smiling.

"You'd not take it. This appeals far too much to your sense of the dramatic; there is a lot that could go wrong, especially if this lot is discovered here before you move it," Jack pointed out, waiving an altar cross in his brother's face.

"I'm being careful," Richard replied.

"How many times have I heard that?" Jack said, shaking his head and adding the polished cross to the line of completed items. "Are we finished?"

"The silverware is, now we just need to clean those?" Richard gestured towards a pile of wooden objects stacked against a wall; they were covered in dust, cobwebs, and a goodly coating of dried bird shit.

"You are jesting?" Jack said incredulously.

# A Queen's Rebel

"I am afraid not. Like Hurcules, we have not just one labour to face," Richard said mischievously.

The Angel was busy as usual. Richard Fitzwarren entered, his sharp gaze cutting through the noise and chaos as he scanned the room. At a private table tucked into the corner, Myles Devereux sat alone, his position affording him a commanding view of the entire room.

The table was infamous—always empty, always available. No one dared occupy it, not even in Myles's absence. It was his by silent decree, offering him the advantage of seeing every entrance, every movement, while ensuring no one could eavesdrop on his dealings.

Richard weaved through the tables and slid into the chair opposite Myles. The other man barely acknowledged him, his attention seemingly fixed on the cup of wine in his hand, the liquid swirling lazily under the light of the Angel's flickering candles.

"Myles," Richard said, leaning forward slightly.

"Richard," Myles replied smoothly, lifting his dark eyes to meet his guest's. A faint smirk tugged at his lips. "You're prompt. A quality I always appreciate."

Richard ignored the pleasantry, cutting straight to the matter at hand. "The church trappings have been cleaned and split into five caches. All are ready for collection and are currently stored under guard at the Fitzwarren house."

Myles arched a brow, setting his goblet down with a soft clink. "Efficient, as always. And the men?"

Richard's mouth thinned into a determined line. "The order remains unchanged. I want the trail to lead precisely as we discussed."

Myles tapped a finger against the edge of the table, his smile widening into something sharper.

"Ah, yes, your little trail of breadcrumbs. I must admit, Richard, it's an extravagant display of theatrics."

Richard frowned. "You're not paid to admire the work, Myles. You're paid to carry it out."

Myles chuckled, his voice a low purr. "Paid, you say? That's an interesting word, considering we've yet to discuss my fee."

Richard's eyes narrowed. "Then name it."

Myles leaned back in his chair, his gaze steady as he considered the man across from him. "The price will be fair," he said, his tone almost casual. "But as yet, I don't know what traps may lie in my path. The harder the task, the higher the cost."

Richard exhaled through his nose, his irritation barely concealed. "Agreed. But I expect results."

"You always do," Myles replied, lifting his cup once more. He took a slow sip, savouring the wine, before changing the subject. "I hear you've been charged with investigating the death of Amy Robsart. Quite the honor."

Richard rolled his eyes, leaning back in his chair. "Is there anyone in Christendom who hasn't heard? It seems even the rats in the gutter are whispering about it."

Myles laughed softly. "Well, it is quite the scandal, isn't it? A beautiful woman, dead under mysterious circumstances, and her husband—Robert Dudley, no less—at the centre of it all. Tell me, do you think he did it?"

Richard's expression darkened. "Dudley's ambition knows no bounds. He would raze heaven itself if it meant a clear path to Elizabeth."

"And yet," Myles said, swirling his wine, "murder is a dangerous gamble. If the truth ever came to light…"

Richard snorted. "The truth rarely sees the light in matters of power. But yes, if Dudley killed her, he would have done so with care. A man like him doesn't leave loose ends."

# A Queen's Rebel

Myles inclined his head, his smirk returning. "A fair point. Still, it makes for an entertaining distraction."

"For some," Richard muttered. "For me, it's just another cursed mess."

Myles drained the last of his wine and set the cup down with a satisfied sigh. "Well, then, I wish you luck in untangling it. And in your other... ventures. I'll ensure your instructions are carried out."

Richard nodded, rising from his seat. "Good. And Myles."

Myles met his gaze.

"Remember, this isn't just a game," Richard said, a warning tone in his voice.

"Have I ever let you down?" Myles was indignant. "In fact quite the opposite."

Richard's tone softened. "Forgive me, my nerves feel as if they have been tied to a lute and plucked by the Devil."

Myles drummed his fingers on the table for a moment before he spoke. "Not long ago, you gave me a warning, one I did not like. It's time for me to return that favour. Do not have me carry out this task; these are steps you cannot retrace. You are playing, Fitzwarren, with men who outrank you and always will."

Richard regarded him for a moment. "You are right I do not like the warning."

A moment later, Myles was watching him leave the Angel.

## CHAPTER ELEVEN

The morning was young, but the promise of another scorching summer day hung in the air. The horses were saddled, their bridles creaking softly as they shifted, and the sharp tang of leather mixed with the faint freshness of lingering dew. Astride his horse, Richard sat tall in the saddle, his gaze sweeping over the men assembling in the yard behind the Fitzwarren house. Jack was in conversation with his lawyer, who seemed to have received an invitation to join them.

"Lord Fitzwarren, I cannot express how delighted I am that you have asked me to accompany you. If there are any legal matters you wish to discuss regarding how I can be of assistance, I would only be to ...." Master Threadmill said.

Jack held a gloved hand up to still his words. "Master Threadmill! Your memory is short."

The lawyer looked slightly taken aback and then paled.

"Exactly, we know each other well. We might no longer be assailed from all sides, but the situation remains the same. If I need your professional advice, I'll ask," Jack said, his tone pleasant, the sun brightening his eyes.

"I hope, my Lord, that we are never again in such a situation," Threadmill replied seriously.

Richard's sharp gaze moved over the ranks of men: a mix of hired guards, servants, and retainers. All seemed in order, but one figure was conspicuously absent.

Richard frowned, his eyes narrowing as he scanned the group again. Moving his horse closer to his brother's, he asked. "Where is Brother Sebastian?" Richard's tone was laced with suspicion.

Jack, busy adjusting his reins with his good hand, didn't meet his brother's gaze. Instead, he focused on his horse as if the animal's bridle demanded his full attention.

Richard's frown deepened. "Don't ignore me, Jack. The monk—where is he?"

Jack let out a long-suffering sigh and finally looked up, the faintest trace of a smirk tugging at his lips. "I sent him away."

Richard stared at his brother, incredulous.

"I sent him away," Jack repeated casually, brushing an imaginary speck of dust from his doublet. "He received an urgent summons to return to the Order's headquarters."

Richard's mouth fell open slightly. "A summons? And I suppose this summons conveniently appeared in your hand when you wanted him gone?"

Jack shrugged, clearly unrepentant. "He is insufferable."

Richard's jaw clenched, his fingers tightening on the reins. "Do you have any idea what Emilio will do when he finds out?"

"Let him find out," Jack replied breezily. "By then, we'll have been to Oxford and back."

Richard shook his head, his irritation simmering just below the surface. "The man was here for your good. You're not invincible, you know."

"I don't need a monk to look after me," Jack retorted, his tone growing sharper.

Richard shot his brother a pointed look, his gaze sweeping over Jack's pale complexion and the stiffness in his movements before saying with sarcasm, "Yes, because you're in such robust health right now."

Jack waved the remark away, unwilling to rise to the bait. "Richard. I have you, don't I? And all these capable men. What more could I need?"

"A brain," Richard muttered under his breath, shaking his head again. He straightened in the saddle, his sharp gaze sweeping the yard one last time. Richard muttered something incomprehensible under his breath and turned his horse toward the road. "Come on, then. Let's see if you can survive without your holy nursemaid. But don't expect me to save you from your own idiocy."

Jack followed, grinning despite himself. "That's what brothers are for, isn't it?"

Richard snorted but said nothing, his disapproval evident in every rigid line of his posture. Jack, however, seemed content, riding out of the yard with the easy confidence of a man who believed he'd outwitted the world.

The horses' hooves clattered rhythmically against the dirt road as the brothers rode side by side, the countryside around them growing greener and denser the more they moved away from London. The early morning air held a fleeting coolness, a fragile remnant of the night soon to be swept away by the blazing heat of the summer day. Jack shifted in his saddle, adjusting the reins with gloved hands that betrayed no hint of unease, though his posture bore the faint stiffness of lingering fatigue. His eyes flicked to Richard, who sat astride his horse with practiced ease, his sharp gaze scanning the line of their small company with an intensity that never wavered.

"Why did you bring Threadmill?" Richard asked, breaking the comfortable silence. "Surely not just to entertain me?"

Jack smiled faintly, his tone light despite the weight of the topic. "I actually thought he might be of use. Despite his vocation, I do trust him, and he would not, I think, betray our cause."

"Our cause?" Richard echoed, arching a dark brow.

"I'm here, aren't I?" Jack replied, a touch of humour in his voice. "So it's our cause now."

Richard smiled but didn't immediately respond. He glanced over his shoulder to where Threadmill rode near the rear of the group, his slight frame bouncing awkwardly in the saddle. "As you say. Our cause. And yet, he might not willingly betray us, but persuasion can be a painful art, and there's nothing to say he might not say something harmful under pressure."

Jack frowned, his lips tightening briefly. "He's thorough and organised, and I trust him."

Richard nodded, his expression unreadable. "Fair enough. Though I do hope your trust in him is well-placed."

Jack chuckled softly, though there was no humour in it. "You're beginning to lecture me like that damned monk. I am sure of my decision, there is nothing wrong with my mind."

"You should listen to him, he's probably right, even if you find him insufferable," Richard replied. He glanced sidelong at his brother. "Speaking of which, I imagine he won't be too pleased when he finds out you have evaded him."

Jack's grin widened, a mischievous glint in his eye. "I'm sure he won't. But I've managed to convince him his services were urgently required elsewhere."

Richard barked a laugh, shaking his head. "You mean you lied to him."

"I wouldn't call it lying," Jack replied smoothly. "I'd call it strategic redirection."

Richard snorted, leaning slightly forward in his saddle. "I'd pay to see his face when he finds out.

No doubt you'll have to endure his righteous indignation when he tracks you down."

Jack waved a dismissive hand, though the gesture was slow and deliberate. "By then, we'll have our answers—or at least the threads of them. Yesterday, the fool had me balancing a jug on my head! I can live without his company for a few days."

"A jug?" Richard queried.

"Indeed."

"Were you any good?" Richard asked.

Jack shot his brother a sour look.

Richard grinned back in reply. "So we won't see you perform amongst the jugglers at the Christmas revels then?"

The two rode for another hour, the noise of their retinue filling the gaps between their conversation. Jack shifted slightly in his saddle; his left side was aching more than he cared to admit, despite his best efforts to hide the fact Richard had noticed.

Jack felt a heaviness settle over him as the journey progressed, and it was worse than he had anticipated. The rhythmic sway of the horse beneath him, once a familiar and comforting motion, now seemed to sap his strength with every step. His muscles ached, his left arm throbbed faintly beneath his doublet, and his grip on the reins felt tenuous at best. By the time they reached the tavern, every movement felt like a Herculean effort.

Richard had dismounted first, his movements fluid and practised. His sharp eyes immediately turned to observe Jack. He held the bridle of Jack's horse, waiting. Jack, determined not to show weakness, gripped the pommel tightly and swung his leg over the saddle.

The dismount lacked any grace. His feet hit the ground heavily, and he stumbled slightly, catching himself with a hand on the saddle. Richard, still holding the bridle, said nothing for a moment, his gaze steady. Then, with a slight smirk, he remarked, "I'm glad we're not in a hurry."

Jack shot him a glare, his pride smarting more than his aching body. "I told you I'd be fine, and I will," he growled, brushing past his brother as he headed toward the tavern door.

Richard handed the reins to one of their men but waited to follow. He stood for a moment, watching Jack's stiff gait and how his shoulders slumped slightly more than usual. His pale complexion and the fine sheen of sweat at his temple didn't escape Richard's notice either, and a flicker of concern passed through him.

Richard overtook, and Jack let his brother go through the door into the tavern. Threadmill came to stand next to Jack. "My Lord, would you like me to announce your arrival?"

"Don't worry, that's in hand. My brother is well able to command any landlord, and he enjoys it," Jack said to Threadmill, who looked a little bemused by the answer, so Jack added. "We shall just wait here."

From inside the tavern came the noise of boots on the stone floor, the scrape of tables, chairs and benches as they were rearranged and shouts of command. Jack sidestepped two men who were ejected over the threshold, cursing the landlord; they looked at Jack, caught sight of the other men, and vanished quickly around the corner.

"If you will, My Lord," Richard announced formally, reappearing at the doorway.

Jack turned to Threadmill before he ducked inside and said quietly. "He's out of practice, that took far too long."

Inside, half the tavern had been cleared, tables and benches rearranged, and Jack was led towards one near the fire by his brother. On one side of the table, a wainscot chair had been placed, and

Jack looked at it with relief. It meant he could rest his weight on the chair arm.

"Join us," Jack beckoned Threadmill from where he was about to take a seat with the other men.

Threadmill, still slightly nervous, approached the table. It had been set for two, and he cast his eyes around for a spare chair or bench, his cheeks flushing.

Richard's eyes had already locked with the landlord's, and he nodded towards Threadmill. A moment later, a stool was carried from the other end of the tavern. Threadmill lowered himself onto it, his eyes on the table.

Jack made to lean towards the lawyer, but his body made him halt in the act. "We know each other well. I hauled your arse from no man's land and saved your skin if I remember rightly," Jack beckoned him closer. "Do not treat me like this."

Threadmill's cheeks flushed. "My Lord ... "

Richard came to his rescue. "My brother hates his foes, deals with his enemies swiftly and holds his friends close; I feel he is trying badly to say that you are in the latter category."

Threadmill looked between Richard and Jack. "I am honoured ..."

"One more fawning word from your lips, and you'll be sat at another table," Jack said.

"Oft times, my brother does not realise that a change in environment necessitates a change in propriety," Richard explained. Then, extending an open hand towards Threadmill, he said, "You have my brother's friendship and mine also. There is no need to stand on formality. Indeed, my brother would rather trample it into the dirt than adhere to it."

Threadmill took Richard's hand briefly in his own.

"He's got an amusing first name," Jack said when they released their grip.

Richard raised an eyebrow.

"Argurran," Jack mispronounced the name.

## A Queen's Rebel

"Angharad," Richard pronounced the Welsh name correctly.

Jack smiled. "De Nevarra was adamant Argurran was correct, and who are we to argue with an opinionated Italian?"

"Who, indeed?" Richard replied, then he turned towards Threadmill and said, "Ydych chi'n dod o Gymru?"

"I'm afraid I have little of the language, sir, I have lived in London all my life," Threadmill replied apologetically.

Mildly annoyed by his brother's grasp of Welsh, Jack picked up his cup and banged it on the table. "We are to investigate an issue we will discuss when we arrive, but I also brought you here to entertain my brother."

Richard frowned. "How so?"

"Ask him about the falling cup that makes no noise," Jack suggested.

Richard looked at Jack blankly for a moment before realisation dawned. "I see you are still pondering that! Well done."

"I'm not pondering it. If it falls, it makes a noise. I might not hear it, you might not hear it, but a dog will start, a horse will spook, and birds will take flight. So there is a sound," Jack said with finality.

"You have been pondering it!" Richard said with delight.

"No. There is nothing to ponder, but feel free to argue the point with Argurran," Jack replied.

Jack hadn't realised how tired he was. The food had been good. The wine had been acceptable, and he had fallen asleep in the wainscot chair. The conversation around him, the voices a quiet lull that ebbed like the tide. It was only when a cup was knocked from a table to clatter on the floor that he was woken. Richard was absent, and so was Threadmill.

Jack rubbed his eyes.

How long had he been asleep?

"The horses are stabled, the men billeted, and your room is upstairs," his brother's familiar voice said from behind him.

"I'm sorry," Jack said. They had covered no more than ten miles today, and if they had found a hill, London would have been in plain sight.

"Why? I have no liking for the task, and your lawyer has educated me while you snored!" Richard said, extending a hand to help Jack from the chair.

"How so?" Jack said, grunting against the stiffness in his limbs.

"Well, apparently, there is always a witness to every sound," Richard said, then in reply to Jack's raised eyebrow, he added, "The Lord hears all."

Jack rolled his eyes. "Did you take him to task on anything else while I slept?

"We did discuss some issues of equity and the law," Richard replied.

"Thank God I was asleep," Jack said wearily as he reached the bottom of the stairs, then asked. "Which room?"

"First on the left," Richard said, following his brother's slow trudge up the stairs.

"Are we sharing a room?" Jack asked as his brother followed him in.

Richard laughed. "No. I have had my fill of your snoring already today."

Jack sat down on the edge of the bed and grunted as he reached down to pull his boots off. It wasn't an easy task. "Do you remember when we arrived in France? It seems so long ago, with the cases of weapons from Christian Carter. Where are we now?"

"The wine has gone to your head. We are just outside London," Richard replied.

"You know that's not what I meant," Jack replied grumpily.

"Honestly? I don't know, Jack, I really don't," Richard replied.

Jack sat on the edge of the bed, his hands pressed to his face. "I need to know, Richard, I'll be a father soon enough, and I will not fail, I cannot be like our father."

"Jack, that would be impossible," Richard said.

"Would it?" Jack said, his hand dropping from his face.

"Our father, Lord, rest his soul, left you to be raised like a pig in a stye, and he tried to murder me with his own hands, twice if I recall correctly. If, at any point, I see you heading down that path, I will be sure to stop you myself," Richard said bluntly. "Now go to sleep."

## CHAPTER TWELVE

Jack awoke in an empty room, the weight of sleep still pulling at his senses. With a loud yawn, he closed his eyes again, savouring the fleeting comfort of the bed. Outside, the sounds of the day filtered through the thick wooden shutters. A barrel rolled noisily across the inn yard, its rhythmic thumps interspersed with the muffled laughter of two men in conversation below his window. Though their words were lost to the distance, their mirth carried easily. Somewhere nearby, a door slammed, and the corridor outside his room echoed with the deliberate tramp of boots.

He frowned slightly, the ambient noise stirring a vague unease. What time was it? He glanced around the room, noticing the deep shadows stretching along the floorboards.

Late, too late.

Cursing under his breath, Jack pushed himself up, his intent clear: make it to the window, throw open the shutters, and see for himself what the day had brought.

Before he could swing his legs over the side of the bed, the door to his room flew open without so much as a knock.

Jack's mouth opened, ready to admonish his brother for barging in unannounced, but the words died on his lips. Instead of Richard's sharp wit, he was met with Brother Sebastian's firm, unyielding presence. The monk's eyes, sharp beneath his furrowed brow, fixed on Jack like a hawk's on its prey. His expression was not one of amusement but a stern, undeniable displeasure. He deposited a bulging bag on the floor with a thud that shook the small table near the bed and crossed his arms, fixing Jack with a glare that could have curdled milk.

Jack blinked, startled. "What are you doing here?"

The monk closed the door loudly. "That is a question I should be asking you.

What in the name of all that's holy are you doing riding to Oxford?"

Jack looked confused.

Sebastian pointed a thick finger towards Jack. "You are in my care, in the Orders care no less. So what are you doing here? Were you given leave to go, eh?"

Jack was, for a moment, without words.

"No, you weren't. And now look what you've done! This arse," Sebastian pointed towards his own rear, "Hasn't sat a saddle for a year or two, and I can tell you I'll be wallowing in regret by the time the day is out."

"You didn't need to come," Jack said lamely.

"Didn't need to come! Are you mad! You are under the care of the Order of St John. I have strict orders to ensure your health and well-being, and I will ensure them!" Sebastian finished.

Jack could only sit there, his eyes blinking rapidly as he tried to process the torrent of words. For a moment, silence filled the room. Then, with a long-suffering sigh, Sebastian bent to retrieve the bag he'd dropped earlier. He hoisted it onto the small table near the window with a thud and began rifling through its contents, muttering something under his breath.

"I thank the order for their care, but there needs to be an end to it," Jack said slowly, determined to stand his ground and not about to bow to the monks demands.

Sebastian stopped, slowly straightening as he turned back to face him. "Ah, so you think you are well now, do you?" he said, his voice laced with scepticism. "You can barely sit up without huffing? You're as pale as a ghost and about as sturdy. And I'll wager you haven't been up at all today. Your body is weak; you lack strength. Do you want to remain like that? Do you want to lie in bed until the bells toll for Sext like an old man? Eh? Is that what you want for the rest of your life?"

Jack pointed towards the monk. "That is my business and none of yours."

Sebastian didn't appear annoyed. "Is that so."

The monk dug into the sack, pulled out a sword, and discarded the sheath on the floor. His eyes cast an admiring gaze over the blade before he held it towards Jack. "Take it," he said.

"Why? Do you want me to balance that on my head as well?" Jack growled in reply.

"Take it," Sebastian's words were an order.

Jack accepted it, wrapping his hand around the hilt. A Knight's blade, the cross of the Order in black and white enamel, shone from between the quillons.

"If you can't hold a milk jug before you how do you expect to be able to hold that?" Sebastian said.

The words were cruel. The tip of the blade had already begun to sag towards the floor. "Take your blade back."

"If you say so," Sebastian replied. He stepped towards Jack, his right hand slammed into Jack's forearm, and an elbow sent him to fall backwards onto the bed, the monk's gloved right hand caught the blade before it hit the floor. Sebastian shook his head sadly. "A maid could disarm you. Think on it."

Jack glared up at him.

"Your wounds have healed, but that process drains the strength from a man. I'm here to put you back on your feet and return your strength to you," Sebastian continued, his tone reasonable.

"You're worse than a nursemaid," Jack muttered.

"And you," Sebastian replied, his tone as dry as parchment, "are worse than a child."

Jack descended the stairs with deliberate slowness, each step testing the stiffness in his body. His confrontation with Sebastian had left his blood simmering, the monk's pointed remarks still echoing in his ears. Pausing halfway down, he found his brother and Threadmill near the fire, seated at either side of the bench, almost exactly where he had left them the previous evening, engaged in a game of cards.

Threadmill was leaning slightly forward, his cards were in a tight fan before him, his face a study in concentration, at some point during the game, he'd run a hand through his hair, and it stood up in short uneven spikes at the front. Richard had one foot propped up on another stool, and his cards were held

# A Queen's Rebel

loosely in his right hand; his attention was not on them but on Threadmill.

Jack, shaking his head, descended the rest of the steps and crossed to them, standing behind Threadmill.

Looking down at his cards, Jack could quickly see Threadmill's dilemma. It was, on the face of it, a good hand: two queens, a ten, and a king of spades—high-ranking cards. Jack looked over the top of Threadmill's head at his brother's impassive face.

"Did I advise you not to play cards with my brother?" Jack announced.

Threadmill, suddenly aware of Jack's presence made to rise, but Jack's hand on his shoulder kept him seated. Jack leaned around and plucked the cards from the lawyer's grasp.

Richard looked mildly annoyed. "Don't spoil the game."

"It's not a game," Jack said examining the cards, then to Threadmill. "I'd fold if I was you."

Threadmill took the cards he was handed back, a look of confusion on his face.

"You need another queen or a knave. You'll not get it," Jack said.

Richard removed his foot from the stool, and Jack took a seat at the table between them, his eyes on the slightly crestfallen Threadmill now that the game had been ruined.

Between the two players sat the rest of the deck.

"Let me explain," Jack said, reaching over to lift the top card from the deck. Then, with an enquiring gaze, Jack looked at his brother.

Richard cast his now useless cards on the table and met his brother's blue gaze. "Three of clubs."

"Thank you," Jack said, without looking at the card he held. He turned it over and let it fall to the table, then selected the next card from the top of the pack.

"Seven of diamonds," Richard said.

Jack let it fall and selected the next.

Richard found another stool to place his feet on as he began to reel off the cards one by one. "Six of spades, eight of hearts, three of hearts, which would have given me primero by the way and the game, two of diamonds, then the fateful queen of clubs Master Threadmill needed, then seven of spades, nine of spades, ace of clubs ....."

Jack continued to turn over each card from the deck and drop them before Threadmill as Richard counted them off one by one.

Threadmill stared open-mouthed as the deck was revealed card by card. Each one correctly predicted before it was dropped on a pile before him.

Jack, grinning, collected the cards back in with one hand and squared up the deck before pushing them towards Richard. "Don't worry; you're not the first and certainly not the last."

"But how?" Threadmill said, still looking dumbfounded.

Richard shrugged. "An old habit."

"He tells me it keeps his mind agile," Jack supplied. "Not that I am sure it needs any more exercise than it already gets. Are we moving on today?"

Richard looked at Jack and shook his head, an incredulous expression on his face. "We have been waiting for you. Master Threadmill and I have been about since cocks crow."

"It's not that late," Jack said, suddenly defensive.

"If we are to leave, please excuse me while I make my arrangements," Threadmill said, leaving them alone.

"At least you've arrived on your own," Richard said, leaning back in his chair. "I had thought

# A Queen's Rebel

Sebastian was going to march up and drag you down by your ears."

Jack scowled, moving toward the table. "He wouldn't dare."

Richard raised an eyebrow, his tone taking on a dry edge. "Judging by the raised voices I just heard, I think he very much would dare. I take it you're pleased to have him back with us?"

Jack sighed, his irritation ebbing slightly. "He's already planning some regime to 'restore my strength,' as he puts it."

Richard's gaze softened for a moment. "And you'll endure it, Jack. Because as much as you hate to admit it, you need someone like him right now."

Jack didn't reply immediately, he began to collect the cards together and reunite the pack. "I suppose you're enjoying this, aren't you?"

Richard smirked. "Thoroughly." Richard lifted his glass in a mock toast. "To meddling monks and reluctant patients. Long may they clash."

Jack clinked a cup against Richard's, his grin widening despite himself. "You're impossible, you know that?"

"Runs in the family," Richard replied smoothly, sipping his wine.

The group of riders moved steadily along the dusty road, the rhythm of hooves a constant backdrop to their journey. Despite Brother Sebastian's earlier complaints about his rear and the saddle, Jack noted with some surprise that the monk rode with a relaxed air of competence. His posture was straight, his hands light on the reins, and his mount moved easily under him. Clearly, this wasn't a man new to the saddle—his horsemanship was second nature, the mark of someone who had spent years riding across various terrains.

Jack found his gaze lingering on Sebastian, curiosity sparking. There was something incongruous about the monk's austere habit and his ease in the saddle, the way he seemed more knight than monk.

As if sensing Jack's eyes on him, Sebastian turned his head slightly and met his gaze. A wry smile tugged at the corner of his lips. "You're thinking, 'He's managing quite well to keep up for an old man.' Am I right?"

Jack nodded, he'd still not forgiven the monk for his appearance. "Something like that."

Sebastian shook his head, chuckling softly. Easing his mount closer to Jack's, he reached for the loose sleeve of his robe and tugged it up to his elbow, revealing a thick, muscled forearm. It bore a pale white scar that ran jaggedly from just behind the wrist bone all the way toward his elbow. The skin around the scar was weathered, the mark itself a striking contrast against the monk's tanned flesh.

"See that?" Sebastian said, holding his arm out briefly before letting the sleeve drop back down. "Saracen blade at Mdina. Down to the bone." He paused, a mischievous sparkle in his eye. "That was the last thing the heathen ever did, mind you."

Jack's brows lifted in surprise, his interest piqued. "You were at Mdina, in Malta?"

Sebastian leaned back in his saddle. "I spent five years in Malta. I was part of the force fortifying Mdina against the Ottomans?"

"You? In Malta?" Jack failed to keep the incredulity from his voice.

Sebastian, ignoring it continued. "It was 1551. The Order knew the Ottomans were coming. Tripoli had fallen, and they were riding high on that victory. They wanted Malta next. We'd focused much of our strength on protecting the harbours at Birgu, Senglea. Mdina was inland, poorly defended, and

# A Queen's Rebel

with a garrison that could hardly be called an army. Just farmers, merchants, and a handful of Knights, myself among them."

"So, what did you do?" Jack asked.

Sebastian's gaze sharpened. "We had to make them think we were stronger than we were. We reinforced the walls with what we had—wooden beams, stone from the building inside, anything that could hold together under fire. We made sure cannons were visible from the walls, even if we didn't have enough ammunition to fire them more than a few times. And we kept moving them to different parts of the bastions. It was all about illusion."

Jack's grin widened. "Clever."

"But it wasn't enough just to look strong," Sebastian continued. "We had to act strong. That meant skirmishes. We sent out small groups at night, harassing their supply lines and burning their tents. We made sure they didn't sleep well."

Jack raised an eyebrow. "And you were part of these skirmishes?"

Sebastian raised his left arm again, revealing the scar. "Oh, I was. That's where this beauty came from."

Jack winced. "A Saracen blade?"

Sebastian nodded, his expression turning grim. "A lucky swing on their part. We'd hit one of their outposts near the coast, aiming to destroy their food stores. It was going well until we got ambushed. One of their soldiers came at me. I blocked, but he was fast—too fast. The blade slipped past my guard, sliced through the muscle. I dropped my sword, blood pouring everywhere."

"How did you survive?"

Sebastian shrugged a wry smile on his lips. "Luck, mostly. One of my men dragged me back to the city. By the time we got inside, I was barely conscious. The wound festered, and fever set in. The Order—God bless them—cared well for me."

"And yet, here you are," replied Jack.

"Here I am," Sebastian agreed. "It took months to recover. My arm was useless for a long time. I had to relearn how to hold a sword and how to fight. But I did it. Recovery isn't just about the body. It's about the mind. I was stubborn, reckless, a fool who thought he was invincible. That blade taught me otherwise."

Jack laughed, shaking his head. "You, reckless? Hard to believe."

Sebastian grinned. "Oh, I was. Just like you are now. But I learned. And you will, too. I had been out five nights in a row harassing their lines, five nights fighting, and then the days moving cannon, keeping up the illusion we were well garrisoned. I was tired and too foolish to admit it. Two days later, they left. We'd given them just enough of a taste of hell to make them think twice. They left Mdina untouched. But they took their vengeance on Gozo, enslaving the entire population. War is never clean."

Jack nodded slowly. "And now you ride with me, playing nursemaid."

Sebastian chuckled, the sound low and warm. "Life takes us to strange places. But don't mistake my current vocation for a lack of steel. If it comes to it, I can still hold my own."

Jack smiled faintly, leaning forward slightly in the saddle. "I don't doubt it."

Sebastian cast him a sidelong glance, his expression softening. "You're a curious one. Remind me of myself at your age—restless, sharp-tongued, and far too stubborn for your own good. Let's just hope you fare better than I did when it comes to listening to advice."

Jack snorted, but the glimmer of amusement in his eyes betrayed his growing fondness for the monk. "I'll take that under consideration."

"De Nevarra tells me that you were a man with considerable skill with a blade, and that is high praise from someone who was trained by Salvator Fabris," Sebastian said.

Jack frowned.

"Ah, you didn't know he owed his skill to Fabris?" Sebastian said with some satisfaction.

"He'd not mentioned it," Jack said, slightly annoyed.

"It will be interesting to see what skill you have when your strength returns," Sebastian chuckled again and nudged his horse forward, leaving Jack to his thoughts.

Emilio hadn't mentioned he had been trained by Salvator Fabris, although on reflection, it, of course, made perfect sense. Fabris was Italian from Padua, and his skill with a blade was legendary across Europe, and that he would have been sought out to provide training to princes would be natural. Still, it rankled that Sebastian knew and Jack hadn't.

They made more progress the second day, despite not leaving the tavern until late in the morning. Jack obstinately refused to stop, and the small contingent moved further from London. By the time the sun was beginning to dip towards the horizon, they were close to the market town of Wycome on the river Wye. A rider, unknown to Jack, had gone ahead, and on their arrival, rooms had already been acquired at High Wycombe's most prestigious inn, The Wheatsheaf.

Invited over, Threadmill sat at the table where the brothers had just finished their meal. A platter of cheese remained on the table, a knife on its side next to it. The trenchers had been cleared, but Jack motioned for the serving boys to leave the cheese.

"Sit down." Jack said to Threadmill, as he angled the knife to take another slice from the yellow slab of cheese when the platter was raised from the table.

Jack turned in complaint, opened his mouth and stopped. The platter had not been removed by the tavern boys but by Sebastian.

"If I let you eat that, we'll be needing chains and tackle to get you into your saddle," Sebastian said curtly; he didn't wait for a reply but turned on his heel, carrying the platter back to the table he was sharing with the other men.

Richard's lips were pressed tightly together. It was obvious he was trying not to laugh, and Threadmill was wisely observing the floor.

"Not a bloody word," Jack growled, letting the knife fall from his hand and taking up an ale cup instead.

Richard, addressing Threadmill, said. "I believe a wise change of conversation is needed rapidly."

Threadmill flushed.

Richard continued. "We three happy fools are to investigate a murder, Master Threadmill. Are you familiar with the proceedings of the coroner?"

Threadmill nodded, delighted to be able to turn to a safer topic of conversation. "I have attended quite an amount of ….."

The door to the tavern was flung open, and two boys yelled from the doorway. "There 'a weighin' the Mayor. Come on da'."

A man dressed in a smiths apron separated himself from his companions and hurried towards the door. The landlord appeared, and, along with other patrons, they hurriedly left the tavern.

Richard weigh-laid a woman who was heading to follow them. "What's he mean weighing the mayor?"

"It's just a custom, sir," she said nervously.

Richard stood. "It's a popular one by all accounts."

# A Queen's Rebel

"Aye, sir it is," she performed a clumsy curtsey and headed towards the door, Richard following.

Jack watched his brother leave. "He's a curiosity that would outdo a cats."

Jack noted sourly that Threadmill also looked as if he wanted to go and find out what was happening outside. He was about to release him when Richard returned.

"Come on, Jack, this will appeal to your sense of justice," Richard said, grinning.

Jack rolled his eyes.

"Up, or do you need help?" Richard said, arriving back at the table.

"I don't need help, especially not yours," Jack said, rising stiffly.

"I thought not," Richard said, turning back towards the door. "They weigh the mayor."

"What?" Jack said, confused.

"You'll see," Richard said, holding the door open.

Jack emerged, squinting into the light outside. The Wheatsheaf Tavern faced the green, when they had arrived there had been a few sheep grazing there, but now it was filled with townsfolk and in the middle a wooden frame where the gallows or pillory would usually be found was filled with the town dignitaries, and with his chain of office around his neck, the Mayor. However, the man was not decked out in his finery; apart from the chain denoting his office, he wore only a linen shirt and hose, and even his shoes were missing.

Jack looked between the badly dressed Mayor and Richard.

"They weigh him at the start of his tenure and a year later," Richard explained.

"Why?" Jack asked, confused.

"Apparently it's a tradition that dates back to the time of King John, it was the way the town made sure that the mayor had not been getting fat on their taxes," Richard said then pointed towards a chair on the platform and next to it a pile of sacks. "Those sacks are filled with rocks, and weighed the same as the Mayor when he took up his office. So after a year, they weigh him again and see if he's fattened himself up."

Jack's blue eyes rested on the Mayor, who was engaged in a jovial conversation with the town's elders, who were readying the chair for him to sit on. "He doesn't look too bothered about the outcome."

The landlord of the Wheatsheaf leaned towards Jack. "It's become a tradition for him to lose, and he pays for two hogs heads of ale for the town."

"That at least explains why there's so many here," Jack replied, then added, "And I am guessing you are supplying the ale."

The Wheatsheaf's landlord's grin confirmed that. "We share it around. Last year, it was the Drovers Inn, and next, the Swan. Here we go!"

A man dressed in a long lawyer's robe and wearing a cap declaring his profession stepped to the platform's edge. He had in his hands an unfurled scroll but didn't glance at it as he delivered his words.

"Good people of Wycombe, as is the custom of the town to safeguard against abuses of power, the time has come to judge the mayor."

A huge cheer went up from the crowd. The landlord next to Jack waved his arms in the air and began a chant that was soon taken up by those around him.

"Expendas .... expendas .... expendas .... expendas.

The shout was a demand. The lawyer rolled up his scroll, handed it to an assistant, and waved theatrically towards the Mayor and the chair he was to take.

The chant reverberated around the good-humoured and eager crowd.

# A Queen's Rebel

"Expendas .... expendas .... expendas .... expendas."

Jack had no idea why, but he joined in. A grin on his face at the ridiculousness of it.

The Mayor took his seat, and the sacks of rocks were set on the opposite side of the scales. There were six stacked up, and when each one went onto the scales, the chant increased in ferocity. Five were in place, and the Mayor, smiling happily, remained in his chair, which was firmly still on the ground. The final sack was lifted up and placed on the scales. As it was planted on top of the others, the chair the Mayor was seated in rose a little unevenly a few inches from the platform but then rattled back down again.

The crowd howled with delight.

The major looked suitably shamefaced.

The lawyer stepped towards the edge of the platform and pronouned, "Iudicatus est." And pointed towards the Wheatsheaf.

"Judged and found guilty!" Jack said, laughing.

The landlord had disappeared, and the reason was soon apparent. Hastily moved tables had been placed outside the tavern along with the promised hogs heads of ale for the people of Wycombe.

Richard tapped Jack's good arm conspiratorially and said, "Free ale always tastes better. Shall we?"

And they did. The tavern was crowded but Richard rapidly reclaimed the table they had been seated at, ousting those who had thought to stake a claim to it and slipping a coin to one of the serving boys he ensured a steady stream of ale was brought to their table, as one jug emptied the attentive lad, hoping for a second coin, had a replacement ready.

They didn't leave Wycombe that day. And neither of them cared.

Sam Burnell

Richard retired back to his room. The weighing of the Mayor had been a happy coincidence, and Jack, dozing off the afternoon's ale, was back in his bed, and Richard could hear his snoring through the walls.

Richard took a book from his pack, he wasn't even sure why he'd brought it. He could still remember quite clearly when he'd stolen it, and sometimes it felt as if the punishment for that act were ongoing.

It was in Venice when he'd seen it, he was maybe sixteen, or fifteen. It was hard to remember. But what he did remember was the desperate desire to hold it, to possess it, to make it his.

The outer cover was a hard binding, red and rich like colour of a good wine. The boards protected the contents, held them together, ordered them. It wasn't written by hand, copied out in ink by a clerk or monk in some dimly lit room. The pages had been printed with the words. The ordered lines the neatness the lack of a crossing out or correction had always fascinated him. Lines of flawless prose. And the lines existed on virgin sheets, seeming to exist in perfect geometric precision. Older books had guidelines on the pages, the ruled marks segmenting the page before the scribe began to fill it with his text. The guidelines holding the text in place, securing it to the middle of the page. The ends of the lines of text ragged and uneven like a broken combe on the right side of the page. But this book, this was neat. The lines in perfect arrangement.

And there was more than just words.

It held pictures, images printed with woodcuts on various pages. Diagrams of explanation and intrigue to be gazed at in wonder. That's when he'd seen the book first, it had sat in the owners lap, and he was delighting in showing the gruesome illustrations to his comrades. He cared not for the text, the printed pages, he revelled in the intricate horrible woodcuts.

Richard remembered telling himself he would not have treated the book like this if it had been his. He would have loved the beauty of the words, printed with skill and craftmanship and written with depth and meaning. He would not have idled his time gazing at the broken images of man. He was better than that. Surely?

He wasn't. He was, after all, human. So used to the eager gazes of men the book obediently fell open at the cone shaped image of torment. Richard's eyes ran down Dante's funnel of hell to where those, like the mayor, were accused of gluttony. When he was a child he was drawn to Canto six, not because of the damned writhing for eternity in the icy mud but because of the dog. Three headed Cerberus. What a fantastical creature. It growled, snapped, howled and tore the damned apart. Virgil silenced it, by feeding it handfuls of mud so they could pass.

This had always perplexed him as a child, if such a beast existed why would it be fooled by mud? No mortal dog would take mud, why would a hell hound? And more, Cerberus had three heads and Virgil two hands, how did he feed the dog to make it quiet? Dante had obviously never fed a starving hound before, food went from the mouth to the stomach with great speed. Unless of course Virgil had great experience with dogs, but this Richard had doubted as the Roman poet's reputation was not one that would see him dealing with vicious hell hounds. Flicking through the book he found Canto six, his finger running down the neatly printed page until he found the words he wanted.

*"A hungry mongrel, yapping, thrusting out – intent on nothing but the meal to come – is silent only when it's teeth sink in."*

But there was more to it now than what he had read as a child. Cerberus, many headed, was more than just the dog, he felt as if it was the dog who pursued him. Hungry, snapping always at his heels. Feed him, give them what they wanted, and in that single moment while they gobbled down the offerings the pursuers fell silent.

Never though, for very long.

## CHAPTER THIRTEEN

Nicholas Adams, member of Parliament for Dartmouth in Devon, had initially thought the summons from William Cecil was of some moment, and related perhaps to his views on the making one realm by joining England to Scotland.

An ambitious plan some may say given that his seat in the Commons related to one of the most southerly of England's towns. Nicholas Adams, MP for Dartmouth, was a man of middling stature, though his presence in a room often felt larger due to his booming voice and an overconfidence that outstripped his intellect. His face, ruddy and lined from years spent battling the brisk Devonshire winds, carried an air of self-importance. His thinning hair was swept back in a way that suggested an effort to convey dignity, though the effect was undone by the perpetual sheen of perspiration on his brow and shoddiness to his dress that spoke of empty pockets.

Around his neck hung the pièce de résistance of his ensemble: a fur-trimmed collar affixed to a cloak that was just slightly too grand for the man wearing it. The fur, likely rabbit and of questionable quality, was moulting visibly, leaving a faint trail of fine hairs wherever Adams went. These hairs clung stubbornly to his doublet and hose, adding an unkempt aspect to what was clearly intended to be a display of status.

Adams, however, appeared either oblivious to or undeterred by the fur's shedding, though it was not without consequence. Every few moments, he would stifle a wet, wheezing cough or bark out a snuffling sneeze that startled those around him. His attempts to mask these interruptions were ineffective at best, and the occasional wipe of his nose with a handkerchief only seemed to distribute the fur further. Still, he clung to the garment as if it were the very emblem of his station, his fingers occasionally brushing over the fur as though reassuring himself of its presence.

William Cecil, observing Adams with a gaze that could curdle milk, found the man's pretense wearisome. Adams had the unfortunate combination of misplaced ambition and a propensity for long-windedness, both of which grated on Cecil's finely honed patience. The man's loud and unnuanced support for merging England and Scotland—a topic far removed from his coastal constituency's immediate concerns—had not earned him any friends among his peers. Instead, it underscored his habit of attaching himself to lofty ideas without the necessary depth to defend them intelligently.

As Adams cleared his throat again, a sound like a wheezy bellows, Cecil allowed his gaze to linger on the offending fur trim. The Secretary of State's lips tightened imperceptibly. It was not the garb of a serious man, and in Cecil's mind, neither was Nicholas Adams.

Cecil's gaze shifted briefly from Adams to the objects displayed on his desk: a small altar, a chalice, and an altar cross. The gleaming silver, polished to perfection, caught the candlelight, casting faint reflections onto the dark oak. Their mere presence in Adams' house was damning. "These were found at your house, Adams."

Adams, who had been blustering with the sort of faux confidence that might have impressed a lesser man, faltered when his eyes landed on the objects. His face suddenly pale. For a moment, he sat frozen, his lips parting in a silent protest that he clearly struggled to form.

"I see you recognise these," Cecil said evenly, his voice devoid of any emotion that might suggest leniency or cruelty. He gestured to the altar cross

# A Queen's Rebel

with a subtle movement of his hand. "Perhaps you would care to explain their presence in your house? It is not every day one finds such...Catholic relics in the possession of a loyal servant of the Crown."

Adams' mouth worked as though he were chewing over an unpleasant piece of gristle. "I—those aren't mine. I've never—" He stopped, swallowing hard as Cecil's unblinking stare met his. "This is a misunderstanding, my lord. I assure you, I am a devout Protestant. These must have been...put there by someone!"

"Put there," Cecil echoed, his tone as flat and cold as a frozen pond. He picked up the chalice, turning it in his hands with the precision of a jeweler inspecting a flawed gemstone. "An interesting claim, Adams. But I wonder, did your neighbors place them there? Or your household staff? Or do they belong to your wife?"

Adams flinched. He had clearly underestimated how deeply Cecil's reach extended. He attempted to compose himself, straightening his posture and fixing his expression into one of righteous indignation. "My lord, with respect, I have never seen these before. There are those who would wish to see my name dragged through the mire for their own gain. You must see this!"

Cecil's lips twitched—barely—but the faint movement spoke volumes of his disdain. "Oh, I see many things, Adams. For instance, I see a man whose enthusiasm for bold ideas has outpaced his capacity for discretion. A man whose ambitions have blinded him to the enemies he's made among his peers. And now I see a man sitting in my chamber, sweating like a thief caught in the act, attempting to deny what I already know to be true."

Adams' protests crumbled in his throat, his gaze darting back to the altar cross as though it might somehow exonerate him. He began to stammer. "It—it isn't—I wouldn't—"

"You wouldn't," Cecil interrupted smoothly, setting the chalice down with a decisive click. "And yet, here we are. These items were found in your possession, attested to by reliable witnesses. Witnesses who, I might add, have no incentive to lie."

Adams' shoulders slumped, his bluster replaced by a simmering panic. "My lord, I beg you, I have been loyal—"

"Loyalty, Adams, is a word best demonstrated through action rather than lip service," Cecil said, his voice slicing through the man's pleas like a razor. "You are fortunate that I am not an impulsive man. There are those who would see you hanged for less."

The silence that followed was suffocating. Adams' chest rose and fell rapidly as he sought a way to recover, to salvage whatever shreds of dignity or favor he could. But Cecil offered him no escape, no handhold to cling to.

"Now," Cecil continued, folding his hands neatly on the desk, "I suggest you consider very carefully how you proceed from here. You may yet prove useful to the Crown, though I would advise a marked improvement in your judgment. The times, as you so often like to remark, are not kind to fools."

Adams nodded stiffly, his face a mask of defeat. Cecil leaned back, his expression impassive as he watched the man shrink into himself. The Secretary of State's purpose had been served, and the once-boisterous Nicholas Adams was reduced to a cowed shadow of his former self.

Cecil had licked his lips, the situation was delicious, he had no liking for Nicholas Adams, he was too much liked by the queen, and complained endlessly that he was not amongst those appointed to the privy council. And with good reason, he was impetuous and self-serving and a fool, the council chamber could do without him. What had been unearthed gave Cecil a hold over the man that nothing else could, he'd still not weighed up the options and Nicholas Adams had been returned to his

## A Queen's Rebel

home, while Cecil debated over what to do. Should he disclose the discovery, or wait until later, or just keep the information close and keep Adams in the palm of his hand.

When Adams had left Cecil had looked again at the items he had been brought. The portable folding wooden altar was wrapped inside cloth that was tied closed with a thick twisted leather cord. Cecil untied it and unwrapped the wooden boards. They were hinged and when opened the sides, at an angle offered support for the structure, in the middle a wooden flap fell forwards. A silver dish fitted into the middle of this, polished, although a little dented around the rim.

Cecil's eyes scanned his desk, a pair of nib clippers, came to hand and he inserted them beneath the dish where the rim was creased and it popped out easily enough. Beneath the dish was a small space. Empty.

Cecil dropped the dish back into place and sat back in his chair reviewing the altar. In the middle, the virgin, seated on a simple wooden stool swathed in a rich blue cloth, in her arms wrapped and painted was the child, a short fat arm reaching towards the mother. Both their heads were surrounded by a golden glow, added with the use of foil after the painting had been finished. On either side of the virgin were kneeling saints both holding forth offerings.

It wasn't new. The style of the artwork belonged to a time long since past. But that meant very little, items like this were passed down from generation to generation, there was even a chance such a portable piece as this could have been included in a campaign chest in the times of the crusades. Cecil stroked his hand down the carvings on the right hand side of the frame, darkened with the patina of age, but still well cared for.

Sam Burnell

Cecil's glasses had slid down his nose and when he went to push them back up he could smell the polish that had been used on the wood. To the right stood an altar cross, it was stood about half the height of the wooden panels, and lifting it told Cecil it was a weighty piece. It had, over time, it seemed lost a few of the gems that had adorned the points of the cross. That in itself wasn't strange, they could have fallen out, been traded or stolen over the long life of the relic. The item had been well polished and his fingers had left imperfections on the mirror finish.

Cecil turned his attention to the final damning item, a chalice and in the bottom, now dried were the unmistakable remnants of wine. Cecil dabbed his finger in the residue, far from being dry and rough, it retained still a stickiness, the blood of Christ had not long since been drained from it.

Cecil banged on his desk and a moment later the door to the scribes room opened and one of his attendants appeared. "Find somewhere for this to go. Keep it together and make sure each item is tagged with the name Nicholas Adams."

The man nodded, and Cecil watched him fold away the Madonna and child, tuck it under his arm, and collecting the chalice he backed from the small room closing the door behind him.

They were all clean, and had seen polish in the recent past, on the silver dish lay drops of fresh candle wax, wine had been in the chalice recently and he could smell the wooden polish that had been applied to the wooden frame. They were not covered in the dust of neglect. These had been used recently, not stored away and forgotten. The question was by whom? Was it Nicholas Adams, perhaps his wife, or someone else within his household. Whoever it was they had provided Cecil with a firm hold on Adams.

A Queen's Rebel

## **CHAPTER FOURTEEN**

They left High Wycombe the following morning just after the bells rang for Tierce. Jack, rested, looked less tired. Today's ride would be short; they should reach their destination by mid-afternoon.

They made slow progress, the weather was good, the ride pleasant, and the lack of haste, of urgency, felt so alien, something so unaccustomed to them both that there was a newfound joy on the journey.

They talked about everything and anything, inspired by what they saw. A goshawk hovering over a mouse, stationary in the air, sparked a debate about hunting. They passed a child riding a small stout cob, and Jack launched into a long and detailed exposition of the horses he'd buy his son, should it be a son. A mill on the banks of a river to their right, the sails turning in the light breeze, reminded Richard of Burton's mills, and he engaged in a debate with Threadmill about gears and maths; Jack was happy to listen, declaring he was not interested in the mill workings. But Richard skillfully turned the conversation from mill wheels to machines of war, which Jack had some recent experience of, and the debate raged for another hour, Brother Sebastian joining in.

As Richard, Jack, and their retinue neared Cumnor where Lady Amy had taken her fateful fall, the sky darkened with looming storm clouds and a chill wind heralded impending rain. Jack laughed and remarked, "I hope this isn't a bad omen."

Sam Burnell

"Cumnor Place, is outside the village, so I am told," Richard said, "there's a tavern by all accounts, we can halt there until the rain passes."

The village of Cumnor was modest at best, a collection of timber-framed cottages huddled together along a single muddy road. Smoke curled lazily from chimneys, mingling with the smell of damp earth and livestock. As Jack and Richard rode down the main thoroughfare, their men following behind, villagers paused to watch the unfamiliar procession, their gazes a mixture of curiosity and suspicion.

The inn was impossible to miss. Its sign, faded and creaking in the autumn breeze, read The Black Swan. The building leaned slightly to one side, its thatched roof sagging in places. It was not a place of grandeur, but it was sturdy, and the sounds of laughter and clinking mugs from within suggested it served its purpose well enough.

By the time they reached the Swan Tavern, the heavens had opened, releasing a torrential downpour. The tavern, a modest establishment frequented by locals, was small and timeworn. Its thatched roof sagged under the weight of age, with rainwater seeping through in several places, forming puddles on the uneven wooden floor. The dimly lit interior, illuminated by a few sputtering candles, revealed rough-hewn wooden tables and benches, some of which wobbled precariously. The air was thick with the mingled scents of damp wood, stale ale, and past meals' faint, lingering aroma.

They stepped inside, ducking beneath the low lintel, and were immediately greeted by a wave of warmth, smoke, and the sharp tang of stale beer. The inn's common room was a cramped space filled with mismatched tables and benches, most of which were occupied by local labourers. The landlord, a rotund man with a balding head and an apron that had once been white, glanced up from where he was filling a

# A Queen's Rebel

jug with his, his face lit up when he saw the finely dressed visitors.

Jack glanced around, his expression a mix of amusement and mild distaste. "I'm glad we're not staying here," he said, shaking the rain from his cloak and sidestepping a stream of drips from the leaking thatch. "Let's hope Cumnor Place doesn't have a leaking roof."

Richard remained silent, his thoughts guarded. He suspected that their reception at Cumnor Place might not be as welcoming as Jack anticipated, but he kept his reservations to himself.

They were served a poor meal of coarse bread and hard cheese, accompanied by mugs of thin, sour ale. The bread was stale, the cheese crumbly and lacking flavour, and the ale did little to wash down the unappetising fare. As they ate, droplets of water occasionally splashed onto their table from the leaking roof above, adding to the discomfort.

Jack took a tentative sip of the ale, grimacing at its bitterness. "Well," he said, forcing a smile, "at least it's wet."

"I think using the definition of ale may be a breach of a law," Richard replied, pushing his ale cup away from him.

"Yesterday you began to ask Threadmill if he had experience with coroners courts, it is after all, the reason for the journey," Jack said, changing the subject.

Threadmill's eyes were alight with curiosity. After introducing the subject of murder the previous day and then being interrupted by the mayor's weigh-in, Richard had not returned to it.

Richard leaned slightly forward, his gaze sharpening as he addressed Threadmill. "What do you know of Amy Robsart?"

Threadmill blinked in surprise, the name clearly familiar. "Lady Robsart?"

"The very same," Richard replied.

"She was …. the wife of Robert Dudley …. the Earl of Leicester," Threadmill stammered.

Richard nodded. "Her death is what brings us to Oxfordshire."

Threadmill's expression shifted to one of grave intrigue. "I remember hearing whispers about her death. She was said to have fallen down a staircase. There were rumours… unpleasant ones."

"That she was pushed," Richard said plainly. "Or worse, that her husband had a hand in it."

Threadmill exhaled slowly. "I had heard such talk, of course. But as a lawyer, I regard this as speculation and gossip at best. Is there a reason to revisit the matter now?"

Richard's lips pressed into a thin line. "The reason lies in the court of Queen Elizabeth. Dudley's star rises, and there are those who find his ascent intolerable. Old whispers are being given fresh breath, and we have been asked to determine if there is any truth to the accusations—or if they are merely tools for political manoeuvring."

Jack, who had been lounging back in his chair, now spoke up. "You've dealt with coroners' proceedings before, haven't you, Threadmill?"

Threadmill nodded, his face serious. "Yes, my lord. I have prepared depositions and advised during inquests, though never on a case as important as this."

"Good," Richard said firmly. "You'll need to put that experience to use. What we're dealing with is no ordinary inquiry."

Threadmill hesitated. "You're asking me to involve myself in a matter that touches the Queen's court? It's a dangerous endeavour."

Jack gave a dry laugh. "You've already involved yourself by coming with us, whether you realised it or not."

Threadmill cast a glance at Richard, who regarded him steadily. "If I may speak plainly," Threadmill ventured, "Lady Robsart's death was ruled an accident. The coroner at the time found no evidence of foul play. If that ruling is to be questioned, it will require more than speculation."

"Precisely," Richard said. "Which is why we need your sharp eye and knowledge of procedure. The evidence must be weighed carefully, without bias or assumption. We're not here to convict anyone—only to uncover the truth, whatever it may be."

"And you trust me to aid in such a sensitive matter?" Threadmill asked.

Richard leaned back, his gaze unwavering. "I trust your discretion and your intellect. That is why my brother invited you."

Threadmill's mouth tightened, but he nodded resolutely. "I understand, my lord. If I can assist, I will."

Jack smiled faintly, lifting his cup. "There you have it, Threadmill. Welcome to the adventure. Finally, I have found work more favourable to your profession."

Threadmill gave a small, uneasy laugh, his hands clasped tightly in his lap. "I shall do my best, my lord."

"It does not look as if the weather is going to improve this afternoon, it seems we shall be arriving at Cumnor Place in the rain," Richard said dourly.

An hour later they left the Swan tavern, it was only slightly wetter outside that it was inside. The ferocious downpour had drained through the roof and sluiced across the flagged floor before heading towards the door.

## CHAPTER FIFTEEN

As Richard and Jack approached Cumnor Place, the rain intensified. Their cloaks clung heavily, and water dripped from the brims of their hats. The once-grand structure loomed ahead, its silhouette blurred by the downpour. The grey stone walls, darkened by moisture, stood as a somber reminder of its ecclesiastical origins. Formerly part of Abingdon Abbey, Cumnor Place had suffered during Henry VIII's dissolution of the monasteries. The air around the manor felt thick with history as if the very stones mourned their fall from grace.

Jack pulled his sodden cloak tighter around himself, shivering against the chill. "I hope this isn't a bad omen," he muttered, glancing at the darkened sky.

Richard remained silent, his eyes fixed on the manor. He suspected that their arrival would greeted with a cool reception to match the weather, but he kept his concerns to himself.

"I didn't realise Dudley was living in a monastic property?" Jack continued, his voice laced with curiosity as he took in the building.

Richard glanced at him, his expression unreadable. "It belongs to him, or rather, he acquired it after the dissolution. He leases it to Anthony Forrester, his steward. Forrester's been in Dudley's service for a decade or more."

"So Amy was living here as Forrester's guest?" Jack said, his brows furrowing as he tried to reconcile the image of a noblewoman residing in such a place.

"Apparently so," Richard replied, his tone clipped. "By all accounts, she often did."

Jack studied the structure as they approached. Its buttressed walls gave it an austere, church-like appearance, and the stone arches of the windows gave it the solemnity of a chapel. The squat, sprawling building was low to the ground, its horizontal expanse broken only by the occasional buttress and a few chimneys that jutted modestly from the roofline. In every inch of its design, it was an abbot's dwelling—a house of quiet dignity rather than grandeur.

Stone-built and well-constructed, the house was clearly intended for comfort and functionality rather than ostentation. The central section stretched long and low, with two sturdy doors flanking either end of the main facade. Above the main floor, three dormer windows punctuated the steeply pitched roof, their pointed arches crowned by intricately carved stone crosses that spoke of its religious past. The otherwise unbroken roofline gave an impression of stark simplicity, as though the structure had been designed to fade into the landscape rather than dominate it.

The grounds around the house reflected the same restrained sensibility. A modest garden edged the approach, its hedges neatly trimmed but lacking the flamboyance Jack might have expected of a residence tied to one of the Queen's favourites. A narrow gravel path led to the main entrance, where ivy crept up the stone walls, its green tendrils softening the severity of the architecture.

Jack frowned, his gaze sweeping over the building. It was not what he had anticipated. This was no grand residence befitting the wife of Robert Dudley, Elizabeth's Master of the Horse, whose name had become synonymous with ambition and courtly intrigue. Instead, it was a house of quiet efficiency. It was seemingly at odds with the man whose ambitions often set tongues wagging across the kingdom.

"Comfortable accommodation for an abbot, perhaps, but not what I imagined for Dudley's wife," Jack muttered, half to himself.

Richard's eyes narrowed as he, too, examined the structure. "Perhaps that's the point. It's modest, unassuming—a retreat, not a display of power."

"Or a place to hide your wife out of sight," Jack added, his voice low.

The brothers exchanged a glance, the weight of their purpose settling heavily between them. Cumnor Place might not be ostentatious, but its history and its current residents promised intrigue—and perhaps danger—beneath its humble facade.

It was clear from the moment they arrived that their presence had been anticipated. The steward, Anthony Forrester, stood at the entrance of Cumnor Place, flanked by two servants. Forrester's arms were crossed, his back stiff, and his expression one of forced civility. His dark eyes flicked over Jack and Richard as they dismounted, assessing them like a merchant appraising flawed goods.

"Fitzwarren," Forrester said, his tone as cool as the damp air. He bowed, but it was shallow, more an obligation than a genuine gesture of respect. "I have been informed of your impending visit."

"How fortuitous," Richard replied with a sharp smile, tossing his reins to one of his men. "It seems word travels faster than we do."

"Indeed," Forrester said, his lips tightening into something that could not be called a smile. He gestured toward the house. "You will forgive me, I hope, for the limited hospitality we can offer. I am instructed to inform you that Cumnor Place will not be hosting you during your time here. There is an inn in the village that should suffice."

Richard raised an eyebrow, his gloved hand resting on the pommel of his saddle. "Not hosting us? On whose authority?"

Forrester's tone grew frostier. "The Earl of Leicester himself. He has sent a letter, which I believe you will find unequivocal in its instructions. I shall fetch it momentarily." He turned sharply, motioning to one of the servants to retrieve the letter.

# A Queen's Rebel

Richard watched him go, his mouth quirking into a dry smirk. "A warm welcome indeed," he murmured, his voice low enough for Jack alone to hear.

"Warm or not, we're here. If he thinks he can send us on our way with sharp words and a dictated note, he's in for a disappointment," Jack replied quietly.

The servant returned with a folded piece of parchment, the Dudley seal prominently displayed. The steward took it and held it towards Richard. "The Earl's instructions," Forrester said with clipped precision.

Richard scanned the contents quickly before handing it to Jack. "As expected. We are to conduct our investigation without burdening the Earl's hospitality. How very magnanimous."

Jack took the letter. Dudley's words were formal but firm, reminding them in no uncertain terms that their purpose at Cumnor Place was not to interfere with his steward's management of the property or to impose on his resources.

"Generous, isn't he?" Jack said, his voice laden with sarcasm as he folded the letter and handed it back to Forrester.

"No doubt, Forrester, you'll be pleased to hear we have no intention of 'burdening' the Earl's hospitality. Though I suspect we'll still need your cooperation during our inquiries," Richard replied evenly.

Forrester inclined his head though his jaw tightened. "Good. As the Earl has instructed, I will provide any assistance you require—within reason."

"Within reason," Richard repeated, his tone neutral but his eyes sharp. "And where exactly does your reason begin and end, Forrester?"

The steward's smile was thin, almost serpentine. "It begins with my duty to the Earl and ends when that duty is fulfilled."

Richard took a step closer, his expression unreadable but his presence unmistakably commanding. "Then you'd best hope our inquiries align with your 'duty,' Forrester. If not, well, we're here on the Queen's orders, not Dudley's."

Forrester hesitated, but only for a moment before recovering his composure. "I will be available tomorrow should you have any questions you wish to ask, and I shall have someone show you the way to the village inn."

Turning sharply on his heel, he disappeared back into the house, leaving Jack and Richard outside.

Jack grinned. "If this is the Earl of Leicester's idea of hospitality, I'd hate to see his version of outright hostility."

Half an hour later, they were back at the only tavern in the area. The Black Swan.

Richard dismounted first, handing his reins to one of their men, and eyed the inn with mild distaste. "Charming," he muttered. "I'm sure the sheets will be crawling with as much life as the village."

Jack slid down from his horse with a wince, his hand briefly pressing against his side. "Needs must," he said, his tone resigned. "Let's just hope they've enough ale to keep the men from mutiny."

"Sir!" the landlord exclaimed, his delighted voice booming across the room. "What an honour to have you back so soon in my humble tavern!"

Jack raised an eyebrow but said nothing, allowing Richard to take the lead.

"We need rooms," Richard said, his tone curt but polite. "For ourselves and our men. Food, drink, and stabling for the horses as well."

The landlord's grin widened, revealing a set of crooked teeth. "Sir, you've come to the right place!

# A Queen's Rebel

We've the finest ale in the village and beds that'll have you sleeping like babes!"

"You forget we've already sampled your ale!" Jack muttered darkly, moving sideways to avoid a stream of water making its way across the middle of the room.

The landlord didn't seem to hear—or chose not to. "How many men, sir?" he asked, addressing Richard, already wringing his hands in anticipation of the coin to be earned.

"Eight, including ourselves," Richard replied. "We'll take whatever rooms you have."

The landlord hesitated, his grin faltering slightly. "Ah, we've only four rooms upstairs, but I'll make arrangements. The common room benches can serve the rest, and I'll have the stable cleared out for your horses, and they'll provide good accommodation for the rest of your men."

Jack's eyes narrowed. "Four rooms? That's generous. I presume they each come with a bed?"

The landlord laughed nervously. "Of course! Though, er... one of the beds is a trundle, but it's sturdy enough for a grown man!"

Jack sighed. "It'll have to do. See that the men are settled and that the horses are well looked after."

The landlord nodded vigorously, shouting orders to a boy lingering by the bar. "Go, fetch fresh straw for the stables! And tell your ma to bring more stew to the pot!"

Turning back to Jack and Richard, he said, "Please, sit by the fire. I'll bring you the best we've got—ale, bread, and stew."

Jack and Richard exchanged a glance, and Jack gestured toward an empty table near the hearth. They sat, the fire's warmth seeping into their travel-chilled bones.

"I'm missing the Wheatsheaf," Jack said sourly.

The landlord bustled over a moment later, placing a jug of sour ale and a plate of coarse bread on the table. "Enjoy! The stew'll be out shortly."

Jack took a sip of the ale, grimacing at its sourness, but drank it nonetheless. Richard poked at the bread with a finger as though expecting it to move.

"Well," Jack said with a faint smile, "if this is where Dudley's generosity leaves us, I can't wait to see how Forrester tries to halt the investigation tomorrow to prolong our suffering."

Richard stood. "I will be back soon."

A moment later, Jack and Threadmill were left alone in the room. Richard and the landlord had a short conversation, which was followed by the few other patrons leaving the tavern.

Jack watching smiled. The landlord, his face deadly serious, was listening to a list of instructions Richard was evidently giving him, ticking each one off on his fingers.

The faint light of late morning filtered through the small window of Jack's room at the Black Swan, casting uneven patterns on the rough-hewn walls. Jack lay sprawled on the bed, one arm draped over his eyes, the other resting lazily on his stomach. His boots were still on, and a half-empty jug of ale sat on the floor next to the bed.

The door creaked open, and Sebastian stepped inside with the quiet authority of a man who knew he wasn't welcome but also didn't care. Jack peeked out from under his arm and groaned.

"What now?" Jack muttered. "If you're here to tell me to meditate or pray, save your breath."

Sebastian clasped his hands in front of him, the long sleeves of his robe brushing the doorway. "I'm here because Emilio De Nevarra tasked me with a very specific mission."

# A Queen's Rebel

"Let me guess," Jack drawled, shifting slightly but not bothering to sit up. "Something about saving my soul?"

Sebastian's gaze didn't waver. "That, too. But more immediately, I've been ordered to restore your former skill at arms."

Jack lowered his arm fully and sat up, scowling. "What?"

"You heard me," Sebastian said calmly. "Your broken ribs may have healed, and your burns may no longer be raw, but your strength has diminished. Your movements are stiff. Your reflexes dulled."

Jack's scowl deepened, his voice laced with irritation. "Is that what he thinks? Is that what you think?"

Sebastian said, stepping further into the room. "I state only the facts of the matter."

Jack opened his mouth to retort, but Sebastian cut him off with a pointed look. "You can wallow here, pretending you don't need to be ready for what's coming, or you can get up and do something about it."

Jack stared at him for a long moment, anger flashing in his eyes. But beneath the anger was something else—something he didn't like to admit. A flicker of doubt. A memory of how easily he'd been out of breath the last time he tried to mount a horse in a hurry.

Sebastian's voice softened, though his tone remained firm. "You may hate the idea, but if you don't take this seriously, you'll find yourself at a disadvantage. And I doubt very much, from what I have heard of you, that you like to be in that position."

Jack swung his legs over the side of the bed, boots thudding on the wooden floor. "Damn you and your lectures."

Sebastian allowed himself a small, knowing smile. "I'll take that as a yes."

"You can take it as me wanting to shut you up," Jack grumbled, grabbing his doublet. He stood slowly, rolling his shoulder to ease the familiar tightness in his back. "Lead the way, monk."

Sebastian stepped aside, gesturing toward the door. "Good. Let's start with the basics. Outside."

Jack muttered something under his breath but followed, his steps heavy but reluctant curiosity creeping into his gait. If nothing else, he thought, it would feel good to hold a blade again. Even if it meant tolerating Sebastian's smug wisdom.

The morning air was brisk as they stepped into the yard behind the inn, the faint scent of rain lingering. Jack squinted at the wooden practice swords leaning against the wall, his irritation simmering again.

"Wooden swords?" Jack asked, incredulous. "What am I, a child?"

Sebastian raised an eyebrow, tossing one of the wooden blades toward him. Jack caught it reflexively, though his grip was awkward. "Fine, are you? Your back stiffens every time you sit too long, and your footwork has the grace of a mule," Sebastian replied, his tone maddeningly calm. "If you're not careful, you'll end up useless in a fight. Is that what you want?"

Jack stood in the courtyard behind the Black Swan, scowling at Sebastian as if he'd been asked to dance a jig naked in front of the whole village.

"This is ridiculous," Jack muttered. "I'm fine as I am. I've healed."

Jack glared but said nothing.

"Good," Sebastian said, taking up his stance. "Then let's begin."

Reluctantly, Jack mirrored him. The first clash of the wooden blades jolted through his arm, the weight of the sword unfamiliar in his hand. Sebastian moved fluidly, pressing Jack with quick strikes that forced him to retreat.

# A Queen's Rebel

"Keep your feet moving!" Sebastian barked, circling Jack like a wolf.

"I am moving!" Jack snapped, his breath already coming in short gasps.

"Not enough." Sebastian stepped in with a sudden thrust, tapping Jack's ribs where they'd once been broken. Jack winced and stumbled back, his frustration boiling over.

"Damn it!"

"Control your temper," Sebastian said sharply. "You'll tire yourself out before the real fight begins."

They continued for several more minutes, Jack's breath growing increasingly ragged as Sebastian pushed him harder. Finally, Sebastian stepped back, lowering his blade.

"That's enough for now," he said.

Jack bent over, hands on his knees, his chest heaving. "Enough! That felt like four rounds in the melee."

Sebastian's lips twitched into a faint smile. "You've been out of practice too long. But you still have the instincts."

Jack straightened slowly, rolling his shoulders. Despite the sweat and the ache in his ribs, he found himself smirking. "I'd forgotten how good this felt."

Sebastian clapped him on the shoulder. "Good. Because tomorrow, we'll do it again."

Jack groaned, though a part of him was already looking forward to it.

Sam Burnell

## CHAPTER SIXTEEN

Jack, released from Sebastian's tasks was more awake than usual and ready to leave the Black Swan.

Richard sidled up to his brother. "I see Brother Sebastian has moved on from having you fight with crockery."

Jack scowled at his brother. "I don't find it amusing."

Richard grinned. "That's a shame because I do. I enjoyed providing Master Threadmill with a commentary on your exertions."

"You were watching?" Jack blurted, annoyed.

"Some things cannot be missed," Richard replied, laughing.

"Give me a few weeks, and I'll give you a few bruises ...." Jack paused, an evil grin on his face. "Perhaps I shall suggest to the damned monk that you, too, would appreciate his instruction. After all, as he keeps telling me, life is a pathway of learning that never ends."

"There is no need ....."

"Don't you also keep telling me – a gift freely given is one to be cherished. Your words, if I remember. Yes, I shall suggest it .... Nay, I shall insist on it," Jack said happily, his blue eyes glinting with mischief.

Their conversation was interrupted by the appearance of the landlord fussing over their departure and pressing a bundle of stale bread and cheese into Richard's hands with the fervour of a man eager to keep his noble guests happy.

They rode out of the village in silence, the hooves of their horses muffled by the damp ground. Summer, it seemed, was temporarily over. Ahead, the weathered outline of Cumnor Place emerged from the mist, its squat, buttressed frame as sombre as the day before. The building seemed to loom larger as they approached, its arched windows dark and unwelcoming, like the hollow eyes of a skull.

Richard reined in his horse as they neared the gates, his gaze sweeping the grounds with a practised eye. "Forrester will be waiting," he said grimly. "If he's as hospitable as he was yesterday, this should be a lively conversation."

Jack, his expression wry, adjusted his grip on the reins. "Let's hope his mood has improved overnight. Though I somehow doubt it."

Threadmill said nothing, though his apprehension was evident as he glanced nervously at the imposing structure. The trio dismounted, handing their horses to a stable boy who emerged from the mist like a phantom and made their way to the main door. As Richard raised his hand to knock, the heavy oak swung open, revealing Andrew Forrester, his expression as cold and hard as the house's stone walls behind him.

"Ah," Forrester said, his tone clipped. "I see you've returned. Shall we dispense with the pleasantries?"

They followed Forrester into a small hall. The fire was not lit, and the room was cold and inhospitable—no doubt on purpose. Threadmill, who had carried his portable scribe's desk, set it up quickly in one corner.

"I have, of course, read the coroner's report," Richard said evenly, his eyes fixed on Andrew Forrester, the steward. The man nodded stiffly, a gesture that carried more resignation than agreement. "But I find it raises more questions than it answers. I'd like to ask a few of my own."

"They'd be questions better directed to the coroner, wouldn't they?" Forrester replied, his tone as cool as the air in the room.

# A Queen's Rebel

"In time, I'm sure I will," Richard said, a faint smile playing on his lips though his eyes remained sharp.

Forrester's gaze flicked to the corner of the room, where Threadmill sat poised, pen hovering over a sheet of parchment. The steward's expression darkened. "And what's he scribbling down?" he asked with a touch of irritation.

Richard's tone grew firmer. "He, Master Steward, is Lord Fitzwarren's lawyer. His task is to record our conversation for the benefit of Lord Burghley. I trust that won't be a problem?"

Forrester's mouth tightened, but he gave a curt nod.

"To my first question," Richard continued, his voice calm but insistent. "The report states there were no servants in the house at the time of Lady Amy's fall. Is this true?"

Forrester's eyes lingered on Threadmill, whose pen hovered expectantly over the page. "That's correct. There was a fair in Abingdon. Lady Amy gave the servants leave to attend."

Richard nodded thoughtfully. "And she did not wish to attend the fair herself?"

"I couldn't say," Forrester replied with a shrug. "She didn't discuss such things with me."

"But she had attended in previous years, had she not?"

Forrester hesitated, his brow furrowing slightly. "It's an annual event. Yes, she has gone in the past."

"But not this year," Richard pressed. "Did that strike you as odd? That Lady Amy would choose to remain behind?"

The steward's expression hardened. "It's not my place to speculate on her wishes, sir. My duty is to carry them out."

"Of course," Richard said, inclining his head. "I understand. It is, after all, quite a journey to the fair—nearly two hours, so I'm told."

Forrester shook his head. "Not so long, sir. The weather was fair that day. For those on horseback, it's no more than half an hour."

Richard's brow lifted slightly. "And how many servants were in the household that day?"

"Five, in addition to myself and my wife," Forrester answered promptly.

"The names of the servants please," Richard asked.

"Mrs Odingsells, housekeeper and her daughter Mary the cook, Molly Woodly, Lady Robsart's maid, John Marsh servant to Lady Robsart and Jed Farnley, groom," Forester provided bluntly.

Richard leaned forward, his tone sharpening. "So all seven of you left the house, even the cook and the maids?"

Forrester shifted uncomfortably. "I rode, as did my wife. The rest walked."

Richard raised an eyebrow. "Ah. So for the majority of the household, it was indeed a journey of some length—perhaps two hours or more each way?"

The steward bristled. "Does it matter? The fact remains that there were no servants present, as the coroner recorded."

"It matters very much," Richard replied, his voice cool. "It tells us how long Lady Amy was left entirely alone that day. And from what you've just said, it sounds as though it may have been for quite some time."

Threadmill looked up from his parchment. "Shall I note the estimated travel time, sir?"

"Yes," Richard said, his gaze unwavering as it rested on Forrester. "Make a note. We'll confirm the timing ourselves tomorrow."

Forrester's face reddened, his eyes darting between Richard and Threadmill. "You're wasting your time with this nonsense," he muttered. "The coroner's verdict was clear."

"Was it?" Richard countered, his tone cutting. "The coroner's verdict may tell us what happened after Lady Amy was found, but I'm far more interested in what happened before."

The steward said nothing, his lips pressed into a thin line.

"Can we see where the poor lady fell?" Richard asked, his tone devoid of the politeness expected, as if the tragedy demanded clarity over courtesy.

The steward waved a hand dismissively toward the door leading out of the room. "You've already passed that point."

Richard moved to the door and opened it, revealing a small hall beyond. To the left, a flight of wooden steps rose sharply upward. His hand rested lightly on the carved newel post. "May I?"

The steward shrugged indifferently. "There's naught to see now."

Richard ascended the steps, his fingers sliding along the oak bannister. The wood was smooth and polished from years of use, and its craftsmanship was evident in the careful grooves of its design. Jack, curiosity piqued, followed close behind. Halfway up, Richard stopped abruptly, his hand pausing on the wood. Caught off guard, Jack muttered a curse as he stumbled into his brother's back.

"Nine," Richard announced, drumming the fingers of his free hand on the bannister.

"Nine, what?" Jack asked, stepping back to regain his balance.

"Steps," Richard replied. He turned slightly and addressed Threadmill, who was lingering at the base of the stairs. "Make a note, please, Master Threadmill."

Threadmill nodded, hastily scribbling in his notebook as Richard continued his observations. "A sturdy bannister on the left, oak and solidly constructed. On the right, another bannister, ash perhaps, affixed to the wall. Two handrails for support, whichever side the poor lady chose to tread."

Jack's gaze followed Richard's gestures, noting the craftsmanship of the rails. His brow furrowed slightly.

Richard took the final step onto a small landing. A simple wooden door stood before him, its iron latch catching the light faintly. He tapped the door with his knuckles. "Was this the lady's chamber?"

The steward nodded curtly. "It was. It's not been used since."

Richard's hand moved to the iron ring of the latch. He lifted it, the mechanism clicking softly, and pushed the door open. It swung inward with surprising ease, the well-oiled hinges making no sound. Beyond lay a bed-chamber, its air heavy with the musty stillness of disuse.

The room spoke of its former occupant with quiet eloquence. A four-poster bed stood against the far wall, the counterpane still arranged neatly as if waiting for its owner's return. The hangings were drawn back, their fabric slightly faded but richly embroidered. A silver gilt mirror lay on a dresser near the bed, its once-pristine surface dulled by dust. Beside it rested three brushes, their bristles splayed from use. A brass candlestick stood nearby, the wax partially melted and hardened in uneven rivulets that had spilt onto the surface of the dresser.

Richard moved further into the room, his gaze sweeping over the details. "Curious," he murmured, running a finger along the edge of the dresser. Jack lingered near the door, his eyes narrowing as he took in the scene. Richard's expression was thoughtful as he stepped closer to the bed, his hand grazing the carved post.

The tension in the air was unmistakable as Andrew Forrester crossed his arms and stood firm in

# A Queen's Rebel

the doorway, extremely unhappy at their presence in the bedroom. "I trust," Forrester began, his tone edged with a practised courtesy that barely concealed his irritation, "that you've completed your inquiries here. You've seen the house, questioned me to your satisfaction, and turned every stone that I will permit. There is nothing more for you here."

Standing just a step away, Richard raised an eyebrow, a faint smile touching his lips but not reaching his eyes. "The investigation is far from complete, Forrester. There are still many questions left unanswered."

Forrester's jaw tightened. "Questions you may ask elsewhere. I have given you what I can. If you wish to interview anyone else connected to this matter, you may do so outside these walls. This house has hosted enough intrusion."

Standing against a wall nearby, Jack regarded Forrester with a faint grin that carried more curiosity than humour. "You're awfully quick to show us the door. One might think you have something to hide."

Forrester's eyes narrowed, and the air between them bristled for a moment. "I have nothing to hide, my lord. But I have my responsibilities, and they do not include accommodating every prying eye that wanders to this place. I serve the Earl of Leicester, and my duty is to him, not to any outside party."

Richard stepped closer, his calm demeanour unshaken by Forrester's thinly veiled hostility. "And yet, the Earl of Leicester's reputation might rest upon the outcome of this inquiry. I would think you'd want to ensure we have everything we need to arrive at the truth."

Forrester's lips pressed into a thin line. "You have what you need, sir. More than enough, I'd wager. If you require anything further, or if you wish to question other household members, you can do so—but not here." His tone left no room for negotiation.

Jack straightened, the movement slow and deliberate. "A hospitable man, aren't you?" His words dripped with sarcasm, but he didn't push further. He could sense the futility of arguing with the man.

"Before we leave," Richard said, "There is a question I would like to ask?"

The steward's eyes narrowed. "If it will bring an end to this interview then ask it."

"You lease Cumnor Place from the Earl, is that right?" Richard asked, then waving his arm around.

Forrester nodded. "I do."

"And much of the furniture, silver and household trappings we see are your property," Richard continued.

"They are," Forrester replied carefully, primed for the trap.

"It seems strange to me that a man would leave his wealth unguarded, his house without servants, anyone could have walked in and taken anything they wish," Richard replied.

Forrester's eyes were fixed on Richard. "It was not empty."

"Ah, so you were in the habit of using the Lady as your guard?" Richard said smiling.

Forrester did not reply. He gave a stiff bow. "If there is nothing else, I'll see to my duties and you to the door."

## CHAPTER SEVENTEEN

Charles Walls was a man who thrived on proximity to power, though he had yet to breach the inner sanctum of the Privy Council chambers. To him the invitation to Cecil's private office was not merely a matter of prestige but a validation of his perceived worth as an advisor of consequence. He was always well-turned out, his doublets tailored just enough to suggest wealth but not extravagance, his ruff stiff and carefully pleated, though his fashion sense belied a more threadbare political acumen. Walls had cultivated a reputation as a sycophant whose opinions were invariably aligned with the Queen's. Whether the topic was military strategy, religious policy, or the import of Scottish affairs, Walls' stance would echo Elizabeth's sentiments, his voice chiming with enthusiasm for her every decision.

This strategy had served him well. It was difficult to lose favour when one's every utterance reinforced the monarch's authority, and yet, Cecil noted with some satisfaction, Walls' star seemed to be waning. The Queen, sharp as ever, was not a woman easily blinded by flattery, and in recent months, she had begun to view Walls' fawning sycophancy as tiresome rather than loyal. The whispers of court suggested he had lost the spark of relevance, his presence more an irritation than an asset.

The connection between Walls and Nicholas Adams was one that Cecil had always considered harmless, if annoying. Adams, too, was a man of mediocrity propped up by his proximity to better minds, and the two men seemed to share an unspoken pact of mutual flattery and self-congratulation. It was a predictable alliance: Walls' opinions, as malleable as clay in the potter's hand, found an eager audience in Adams, who was too vain to see through the artifice. If there had ever been a more ineffectual pair in Elizabeth's court, Cecil could not recall them. And yet, here they were, the subjects of rumours linking them to Catholic intrigue.

Cecil leaned back in his chair, pulling his cap from his head and tossing it onto the desk with a sigh. His ink-stained fingers raked through his thinning hair as he stared at the pile of correspondence before him. Something gnawed at the edges of his thoughts, a sense that he was missing a crucial piece of the puzzle. It was maddening, like a worm burrowing through his mind, just out of reach.

Walls and Adams lacked the wit to mastermind a serious conspiracy—of that Cecil was certain. But that was precisely what made the situation so troubling. Men of such limited capability were easy prey for those who sought to manipulate them. Adams' ambition and vanity, coupled with Walls' desperate need to remain relevant, made them ideal pawns in a larger game. And if there truly was a Catholic plot to undermine Elizabeth's rule, these two might unwittingly hold the threads that led to its architect.

Cecil's hand hovered over the latest report from one of his informants. Could it be true? Yesterday, the idea of Nicholas Adams and Charles Walls being involved in treason would have made him laugh. Adams was too foolish, and Walls too spineless. But power was a great corrupter, and Adams, for all his superficiality, could easily be tempted by the promise of influence. A clever man—someone with charm, guile, and a talent for persuasion—could turn Adams into a weapon without him even realizing it.

Walls, too, might be persauded. His obsession with currying favour made him blind to nuance, and his desperation to regain the Queen's regard could be exploited by a whisper in the right ear or a nudge toward the wrong decision.

Cecil sat forward, tapping his fingers on the desk. His instincts told him there was more to this than the surface suggested. The Catholic relics found in Adams' home, then whispers of treason surrounding Walls and a traveling case found in his London home containing popish trappings—these could not simply be dismissed as coincidence. But why these men? Why now?

He picked up the report and scanned it again, searching for the elusive thread that would pull the pieces together. There had to be a reason why these two hapless courtiers had been drawn into the centre of something so sinister. Perhaps they were being used as bait, their downfall meant to distract from a larger target. Or perhaps, despite their lack of intelligence, they had stumbled onto something they were never meant to see.

Cecil's lips pressed into a thin line. The answers would come, but he would have to be patient. For now, he would continue to watch Walls and Adams closely. If they were pawns, then somewhere in the shadows was the hand that moved them. And Cecil intended to find it.

Cecil sat in his study, the air thick with tension as the knock he had been expecting finally sounded at the door. He set the report in his hand down deliberately, smoothing the creases in the parchment, and adjusted his doublet with a practiced motion.

"Enter," he called, his voice even, but with an undertone that suggested no tolerance for delay.

The door opened to reveal Charles Walls, his posture a careful mix of self-assuredness and unease. His doublet, as always, was tailored to perfection, the ruff at his neck stiff and pristine. Yet, to Cecil's discerning eye, there was something faintly desperate about the man's appearance, as if he'd spent too long polishing the veneer to conceal the cracks beneath. Walls stepped forward, his expression a mask of respect tempered by a hint of confusion.

"My lord," Walls said, bowing slightly. "You sent for me?"

"I did," Cecil replied, gesturing toward the chair opposite his desk. "Sit."

Walls hesitated, his eyes darting around the room as if searching for an unseen ally. When none appeared, he moved to the chair and lowered himself into it with the caution of a man unsure of his footing.

"Do you know why you're here?" Cecil asked, his tone calm but unyielding.

Walls licked his lips nervously. "I... I assume it has to do with recent whispers, my lord. Rumours travel quickly in court."

Cecil leaned forward, his hands folding neatly atop the desk. "Then let me dispel any misunderstandings. This is not about court gossip, Walls. This is about treason."

The blood drained from Walls' face, his carefully composed demeanor faltering for a moment. "T-treason?" he stammered. "My lord, I assure you, I have no involvement in—"

Cecil held up a hand, silencing him. "You will save your denials until I've asked my questions. And I suggest you consider your answers carefully."

Walls swallowed hard, his knuckles white as he gripped the arms of the chair. "Of course, my lord."

"Good," Cecil said, his tone softening slightly, though his eyes remained sharp. He reached for a small box on his desk and opened it, revealing several items within. He withdrew a silver crucifix and placed it on the desk between them. "Do you recognize this?"

Walls' eyes widened, and he leaned back as if the object itself might burn him. "I... I've never seen it before," he said, his voice trembling.

## A Queen's Rebel

Cecil's gaze didn't waver. "It was found in a traveling case at your London residence, along with other items of a Catholic nature. A chalice, an altar cloth. Shall I continue?"

Walls shook his head, his face pale. "I swear, my lord, I have no knowledge of those things. They are not mine."

"Not yours," Cecil echoed, his voice devoid of inflection. "And yet, they were found in your possession. How do you explain that?"

Walls opened his mouth, then closed it, his mind clearly racing. "Perhaps... perhaps they belong to John Titch, I rent rooms from him in Stand Street in the City. I would never—"

"John Titch," Cecil repeated, his tone almost amused. "A bold accusation, Walls. Why would he hide these in with your belongings?"

"I... I don't know, my lord," Walls admitted, his voice barely above a whisper. "But I would never involve myself in such things. My loyalty to Her Majesty is absolute."

Cecil leaned back, his fingers steepling as he studied the man before him. "Your loyalty may be absolute, Walls, but your judgement has been questionable at best. Your associations, particularly with Nicholas Adams, have not gone unnoticed."

Walls' head snapped up, his eyes wide. "Adams? My lord, he's a friend, nothing more. A harmless man with no ambition beyond his own self-importance."

"Harmless," Cecil murmured, his gaze narrowing. "And yet, he too is implicated in this matter. Catholic relics found in his home, whispers of treason tied to his name. Tell me, Walls, do you truly believe this is all coincidence?"

Walls faltered, his mouth opening and closing as he searched for a response. "I... I don't know what to believe, my lord. But I swear to you, I have no part in any treachery."

Cecil studied him for a long moment, the silence in the room growing heavy. Finally, he spoke, his voice measured. "You may be innocent of intent, Walls. But innocence does not absolve you of responsibility. You and Adams may be pawns in a larger game, but pawns can still be sacrificed."

Walls paled further, his hands trembling slightly. "My lord, please—"

Cecil rose from his chair, cutting him off with a wave of his hand. "This conversation is over. For now. You are to remain in London and keep yourself available should I have further questions. And Walls..."

Walls looked up, his eyes filled with fear.

"Pray that your ignorance does not cost you your head," Cecil finished, his tone cold.

Walls stood, bowing shakily before retreating from the room, his steps hurried and uneven. Cecil watched him go, his expression unreadable. When the door closed, he turned back to his desk, his gaze falling on the crucifix. The pieces were moving, but the game was far from over. Somewhere in the shadows, the true players waited. And Cecil intended to unmask them all.

A Queen's Rebel

## CHAPTER EIGHTEEN

The dimly lit Black Swan tavern reeked of damp straw and spilt ale. A sputtering fire did its best to chase away the chill of what should have been a warm summer evening, but the effort was half-hearted at best. The three men sat at a rough-hewn table pushed against the far wall, Richard leaned back in his chair, the coroner's report held casually in one hand.

Jack, seated across from him, tapped his fingers idly on the table, his expression one of faint irritation. Threadmill, seated beside Jack, had his parchment and quill ready, his brows knit with focus as he prepared to take notes.

Richard straightened, holding up the report. "The coroner's findings," he began, his voice cutting through the muted chatter of the tavern, "are as dry as the ale here. But the names of those involved—those are what interest me." He glanced at Threadmill, who dipped his quill into the inkpot and poised it above the parchment.

"Ready?" Richard asked.

Threadmill nodded briskly. "Ready."

Richard began to read, his tone steady and deliberate. "John Pudsey. Richard Smith, foreman of the jury. Humphrey Lewis. Thomas Moulder. Richard Knight. Thomas Spyre. Edward Stevenson. John Stevenson. Richard Hughes. William Cantrell. William Noble. John Buck. John Keene. Henry Langley. Stephen Ruffyn. And John Sire."

Threadmill's quill scratched against the parchment as he hurried to capture each name.

Richard lowered the paper slightly and added, "And we'll need to add the names of the household servants provided by Andrew Forrester. Make a note of that, and we want to know if the jurors had any connection with them or Forrester."

Threadmill glanced up, his quill pausing. "You want me to list the servants alongside the jurors?"

"Yes," Richard replied curtly. "If we find any link between them, I want to know."

Jack leaned forward, resting his elbows on the table. "What's your thought, brother? That someone on the jury might have been swayed or coerced?"

Richard's eyes flicked to Jack. "I'm not suggesting anything yet, but it's prudent to consider all possibilities. The coroner's report raises more questions than it answers. For one, it states there were no servants present at the time of the fall. Yet, we know the servants had to pass through the village to attend the fair. Who saw them? How long were they gone? These details matter."

Threadmill nodded, his quill already moving to add the task to his growing list.

Jack leaned back in his chair, his hand resting lightly on the table. "So, we track down these jurors and interview them, one by one?"

Richard nodded. "Precisely. Each man will have a perspective, and perhaps one of them will reveal something the others did not."

Threadmill glanced between the brothers. "And the servants, my Lord?"

"Every last one," Richard said firmly. "Their stories will either confirm the details of the events Andrew Forrester gave us—or contradict it."

Jack exhaled. "I don't imagine Forrester will appreciate us stirring the pot like this."

Richard allowed himself a faint smile. "No, he won't. But his discomfort is not my concern."

Threadmill finished his notes and looked up. "It will take some time to track everyone down."

"We have time," Richard said simply. "For now, you can start with the jurors."

# A Queen's Rebel

Jack pushed his chair back with a scrape, and said to Threadmill, "If you're to find everyone on this list the landlord might be a good start."

Richard arched an eyebrow. "A sound idea, Jack. Though I expect the price of his help will be another round of that swill he calls ale."

Jack rolled his eyes and watched as Threadmill, holding his list, went in search of the landlord. "Richard, this is going to take more than two weeks."

Richard let his eyes roam around the Swan's rotting interior. "It won't."

Threadmill wound his way back to their poor table shortly afterwards a smile on his face. "I have some good news."

"Go on," Jack said without enthusiasm.

"John Marsh, one of Amy Robsarts servants, died of an ailment of the heart, and two of the jurors have also deceased,"

"Hardly good news for them," Jack shot back.

"I rather think Master Threadmill was alluding to the fact that we can strike three people from the list that we need to talk to, am I right?" Richard replied.

"Actually, it will be five," Master Threadmill replied. "The groom left Cumnor Place shortly after Marsh died, and no one seems to know where he went. Mrs Odingsells now lives in Oxford, where she is a servant in the Price household."

"Good work. I will provide two men to accompany you tomorrow. Find as many as you can, I will give you a list of questions to ask each of them."

"Cetainly, sir," Threadmill replied.

"If you will excuse me," Richard said suddenly.

Brother Sebastian stood at the edge of the tavern's common room, his imposing figure silhouetted against the flickering light of the hearth. The damp clinging to his robes, his expression was a mix of displeasure and resignation.

"Sir," Sebastian began, his tone both firm and exasperated, "I cannot for the life of me understand why you've seen fit to keep your brother in this miserable hovel. The air is damp, the floors are near to rotting, and the smell—" he waved a hand, as though trying to disperse the offensive aroma—"is enough to make a man question his stomach. I had thought we would leave after a night."

Richard fixed Sebastian with a hard stare. "It's not ideal, Brother Sebastian, but it will have to suffice for a few days."

"'Suffice!" Sebastian spluttered, stepping closer. "You've seen his condition. This place will do him no favours. Better accommodation can be found in Oxford."

"It will only be for a few days. Better food has been soured, there is dry wood for the fire, and at the moment is it near to Cumnor Place where we need to be. If I suggested moving him to more comfortable accommodation for his health, he'd take it as an insult—or worse, a challenge."

Sebastian sighed heavily, his arms crossing over his chest. "The man is stubborn, but stubbornness won't mend his health. He needs rest, dry air, and proper care. This place offers none of those things."

Richard snorted softly. "Jack listens to no one, least of all me."

Sebastian shook his head but said nothing further, his lips pressed into a thin line. He glanced toward the corner where Jack sat, deep in conversation with Threadmill.

"I'll pray he doesn't catch his death in this place," Sebastian muttered before turning away, his heavy steps retreating toward the door.

"Pray all you like, Brother," Richard replied; however, he had to agree that Sebastian did have a point. The tavern offered little more comfort than a tent in a field, and the floor was a mire of rotting reeds, piss and split ale and food. He, too, would be glad when they were gone. Richard looked around the place and sighed.

The sound of Brother Sebastian's steady knocking at the door was enough to rouse Jack from his sleep, though his first inclination was to pull the blankets over his head and pretend he hadn't heard. It was early. Too early.

"Up, my Lord," came the monk's resonant voice. "The day waits for no man, and neither do I."

Jack groaned, muttering something unintelligible as he swung his legs over the side of the bed. The chill of the floorboards did nothing to improve his mood. He rubbed his face with his hands, then, his voice serious, he called out, "Brother Sebastian, since you're so keen on company, perhaps you'd do me the favour of waking my brother as well. He has expressed an interest in joining us."

Sebastian's enthusiasm was immediate. "Did he now? Excellent. I shall see to it!" Without waiting for further comment, the monk's heavy footsteps retreated down the hall.

Jack chuckled to himself as he dressed. If Sebastian's zeal was anything to go by, Richard wouldn't have long to lament his words. Jack took his time pulling on his boots, enjoying the mental image of his brother being roused from sleep by the tireless monk.

When Jack finally made his way down to the yard at the back of the Black Swan, the sight waiting for him was worth the effort. Richard was already there, leaning against the low stone wall with a faintly disgruntled expression. His dark hair was tousled, and his cloak draped unevenly over one shoulder. Brother Sebastian stood nearby, holding a pair of wooden training swords and two bucklers.

"Good morning, Richard," Jack greeted him with a wide grin. "You look as if you're enjoying the fresh air."

Richard shot him a withering look. "I'll remember this, Jack."

"Come now," Jack teased. "You said you wanted to join us."

"I said I might, in jest," Richard corrected, his tone dry. "Apparently, jesting is lost on Brother Sebastian."

"On the contrary," Sebastian interjected, his expression unyielding but his tone pleasant. "I simply took your words at face value. Honesty is the cornerstone of a disciplined man."

Jack laughed outright, taking one of the wooden swords Sebastian offered him. Richard accepted the other with obvious reluctance, testing its weight in his hand with a grudging flick of the wrist.

"Let's start with something light," Sebastian instructed. "No need to overexert yourselves." His pointed glance at Jack didn't go unnoticed.

The session began with slow, deliberate movements. Sebastian had them practice basic strikes and blocks, ensuring their footwork was steady and controlled. Richard carried out the exercises with precision, although his dissatisfaction at being in the yard early in the morning was evident from his occasional grumbles.

Jack, for his part, kept the grin plastered on his face, especially when Richard's footwork drew a sharp correction from Sebastian. "The ground's not going anywhere, Richard," Jack quipped.

"Keep talking, and I'll introduce you to it," Richard retorted, swinging his practice sword a little more forcefully than necessary.

"Easy, gentlemen," Sebastian chided, his voice calm but firm. "The goal here is refinement, not injury."

The session didn't last long—Sebastian mindful of Jack's recovery, called it to a halt, both brothers were breathing harder than they'd anticipated.

"You're improving," Sebastian remarked, nodding approvingly at Jack. "But don't think for a moment this means you can neglect tomorrow's session."

Jack groaned theatrically. "Tomorrow? Surely, Brother, you've exhausted all your wisdom for the week."

Sebastian's expression didn't waver. "Wisdom, my Lord, is inexhaustible. I'll see you both here at the same hour."

Jack glanced at Richard, whose lips twitched with what could have been a smile or a grimace—it was hard to tell. As they left the yard together, Jack clapped his brother on the back.

Richard shook his head. "You'll pay for this, Jack."

"I don't doubt it," Jack replied with a grin.

## CHAPTER NINETEEN

Richard picked up the list from before Threadmill. "The jury's foreman is Richard Smyth, I would imagine this is as good a place to start as any."

Threadmill shuffled the papers on the table before him, searching his notes. "I have it, Richard Smyth, he lives at Mount Rake Farm, Abingdon."

Threadmill left shortly afterwards, followed by two of the men, his task to track down as many of the jurors as he could.

Richard watching Threadmill leave said to Jack. "Shall we ride to Abingdon? Or shall I send for him?"

Jack looked up from where he was seated near the fire, his legs crossed at the ankles, resting on the top of one of the fire dogs. Then he glanced towards the window, where rain sluiced down the panes. "Send for him. Summer appears to have forsaken us."

Richard Smyth, a gentleman of notable standing, arrived at The Black Swan a few hours later than anticipated. The relentless rain had caught him on the road, leaving his fine attire in a sorry state. His outer cloak, once a rich, deep woollen fabric, was now soaked through, clinging uncomfortably to his shoulders. The grand plumes in his hat, which had been a proud emblem of his rank when he left that morning, now drooped pitifully down his back like bedraggled feathers on a waterlogged bird.

If he had set out the picture of a well-dressed gentleman, this was certainly not how he arrived. Once polished to a shine, his boots were now coated with layers of mud, and the finely woven hose beneath them were splattered and soaked, clinging uncomfortably to his legs with each step. The weather had clearly done its best to humble him.

He paused at the tavern's threshold, shaking droplets of rain from his hat and attempting to regain some semblance of dignity. He straightened his posture, though his waterlogged clothes sagged against him, and he gave a frustrated sigh.

Richard Smyth was greeted by Richard Fitzwarren's sharp grin. Fitzwarren stood impeccably dressed in dry, clean clothes, which made Smyth's dishevelled state all the more glaring.

"Richard Smyth," Fitzwarren said with a mock cheeriness that did little to disguise the frost in his tone, "soaked through to the bone, I see. I do hope your journey wasn't too unpleasant." His eyes flickered over Smyth's sodden cloak and muddy boots with thinly veiled amusement. Fitzwarren himself, in contrast, looked as though he had just stepped out of a portrait, perfectly composed.

Smyth's jaw tightened as he removed his ruined hat, shaking water from the sad, drooping plumes. "The rain was no kinder to me than I imagine this meeting will be," he muttered, his voice low and edged with wariness. He could feel the tension humming in the air between them.

Fitzwarren's smile barely shifted, but his eyes were sharp. "Let's not waste time, shall we? Forrester would not afford us the pleasure of using Cumnor Place, so we have been forced to make our offices in the humble Black Swan, but we can offer a seat by a warm fire."

Richard gestured grandly towards the fire, which crackled invitingly—though it was clear neither man felt the warmth in the other's presence. Drenched and weary, Smyth followed with heavy steps, leaving muddy footprints behind him.

"Sit, sit," Fitzwarren said with faux politeness, gesturing toward a chair near the fire. His tone was light, but both men could feel an undercurrent of tension. Smyth remained standing, his hands still clutching his soaked hat, rainwater dripping slowly from the brim onto the floor. He wasn't here for pleasantries, and they both knew it. The heat of the fire crackled, but it did nothing to ease the growing chill in the room.

With a tight smile, Fitzwarren's gaze flicked to the other man seated in the room. "Let me introduce you to my brother, Lord Fitzwarren," he said, indicating the man by the hearth. Jack sat comfortably, his legs outstretched toward the warmth of the flames, the image of leisure. His eyes, however, were anything but relaxed, ice blue and watching Smythe carefully. He didn't bother standing or even acknowledging the introduction beyond a curt nod.

The room was thick with expectation, the fire casting shadows that danced across the faces of those present. Jack Fitzwarren's feet shifted slightly, the leather of his boots creaking as he stretched his legs, his gaze still firmly on Smyth, dissecting him with an unnerving calmness.

Smyth felt the weight of their stares, his soaked clothes a reminder of the discomfort and unease of this meeting. He glanced at the chair near the fire but did not move. His spine stiffened, and he raised his chin slightly. "I'll stand," he said, his voice rough but firm.

Fitzwarren's smile didn't falter, but the cool gleam in his eyes sharpened. "As you wish," he replied, the words dripping with an air of subtle condescension.

"So," Richard began, stepping closer to the fire and clasping his hands behind his back. The casualness of the gesture was at odds with the intensity of the room. "We are here to discuss the matter of Lady Amy Robsart's unfortunate demise. As you were the foreman of the jury that ruled her death an accident, I trust you will have no objections to us reviewing the details of that decision?"

# A Queen's Rebel

Smyth tightened his grip on the brim of his hat, his knuckles whitening. "The decision was made after thorough deliberation of the facts. There was no evidence of foul play, only that she fell down the stairs."

Richard's smile remained, but it was Jack who spoke, his voice low and dark, contrasting with his relaxed posture by the fire. "And yet, many whisper otherwise, do they not? It seems to me, Mr. Smyth, that sometimes what is not said in court speaks louder than what is."

Smyth bristled, his heart hammering in his chest, but he refused to be drawn in so easily. "The jury was presented with no evidence that suggested anything but an accident," he repeated, more firmly this time, his voice tight. "Whispers and rumours are not enough to sway the law."

"True," Richard chimed in smoothly. "But there are those of us who find it rather difficult to believe that a young, healthy woman could fall to her death so conveniently, particularly when her husband, Robert Dudley, stands to gain so much from her sudden departure from this world."

"Again," Smyth said, forcing calm into his voice, "there was no evidence of Dudley's involvement. The inquest was thorough."

"Perhaps," Richard replied, turning toward the fire, his back now to Smyth. "But thoroughness, Smyth, does not always uncover the truth. Especially when powerful men have a vested interest in keeping certain truths buried."

Richard turned back, his eyes locked onto Smyth, and a hint of something dark flickered behind his cold demeanour. "Tell me, Smyth," he asked, his voice low but sharp, "did you never question why Lady Robsart fell? Or were you so eager to be done with it all?"

Smyth felt the pressure mounting, a storm of accusation and implication gathering around him. He straightened, his voice as steady as he could make it. "I followed the evidence. The jury followed the law."

Richard's smile was gone. "Did you?" His voice was like a blade cutting through the air between them. "Or did you follow the shadow of Robert Dudley's influence?"

"I will not be accused of corruption or cowardice without cause," he said, his voice rising, his eyes locked on Richard's. "If you have any evidence to support these claims, then by all means, present it. But if you're here to drag my name through the mud based on nothing more than suspicion, I'll have no part of it."

For a moment, the tension hung in the air like a drawn bowstring. Then Richard's smile returned, cold and calculating. There was a pause for a moment; if Smyth thought for a second that the interview was over, he was wrong.

"Did you examine the stairs she fell down, may I ask? Did the jury visit Cumnor Place where this 'accident' occurred?" Richard's voice was sharp, every word cutting into the silence of the room.

Smyth shook his head, the motion sending more droplets of rainwater splattering onto the floor. His discomfort grew by the second, but it wasn't just from his soaked clothes. There was an air of accusation in Richard's words that felt inescapable.

"No," Smyth admitted, his voice low but firm. "We were not required to visit Cumnor Place. We relied on the testimonies provided to us."

Richard's eyes gleamed, his voice taking on a hard edge. "Ah, no visit to where the so-called accident took place." He paced slowly as though considering every word carefully before letting it fall. "Did you, or any of the jury, even know that there were only eight steps? Eight. Not a grand staircase but a simple, modest set of stairs with two handrails." He paused, letting the words hang in the air, watching Smyth closely. "Eight steps, Smyth. That's not so many to fall down, is it?"

# A Queen's Rebel

Smyth opened his mouth, but no words came out immediately. His thoughts tangled as Richard's insinuation took root. Eight steps. He hadn't known that. It hadn't seemed necessary at the time. The testimonies had described a fall—fatal, tragic—but not remarkable. Certainly not enough to warrant additional questioning from the jury.

Richard continued his voice now almost a whisper, leaning closer. "Two handrails, Smyth. Lady Amy, a woman of good health, fell down those eight steps to her death, and not a single soul in your jury thought to ask how?"

Smyth felt a flush of heat rise up his neck. "We considered all the information presented to us," he replied, his voice tight and defensive. "There was no evidence ...."

"No evidence," Richard interrupted, his tone mocking now. "No evidence because none of you thought to look for it. Eight steps. A woman who, by all accounts, was capable of steady movement and health. And yet, she is dead. And Robert Dudley...."

"Stop," Smyth said abruptly, his voice louder than he intended, cutting through Richard's words. He could feel his pulse in his temples. "The jury ruled as they saw fit. If you believe there was more to it, why was nothing brought before the court?"

Richard took a step back, his gaze never leaving Smyth's face. "Tell me, Smyth," he said softly but with menace in every word, "if your jury had known about those eight steps, the handrails, the sheer improbability of such a fatal fall, would you still have ruled it an accident? Or would you have had the courage to challenge the version of events Dudley wanted you to believe?"

He swallowed, trying to steady his voice. "The jury ruled on what was given to us. We had no reason to doubt ...."

Richard cut him off again, his voice a venomous whisper. "Perhaps you should have."

"Which brings me to the other injuries," Richard continued, his voice sharp with incredulity. "The lady had two dents in her head. One is not so deep, an inch, perhaps, but the other, Smyth, is two and a half inches deep. Both on the back of her skull."

Smyth stood still, his face pale. He could feel the weight of the accusation growing.

Richard pressed on, his voice rising. "Two and a half inches, Smyth! And yet, the stairs she supposedly fell down had rounded edges, smooth newel posts and bannisters. Nothing sharp, nothing that could cause such injuries. Did no one think to question this? Did your jury not pause to wonder how such wounds could have been inflicted from a fall down eight modest steps?"

The room fell silent for a moment, the only sound the fire crackling in the hearth. Smyth's throat felt dry, his thoughts scrambling for defence, something that would explain why they hadn't questioned it further.

"We were presented with the medical evidence," Smyth said quietly, but even he could hear the strain in his voice. "The physician explained the injuries as consistent with a fall. There was no indication...."

"No indication?" Richard interrupted, stepping closer, his eyes blazing. "A fall? Down eight steps? With two separate dents in her skull, one deep enough to crush it? No indication, Smyth? Or was the jury too eager to accept the most convenient conclusion?"

Smyth's breath caught in his chest. The thought had crossed his mind during the inquest, he admitted to himself now, but at the time, the jury had trusted the physicians' testimonies. They hadn't had the courage to question further, to dig deeper into what had happened in Cumnor Place. But now, faced with Fitzwarren's words, it seemed like a glaring oversight.

# A Queen's Rebel

"Tell me," Richard demanded, his voice cold now, every word measured. "Did none of you consider that those injuries might have been caused by something other than a fall? Something deliberate?"

The suggestion hung in the air like a blade poised to strike. Smyth felt his pulse quicken, but he couldn't bring himself to meet Richard's piercing gaze. His mind raced back to the inquest. How had they let those injuries pass without proper scrutiny?

Richard continued, relentless. "Lady Amy Robsart didn't simply fall, Smyth. Someone made sure she wouldn't rise again. And you ...." he paused, his voice dripping with contempt, "and your jury allowed them to get away with it. That does remain a very real possibility."

Smyth opened his mouth, but no words came. The weight of the accusation crushed him, the realisation of what might have been lost in their hasty conclusion swirling in his mind. Had they been blind to the truth? Had they, in their desire to be done with the case and avoid the shadow of powerful men like Robert Dudley, ignored the very facts that now seemed so glaring?

Richard stepped back, his voice soft but filled with fury. "You were supposed to deliver justice, Smyth. Instead, you delivered a lie."

"Her neck was broken by the fall," Smyth said, his voice tight, defensive. "Even eight steps is enough to do that." He grasped at the medical testimony that had been presented at the inquest, the facts that had seemed so clear then. He clung to them now, trying to justify the jury's decision, trying to explain how they had come to their conclusion.

Richard's eyes narrowed, his lips curling into a thin smile that held no warmth. "Ah, yes," he said, his voice dripping with sarcasm. "The broken neck. Convenient, isn't it? But let's not forget, Smyth, that people fall all the time—down steps, over rough ground. And yet, they rarely break their necks unless something more violent occurs."

Smyth's breath caught in his throat, but Richard wasn't finished.

"Even if we accept that a fall from eight steps could break a woman's neck," Fitzwarren continued, his voice low and deliberate, "how do you explain the other injuries? The deep dents in her skull? You tell me, Smyth, what kind of fall leaves both a broken neck and two separate head wounds, one severe enough to crush part of her skull?"

Smyth opened his mouth to respond, but no words came. Richard had backed him into a corner, and he knew it. The explanations that had seemed sufficient during the inquest now felt thin and insubstantial.

"And what of the smoothness of the stairs and bannisters?" Richard pressed on. "Rounded edges, no sharp surfaces, nothing to account for such injuries. So I ask you, Smyth, how do you reconcile that? What did she fall against, if not the steps?"

Smyth felt his pulse quicken. "We were told... we were told the force of the fall was enough..."

"Told by whom?" Richard shot back, his voice rising.

"By the physician," Smyth stammered. Smyth's hands trembled slightly as he clutched his soaked hat. He had no other answer. None that could stand up against the growing weight of Richard's accusations. The pressures, the whispers of Dudley's power, had loomed over them all during the case.

Richard stepped forward, his face inches from Smyth's, his voice dropping to a cold whisper. "There is more than a chance that Lady Amy Robsart didn't die by accident. Someone killed her, Smyth. And you, along with your jury, may have allowed them to walk away free."

The room fell silent again, the fire's crackling the only sound as Richard's words hung heavy in the air. Smyth felt the weight of it all pressing down on

# A Queen's Rebel

him, the truth—or what he had believed to be the truth—slipping away under this relentless questioning.

"There are often as few as eight steps to the scaffold. Remember that, Smyth," Richard said, his voice laced with cold finality as he folded his arms across his chest. His gaze was sharp, unrelenting, the veiled threat hanging heavy in the air.

Smyth's heart pounded in his chest, the weight of Richard's words settling over him like a dark cloud. The implication was clear, if the truth came out, if Lady Amy Robsart's death was ever proven to be more than an accident, there would be consequences, not just for Robert Dudley, but for everyone involved in the inquest. And that included him.

Smyth swallowed hard, his mouth suddenly dry, his mind racing. Richard's eyes stayed locked on his, unblinking, daring him to respond. The crackling of the fire seemed louder now, filling the tense silence as Smyth tried to find words that wouldn't betray the sudden panic rising in his chest.

"You think me a fool, Fitzwarren," Smyth finally managed, though his voice wavered slightly. "We followed the evidence. We did what was right based on what was presented to us."

Richard's lips twitched into a cold smile, but his arms remained folded, his posture unyielding. "Did you? Or did you simply close your eyes to what you didn't want to see?"

Smyth shook his head, feeling the sting of Richard's words. "I have done my duty. If there is more to this than I know, it was not my failing."

Richard leaned forward slightly, his voice dropping to a near whisper. "Duty, Smyth, doesn't absolve you of guilt. Turning a blind eye, choosing the easy answer... that's not justice. And you know it."

Smyth's hands tightened around the brim of his hat. The pressure in the room was suffocating, the fire's warmth doing nothing to ease the chill running through him. Richard's threat, the subtle reminder of the scaffold, stayed with him, gnawing at the edges of his thoughts.

"Lady Amy is dead," Richard continued, his voice soft but filled with a hard edge. "But you are still very much alive. Be sure that you stay that way, Smyth."

Smyth stared at him, frozen by the weight of those words.

As soon as the door closed behind Richard Smyth, the tension in the room seemed to shift. The crackling of the fire softened in the sudden silence, and for a moment, neither Jack nor Richard Fitzwarren spoke. Jack, still seated by the fire, stretched his legs out and glanced at his brother, who remained standing with his arms folded, staring at the door with an unreadable expression.

"Well," Jack finally said, drawing the word out with a hint of amusement. He tilted his head toward the door. "He looked like a drowned rat by the end of that."

Richard didn't respond right away. His eyes were still fixed on the door, his brow furrowed as though replaying every word of the interview in his mind. Slowly, he let out a breath and unfolded his arms, pacing toward the fire and standing beside his brother.

Richard shook his head, clearly dissatisfied. "The way he stammered when I brought up the injuries, he never even questioned those details during the inquest. And the stairs. How could he not have gone to Cumnor Place? He ruled on a death without even seeing where it occurred."

Jack leaned back in his chair, casually studying the fire. "Not everyone has your curiosity for justice, Richard. Smyth and his jury saw what they were meant to see. A convenient accident for a troublesome woman and the matter was settled."

Richard's eyes flashed with frustration, and he turned away from the fire, pacing again. "Dudley's shadow looms over everything. I don't believe for a moment that Lady Amy's death was an accident. But I do believe Smyth, he, and his fellow jurors made their decision on what information they had, and that was very carefully controlled. No visit to where the accident occurred, the emphasis on the broken neck etc. The fault of this, if there is a fault, lies at a higher level than the jury."

"You are enjoying this far too much," Jack said accusingly.

Richard turned to him, a slow smile spreading across his face. It wasn't a pleasant smile but one filled with a sharp, almost predatory edge. "I am," he admitted, his eyes gleaming with satisfaction. "Aren't you?"

"Indeed, you are providing worthwhile entertainment – the court should consider your talents for Christmas. Who is next on your list for a verbal roasting?" Jack grinned.

Richard's smile didn't fade. "Justice is a game, and like any game, it has to be played with a little pleasure?"

Jack chuckled. "That's the difference between you and me. I prefer to keep my pleasures and my principles separate. You seem to enjoy the way they mix."

Richard stopped pacing and turned fully toward Jack, his grin sharpening. "Perhaps. But you can't deny that the game's more exciting when there's something on the line, can you?"

"Just don't let your enjoyment get us both killed," Jack said. His smile dropped when he saw Sebastian standing near the door, his riding cloak over one arm. "The rain has stopped. Shall we?"

The late afternoon sun cast long shadows across the yard as Jack mounted his horse, gritting his teeth against the pull in his back. Sebastian stood nearby, watching with his usual air of calm authority.

"Posture, Jack," Sebastian said, his tone clipped. "You're sitting like an old man."

Jack adjusted in the saddle, wincing as the scarred skin on his back pulled uncomfortably. "Easy for you to say. Your back doesn't feel like it's made of parchment."

"Pain is part of the process," Sebastian replied. "Now, take the reins properly. Loosen your grip. We're working on control, not brute strength."

With a sigh, Jack obeyed. Sebastian led him through a series of manoeuvres—sharp turns, stops, and starts—forcing Jack to engage muscles that had gone stiff with disuse. By the end, Jack's thighs burned, and his hands trembled from holding the reins.

"Not bad," Sebastian said.

Jack dismounted, his legs nearly buckling. Jack scowled, but as he stretched his back, he realized it didn't feel quite as stiff.

## CHAPTER TWENTY

The following day Richard and Jack arrived at John Pudsey's home in Oxford, Pudsey had been the coroner in the case. The weather had turned to rain again and their cloaks were heavy with water and mud from the unpleasant journey. The wind howled through the narrow streets as Richard rapped sharply on the door. Threadmill was not with them, he was still seeking out the remaining jurors on his list.

The door swung open almost immediately, revealing a tall, thin man dressed impeccably in a dark coat; Pudsey's pale, angular face betrayed no warmth as his sharp eyes flicked over his visitors.

"Fitzwarren, I presume," Pudsey said, his voice clipped and precise. "And your... companion."

"My brother Lord Fitzwarren," Richard replied, pulling his soaked hat off and giving Pudsey a curt nod.

"Do come in," Pudsey said, stepping back to allow them inside. "I dislike keeping people waiting in this weather, though I imagine your business here will be brief."

The house was as austere as its owner. Sparse furnishings, dark wood paneling, chairs and tables, but nothing that was more than essential. Pudsey led them into a room where a fire burned low in the hearth, a table neatly arranged with books and documents.

"You are here about the unfortunate matter of Lady Amy Robsart," Pudsey began, taking his place in a chair opposite them. He rested his hands on the arms of the chair, his long fingers draping over the wooden ends. "I had expected your arrival, a message arrived from Leicester's man at Cumnor. Shall we proceed directly to the facts?"

Richard settled into the chair. "I'd like to go over the findings in your report, specifically regarding the injuries to Lady Amy."

Pudsey inclined his head slightly, reaching for a sheaf of papers on the table. "Very well. The jury, as you know, determined that her death was the result of misfortune—a fall down the stairs. My duty, as coroner, was to document the evidence presented and ensure the inquest adhered to proper legal standards. The report reflects that."

He handed Richard a copy of the report, identical to the one Richard had already studied. "It details the injuries consistent with a fall, including a broken neck and head wounds, as presented by Theodore Wood. The jury reached its verdict accordingly."

Richard skimmed the pages before looking up. "There are eight steps in that staircase. With such a short fall, isn't it unusual for the injuries to be so severe?"

Pudsey's expression did not change. "Unusual, perhaps. But not impossible. Accidents are often unpredictable, sir. A fall from a horse can snap a man's neck, and that distance is far less than eight steps."

"And yet," Richard pressed, "the head injuries, they did not bleed. The poor lady was not found in a pool of blood. Or was that omitted from the report?"

Pudsey's eyes narrowed slightly. "Dr Wood's findings were presented during the inquest. It is not my role to question a physician's expertise nor to speculate beyond the evidence. The jury was satisfied with the explanation given, and so was I. The reason there was no mention of it was simply because there was no pond of blood where the lady lay. If there had been, it would have been noted.

"Did Wood himself think that the lack of blood was strange given the severity of the injuries?"

# A Queen's Rebel

Richard countered, leaning forward. "Would you not agree that this should have warranted further investigation?"

"I would not," Pudsey said coolly. "It is not the duty of a coroner to entertain conjecture. My role is to ensure the process is followed, to document the facts as they are presented, and to submit them for the jury's consideration. That is what I did."

"So you are saying, even if something looked wrong, you wouldn't lift a finger to look into it?" Richard said, an eyebrow raised.

Pudsey's hard expression remained unchanged. "I am saying that I followed the law. The jury made its decision based on the evidence and Wood's report. I am not here to indulge in unsupported theories or conjecture."

Richard chose his next words carefully. "But if there were evidence—something that cast doubt on the conclusion of the inquest—would you revisit the case?"

Pudsey rose from his chair, the movement deliberate. "If compelling new evidence were brought forward, it would be my obligation to act. However, until such evidence is presented, this matter is closed."

The dismissal was clear, but Richard wasn't finished. "You understand the implications if this wasn't an accident," he said quietly.

Pudsey's expression remained impassive, but there was a flicker of something—annoyance? Concern?—in his eyes. "I understand that rumours and speculation can be dangerous, Fitzwarren. My duty is to deal with facts, not gossip. Unless you have something more substantive to discuss, I suggest we conclude this meeting."

Richard stood, carefully tucking the report under his arm. "Thank you for your time, Mr. Pudsey. We may yet find something more substantive."

Pudsey gave a curt nod, showing them to the door without another word. As they stepped out into the rain, the wind biting at their faces, Jack pulled his hat low over his brow.

"Well, that was another pointless conversation," Richard said after the door had closed, and they were back in the rain once more.

"Whose next?" Jack asked, rubbing his hands together to remove an ache that had settled in the back of his hand.

"We shall speak to the medical examiner, Wood," Richard replied, a faint smile tugging at his lips. "I'd imagine you'd be quite curious to know what he made of the dynts, wouldn't you?"

Jack was unable to hide the glimmer of interest in his eyes. "Curious? I'd say suspicious. You saw the coroner's report—it barely mentioned anything beyond 'natural causes' and a fall. Doesn't that seem a bit... lacking?"

Richard folded his arms, his smile thinning. "It's more than lacking, Jack. It's evasive. And I suspect the good examiner may have had his reasons not elaborating on the details."


Theodore Wood swept into the dimly lit Black Swan with the air of a man whose time was far more valuable than those around him. His silver hair, neatly combed back, shone in the candlelight, and his sharp eyes darted to Richard impatiently. He carried a leather satchel, worn but sturdy, slung over one shoulder.

"I'm a busy man, sir," Wood said brusquely, depositing the bag on the table. "I have no desire to linger in taverns or be interrogated like a criminal. State your questions."

Richard rose from his seat, extending a hand in greeting that the elderly physician ignored. Unfazed,

# A Queen's Rebel

Richard gestured to the chair opposite him. "Dr. Wood, I appreciate your time. I'll keep this brief."

"You had better," Wood muttered, lowering himself into the chair with a grimace. He pulled out a sheaf of yellowing papers from his satchel. "I brought my notes, as requested. Though I'm not sure what good it'll do you. The matter is long closed."

Richard poured a cup of wine and slid it across the table, but Wood waved it away irritably. "I prefer to keep a clear head."

"Very well," Richard said smoothly, leaning forward. "You examined the body of Lady Amy Robsart on the day she was found at the bottom of the stairs. I need to understand exactly what you saw."

Wood's brows furrowed. "I confirmed what anyone with eyes could see. The woman's neck was broken—snapped cleanly, most likely by the fall. And there were injuries to her head, consistent with striking the steps as she went down."

"And yet," Richard said, his tone measured, "you found something unusual about those head injuries, did you not?"

Wood exhaled sharply, clearly annoyed at being drawn into details he felt were beneath him. "Yes, yes, I told the coroner as much. The head wounds were peculiar. There was no bleeding."

Richard straightened, surprised by the frankness. "No bleeding?"

"None," Wood said firmly. "The scalp should bleed profusely, even from a relatively minor wound. Yet her injuries—while severe—had not bled at all. No pond of blood on the steps, no evidence of the heart pumping its last under the strain. It struck me as strange, but what would you have me do? I noted it in my report and told the coroner."

Richard produced a neatly folded document from his coat, unfolding it with deliberate care. "This is the coroner's report," he said, sliding it across the table toward Wood. "There's no mention of your observation. Nothing about the absence of blood."

Wood took the report, his lips tightening as he scanned the lines. His frown deepened, and he shook his head. "Typical. Shoddy work. If they failed to include it in the official findings, that's hardly my fault."

"You admit there's a discrepancy here?" Richard pressed.

Wood handed the paper back with a shrug. "I admit nothing except that I did my duty. I examined the body, recorded my findings, and shared them. If the coroner neglected to include them, that's his responsibility, not mine."

"But surely," Richard said, leaning in, "the lack of bleeding is significant. It suggests—"

"It suggests nothing conclusively," Wood snapped, cutting him off. "I've been a physician for over forty years, sir. I know what I saw, and I know when speculation begins to outpace evidence. Could it mean something more? Possibly. But I've no intention of losing sleep over it. My role in this matter is finished."

Richard studied Wood weighing his frustration against the potential truth in his words. "And yet," he said slowly, "you do agree that the absence of blood raises questions?"

Wood sighed, rubbing a hand over his lined face. "Yes, I agree. But questions without answers are just that—questions."

Richard leaned forward, fixing Wood with a steady gaze. "You mentioned head injuries. Can you tell me more about them?"

Wood sighed, clearly displeased at the prospect of further questions. "I've already told you—there were injuries consistent with a fall."

"You also said they were peculiar," Richard pressed. "If you wouldn't mind consulting your notes, perhaps there's something more precise you could share?"

# A Queen's Rebel

Wood muttered under his breath but obliged, pulling out his yellowed pages and flipping through them. His movements were methodical, his finger trailing over the cramped handwriting until he stopped and adjusted his glasses.

"Here," he said, tapping the page with one bony finger. "There were two primary depressions to the skull. One was deeper, more significant—a definitive blow to the back of the head. The other was shallower, just above it."

"And you measured them?" Richard asked, his interest sharpening.

"Of course," Wood said stiffly as if the question insulted his professionalism. "The deeper injury measured roughly an inch across and nearly two and a half inches in depth. The lesser one had a depth of no more than half of an inch."

Richard frowned, considering the implications. "Would the steps have caused such injuries?"

Wood's gaze snapped up from his notes, sharp and unwavering. "My duty, sir, was to document the injuries, not to speculate upon how they were caused. I'm a physician, not a dramatist."

"But surely," Richard pressed, "you must have had some thoughts on it. An injury that deep—did it seem plausible to you that she might have struck her head on the edge of a step with such force?"

Wood pursed his lips, closing his notes with deliberate care. "As I said, it is not my role to determine plausibility. I examined the body, I recorded what I observed, and I passed those observations to the coroner. Anything further would be conjecture, and conjecture is not medicine."

"Even so," Richard said, his voice firm, "your expertise must have led you to some conclusions, if only in private."

Wood's face hardened, and he rose from his chair with stiff precision. "If I have conclusions, sir, they remain mine alone. Now, unless you have further questions about my *actual findings,* I would like to conclude this meeting."

Richard leaned back, watching as the physician began to gather his papers with brisk efficiency. "No more questions."

He stood abruptly, gathering his papers and slinging the bag back over his shoulder. "If you'll excuse me, I have other patients to attend to. Good day.."

"That went well," Jack said jovially from behind him. "Though I think you might have better luck getting blood from a stone than answers from that old curmudgeon."

Richard sank back into his chair, pinching the bridge of his nose. "He's a relic of another age, Jack. Complacent. Arrogant. But what he said about the lack of blood... that's not something to dismiss lightly."

Jack shrugged as he pulled out a chair and sat down, crossing his legs lazily. "It's strange, but you know as well as I do that strange doesn't always mean sinister. Maybe she fell just right—or wrong, depending on how you look at it. Who knows how a body reacts to such things?"

"The lack of blood isn't just strange," Richard said. "It's damned unnatural. You cut a pig's throat, and it bleeds while it dies, does it not? You kill a man with a blade, and blood pours from him."

Jack leaned forward, his interest sharpening. "You think she was dead before she fell?"

Richard nodded slowly, his jaw tight. "It fits the facts, and the way Wood described those head injuries, they sounded severe."

"Then why didn't he say so outright?" Jack interjected, clearly skeptical. "If he suspected foul play, why not say so?"

Richard gave him a grim smile. "Because men like Wood don't step out of line unless there's no other choice. He told the coroner what he saw, but when they ignored it. Easier that way. Safer, too."

# A Queen's Rebel

"Safer?" Jack repeated, his brow furrowing.

"We both know this isn't just about a woman falling down the stairs," Richard said, his voice low and measured. "Amy Robsart wasn't just anyone—she was Robert Dudley's wife. And Dudley's fortunes rest on his relationship with the queen. If there's even a whisper of suspicion that he had a hand in her death..."

Jack nodded. "Yes, I know. It could bring everything crashing down. For him, for the queen, for anyone remotely tied to the court. It's a simple question of whether she was pushed or fell that led to her breaking her neck."

"Did you actually read this?" Richard waved the coroner's report in Jack's face.

Jack paused for a moment before taking it.

"Pay attention this time," Richard said, folding his arms and leaning back in the chair.

"It's in legal Latin," Jack grumbled as he read.

"And you can read it perfectly well, so read," Richard said.

Jack paused and looked up.

"Go on, read it aloud for my entertainment," Richard shot back.

"Lady Amy there and then sustained not only two injuries to her head, in English called dyntes – one of which was a quarter of an inch deep and the other two inches deep..." Jack's voice trailed off.

"Precisely. It is an issue of 'dyntes' at the moment, is it not. A quarter of an inch is thus," Richard held his fingers apart in the air, "but two inches."

Jack raised his own hand and viewed the gap between his fingers.

"How hard would you have to strike a skull to create a dent so deep?" Richard asked.

"Damned hard," Jack replied, lowering his hand.

"And let us consider the scene. The top of the newel post is rounded and smooth, not likely to have caused a dent," Richard said.

"Her head could have struck the edge of the steps," Jack interjected.

"Yes, and also rounded on the edges, again unlikely to cause a dent," Richard replied.

"It's hard to know; it could have been a depression; we only have words on a page to go by," Jack said.

"Not so, Wood confirmed the depth of them in his report," Richard replied then said. "Everyone you talk to speaks of a broken neck. Rumour the length of the country only ever refers to the ladies snapped spine, never are these dents spoken of, and yet here they are recorded in the report. And not just one but two. The lady struck her head not once but twice, and one of those blows was a lot worse," Richard said, tapping a finger thoughtfully on his chin. "A broken neck may have killed her, but if it hadn't I'd wager these other injuries would have surely led to the same state of affairs. She died on the 8$^{th}$, then laid out to rest in Oxford until she was buried in St Mary's on the 22$^{nd}$ of September," Richard laid out the timeline.

"I know, and Dudley didn't attend the inquest or the funeral. You already told me," Jack said.

"So that is how long ago?" Richard said.

"Nine months, give or take," Jack replied.

"Give or take, more like ten, but who is counting," Richard said.

Jack laughed. "Dudley is counting; I am damned sure that by now, he would have hoped that this would no longer be the subject of gossip."

"True …. True," Richard said slowly, then, "St Mary's Church is, as it happens, directly opposite Oreil College in Oxford."

"And this is relevant, why?" Jack's blue eyes had narrowed, and he was regarding his brother with an inquisitive gaze.

## A Queen's Rebel

"There is a tunnel between the third quad at Oreil and the island site to the west, but half way along this and running directly north under Oreiel street is another tunnel that lead directly to the vaults beneath St Mary's," Richard replied, a slight smile playing on his face, it's all a matter of "dyntes."

"You can't be serious?" There was a look of horror on Jack's face.

"Never more so. Shouldn't be too bad, it's been give or take ten months," Richard said.


If Jack had thought he'd spend the afternoon in the glow from the fire while Threadmill was out speaking to the jurors he was wrong, instead he found himself in the damp yard at the back of the tavern again where the peace was broken by the rhythmic clack of the practice swords as Jack and Sebastian moved in a steady dance of attack and defence.

Jack's breath became easier now, and his movements became fluider. He ducked under a swing and countered with a quick strike that Sebastian blocked with a grunt of approval.

"Better," Sebastian said, pushing Jack back with a series of sharp thrusts. "But you're hesitating. Commit to your attacks."

Jack grinned, sweat dripping down his face. "And here I thought you'd be impressed."

Sebastian's only response was to feint left and land a sharp tap on Jack's shoulder. Jack hissed, shaking his arm out, but his grin widened.

They went another round, and by the end, Jack was grinning despite his aching muscles. The movements felt more familiar now, and the weight of the blade was less foreign in his hand.

When Threadmill returned, his cloak hung heavy with rain, water dripping steadily from its hem, and his boots carried the evidence of long hours trudging through mud-soaked streets. He pushed open the tavern door with a weary sigh, the warm air doing little to lift the exhaustion etched into his features.

Richard looked up from his corner table, where papers were spread haphazardly in the candlelight. A glass of wine, barely touched, sat at his elbow. Jack lounged nearby, sharpening his dagger with the methodical scrape of steel against stone. Richard's eyes met Threadmill's as the lawyer entered, and though his expression remained unreadable, there was no mistaking the anticipation behind it.

"You're late," Richard said, his tone neutral but pointed.

Threadmill grunted in reply, slapping his sodden hat onto the table with little regard for the mess it made. "Aye, and you'd be late too, slogging through half of Oxford to chase down stubborn jurors."

Threadmill sank into the chair opposite Richard. "I found most of them—those who could be found, that is. Three in Abingdon, a couple more in Oxford. The rest were either conveniently absent or had no interest in being disturbed."

"And?" Richard prompted, his fingers lacing together as he leaned back in his chair, his eyes sharp in the dim light.

Threadmill let out a heavy breath, his shoulders slumping. "I've learned little. I pressed them and tried to dig beneath their answers, but they all said the same thing. They made their decision based on what they were given, and they were given only enough to determine that it was a death from a fall."

"An accident." Richard echoed the word softly, a note of derision in his voice.

Threadmill nodded. "Lady Amy found at the bottom of the stairs. Broken neck. Wounds on her head, they say, were consistent with the steps. That's what they were told, and that's what they ruled. They weren't there to question it—just to agree."

Jack stopped sharpening his blade, the sound suddenly absent. "So they all just nodded along like cattle at the market?"

Threadmill glanced at him and shrugged. "They're jurors, not inquisitors. None of them saw a reason to doubt the coroner's words, and the coroner gave them no cause to. If you don't tell a man there's something wrong, he doesn't look for it."

Richard's gaze drifted to the faint glow of the fire, his fingers drumming rhythmically against the tabletop. "No mention of the severity of the wounds? The lack of blood?"

"Not a whisper," Threadmill replied. "It wasn't in the evidence presented. So they ruled as they were led to rule."

"And the coroner?" Jack asked, his voice hard.

"Officially? Thorough. Unquestionable. And as far as the jurors are concerned, a man beyond reproach." Threadmill's tone was dry, his frustration evident. "Unofficially? The man's blind as a bat or too afraid to see."

Richard sighed, his expression carefully controlled. "And that's how it's done. Leave out the inconvenient details, present only the simplest explanation, and let everyone wash their hands clean of it." He glanced back at Threadmill. "And none of the jurors hinted at anything unusual? Pressure or threats?"

"Not one," Threadmill replied. "They seemed honest enough, just men doing their duty. But honest men don't need much convincing when the right facts—or lack of them—are placed under their noses."

Richard's mouth tightened, though he gave a faint nod of approval. "It's not their fault, then. The decisions were made well before the evidence was presented to the jury."

Jack leaned back in his chair, resting his hands behind his head. "So where does that leave us, Brother? The jurors ruled. The coroner scribbled his verdict. Everyone seems happy enough to forget the thing ever happened."

"It leaves us," Richard replied quietly, his eyes fixed on the flickering embers, "with more questions than answers, but now we know the shape of the lie. Someone along the way decided the truth was too dangerous to be spoken. They fed the jurors a very simple and plausible story."

Threadmill nodded slowly. "And whoever decided that had enough influence to ensure no one asked for more."

Jack exhaled sharply. "Someone who wanted Lady Amy's death to be forgotten and buried deeper than her coffin."

Richard didn't respond immediately, his thoughts circling as the fire cracked softly in the hearth. Finally, he said, "Then we look elsewhere. The jurors are a dead end, but someone knows why this happened and who stood to gain."

Jack lifted his cup, tipping it toward Threadmill. "At least you're not wasting your time talking to the jurors anymore."

Threadmill cracked the faintest of smiles.

Richard pushed back from the table, gathering up the papers in front of him. "Tomorrow we'll start again."

Threadmill rose wearily to his feet, tucking his hat under his arm. "Let's hope tomorrow brings answers and not more questions, and better weather."

Jack, watching him go, muttered under his breath. "Tomorrow always brings questions."

# A Queen's Rebel

Richard glanced at his brother, the flicker of a smile in his expression. "And brother Sebastian, maybe you should get some rest before then as well."

"It is a joint venture now, remember?" Jack shot back.

## CHAPTER TWENTY-ONE

William Cecil sat in his office, the air thick with the scent of old parchment and the faint tang of candle wax. The latest report from his informants lay open before him, the name at the centre of it sparking both intrigue and unease: Alex Gill.

Cecil read the report twice, his sharp eyes scanning the careful script for any detail he might have missed. Gill was a name he knew well, though not one that had drawn his immediate suspicion until now. A wealthy merchant, a landowner of significant acreage, and a man who, more concerningly, controlled half the printing presses in London. He was not a man who raised his voice in public debate, nor one who openly decried the Queen or her policies. And yet, the absence of overt opposition made him all the more dangerous.

It was easy to spot a fool like Nicholas Adams or a sycophant like Charles Walls. Men like Alex Gill, however, operated in the shadows, subtle and deliberate. They were the kind of men Cecil distrusted most, for they rarely left traces of their true intentions.

Cecil pushed the report aside and stood, pacing the length of his office. The oak floor creaked faintly underfoot as he mulled over what he knew of Gill. Gill's wealth came not just from trade but from his stranglehold on London's printing industry. His presses produced everything from pamphlets to books, shaping public opinion as effectively as any speech in Parliament. A single rumour, whispered and spread through the pages of his publications, could ignite unrest or plant doubt in the minds of the Queen's subjects. And while Gill had never outwardly spoken against Elizabeth, Cecil knew that silence was not the same as loyalty.

"Gill..." Cecil muttered under his breath, his fingers tapping against his thigh. Could this man be behind a plot to undermine the crown? It would make sense. Gill had the resources, the connections, and the influence to orchestrate something far-reaching. More than that, he had the cunning. He would not be so foolish as to be caught with Catholic paraphernalia in his home like Adams or to spout treasonous opinions in public like so many lesser men.

Cecil stopped at the window, looking out over the grey rooftops of London. If Gill truly harboured treasonous ambitions, he would not act alone. Men like him surrounded themselves with pawns and proxies, shielding their own hands from the dirty work. He would fund and guide, but others would take the fall. Adams, Walls—they could easily be tools in Gill's larger game, unwitting players in a plot they barely understood.

Returning to his desk, Cecil picked up the report again. His informants had uncovered little concrete evidence against Gill, but the hints were there: unusual gatherings at his printing house, a sudden increase in private shipments that bypassed the usual customs inspections, and, most intriguingly, a series of coded messages intercepted by one of Cecil's agents. The messages were short, almost innocuous, but the language suggested careful planning.

One phrase in particular caught Cecil's attention: *"The ink is laid; the press awaits."*

It could refer to nothing, a simple reference to Gill's trade. Or it could be something far more sinister—a signal that plans were in motion.

A knock at the door interrupted his thoughts. Cecil's secretary entered, bowing slightly. "A messenger has arrived from one of your agents, my lord. He says it concerns Alex Gill."

"Send him in," Cecil said, his voice calm but sharp.

The agent entered, a wiry man with a weathered face and quick eyes. He handed over a sealed document, which Cecil broke open immediately.

"Gill has been meeting with Jesuit sympathisers," the agent reported as Cecil read. "At least two of the men have ties with Adams. There's also word that he's been funding pamphlets critical of Protestant reforms, though none bear his name."

Cecil nodded, his mind racing. "And the presses?"

"Still operational, my lord. But we believe he has hidden printing blocks—ones that could produce seditious material without being traced back to him."

Cecil set the document down, his decision forming. "Gill may not speak treason, but his actions speak for him. He is too careful to leave much evidence, but even the most careful man can be undone."

The agent hesitated. "Do you wish to move against him now, my lord?"

"No," Cecil said, his tone firm. "Not yet. Let him think he is safe. Keep the presses under surveillance, and watch his associates closely. If he is the spider at the centre of this web, I want the whole thing unraveled before we move."

As the agent left, Cecil leaned back in his chair, his gaze distant. Alex Gill might be the key to understanding the broader scope of the threat facing Elizabeth's reign. But catching a man like him would require patience and precision. Cecil was determined to ensure that when the moment came, Gill's web would collapse entirely—and with it, any hopes of rebellion.

# A Queen's Rebel

The hour was well past midnight when the shadows outside Alex Gill's print rooms stirred with the movement of Cecil's men. Hidden among the alley's darkness, the agents observed the building in silence. The soft glow of light leaking through the cracks in the shutters betrayed activity within, an unusual sight for so late an hour.

The leader of the group, a man seasoned in Cecil's clandestine operations, motioned for the others to hold their position. They watched as figures moved behind the warped glass of the windows, their silhouettes distinct against the golden lamplight. Low murmurs filtered through the night, too faint to discern words but clear enough to indicate a gathering. One of the men shifted, his leather boots scuffing against the cobblestones, and was immediately stilled by the sharp gaze of his superior.

"Wait," the leader whispered. "Give it time. Let's see if anyone else arrives."

For nearly an hour, they watched the comings and goings. The light inside flickered occasionally as shadows passed in front of lamps, and once, the sound of hurried voices reached them before fading into silence. No additional visitors appeared, and eventually, the activity within began to quiet.

The leader nodded to his men. "We move now."

The agents approached the building swiftly and silently. The leader tested the door and found it barred from within. He motioned for one of the larger men in the group to step forward. With a heavy boot, the man forced the door open, the sound of splintering wood shattering the stillness of the night.

They poured into the room, their weapons drawn, but the space was eerily empty. The lamps, still lit, cast long shadows across the tables and shelves crowded with typesetting trays, ink pots, and reams of paper. The faint smell of ink mingled with the mustiness of damp wood and old parchment.

Sam Burnell

The leader's eyes swept the room, taking in the signs of a hasty departure. A chair lay overturned near a desk, and a scattering of paper led toward a rear exit that stood slightly ajar. Whoever had been inside had fled, leaving behind only traces of their presence.

"Search everything," the leader commanded. "They left in a hurry. They won't have taken it all."

The men moved quickly but methodically, overturning crates and rifling through drawers. It didn't take long to find the first item of interest: a rosary, its beads glinting dully in the lamplight as it was pulled from beneath a pile of discarded parchment.

"Here," one of the men said, holding it up.

Another agent, searching the main workbench, uncovered a silver altar plate, its polished surface engraved with delicate religious symbols. He held it aloft for the leader's inspection.

"Well, well," the leader murmured, taking the plate in hand. "It seems Mr. Gill has more than just an interest in printing."

The men gathered the items and swept through the remaining rooms, but no further evidence was found. The fleeing occupants had clearly known the risks of leaving anything incriminating behind.

"Take these to Lord Burghley," the leader said, nodding toward the rosary and the altar plate. "He'll want to see them immediately."

The group exited the print rooms, the heavy door swinging back on its broken hinges. Outside, the streets were silent save for the soft hum of the wind. The men moved swiftly through the narrow lanes, their shadows stretching long and dark in the moonlight.


Back at Cecil's chambers, the rosary and altar plate were laid carefully on his desk. The Secretary of State, still awake despite the late hour, examined the items with a critical eye. His fingers brushed over the smooth surface of the altar plate, his lips pressing into a thin line.

"They fled?" Cecil asked, his voice calm but edged with dissatisfaction.

The leader of the group nodded. "Yes, my lord. We gave them enough time to feel secure, but they had a rear exit. They must have slipped away as we approached."

Cecil leaned back in his chair, his sharp gaze fixed on the items before him. "The rosary and altar plate... They didn't take these. Why?"

"Perhaps they were left behind in the rush," the leader suggested.

"Or perhaps they were meant to be found," Cecil mused, his tone thoughtful. "These are bold items to abandon, even in haste. They carry the weight of symbolism—enough to cast suspicion without offering proof."

The leader hesitated. "Do you think they're bait, my lord?"

Cecil's expression remained unreadable. "If they are, we'll use them as such. Whether intentional or not, these items deepen the connection between Gill and the Catholic sympathisers we're hunting. It's time to tighten the net."

He turned his gaze to the leader. "Increase surveillance on Gill. Watch his associates, track his shipments, and ensure his presses are monitored day and night. He's careful, but even the most cautious man makes mistakes. And when he does..."

Cecil allowed the words to hang in the air, the weight of his intent unspoken but understood. The leader nodded and withdrew, leaving Cecil alone with his thoughts.

The Secretary of State leaned forward, his fingers steepling as he stared at the rosary and altar plate. The pieces were falling into place, but the full picture remained obscured.

Sam Burnell

A Queen's Rebel

## CHAPTER TWENTY-TWO

It did not come as a surprise to Jack that Richard was on first-name terms with the Master of Oriel College, John Rankin. Jack politely drank the Master's wine while he listened to the Master share reminiscences with his brother. Jack let his eyes run over the opulent and slightly slovenly rooms the Master occupied. His brother would look at home here in this organised academic chaos; of course, it would be neater. Rankin, it seemed, was apt to abandon things; books were left open or were bookmarked with inappropriate items; one on the desk had a plate wedged in the pages, and another on the floor near the fire next to his chair atop a stack of others was wedged open with a knife.

The carpet was worn before the chair, threadbare, and the bed shoes next to it were equally dilapidated. He doubted Rankin had a wife, and it seemed the servants at the college were doing their best to clean around his academic detritus. The few flat and empty surfaces there were, had been cleared of dust, but some of the papers, books, and notes looked like they hadn't been moved in an age. Next to the chair by the fire on either side were two stacks of books. The top of the left-hand one had become a table of sorts, and a plate with the crumbs of whatever Rankin had last eaten were upon them, the servants, it seemed, not daring to remove the plates lest they disturb the Master's work below.

The bells rang outside for midday.

"Right, shall we go?" The Master announced, looking around for somewhere to abandon his wine glass. "Grunto said he would meet us by O'Brien's gate. I'd come with you if I didn't have a meal with the Dean at eight."

Grunto? Jack mouthed to Richard as they left the Master's apartment and descended the steps, crossing the neat quad and heading towards an arch on the opposite side.

"His students bestowed him with the name," Richard said under his breath.

Arriving at the gate they found waiting a small man, wearing round spectacles, and drab and somewhat stained coat.

"I want him back in one piece, do you hear? He has a lecture this evening, and I'll not be pleased if he misses it." Rankin said, laying a hand on the man's shoulder, his eyes on Richard.

"I shall return your professor hearty and whole," Richard said.

Grunto had the keys and a low door was unlocked. On the other side was a darkness that made Jack shiver, and a cool draught that was less than inviting. Richard squeezed his arm and said. "There are lamps."

And there were. Hanging from hooks on the inside of the door were oil lamps, and Grunto and Richard lit them from the lamp that Grunto had brought. Armed with one each, they descended the steps into the tunnel.

The cold air caressed Jack's cheeks as they stepped down a dozen stairs. It was enough of a distance he guessed to put them beneath the level of the quad above.

"This leads under the road to the Island Site, but halfway along, when we are under Oriel Street, Ha ... here it is," Grunto announced. There was a sudden jangle of keys and the rattle of another lock followed by the grate of iron hinges complaining at their lack of use. Jack stepped closer, raising his lamp, and found the grilled gate that was sealing the tunnel. He scowled. Even Grunto was going to have to stoop as he made his way into the tunnel that took them north, and Jack had to bend even further to avoid banging his head on the roughly hewn roof.

"It was primarily made so the choir could make there way from St Mary's to the college and back without being seen," Grunto said as he made his way along the tunnel. "Because, of course, St Mary's was linked with Abingdon Abbey, there was some sympathy you see amongst the college, so the priests could use this to avoid Henry's men."

Jack wasn't listening to Grunto's diatribe on the history of the Abbey and its ties with Oreil. He was instead thinking about what lay at the end in the vault. The darkness of the tunnel, the smell of dampness, and the occasional splash of water underfoot were becoming an unwanted reminder of the room they had sealed in him years ago at Marshalsea. Icey cold it had stored the dead debtors, rotting in cold heaps awaiting disposal, and in that room, breathing in the aroma of death, shackled and alone they had left him. It had been hell, and he had known he was not alone; lurking in the corner, enjoying his fear, had been the worst evil Jack had ever known. It had feasted upon his thoughts, gurgled and laughed when he'd tried to assert himself, and undermined his reason. He still hated the dark; it was not so bad as it had been, but still, the fear and the uncertainty remained. Jack kept his eyes on the lamp as he continued with his stooped journey along the tunnel.

He was drawn to a halt, and ahead of him, he could hear the sound of keys for a second time opening another door. This one, when he arrived at it, was solid wood and let into the vault beneath St Mary's.

"Here we are," Grunto announced.

Richard was holding his own and Grunto's lantern ahead of him as the little man, obviously in familiar surroundings, shuffled into the vault.

Jack shuddered as he straightened up and stood in the low ceilinged crypt. In the far corner stairs disappeared up over into the darkness, and around them were the stored coffins of those deemed worthy of a place beneath the altar. And one of them belonged to a woman called Amy Robsart.

It wasn't hard to identify. Her husband was rumoured to have spent a thousand pounds on her lavish funeral. And it was the newest coffin in the crypt. It sat on two trestles and was draped with a thickly embroidered cloth bearing Dudley's coat of arms. On top of it, dried and brown now, was a handtied posy of flowers, with a small note tied to the stems. A thoughtful final wish from someone who probably cared for the dead lady more than her husband had.

Richard put the lamp down on the top of the coffin and picked up the dried flowers, petals fell from the dead flower heads scattering across Dudley's coat of arms.

"What's it say?" Jack asked.

"The light is not good enough in here to read it," Richard angled it closer to the lamp.

"Try not to set us alight!" Jack commented.

"Quite," Richard replied, twisting the small sliver of paper from the dead bouquet and slipping it inside his doublet. "Now to the poor lady herself."

Jack, who had no taste for this at all, did not step forward.

With a dramatic flourish, Richard removed the heavy heraldic drapery, revealing the freshly made coffin below. It was superbly made. It occurred to Jack that it was a shame no one could see the craftsmanship and that it was wasted on the dead. The sides were carved with a delicate fretted design that reminded Jack of the roof of York Minster when he had seen it years ago. Lace was carved from stone, and this was the same. There also seemed to be no join to show where the top could be removed.

# A Queen's Rebel

"A conundrum," Richard said, running his hands over the wood.

"Hardly," Jack said dryly.

Richard circled the coffin, his hands sliding over the smooth oak edges. "There has to be …. Ahhhh …. Very clever. Very clever indeed."

"Would you like to share?" Jack asked a little sourly.

"You can't see it from over there, come here," Richard beckoned his brother forward. "The lid does not sit on top of the coffin as you would expect, but is actually recessed into it, look it is a perfect fit. I would imagine the lid tapers, so once it is sat in place, there is no need for nails."

"So, how do we get it open?" Jack asked.

"There are two ways. I suspect if we lifted the coffin up and tipped it beyond the vertical, the lid, via pressure from the contents, would pop," Richard replied with a grin.

A look of disgust settled on Jack's face.

Seeing the scowl on Jack's face, Richard grinned and said. "As you object, and doubtless this weighs more than one man can lift, and you are unlikely to help, and Master Grunto by virtue of his age and the promise the master extracted from me to return him hearty and whole for his evening lecture, should not help, I shall use this instead."

Richard held up his knife, then with a look of sadness he wedged it into the almost invisible line between the coffin and the lid. The wood splintered under the force as the blade gouged a hole between the coffin and the lid. Using the knife as a lever Richard managed to raise the end of the lid high enough to get his hands underneath and he slid it along the length of the coffin, then lowered it to prop it against the end.

Jack, regarding the damage, said, "Well, someone is bound to notice that damage now."

"It's not likely, Jack, we'll cover it with the cloth again and I doubt anyone will be removing that in a very long time," Richard said, then peering into the coffin added, "well, that's a relief!"

"What?" Jack, despite his misgivings, found himself taking a step forward.

"The lady is not lead-wrapped; that would have slowed us down considerably. That was at least one expense Dudley forwent. Strange, don't you think?"

"Not really," Jack replied grumpily.

Master Grunto stepped up to the coffin. "Sir, would you like me to make my examination now?"

"We would indeed," Richard said, stepping back and letting Grunto take up a position at the coffin side.

"The funeral was elaborate, a thousand pounds by all accounts, but the spend has been made upon only that which can be seen. The lady wears no jewels, her coffin is not lead-lined, and she has been dressed in a simple linen shroud. A pauper on the inside and a princess without. Strange, don't you think?" Richard said, tapping his chin.

"He didn't care for the contents," Jack said bluntly.

"Very perceptive, Jack. He didn't at all, and to that effect, he wasted no gold upon them. She wears no rings, no time had been expended upon the lady's hair, she has literally been bundled into a coffin, apart from the shroud she has nothing, not even a posy of flowers," Richard spoke from where he had rounded the opposite side of the coffin and was watching Grunto perform an examination of the corpse.

The smell now was beginning to fill the crypt. It wasn't a rotting putrid odour, but it was the stale aroma of death.

"The corpse lay in the guildhall for around twenty-five days, so by necessity, it has been embalmed, the viscera removed and fluids that would

# A Queen's Rebel

have pooled drained. The coffin has been well sealed, as we saw, and that has slowed natural decay as well, so the flesh, as you can see, has begun to dry and shrink around the bones, it is all as we would expect," Grunto said as if already giving his evening lecture.

Jack's face twisted. It was more information than he wanted to know about the deceased lady.

"But it has served us well. There is little flesh around the brain pan, and the skin is thin at this point, and ...." Grunto, leaning into the coffin, continued, "If I could have some help to roll her .... That's it perfect .... Keep your hand there to stop her rolling back. Good. Now then, I'm just parting the hair, and with a simple incision at the base of the neck I can remove the skin and we should be able to see the full extent of the dentes you are so interested in."

Jack turned his back on the proceedings and walked the short distance to the end of the crypt and tried to find something else to focus on, but he couldn't block out the sound of Grunto's serrated blade as it cut through the crusted, dry flesh or the unnerving grunts of exertion that passed from his lips as he worked. Jack was suddenly sickeningly aware of how the little man had earned his name.

"There we go," Grunto replied.

There followed the noise of him grunting as he strained to do something, something Jack definitely didn't want to watch.

"Oh my!" The university lecturer proclaimed suddenly, shock in his voice.

"Oh, my indeed!" Richard agreed, but then Jack didn't want to hear the words. "Come and look at this."

"Do I have to?" Jack said.

"Come over, she's covered with linen, all there is to see is the skull, you need to see this," Richard replied.

Jack twisted his face and then rounded the coffin so he stood next to Grunto; he let his eyes move slowly towards the coffin; he didn't want to take in the image in one go; he wanted to be able to look away if the horror was too much. It wasn't as bad as he had imagined. The body was wrapped in a shroud, and the corpse's face turned away, hidden beneath an untidy tumble of brown hair. The hair was ragged and messy; no time at all had been taken on her appearance. Grunto had peeled away the skin from the back of the skull to reveal bone, creamy white with flecks of skin still attached, but worse, much worse, were the two holes punched through the bone.

"God's bones!" Jack gasped.

The smaller was square in profile, the central section had disappeared, leaving only the hole into the dark interior, around the edges hair was bonded with a dark layer of dried blood. But the second was worse. Again a square hole, but this time all the bone around it was caved in and depressed towards the dark central square. Whatever she had been hit with had been hard and the force had been extreme.

"I would say the smaller was the first; the way this fracture in the bone spreads around the curve at the back of the skull is by virtue of the second impact, making it radiate further when the second blow occurs. The measurements are approximate that they made, I am afraid. There would of course, have been a covering of hair and skin. We can see from here that the blow forced into the broken skull, skin and hair into the depression, plugging it so to speak, so when an measurement was taken as to the depth of the injuries it was a little inaccurate," Grunto summarised as if he was already giving his evening lecture.

"How inaccurate?" Richard said, leaning over the coffin further to examine the exposed bone.

Grunto produced a pen from somewhere inside his cloak and began to prod the holes. Jack, preferring not to watch, turned his head away.

# A Queen's Rebel

"The smaller, I would estimate, has produced a penetration into the brain of two inches and the other around four inches. Either, I am afraid, would have been sufficient to have killed the good lady," Grunto said, shaking his head, then added, "But do not assume that whatever it was that caused the injury was of a continuing thickness, I rather feel that it was, like the lid you removed, tapered."

"So it was something with a point?" Richard said.

Grunto nodded his head.

"Makes sense; the leading edge punctures the bone, and then the rest continues on in," Jack said matter-of-factly. "And it wouldn't be easy. It looks like she was struck with a halbert."

Grunto had extracted his pen and was tapping it thoughtfully against his chin. "I, too, would be thinking along that line, although the profile is square, and such a weapon would usually produce a round hole. But it is a weapon of sufficient size to allow the wielder to inflict such an injury."

"So a square profile, halbert?" Richard mused.

"Something like that," Master Grount said, then added, "You can let her roll back now."

Jack didn't move fast enough and found his gaze had remained stationary for a second too long, and he met the withered and dry gaze of Amy Robsart, her face, in death a dark purple, cheeks hollow, lips drawn back and her jaw hanging open.

Jack jumped back, emitting an involuntary yelp.

"Sorry," said Richard, not sounding at all apologetic.

## CHAPTER TWENTY-THREE

Jack threw his hands up in mock exasperation, but the gesture lacked heat. "Keep me here for much longer, and I will die of boredom. And I promise you my ghost will haunt you. Surely we've no need to remain here? After what Grunto showed you there is little left to find out is there? We know this was a murder, and yet we know we must report it as an accident."

"Duly noted," Richard said with a faint smile, returning his attention to the papers in front of him. "Now sit down and try not to break anything. We have work to do."

Jack muttered something under his breath and slumped back into his chair, his fingers drumming a restless rhythm on the armrest once more.

Richard glanced up, his eyes gleaming with a hint of mischief. "Fortunately for you, I've devised an entertainment that will very shortly end your boredom."

Jack's drumming stopped abruptly, and his interest was immediately piqued. He leaned forward, his expression one of suspicion laced with curiosity. "Oh? And what exactly does this 'entertainment' involve?"

Richard leaned back slightly, feigning nonchalance as he gathered the papers into a neat stack. "Let's just say it's an exercise in patience, observation, and perhaps a touch of charm—all skills you so desperately need to refine."

Jack narrowed his eyes, his scepticism growing. "That sounds suspiciously like work."

"It will involve speaking to someone who might actually enjoy your company," Richard said smoothly, ignoring Jack's grumbling.

# A Queen's Rebel

Jack's grin reappeared, wide and playful. "Ah, you mean there's a lady involved. That's more like it."

Richard's lips twitched, his expression remaining enigmatic. "Possibly. But don't mistake this for a dalliance. It's an interview. Informative, necessary, and, as you so often claim to excel at, an opportunity to win someone over."

Richard's timing could not have been more perfect. Just as Jack opened his mouth to press for more details, the inn door opened. All three men turned toward the sound, and Richard's expression shifted into one of calm expectation as though he had orchestrated this moment precisely.

"Master Fitzwarren, Andrew Forrester sent me, I have brought the servant you wish to question," the man said, his cloak was damp from the persistent drizzle outside, and behind him stood a young woman.

Richard nodded, his demeanour unhurried. "Very good."

The steward's man straightened, his tone firm. "He instructed me to remain present for any questioning."

Richard's brow arched ever so slightly, but his voice remained composed. "I see." He turned his gaze to Jack, who was now sitting upright. Richard then shifted his attention back to the man at the door. "You've delivered her safely, which is all that was required. Your continued presence, I'm afraid, is unnecessary."

The man frowned, clearly prepared to protest. "Master Forrester was most insistent—"

Richard's expression hardened, though his tone remained cool. "Master Forrester may be insistent, but this is a matter of investigation under Lord Fitzwarren's authority. I will not have unnecessary parties interfering."

The man hesitated, his eyes darting nervously between Richard and Jack.

Jack, sensing the man's discomfort, leaned back in his chair, a lazy grin spreading across his face. "You'd best not argue, friend. My brother here has an irritating habit of always getting his way." He let the words hang in the air for a moment, his tone light but his gaze sharp.

The man shifted uneasily, glancing between Jack and Richard. "It's not that I'm arguing, my lord," he began hesitantly.

Jack cut him off with a raised hand, the grin on his face hardening into something more commanding. "Good. Because arguing with me would be a mistake. Allow me to remind you that I am *Lord* Fitzwarren, and my rank far exceeds that of any steward—or his man. My wishes are not to be trifled with, nor are they subject to debate."

The man swallowed, his discomfort plain as Jack continued, his voice dropping to a more deliberate tone. "Your master, Forrester, may have some authority within the walls of Cumnor Place, but beyond them, his word holds little weight. Mine, however, holds considerably more. I trust you understand the difference?"

Richard remained silent, letting Jack's words settle, but the flicker of amusement in his eyes betrayed his approval of his brother's theatrics.

The man finally nodded, his shoulders stiff with tension. "Of course, my lord. I meant no disrespect."

"Good," Jack said, his grin returning but with an edge that suggested the conversation was over. "Now, be a good man and leave us to our business. My brother has questions, and they'll be answered without further interruption."

The steward's man looked between them, his frown deepening, and then, with a curt nod, he stepped back toward the door. "Very well, my lord. I'll wait outside."

"Go back to Cumnor, we will return Molly later," Richard said, closing the door firmly behind him as soon as he left. He turned back to Molly, his demeanour softening. "Please, take a seat by the fire."

Molly stepped forward hesitantly, her hands twisting the fabric of her apron as her eyes darted around the room.

Molly's gaze flickered from Richard to Jack and back again. "Am I in trouble, sir?" she asked in a voice barely above a whisper.

"Not at all," Richard assured her, stepping forward and pulling out a chair with a deliberate gesture. "Please, have a seat."

Molly flushed, bobbing a quick curtsey. "I shouldn't really, sir."

"And why not?" Richard asked, patting the chair with exaggerated patience.

"It's not proper, sir," she murmured, her hands twisting nervously at her apron.

"Ah, worried the steward might catch us? Rest assured, he's not here," Richard replied evenly, his tone disarming. "And if he were, I'd happily explain that I insisted on it."

Jack, sprawled awkwardly in the tavern's only armchair by the fire, gave up his search for comfort and rose with a groan. "Sit, woman," he said, his easy grin breaking across his face. "Unless you'd prefer to have us all craning our necks like geese to speak to you."

Molly hesitated, glancing between the brothers, clearly torn.

"Come now," Jack added, grabbing a plate of griddle cakes from the table and extending it toward her. "At least join us for one of these. I warn you, though, they're not the best I've had."

"Jack!" Richard said with a pointed sigh, folding his arms and leaning back against the wall.

Molly sat down cautiously, smoothing her skirts. "I shouldn't ... but I suppose one couldn't hurt," she said, reaching hesitantly for a griddle cake.

"But you will," Jack said with mock solemnity, his grin turning mischievous. "I insist."

He took one himself, biting into it with an exaggerated crunch before pulling a face. "As I thought. Overbaked, and not a grain of salt to be found. What do you think?"

Molly took a tentative bite, her expression shifting to one of mild disapproval. "You're right, sir. They're dry as the river in a drought. I could do better in my sleep."

"Ah, a bold claim!" Jack leaned forward conspiratorially. "If I weren't already married, my lady, I'd propose on the spot. Good cooking and a bonny face—what more could a man want?"

Molly blushed furiously, but her pride won out, and she gave a small smile. "You flatter me, my lord."

"If I had my way I'd have the cook here turned off," leaning forwards he whispered something in Molly's ear. Molly giggled, covering her mouth with one hand and blushed while Richard rolled his eyes.

Richard, who had been watching the exchange with his arms still folded, sighed deeply. "If you're quite done, Jack," he said, his voice cutting through the laughter like a knife through butter, "perhaps we can return to the matter at hand?"

Jack winked at Molly, his grin unfaltering. "All business, my brother. No wonder the ladies find him insufferable."

Richard said nothing, his patience, as ever, a thread stretched taut but unbroken.

"Is it a good place to work?" Jack asked, changing the subject. "Forrester seems a bit formidable for my liking."

"He can be, sir, I don't see much of him, but Jed used to complain about him. He used to work in the stables, " Molly said, taking a second dainty nibble.

"I used to work in the stables for an evil cur called Farringdon, the worst temper of any man I've ever come across," Jack lamented, adding, "I was oft on the wrong side of his temper."

"Jed has been on the wrong side of Master Forrester's temper as well, a time or two, he had a right black eye just before he left."

"He left? When was that?" Jack asked casually.

"Not long after ...." Molly bit her lip, stopping suddenly.

"Days or weeks?" Jack asked, abandoning the cold oat cake onto the platter.

"A few days, I suppose," Molly said, sensing a sudden seriousness in the room.

"Any reason you can think of as to why he went? Did he say anything to you before he left?" Jack asked.

Molly shook her head. "He just wasn't there, Master Forrester said he'd gone to take up work in Kidlington."

"Do you know who with?" Jack asked.

Molly shook her head.

"And you've not heard from him again, I assume?" Jack questioned.

Molly raised her eyes to Jack, clearly getting nervous. "Kidlington is a long ways north of here, sir, it's not likely he'd pass us by often."

Richard had placed a glass on the table, and next to it an earthenware jug. The glass was plain, simple and smooth sided.

Jack looked from the glass to his brother. "You definitely didn't find that in this tavern."

Richard smiled. "You'd be right, I borrowed it from Pudsey while he wasn't looking."

"I have a question," Richard said, his tone friendly – Jack's nerves were instantly on edge.

"A clear glass, empty, do you agree," Richard held it out towards Molly and Jack.

The woman nodded, confused, and Jack's eyes narrowed.

Richard set the glass down, and lifting the pitcher poured water from the jug filling the glass. Molly watched, and Jack his eyes on the water was wondering also what the point of this was.

"Aristotle said water was a puzzle," Richard raised the glass and held it first towards Molly and then Jack. "A conundrum, there is something there, we know that, and yet we can see through it! How can that be?"

"Really!" Jack said sarcastically.

Richard ignored Jack; taking a small knife from the table, he stirred the water. "It moves, within the glass, and yet that movement cannot be easily seen."

"Get on with it," Jack growled.

Richard threw a disparaging glance at his brother before he turned his back and produced something from inside his doublet, Jack leaned to one side but he couldn't see what was in his brother's hand. And when Richard turned back and Jack saw the gilt comb he had last seen in Amy's bedroom he frowned.

Molly paled, and a tiny noise erupted from between her lips.

Jack looked between the pair.

"Lady Robsart's comb, am I correct?" Richard asked Molly.

Molly nodded her head quickly, her eyes fastened on it, and her hands now wound in the apron on the front of her dress.

"Long chestnut hairs are still wound around the teeth; they would undoubtedly be your mistresses unless you were in the habit of using this?" Richard replied.

Molly shook her head.

"Observe," Richard said and pulled a small clump of hair from between the teeth of the comb. He held it up between thumb and forefinger, the threads were tangled and bound together in a knot.

# A Queen's Rebel

As they watched, he dropped the hair into the glass with a finger, forcing it beneath the surface.

"Behold," was all he said.

Jack was about to tell his brother what he thought of his theatrics when he stopped, a frown gathering between his brows uncertain for a moment if what he saw was real – a faint trail appeared, red in the clear water was weaving its way slowly from the small clump of hair. A tiny whisp, like ethereal smoke, but it began to thicken, as the blood on the hair stained the water.

"My God!" Jack said, his eyes switched from the glass and the swirling line of red to Molly.

The woman's face was ashen, her eyes on the hair as it turned slowly in the water.

"Blood?" Jack exclaimed.

"I think so," Richard replied grimly, then his eyes on Molly , "How do you think these tangled hairs bound together with blood came to be on your mistresses comb?"

Molly swallowed hard; her eyes were wide and fastened on the glass, and the twirling hair that was still caught in the current of water. Molly's hands were wound tight in her apron, her feet shook and her wooden clogs rattled on the floor.

Richard put the comb down next to the glass. "The comb is clogged still with blood and hair. It's not been cleaned. Should that not have been your job, Molly, to keep these clean and to brush and comb your mistress's hair?"

Molly's eyes briefly flicked up to meet Richard's before dropping back to her hands and the rucked apron in her lap. The thin trace of blood in the water had begun to disperse, and all that was left now was a very faint pink tinge around the submerged hair. Richard lifted the glass, swirling it, the three of them watched as the stain in the water completely vanished. "Gone, evidence, like smoke, it seems, can disappear."

"Why didn't you clean them?" Richard asked, his voice level and tone even.

Molly just shook her head but didn't utter a word.

"Alright, I will make some assumptions about what happened, and you can stop me if I'm wrong," Richard said; he hitched himself onto the edge of the table and picked up the comb again, examining it briefly before he spoke. "This was used to comb your mistress's hair, and that hair had to be washed, didn't it? It was soaked in blood; some of the strands had been torn away, snapped off and cut when she was attacked, and these caught in the teeth of the comb. The wound would not have bled for long, only while the lady still lived, then it would have stopped seeping from her. It must have been a terrible mess to clean up, I cannot imagine how you did it on your own."

A small cry escaped from between Molly's slightly parted lips.

"You wish to say something?" Richard asked, folding his arms.

Molly's eyes flitted between Richard and Jack, nothing in them now but the fear of a trapped animal. "I ...."

"Yes .... Go on," Richard encouraged.

Another choking sound escaped her lips, but no words.

"For God's sake, Richard, you are terrifying the poor woman," Jack said, exasperated; leaning forward, he wrapped his hand around one of hers where it lay among the twisted wreckage of her apron in her lap. "I doubt, Molly, that this was your doing, and I am sure any part you played was an unwilling one."

Molly swallowed hard and raised her eyes to meet Jack's; tears were leaking from them and running down her cheeks. "It wasn't me, sir."

Jack squeezed her hand and bestowed upon her what he hoped was his most encouraging smile.

# A Queen's Rebel

"You can tell us, Molly, we know you wished your mistress no harm."

"I can't, sir," Molly managed.

"You can't tell us?" Jack asked.

Molly shook her head, freeing more tears from her eyes.

"If we promise to keep you safe would that make a difference?" Jack said suspecting the reason for the silence.

"No, sir, you can't," Molly replied.

Jack looked at her. Who, or what, could be more terrifying to a poor woman than the two men she now faced? Was it fear for herself or her family?

"Very well, if you cannot tell us, we will detain you no more," Richard said, sighing, then to his brother, who still held Molly's hand. "Jack, let her go."

"We can't just ...."

"We can and we will. I cannot force her to tell us," Richard said then to Molly, "Please, you are free to leave. I am sorry we have caused you such distress."

Molly looked between Richard and Jack uncertainly and then began to rise from the chair; wiping the back of her hand across her wet cheeks, she rose and stepped towards the door.

"Of course, Forrester will believe you have told us. He'll be watching, he'll see your tears and he'll be sure the secret is not safe anymore. Then what will he do?" Richard said conversationally.

Molly stopped dead on her way towards the door.

"You bastard," Jack muttered under his breath.

"Think about it a little longer if you like, but it will not change anything. What will he do to you?" Richard asked again.

Molly turned back, her face stricken with fear. "He'll kill me."

Sam Burnell

They got no more from Molly. The woman collapsed back into the chair, her face hidden behind her apron, and sobbed.

"Now, what do we do?" Jack said, annoyed.

Richard shrugged. "I hadn't thought that far ahead."

## CHAPTER TWENTY-FOUR

The room at the Black Swan was quiet now, save for the occasional crackle of the fire in the hearth and the soft patter of rain against the window. Molly had left, her sobs lingering in the memory of the two men who remained behind. Jack stared at the flames, a rare seriousness overtaking his usually jovial demeanour.

Richard leaned against the table, arms folded, his expression unreadable. Molly had been handed into the care of the landlord's wife with instructions to look after the poor girl.

Jack broke the silence with a sharp exhale. "Well, that was a disaster."

"It was necessary," Richard replied, his voice steady but low.

"Necessary? You terrified the poor girl out of her wits," Jack said, sitting up straight and gesturing toward the door. "She looked like she'd seen the Devil himself."

"She's afraid of whoever was behind Lady Robsart's death, Jack," Richard said, his tone firm. "And if we sent her back to Cumnor Place in that state, looking like she does now—tear-streaked, apron ruined—it would raise more questions than she could answer."

Jack scowled but nodded, running a hand through his hair. "Fine. But what do we do with her? We can't hide her away forever."

"No, but we can find somewhere safe for her to stay for now," Richard said. He pushed off the table and began pacing. "A local inn, perhaps in Oxford. Somewhere out of the way where she won't be recognised."

Jack looked up sharply. "And what about Jed?"

Richard stopped pacing and turned to face his brother. "What about him?"

"Molly mentioned he left a few days after Lady Robsart's death. A black eye, no warning, and vanished off to Kidlington, or so they say," Jack said, his tone laced with suspicion. "That doesn't strike you as odd?"

"Odd, yes," Richard admitted. "But it doesn't tell us much."

Jack scoffed. "It tells us he might've known something, or worse, done something. And now he's conveniently out of reach."

Richard frowned. "We can send Threadmill to see if he can find him. If he's still in Kidlington, he may know more than Molly does."

"And if he's not?" Jack asked.

"Then we'll have to assume he's either been silenced or is hiding for a reason," Richard said grimly.

Jack sighed and leaned back in his chair. "This whole thing gets darker by the hour. Molly's too terrified to speak, Jed's gone missing, and we know the lady received terrible blows to the head, that her maid was forced to clean the blood away, but I still feel we're no closer to finding out what really happened."

Richard's jaw tightened. "We'll get there. But for now, we focus on what we can do. We find Molly somewhere safe."

Finally, Richard broke the silence. "We know Lady Robsart was murdered. Whoever killed her forced Molly to clean up the blood afterwards. The blood on the comb, the tangled hair—it wasn't just from a fall. Those were the remains of a deliberate attack. Lady Robsart's body was then rearranged at the bottom of the stairs to make it look like a tragic fall."

# A Queen's Rebel

Jack leaned forward, resting his elbows on his knees. "Forcing Molly to clean her mistress's body, knowing she couldn't speak of it..." He trailed off, shaking his head. "No wonder she's terrified."

"Exactly," Richard said, his voice low but firm. "They used her. Probably threatened her life—or the lives of her family—to keep her quiet. It's no wonder she's afraid to talk to us. She likely fears whoever did this will come back for her if they think she's betrayed them."

"Poor woman," Jack said. "That outburst at the end—it wasn't just fear. It was guilt. She knows what happened to Lady Robsart, at least in part. She might even know who was behind it, but she's too terrified to say. And Jed, How does he fit into this?"

Richard exhaled slowly. "He's another loose end. If he left shortly after Lady Robsart's death, it's possible he saw or heard something he shouldn't have. Or maybe he was involved in some way and decided to disappear before the noose tightened."

Jack rubbed his jaw, his expression pensive. "And if he's dead?"

"Then we're chasing shadows," Richard admitted, his voice grim. "But until we find him—or at least find out what happened to him."

Jack sat back in his chair, crossing his arms. "And what about Molly? If we're right, she's the closest thing we've got to a witness. What do we do with her?"

"For now, we keep her safe," Richard said. "If she's brave enough, she might come around and tell us what she knows. Until then, we move forward with what we have."

"And what exactly do we have?" Jack asked, his voice tinged with frustration.

Richard turned back to the fire, the flickering light casting sharp shadows across his face. "A comb, a trail of blood, and a maid who's too terrified to speak. It's not much, but it's enough to start."

Sam Burnell

The door at the back of the room opened abruptly, and the landlady swept in, carrying a plate of oatcakes in one hand and a jug of wine in the other. The warm, yeasty smell of the cakes filled the room, but the sight of them—overcooked and as unappetising as the first batch—did little to lift the mood.

"Here we are, gentlemen," she said brightly, setting the plate and jug on the table with an unnecessary flourish. "Fresh from the kitchen. And there's plenty more if you're thinking about it. If there's anything else you need, just call for me."

Richard nodded absently, barely glancing at her as he remained deep in thought by the fire. Jack, however, gave her a charming smile as he leaned back in his chair.

"Thank you, mistress. Though I wouldn't call them fresh," he said, gesturing toward the oatcakes with a grin.

She tsked good-naturedly, ignoring the jab. "My husband's the one with the real knack for cooking. Unfortunately, he's out just now."

Richard turned slightly, frowning. "Out?"

"Oh yes," she said cheerfully, brushing her hands off on her apron. "He's taken Molly back to Cumnor Place on his horse."

The room went still. Jack's grin vanished as he straightened in his chair, his boots hitting the floor with a heavy thud. Richard took a sharp step forward, his eyes narrowing.

"What did you say?" he asked, his tone sharp enough to cut through her pleasant demeanour.

The landlady blinked, surprised. "Why, he's taken Molly back to Cumnor, like I said. She was in quite a state when she came out of here, poor girl. She said she didn't want to stay, and wanted to go back home. So my husband saddled up and took her. Left not ten minutes ago."

"You *let her go?*" Jack said, his voice rising as he stood abruptly.

# A Queen's Rebel

She frowned, looking between the brothers in confusion. "I didn't realise she was to stay. She didn't seem like she wanted to, and no one told me otherwise. Was there... some reason you wanted her here?"

"We need to stop her," Jack snapped, grabbing his cloak. "Now she's on her way to God knows what!"

"Which way will he go?"

"He'll take the main road—it's faster with a horse."

Richard nodded, his mind already working through the next steps. "Jack, I'll go after her, it'll be faster on my own."

Jack pulled on his cloak with a scowl. "If anything happens to her, Richard..."

"I know," Richard said grimly.

As Richard stepped out into the rain, his jaw tightened. How had he let that happen? Molly had been within their grasp, the key to unravelling the truth. Now, she was slipping away.

The rain had softened to a drizzle by the time Richard caught sight of the landlord riding toward him on the muddy road back from Cumnor. The man sat hunched over his saddle, his horse plodding along at a lazy pace. Richard pulled his own horse to a halt, his cloak heavy with water, and raised a hand to flag him down.

The landlord spotted him and reined in, his expression one of surprise. "Sir, I've just taken the lassie back. Couldn't let her walk in this weather," he said, tipping his hat.

"Did you see Forrester, the steward?" Richard asked sharply.

The landlord shook his head. "No, sir. Just handed her off and left. Didn't see much point in lingering."

Richard's thoughts raced. Molly was back in Cumnor Place, directly under the steward's control. She might have been safe for the moment, but if he suspected she'd spoken—even hinted at what she knew—she'd be in danger.

He gritted his teeth, his decision made.

By the time Richard reached Cumnor Place, the manor loomed dark and foreboding against the gloomy sky. He dismounted at the gate and tied his horse to a post, brushing the mud from his boots as he strode toward the main entrance.

"Forrester," Richard said coldly as the steward opened the door. His voice carried the weight of command, the clipped edge of a man who expected compliance. "

To what do I owe this unexpected and unwelcome visit?" Forrester's tone was laced with disdain, but there was a flicker of unease in his eyes.

Richard stepped forward without waiting for an invitation, the force of his presence alone enough to make Forrester take an involuntary step back. "I'm here about Molly."

Forrester's frown deepened. "What of her?"

"A word. In private," Richard said, his words sharp as a blade. The underlying threat was unmistakable.

Forrester hesitated, then reluctantly led Richard into the main room. He shut the door behind them with deliberate care, as though trying to maintain some semblance of control. Richard wasted no time.

"I know Molly was forced to clean Lady Amy's body after her death," Richard began, his voice low and venomous. He took a step closer, his eyes boring into Forrester's. "I know she saw more than she should have, and I know someone made damn sure she'd stay silent."

Forrester stiffened, his hand twitching at his side, though he kept his expression carefully neutral.

# A Queen's Rebel

"That's a dangerous accusation, Fitzwarren," he said, his voice betraying a hint of wariness.

"It's not an accusation. It's the truth." Richard's tone hardened, his eyes narrowing. "And here's another truth: if anything happens to Molly, there will be consequences—ones you won't like."

Forrester's jaw tightened, his gaze locked with Richard's in a silent battle of wills. "You have no proof," he said finally, his voice quieter but no less defiant.

Richard took another step forward, his presence almost suffocating. "Proof is irrelevant, Forrester. I don't need proof to set tongues wagging or to drag your name through the mud in every hall and court from here to London. What I do have are witnesses—people who've heard her tell her story. Tearfully. In detail." His voice dropped to a dangerous whisper. "Do you really want me asking those questions in places where the wrong ears might hear the answers?"

Forrester's hand twitched again, his breath shallow. "You're making a mistake if you think threats will get you anywhere." Richard's lips curled into something that wasn't a smile. "A mistake? Let me be very clear, Forrester. I don't make mistakes. If Molly isn't safe, if I so much as hear a whisper of harm befalling her, I'll personally ensure you regret ever crossing me." He leaned in, his voice dropping to a growl. "You think your master's name will shield you? It won't. Not from me."

Forrester hesitated, his bravado wavering. Finally, he inclined his head, the gesture small but significant. "Molly will be safe," he said through clenched teeth. "You have my word."

"She'd better be," Richard said, straightening to his full height. His eyes lingered on Forrester for a moment longer, cold and unforgiving. Then, without another word, he turned on his heel and strode out of the room, leaving the steward standing stiffly in his wake.

The door slammed shut behind him, the sound reverberating through the house like thunder.

When Richard returned to the Black Swan, Jack is waiting for him by the fire, his boots propped on a stool and a mug of ale in his hand. He looked up as Richard entered, rain-soaked and muddy.

"Well?" Jack asked, sitting up. "What happened?"

"I was too late, she was already back at Cumnor Place. I confronted the steward," Richard said, peeling off his wet cloak and hanging it by the hearth. "Told him I knew what Molly had been forced to do, and that if anything happens to her, there'll be consequences."

Jack raised a brow. "You think that'll keep her safe?"

"I hope so," Richard said, sinking into a chair. "Forrester's no fool."

A Queen's Rebel

## CHAPTER TWENTY-FIVE

Jack woke in the middle of the night, startled and cold. The room was dark, the faint moonlight that seeped through the shutters, slicing the air into long, uneven streaks. His blanket had slipped to the floor, and he shivered. But it wasn't just the cold that unsettled him; it was the wind. Not a gentle breeze but a relentless, buffeting gale that rattled the shutters and swept through the cracks like an invisible hand pressing against his skin. It felt almost deliberate, like something forcing its way in.

He glared at the shutters, their wooden slats quivering under the wind's assault. Once, he would have swung his feet from the bed without a second thought, crossed the room, and slammed them shut. But not anymore. That simple act, so instinctive in the past, now required consideration. Crossing the room, he pressed them closed. The wind ceased instantly, its howling silenced as if the house had swallowed it whole. A hanging on the far wall that had been lifted by the draft fell back into place, its musty fabric settling quietly against the stone.

White.

Shroud white.

Jack froze, staring at the hanging as the image crept unbidden into his mind. The shroud hadn't been white, not anymore. Trapped within the coffin, sealed tight for nine months, it had yellowed, taken on the marks of its grim purpose. Stained where it had touched skin, blackened where decay had seeped through. He squeezed his eyes shut against the thought, but it was no use. The details were too sharp, too vivid.

Sam Burnell

The eyes.

They hadn't been horrific, not in the way he might have imagined. There was no terror in them, no frozen scream or malevolent glare. They had been empty. Hollow sockets in a face ruined by death and the indifference that followed. It wasn't horror that had gripped him when he saw her—it was pity. Deep, gnawing pity. She had been cast aside, discarded like an afterthought in a coffin meant more to display grief than to honour the dead.

Dudley had not cared for what lay inside that coffin. Richard's words echoed in Jack's mind, biting and true. Dudley's concern had been with the exterior, the public face of mourning. The coffin designed to elicit sympathy, to project the image of a bereft husband torn apart by tragedy.

But it was a lie. All of it.

The poor widower. The grieving lover.

Jack clenched his fists, his nails digging into his palms. Yet Dudley was neither. His actions, his carefully constructed spectacle, betrayed the emptiness of his sorrow. If it was all for show, why hadn't he seen it through to its final act? Why hadn't he placed himself at the centre of his macabre theatre? Why had he not followed the coffin of his wife? Why had he not marched at the head of the procession, his eyes red with tears, his cheeks hollowed with sorrow? Why had he not let the world witness his grief, his loss, his despair? Surely, that was the point of all this—the grand display of mourning. It was all for them, for their pity, for their whispers and nods of approval.

But Dudley had been absent.

Why?

Jack's thoughts raced, looping back on themselves like a hound chasing its tail. Dudley must have intended to be there. He wouldn't have gone to such lengths only to abandon the charade at the last moment. So what had kept him away? What had been more important than the performance he had orchestrated?

Jack leaned against the shutters, the wood cool against his forehead. His heart beat heavy and uneven in his chest. He tried to shake the questions from his mind, but they clung to him, insistent and sharp. There had to be a reason, something he was missing.

Why?

The silence in the room was oppressive now, the wind outside muted to a low, distant murmur. Jack turned from the window and let his gaze drift back to the hanging on the wall. The pale fabric was still, but in his mind, it rippled like the shroud in that coffin, heavy with death and unanswered questions.

The image lingered, refusing to fade. He knew sleep would not come again that night.

"Why are we doing this?" Jack demanded, his voice taut with frustration. He leaned forward in his chair, glaring at his brother. "We can't go back to London with evidence that Amy Robsart was murdered! The only way to survive this is to exonerate Dudley."

Richard smiled, a small, enigmatic curve of his lips that only infuriated Jack more. "We will," he said smoothly.

Jack threw up his hands. "Then why are we turning over every filthy stone we can find here and uncovering evidence that points to a very different conclusion?"

Richard steepled his fingers, resting his chin lightly against them as he regarded his brother with an unruffled gaze. "It seems like a lifetime ago," he said slowly, "but do you recall our role in Northumberland's downfall?"

Jack met his brother's eyes, suspicion mingling with weariness. "You were instrumental in it," he said pointedly. "You switched sides, convinced the rest of us to follow, and even persuaded Grey to return to London rather than continue marching to support Northumberland."

"Precisely," Richard replied, his smile widening. "Mary ascended to the throne, and history, as they say, was etched in stone. However..." He let the word hang in the air, a deliberate pause heavy with implication. "However, Dudley is the son of Northumberland, and he has every reason to hold us in profound dislike."

"Us?" Jack shot back, eyebrows arching in disbelief. "You mean you. You were the one who orchestrated that."

Richard waved a dismissive hand. "Us," he insisted. "We supported Mary, placed ourselves against Northumberland, and thus positioned ourselves as obstacles to his ambitions. That fact was advantageous for her Majesty, though she may have chosen to forget it by now."

Jack straightened, alarm flashing across his face. His voice dropped to a near whisper as if the walls themselves might overhear. "Have you lost her favour?"

Richard exhaled slowly, his eyes narrowing. "Favour is as fickle as fortune," he said. "And at this moment, every ounce of the queen's favour rests firmly upon Dudley's shoulders."

"So she'll want you to clear him of any wrongdoing," Jack reasoned. "Surely she wouldn't fault you for that?"

Richard's expression darkened, his smile fading into something far colder. "The very fact that I am here investigating this matter has already drawn Dudley's ire. She needed someone to do it—someone she could trust to ensure her desired outcome. But here's the problem: no matter what I conclude, I risk offending someone. The queen wants Dudley

# A Queen's Rebel

exonerated, but she will resent anyone who dredges up his past, asks difficult questions, and rakes over the ashes of this sordid affair. And then there's Cecil."

Jack frowned. "Cecil?"

Richard's eyes gleamed with sardonic amusement. "Cecil couldn't resist handing me this task. It's a neat little trap, don't you think? A test of loyalty, if you like. One wrong move and I fall afoul of the queen's wrath or Dudley's ambition—or both."

Jack slumped back in his chair, the weight of Richard's words settling heavily on his shoulders. "So we're damned either way?"

"Not necessarily," Richard said, his tone as measured as ever. "The conclusion must be that the poor lady fell and that her death was an accident. Anything else would unleash the queen's displeasure—and that, I assure you, is a far worse prospect than Dudley's anger. However..." He leaned forward, his voice dropping conspiratorially. "If we can uncover the truth, we might yet turn it to our advantage."

Jack raised an eyebrow, scepticism mingling with curiosity. "And how exactly do you plan to do that?"

Richard's smile returned, sharp as a knife. "If we possess the truth, we can use it to keep Dudley firmly leashed. Imagine a public display of appreciation for our work, an acknowledgement that secures our place in Her Majesty's graces while quietly reminding Dudley of what we know."

Jack's frown deepened. "That's a dangerous game, Richard."

Richard spread his hands in a gesture of mock innocence. "Life at court is nothing but dangerous games. The question is whether you play to win or lose."

Jack shook his head, leaning forward. "And you're sure it was murder?"

"Aren't you?" Richard's tone shifted, a faint note of incredulity slipping through his polished demeanour. "You've seen the poor lady's head."

Jack's stomach turned at the memory. The fractures, the violence etched into the bone—details he wished he could forget but knew he never would. "I've seen it," he said quietly. "And if that's not murder, I don't know what is."

There was a moment of silence between them. Jack broke it first.

"Ther is something we have not considered," Jack said suddenly.

Richard's eyebrows raised. "Go on."

"Why was Dudley absent?" Jack said simply.

Richard leaned back in his chair, his expression momentarily unreadable. The flickering candlelight cast shifting shadows across his face, and for once, the ever-composed veneer seemed to falter. He drummed his fingers lightly against the table, his gaze fixed on Jack with something approaching curiosity or perhaps unease.

"Why was Dudley absent?" Jack repeated, his tone low, insistent. "The funeral was an elaborate affair, a thousand pounds spent on mourning the wife he supposedly adored. And yet, the man himself was nowhere to be seen. Why?"

Richard's lips parted as though he were about to reply, but no words came. Instead, he tilted his head slightly.

"You've not shared of something," Jack pressed, his eyes narrowing.

"Perhaps," Richard said, his voice thoughtful, his fingers now steepled beneath his chin.

"Don't keep it to yourself," Jack said, an annoyed tone in his voice.

Richard sighed, after a short pause he said. "It's not just the absence, is it? It's the timing. Dudley's failure to attend the inquest or the funeral

# A Queen's Rebel

wasn't merely a slight oversight or a display of apathy—it was a decision. A deliberate act."

Jack's gaze didn't waver. "Deliberate, yes. But why? If Dudley wanted to display his grief to the world, what better stage than his wife's funeral?"

Richard tapped his fingertips together rhythmically, his voice growing quieter, more introspective. "There could be practical reasons—his obligations to the court, for instance, or maybe he couldn't risk leaving the queen's side during a time of political unrest."

Jack snorted derisively. "Or perhaps he knew what they'd find. Maybe he knew that the inquest would reveal what we've already seen. The marks on her skull. The evidence of violence."

Richard's expression tightened, his gaze shifting slightly as though the thought struck a deeper chord than he cared to admit. "If he knew," he said slowly, "then he must have had a hand in ensuring the outcome of the inquest. The coroner declared her death accidental, after all."

"Convenient, isn't it?" Jack countered. "A tragic fall, no further questions asked. But even so, you'd think Dudley would be there to weep at her graveside, to lend credibility to the illusion."

Richard rose abruptly, pacing the length of the room. His footsteps were soft against the worn wooden floor, but the energy behind them was anything but subdued.

"Unless," Richard began, "his absence was not out of fear but calculation. What if his absence was meant to distance him from the act itself? To suggest that he was so consumed by grief he could not bring himself to face her funeral?"

"You don't' believe that!" Jack scoffed, his tone sharp, "what if he feared scrutiny? What if he worried that every eye on him might see guilt instead of grief? A man who mourns too openly risks the accusation of a guilty conscience."

"Perhaps …. But while conjecture is interesting, it isn't overly helpful. We know the shape of the weapon. I would wager it is still at Cumnor Place, and so is Molly. We forget her. She is the only person so far who we know was closely involved, and she was forced to clean the blood from her mistress's hair."

"How? She's back at Cumnor Place, Forrester isn't going to let you speak to her," Jack pointed out.

Richard smiled. "Then I shall have to go while he is absent."

## CHAPTER TWENTY-SIX

The false summons was crafted with precision, and the magistrate's seal was carefully imitated to ensure no suspicion arose. A nervous-looking messenger delivered it to Forrester, whose irritation was plain in the grumble that escaped his lips as he read the note. Richard watched from a concealed spot among the trees, his breath steady, his eyes tracking every movement. Ten minutes later Forrester adjusted his coat against the chill, muttering under his breath, then mounted his horse. The steward's silhouette shrank into the distance as the muffled clatter of hoofbeats faded on the muddy road. Only then did Richard step from the shadows.

The back entrance to Cumnor Place was just as he remembered. The weathered door creaked faintly as he pushed it open, and he slipped inside, the stale air of the house washing over him like an unwelcome embrace. The corridors stretched out before him, dimly lit by streaks of light filtering through the narrow windows. Shadows pooled in corners, thick and unyielding, and the faint smell of damp wood and cold stone hung in the air. Each step was deliberate, his boots soundless on the stone floor, his senses heightened by the oppressive silence.

He moved with purpose, pausing briefly at intersections to ensure no one stirred in the house. Finally, he reached the kitchen, a low-ceilinged room with worn wooden counters. Molly was there, her back to him, furiously scrubbing at a pot. The harsh, repetitive sound of metal on metal filled the room, a rhythm that stopped abruptly when she sensed his presence. She froze, her shoulders tightening, then turned sharply, the pot slipping from her hands and splashing into the water.

"Master Forrester isn't here," she stammered, her voice trembling. Her eyes darted around the room, wide with fear. "You shouldn't be either."

"I know," Richard said softly. "Molly. I just need to talk to you."

Her hands clutched the edge of the basin as though it were a lifeline. "I've told you everything I know," she said quickly. "Please, I can't say any more."

Richard's gaze softened, but his voice held steady. "You can, Molly. You were there. You cleaned the blood from her hair. What happened?"

Her breathing quickened, her knuckles white against the basin. "I don't know what you're talking about," she whispered, her tone thin and unconvincing.

Richard stepped closer, lowering his voice as if speaking to a spooked animal. "I can help you. But you need to trust me. Whatever you saw or heard—it matters."

Tears welled in her eyes, her lip trembling as she shook her head violently. "No," she choked out. "I can't. I'm sorry, sir, but I can't."

The resignation in her voice sent a pang through him. Richard could see the terror that gripped her, the way her entire body trembled with an effort to hold something unspeakable at bay. She was a prisoner of her own fear, and no amount of coaxing could free her.

"Very well," he said finally, stepping back, his tone tinged with regret. "If you change your mind, you know where to find me."

She didn't respond, her back already turned to him, her head bowed as she resumed scrubbing with renewed desperation. Richard lingered for a moment, watching her trembling hands before turning and slipping out of the room.

# A Queen's Rebel

The house seemed to hold its breath as Richard ascended the creaking stairs, every step deliberate, the silence of Cumnor Place pressing against him like a weight. The air was heavy with the faint scent of beeswax and damp, mingling with the faint memory of something long gone. At the top of the stairs he paused, listening for any sound of movement. Satisfied that the house was still, he turned the latch on Amy's room and slipped inside.

The room was as he remembered: orderly, almost unnaturally so, as though someone had gone to great lengths to erase the signs of life that had once filled it. The air was cool and stale, untouched by a fire for a long time. Richard's eyes roved over the space, taking in the faintly faded tapestries, the draped bed with its canopy and the simple dresser on the far side of the room.

The brushes and combs on the dresser caught his attention immediately. The last time he had been here, they had been matted with hair. Now, however, they gleamed. Their polished surfaces reflected the faint light filtering through the small, leaded window. Molly had clearly cleaned them, meticulously removing all traces of use.

Richard's gaze lingered on the bed for a moment before shifting to the fireplace. He moved toward it slowly, the stillness of the room amplifying the sound of his footsteps. The hearth was cold and bare, swept clean save for a faint dusting of ash in the corners. Whoever had tended to the room had been thorough yet not meticulous enough to eliminate every trace.

The iron tools were propped neatly against the side of the fireplace: a poker, tongs, and a small shovel. Richard picked each one up in turn, weighing them in his hands. They were heavy, and their iron surfaces were smooth from years of use. He imagined how easily one of these could be wielded as a weapon. However, as he examined the tools, he realized they were too narrow to match the impressions left in Amy's skull. The poker was far too slender; the tongs, while heavy, lacked the squared profile of the injuries he had seen.

Richard set the tools back quietly in their place. His eyes drifted downward to the two iron fire dogs positioned before the hearth. The stout, functional supports were adorned with curled twists of wrought iron at the top, and their sturdy, square feet sat solidly on the hearthstone. Something about them drew his attention.

Richard knelt and picked up one of the fire dogs, the cold iron biting into his hands. It was heavy—heavier than it appeared—and as he turned it over in his hands, his breath caught. The square feet were almost exactly the size of the wounds in Amy's skull. He measured the length of one foot against his palm; it was roughly three inches long, consistent with the depth of the fatal injuries.

The iron seemed to pulse with latent menace as if it still bore the memory of violence. He turned the fire dog over again, examining the underside of its feet. His fingers froze as they brushed against something coarse and brittle. He raised the fire dog closer to his face, his pulse quickening.

There, stuck to the bottom of one of the feet, were a few strands brown hair. A wave of grim certainty settled over him. He lowered the fire dog slightly, staring at it with a mix of revulsion and triumph.

This was it.

The weapon.

The fire dog had been used to strike Amy not once but twice. The square feet matched the impressions in her skull perfectly, and the hair—brown and unmistakable—was a damning piece of evidence. The violence of the act played out in his mind, unbidden: the first blow landing with sickening force, the sharp edge-crushing bone. The second a brutal follow-up, shattering any chance of survival.

# A Queen's Rebel

Richard carefully set the fire dog back in its place beside its twin, as though trying to erase the disruption his discovery had caused. He straightened and exhaled slowly, the weight of what he now knew settling over him like a shroud.

Amy had not fallen. She had not tripped or stumbled to her death. She had been struck down with deliberate force, her life snuffed out by the hand of another. And now, holding the truth, Richard understood the chilling precision of her murder.

But the question remained: who had wielded the fire dog, and why? He stared at the empty hearth for a long moment before turning to leave the room, his mind racing with the implications. The house seemed to watch him as he slipped out of the door, leaving behind the scene of a crime that could no longer be hidden.

The corridor seemed darker now as he made his way toward Forrester's office, the office door yielded to his touch, and he stepped inside, drawing the door quietly shut behind him. The room was cramped, lit faintly by the light filtering through a single window. Shelves lined with ledgers and stacks of parchment loomed on either side, the air thick with the scent of old paper and ink.

The desk was locked, as he'd anticipated, but Richard's knife was sharp, and the mechanism gave way with a satisfying click. He rifled through the drawers, his movements precise, skimming through accounts of household expenses and correspondence with merchants, then something different—a folded letter tucked beneath a ledger.

Richard unfolded the paper, his eyes narrowing as he scanned the elegant script. The words were mundane, polite even, but the signature at the bottom sent a chill racing down his spine:

*Robert Topcliffe*

Sam Burnell

He read the letter again, the implications sinking in like lead:

*To my esteemed host,*
*I trust this letter finds you in good health. I wish to express my gratitude for the hospitality extended to me during my brief stay at Cumnor Place. Rest assured, I am eager to return the favour whenever the need arises.*
*Yours,*
*R. Topcliffe.*

Richard stared at the name, his heart thudding in his chest. Topcliffe. The queen's man. A figure of whispered terror, known for his brutal efficiency and unwavering loyalty to Elizabeth. If Topcliffe had been here, the ramifications were staggering. Amy's death wasn't just a matter of intrigue—it was entangled in the shadowy politics of the Crown.

He carefully refolded the letter and returned it to the drawer, ensuring everything appeared untouched. The lock clicked back into place, and Richard straightened, his mind racing.

## CHAPTER TWENTY-SEVEN

The journey back to the Tavern was a haze of cold air and half-formed thoughts. The tavern's warmth was a welcome reprieve as he pushed open the door to the room. Jack was there, hunched over the table, his expression sharpening as Richard entered.

"Well?" Jack asked, his voice taut with curiosity and unease.

Richard shrugged off his cloak and sank into the chair opposite, the weight of his discovery etched into his face. "Robert Topcliffe," he said flatly.

Jack's brow furrowed. "The queen's man, Topcliffe?"

Richard nodded grimly. "He was at Cumnor Place shortly after Amy's death. There's no question now, Jack—her death is tied to the Crown."

Jack's face darkened, his jaw tightening. "This isn't just Dudley's ambition, is it?"

Richard's eyes met his brother's, a silent understanding passing between them. "It's far more dangerous than that. Consider this: if Dudley is innocent of the act itself but complicit in having the jury declare it an accident, who would he risk everything to protect?"

Jack frowned. "It would have to be someone close to him. Someone whose involvement would destroy him if it became known."

"Exactly," Richard replied, his tone quickening. "A family member, perhaps. Or a confidant."

"Cecil?" Jack suggested.

Richard shook his head. "Too dangerous. Cecil would never risk himself for Dudley, and Dudley wouldn't gamble on Cecil's silence. No, it's someone more personal, someone he can trust implicitly."

"A lover," Jack said flatly.

"Yes," he said softly, the word heavy with implication. "A lover. Or someone he hopes to make one."

"The queen?" Jack asked, his voice incredulous.

Richard didn't answer immediately. He crossed to the window and peered into the storm-laden night. The wind rattled the wooden frame with restless fingers, and for a long moment, he said nothing, his silhouette outlined against the weak light.

When he finally spoke, his voice was a murmur, barely above the sound of the storm. "She has always been possessive, hasn't she? Of those she values, of those she keeps close."

Jack frowned, uneasy. "Possessive enough to...?"

"To murder?" Richard's gaze flicked back to his brother, his expression unreadable. "That's the question, isn't it?"

Jack shook his head, disbelief edging into his voice. "No. It doesn't make sense. If she were jealous, if she wanted Amy gone, she wouldn't risk her reputation like this. She's too clever for that."

"She is clever," Richard agreed, stepping away from the window. "But cleverness does not always temper jealousy. Jealousy is a beast, Jack. It gnaws at reason and distorts judgment. And consider the timing. Amy's death comes just as Dudley begins to rise higher in the queen's favour. Coincidence?"

Jack opened his mouth to protest, then closed it again. He didn't like the turn this was taking, but Richard's words clung to him like damp clothes. The queen's temper was no secret; her capriciousness was whispered about in every court.

"If you're right," Jack said slowly, "then why go to such lengths to make it look like an accident? Why not just poison her? That would be simpler, subtler."

# A Queen's Rebel

Richard's expression tightened. "Because poisoning carries its own risks. Especially given Dudley's ambitions, Amy's sudden illness would have been suspicious. But an accident—a fall, a tragedy—casts no such shadow. It allows everyone to grieve openly, to mourn without questioning. A clever way to remove a rival, wouldn't you say?"

"A rival," Jack repeated, the word tasting bitter on his tongue. "You think the queen saw Amy as a rival for Dudley?"

Richard nodded. "Not for his affections, perhaps. But for his focus. For his loyalty. Dudley's ambition has always been a double-edged sword. If he were distracted by his wife, he might not serve her as devotedly as she wished. And if he remained married, she could never fully possess him—not politically, not personally."

Jack paced, his boots scuffing against the uneven floorboards. "It's still a risk. Too much could go wrong. The coroner could have ruled differently, witnesses could have spoken out."

"Ah, but the coroner didn't, did he?" Richard said sharply. "The inquest was swift and conclusive, almost too tidy. And who, pray tell, would dare question the findings? Who would risk accusing the queen herself of such a crime?"

Jack stopped pacing, his jaw tightening. "You're suggesting that she orchestrated the whole thing. That she controlled the inquest, silenced the voices, even arranged the manner of Amy's death?"

"I'm saying it's a possibility," Richard replied, his voice calm but firm. "One we can't afford to ignore."

Jack exhaled slowly, his unease growing. "And what do we do with this possibility, Richard? What can we possibly do?"

Richard smiled faintly, though there was no warmth in it. "For now? We do nothing. We dig deeper, but we tread carefully. Very carefully. If it is true, this truth is a blade sharp enough to cut us both."

Jack didn't reply. He crossed to the fire and stared into the embers, his thoughts churning. The idea that Amy's death might have been orchestrated by the queen herself was almost too terrible to comprehend. But the pieces fit together too well.

Behind him, Richard spoke again, his tone quieter now, almost pensive. "If the queen is guilty, Jack, it changes everything. Not just for Dudley, but for us."

Jack didn't turn around. The firelight danced against his face. "And if she's guilty, Richard, what do we do then?"

Richard's answer came after a long silence, and when it did, it was spoken softly, like a confession. "We survive. Whatever that takes."

Richard straightened, his expression sharp and controlled, a contrast to the storm of implications they had just unearthed. With a flick of his hand, he gestured toward the door.

"Do not mention this to Threadmill," Richard said, his voice low and deliberate. "Not a word."

Jack blinked, startled. "Why not? He's already neck-deep in this mess."

"He's not. All he has done so far is speak with the jurors, remember. He knows nothing more," Richard replied. "This isn't just about Dudley anymore, Jack. If the queen's hand is in this, even indirectly, we're playing a game with stakes far too high."

Jack watched Richard carefully, his brow furrowed in a mix of curiosity and unease. "Fine. I won't breathe a word," he said reluctantly. But the look in his eyes was questioning as if waiting for Richard to reveal what had clearly been weighing on him since his return from Cumnor Place.

Richard leaned back in his chair, his fingers interlaced and resting lightly on his stomach. The faint flicker of the tavern's candlelight danced across

# A Queen's Rebel

his face. "I found what killed Amy," he said quietly, his voice devoid of triumph.

Jack blinked, straightening in his seat. "You did?"

"Yes," Richard replied. "It wasn't some mysterious instrument, nor was it something carried into the house by an unknown assassin. It was already there in the room, waiting for whoever had the will to use it."

"What was it?" Jack pressed.

Richard exhaled, his gaze steady. "A fire dog. One of them had strands of her hair stuck to the bottom of its square feet."

Jack's expression shifted, a mix of disgust and disbelief crossing his face. "You're certain?"

"Positive. The dimensions match the injuries we saw on her skull—the square profile, the depth. Whoever struck her did so with the deliberate force of someone who knew exactly what they intended to do."

Jack frowned, leaning forward. "So what now? You've found the weapon, we've uncovered far too much about Dudley, and we're dangerously close to implicating the queen in all of this. What's left to do here?"

Richard considered the question for a moment, his expression tightening as he weighed the options. "There's little point in us remaining in Abingdon. There's nothing more to learn here that would change the shape of what we already know. Dudley may have wanted her dead, but I don't think he wielded that fire dog. And the queen...her shadow looms over all of this."

Jack sighed heavily, slumping back into his chair. "So that's it? We pack up and leave?"

"For now," Richard said.

Jack's eyes narrowed. "What are you planning?"

Richard's lips curved into a faint smile, though there was no humor in it. "I might just pay a visit to Robert Topcliffe."

The name landed like a thunderclap in the quiet room, and Jack stiffened.

"Topcliffe?" he echoed, his voice low and incredulous. "You can't be serious."

"Completely," Richard replied, his gaze sharp. "If anyone knows the full extent of what happened that night—or whose orders were carried out—it's him."

Jack leaned forward, his voice hushed but urgent. "Richard, this is Topcliffe we're talking about. The queen's hound. A man who tortures and kills without hesitation. He's not going to sit down and have a friendly conversation with you over wine."

"I'm not expecting civility," Richard said, his tone calm but resolute.

Jack ran a hand over his face, exhaling sharply. "This is madness, Richard. You're walking into the lion's den."

"It's a risk I'll have to take," Richard replied.

## CHAPTER TWENTY-EIGHT

John Somer had not wanted this. Hosting foreign dignitaries was a necessary evil in his line of work, but Hans Holdinger, Ambassador to Holland, brought with him the weight of a strained alliance. Relations between England and Holland teetered on the edge of hostility, and while Holdinger's formal introduction to the Queen had gone smoothly enough, it had been Somer's idea to invite him to his home for a more private, and hopefully productive, conversation.

Somer had been confident in his decision. His wife, Eleanor, was more than capable of managing the household in his absence for the first evening. Holdinger would be entertained, fed well, and left with the impression of an English gentleman's refined hospitality. And yet, as Somer rode up the long gravel drive to his estate after several hours of tending to pressing matters at the court, he could feel the tension in the air before he even dismounted.

The steward met him at the door, his face pale.

"My lord," he began hesitantly, wringing his hands.

"What now?" Somer barked, his patience already thin.

"It's—well—it's the ambassador, sir. There's been a misunderstanding," the steward stammered.

Somer's stomach tightened. He handed off his cloak and hat and strode into the main hall, where Eleanor stood waiting, her face a mask of composure that didn't entirely hide her exasperation.

"John," she began, her voice low, "we have a problem."

"What sort of problem?" Somer asked, his tone clipped. He could already tell from the way her lips tightened that this was no minor issue.

Eleanor gestured for him to follow her. "It's better if you see for yourself. The ambassador is taking a meal with his aid at the moment."

She led him upstairs to the set of rooms prepared for the ambassador. Holdinger's appointed chambers were among the best in the house, positioned to catch the morning sun and furnished with fine tapestries and elegant, understated decor. The door to the main room stood ajar, Somer paused outside the door, but Eleanor continued walking, leading him past the main chamber to a smaller door at the far end.

She pushed it open, and Somer stepped inside.

Somer's eyes widened in dismay.

The ante-room, which should have been an innocuous space for storage or quiet reflection, had been transformed. Against one wall stood a gleaming portable altar, its surface adorned with polished gold plate and heavy candlesticks. A small statue of the Virgin Mary, draped in rich blue and gold, dominated the center. Candles, unlit but clearly new, were arranged in meticulous symmetry, and the faint scent of incense clung to the air.

For a moment, Somer simply stared, his mind scrambling to make sense of what he was seeing. Eleanor's voice broke the silence.

"The Ambassador did not bring these, and they were not here yesterday," she said firmly, her hands clasped in front of her. "I had the rooms prepared myself. This—this is a deliberate act."

"Deliberate?" Somer repeated, his voice rising. "By whom?"

Eleanor shook her head. "I don't know. But the ambassador has seen it."

Somer swore under his breath. "And what does he make of it?"

# A Queen's Rebel

"That's the trouble," Eleanor said. "He believes it's a statement—a declaration of your own faith. He seems to think you've set this up to show him your sympathy for the Catholic Church."

Somer's face darkened. "The man knows me better than that! We've worked together for years—he knows where I stand."

"Apparently, he's reconsidering," Eleanor said dryly. "He asked me pointedly whether you've had any recent changes of heart."

Somer let out a growl of frustration and turned on his heel, marching back downstairs to find his guest. Eleanor followed, her expression calm but watchful. When he reached the door Somer pushed it open without ceremony.

Hans Holdinger was standing by the window, his hands clasped behind his back, his bearing stiff. He turned as Somer entered, his expression carefully neutral but his eyes sharp with curiosity—and something darker.

"Ambassador," Somer began, inclining his head. "I trust you've been made comfortable."

"I have," Holdinger said smoothly. "Your wife has been most gracious." He paused, then said. "Though I must admit, I was surprised by certain... decorations."

Somer clenched his jaw. "A mistake," he said flatly. "One that I intend to correct immediately."

Holdinger raised an eyebrow. "A mistake? Such a display is not assembled on a whim, John."

"It was not done with my knowledge," Somer said, his tone firm. "I assure you, I had no intention of presenting you with anything that might suggest—" He broke off, searching for the right words.

Holdinger's lips twitched in a faint smile. "Sympathy for the old ways?"

Somer's eyes narrowed. "Precisely. Whoever is responsible for this will answer for it."

"Of course," Holdinger said, though his tone suggested skepticism. "Still, one wonders how such an elaborate arrangement could appear without the master of the house being aware."

Somer ignored the jab. "You know me better than to believe I would indulge in such theatrics."

"Do I?" Holdinger's voice was mild, but the challenge was unmistakable. "The times change, John. Loyalties shift. Even old friends can surprise us."

Somer bristled, but before he could respond, Eleanor stepped forward smoothly.

"Ambassador, please understand that this matter is as shocking to us as it is to you," she said, her voice steady and measured. "We value the trust between our nations, and I assure you that trust is reflected in our household. Whatever this display is, it does not reflect my husband's beliefs or intentions."

Holdinger studied her for a moment, then inclined his head. "I will take you at your word, Lady Somer."

Somer exhaled, his anger still simmering but tempered by Eleanor's diplomacy. "If you'll excuse me, I have some matters to attend to."

Holdinger nodded, his expression inscrutable. "Of course."

Somer left the room with Eleanor, his mind racing. Someone had done this, and the implications were chilling. Whether the act was meant to sow discord between him and Holdinger or to implicate him in a Catholic conspiracy, the effect was the same: doubt had been planted.

And doubt, in the world of politics, was a weapon as deadly as any blade.

The morning sun filtered weakly through the windows, doing little to warm the air in William Cecil's chambers. The Secretary of State sat at his

# A Queen's Rebel

desk, his quill scratching faintly against parchment as he penned yet another letter to be dispatched with the day's couriers. The room smelled faintly of ink, leather, and a faint trace of the wine Cecil allowed himself when the pressures of court grew particularly heavy.

A knock at the door interrupted his thoughts, and Cecil looked up, his brow furrowing slightly. An aid announced that that Somer was demanding entrance n urgent business.

"Send him in," Cecil replied.

The door swung open, and John Somer strode in, his expression tight, his posture rigid. Cecil noted the deep lines etched across his old colleague's face, the shadow of a sleepless night beneath his eyes. Whatever had brought Somer to him was no trivial matter.

"John," Cecil began, rising from his seat, "to what do I owe—"

Somer didn't let him finish. As soon as the door closed behind him, he reached into the satchel he carried, pulled out a gold cross, and banged it down on the table with enough force to rattle the inkwell. The cross gleamed in the morning light, its polished surface catching the glint of Cecil's surprised gaze.

"That," Somer said sharply, his voice a growl, "is why I'm here."

Cecil's brow lifted, and he moved around the desk, his hand hovering briefly over the cross before withdrawing. He glanced up at Somer, then back to the artifact. "You'd best explain."

"I found this," Somer said, his tone clipped, "on a portable altar in a room adjoining the ambassador of Holland's chambers in my own house."

Cecil's eyes narrowed, the weight of the words settling over him. "A portable altar," he repeated, his voice cool and deliberate. "And this was part of it?"

"Yes," Somer spat. "Holdinger denies bringing it, and I believe him. Gold plate, candles, the Virgin

Mary surrounded by saints, a chalice with wine still clinging to the bottom. Set up as if I'd invited the Pope himself to dinner!"

Cecil folded his arms, his expression darkening. "And the ambassador? What did he say?"

"What do you think?" Somer snapped. "He thinks I did it. Thinks I'm a Catholic sympathiser with a hidden chapel in my own home. I tried to explain, but you know how these men are—they hear what they want to hear, see what they want to see."

Cecil stepped back, his gaze on the cross as if it might speak to him. "Why bring this to me?"

Somer leaned heavily on the edge of the desk, his shoulders hunched. "Because this isn't just some prank or misunderstanding. Someone put those items there deliberately. They knew the ambassador would see it. Knew what conclusions he'd draw. And they did it to discredit me."

Cecil's gaze sharpened. "Discredit you? Or warn you?"

Somer blinked, the anger in his face giving way to uncertainty. "Warn me?"

Cecil turned and moved across the room, his hands clasped behind his back. "Consider the timing. The ambassador arrives, tensions are high, and suddenly, a display like this appears in your home. It's bold, too bold for a subtle smear. Whoever did this wanted you to know they had done it. Wanted you to see their hand at work."

Somer frowned, his mind racing. "But why? What purpose does it serve?"

Cecil returned to the desk, his gaze cold and calculating. "What better way to undermine the queen's rule than to sow doubt among her officers? To suggest, even faintly, that her most trusted servants might not be as loyal as they seem?"

Somer shook his head. "You think this is about the Queen?"

"No," Cecil said firmly. "Not directly. If this were a plot against her, the target wouldn't be you. This is

# A Queen's Rebel

more insidious. This is about us, John. Her council, her advisors. They don't need to attack her if they can make us look like traitors in her eyes."

The room fell silent for a moment, the weight of Cecil's words settling between them. Finally, Somer broke the silence.

"Do you think the Queen knows?" he asked, his voice low.

Cecil considered the question carefully before answering. "Not yet. And I intend to keep it that way until we know more. Panic and uncertainty are their weapons, John. We can't let this spread."

"What do we do?" Somer asked, his voice steady now, his anger tempered by resolve.

Cecil reached out, picking up the cross and examining it closely. "Leave this with me. In the meantime, keep the ambassador calm. Assure him this was a mistake, an unfortunate misunderstanding. I too will speak with him, assure him of our investigations into this. And, John—" Cecil's gaze hardened. "Be careful. Whoever orchestrated this is watching."

Somer straightened, the fire returning to his eyes. "Let them. I won't be cowed by shadows."

Cecil allowed himself a faint smile. "Good."

The door to Cecil's chamber closed softly behind Somer, leaving the Secretary of State alone with his thoughts and the gold cross still glinting on the desk. He remained standing, one hand resting on the edge of the table, his eyes fixed on the artifact as though it might yield its secrets to his scrutiny. The faint noise of activity in his outer office carried through the thick oak door, but inside the room, all was still.

Cecil reached out and lifted the cross, its weight solid in his hand. The craftsmanship was intricate, the kind of detail that spoke of a bygone age and devout care. This wasn't the sort of trinket one stumbled upon in a marketplace or acquired from a casual collector. No, this was deliberate—chosen, placed, and staged to send a message.

He set the cross down carefully.

He could have told Somer about Nicholas Adams and Alex Gill. The parallels were glaring—each of them had been implicated with Catholic treasures, each of them found their reputations under siege. It would have comforted Somer to know he wasn't alone, that this wasn't an isolated attack targeting him specifically. But Cecil hadn't. Somer's nerves, as frayed as they might be, were not his responsibility.

The truth was simpler, and colder: Somer had allowed this to happen. His household, his responsibility, his failure. Cecil had no interest in hand-holding men who should have been more vigilant, more capable. The matter of blame, however, was secondary. What mattered now was why.

The incidents—Adams, Gill, and now Somer—were clearly connected. The pattern was too precise to be coincidence. The portable altars, the carefully selected relics, the fresh signs of use—they weren't simply planted, they were staged. Whoever was behind this was methodical, aware of what such discoveries would mean, not just to the Queen, but to the Privy Council.

Cecil's eyes narrowed as he considered the implications. This wasn't about a Catholic uprising. That much was clear. The signs were too theatrical, the trail too neatly laid. No, this wasn't an attack on the Protestant faith or Elizabeth herself. It was something far more basic—far more human. Was it personal, had it all been leading to Somer?

Why Somer? The question gnawed at him like a worm burrowing through his thoughts. Somer was gruff, opinionated, and difficult to work with, but he was loyal. Loyal to the Queen, to England, and—more importantly—to Cecil himself. If someone wanted

# A Queen's Rebel

Somer out of the way, it wasn't to weaken the Protestant cause. It was to remove him specifically. Someone wanted him discredited, stripped of his position, and cast out of court.

But who? Cecil frowned, his fingers drumming lightly on the desk. Who would benefit from Somer's disgrace? And to what end? The possibilities stretched before him like a labyrinth, each path darker and more treacherous than the last.

A flicker of unease crept into his thoughts. Would it end here? Somer was not the only man with influence and power among Elizabeth's advisors. If this was about destabilising the Privy Council, there could be others already marked, others whose households were being infiltrated even now.

Cecil turned away from the window, his jaw tightening. He couldn't wait for the next move; he needed to act. The key, he was certain, lay in understanding the connection between the targets. Adams, Gill, Somer—very different men, but someone had chosen them deliberately. There had to be a thread linking them, something he was missing.

He returned to his desk and sat down, his gaze once again falling on the cross. Its golden surface gleamed in the dim light, a cruel mockery of faith and devotion. Slowly, deliberately, Cecil reached for a fresh sheet of parchment and dipped his quill into the ink.

If this was a game, he would not be a passive player. The next move would be his.

## CHAPTER TWENTY-NINE

Myles Devereux sat at his desk, the soft rustle of a bedgown draped over his shoulders the only sound in the room apart from the scratch of his quill against parchment. He had been determined to ignore the ceaseless toll of the church bells pealing behind him, their relentless clangor a harsh counterpoint to the orderliness of his ledger. Numbers, clean and precise, were the only balm against the chaotic world outside.

The door creaked open without warning, interrupting his focus. Myles didn't look up, his annoyance sharpening as he heard the sound of a knock followed belatedly, perfunctory and meaningless.

"What is it?" Myles asked tersely, his eyes fixed on the ledger.

"A letter," Matthew replied, stepping fully into the room. In his outstretched hand, he held a folded missive bearing a wax seal.

Myles' head snapped up, his expression darkening. "I can see that," he said coldly. "Who's it from?"

"Fitzwarren," Matthew said simply. Without ceremony, he flicked his wrist, sending the letter spinning through the air. It landed squarely atop the ledger Myles had been working on, obscuring the neat columns of figures.

Myles groaned audibly, his irritation barely contained. He picked up the letter and waved it at Matthew. "Is this it? Or is there a messenger downstairs waiting for some witty reply?"

"Just the letter," Matthew replied evenly, though his lips twitched in something close to amusement.

# A Queen's Rebel

Myles discarded the letter, sending it sliding to the corner of the desk. He retrieved his quill, dipping it into the inkwell with exaggerated care. "I'll deal with it later," he muttered, more to himself than to Matthew.

Matthew stood for a moment longer, his gaze sharp and faintly reproachful. When it became clear Myles wasn't about to acknowledge the letter, Matthew shook his head and left the room, the door clicking softly shut behind him.

For a brief moment, the room returned to silence, broken only by the faint scratching of Myles' quill. But his concentration faltered almost immediately, his thoughts drifting toward the letter. The presence of it on his desk was like a whisper in the back of his mind, insistent and nagging.

Amica, his black cat, seemed to sense his distraction. She leapt gracefully onto the desk, her tail curling upward as she padded toward him. With a soft meow, she rubbed against his shoulder, her sleek body arching with elegant insistence.

"Yes, yes, in a minute," Myles murmured, setting the quill aside. He reached out, his ringed fingers trailing absently down the cat's back. "After we've read this, hmm? What do you think Fitzwarren wants now?"

Amica purred, her golden eyes narrowing in contentment as Myles retrieved the letter. He broke the seal with deliberate slowness, unfolding the parchment as though it might contain a trap. His gaze swept over the lines of text, his expression darkening with each passing second.

"The arrogant bastard," Myles muttered at length, his voice low but filled with incredulity.

He tossed the letter onto the desk with a sharp motion and scooped Amica into his arms. The cat settled against his chest, her purring a steady vibration that offered no answers to his rising irritation. Crossing the room, Myles sank into the chair near the fire, the flames casting flickering shadows across his sharp features.

He stared into the fire for a long moment, his mind considering the implications of what he had just read. Fitzwarren's proposal was as audacious as it was dangerous. The political stakes were obvious. The mere suggestion bordered on lunacy—and yet Fitzwarren had framed it as a challenge, as though daring Myles to prove his skill and cunning.

Myles scoffed, the sound sharp and bitter in the quiet room. "As if I would balk at such a task," he said aloud, though the firelight concealed the calculating gleam in his eyes.

Amica shifted in his lap, nuzzling against his hand as though sensing the shifting tide of his thoughts. Myles allowed himself a faint smile, his fingers stroking her soft fur as he considered the challenge Fitzwarren had laid before him.

Whatever Fitzwarren was planning, Myles knew one thing for certain: it would not be straightforward, and it would demand every ounce of his ingenuity. Still, a part of him relished the prospect. The stakes were high, but so too was the opportunity for power—if played correctly.

## CHAPTER THIRTY

The afternoon light waned as Jack and Richard rode through the gates of London, the city humming with the ceaseless rhythm of its people. Merchants called their wares from market stalls, and the streets were alive with the clatter of carts and the murmur of a thousand conversations.

At the crossroads near Cheapside, Jack reined in his horse. "I'll head home," he said, his voice lacking its usual bravado. "Catherine will be still in confinement, but she will expect me, and I need to know all is well with her."

Richard gave a nod. "And when you find yourself restless and ill-suited to domesticity?"

Jack smirked, though there was little mirth in it. "I'll meet you at the Angel later."

"Of course you will. I have business with Devereux first." Richard replied, his tone dry. He nudged his horse forward, leaving Jack to navigate the bustling streets toward home.

The room at the White Hart was dimly lit, a single candle sputtering on the table as shadows danced on the wooden walls. Myles reclined in a chair, his legs stretched lazily in front of him, one booted foot tapping against the floor in an uneven rhythm. His cat, ever capricious, had once again betrayed its supposed loyalty, and now curled comfortably on Fitzwarren's lap. The nobleman absentmindedly stroked the creature, his sharp eyes fixed on Myles.

Myles grinned, the expression both smug and boyish. "You'd think it would have been difficult, the lot of them being so careful. But no, my dear Fitzwarren, it was almost laughably easy."

Fitzwarren raised an eyebrow, his fingers scratching behind the cat's ears. "Do enlighten me. How does one implicate half the court in treason before Prime?"

"Adams first," Myles said, leaning forward to pour himself a glass of wine. He swirled the liquid, watching the light play off its surface. "The man's vanity is only matched by his parsimony. Underpaying servants is a risky game, as it turns out. One quiet word and a coin slipped into the right hand, and voilà—Catholic relics appear in his house as if by divine intervention."

"And Walls?" Fitzwarren prompted, his tone as casual as if they were discussing the weather.

"Ah, Walls." Myles chuckled, setting his glass down. "His was even simpler. The man prides himself on appearances, yet his belongings are guarded with all the vigilance of a drunkard at the gates. A broken lock, a case left ajar, and inside—well, let's just say the contents suddenly became less Protestant than he would like."

The cat purred loudly, as if in agreement, and Fitzwarren smirked. "Gill, then? That name was not part of my original request."

Myles' grin widened, a flicker of something darker crossing his features. "Gill was my addition. A personal touch. You see, the man had the gall to print a pamphlet last year accusing me of heresy. Nearly had me roasted alive for a crime I did not commit." His voice cooled, the grin fading. "So, implicating him? A little sweet revenge. The gathering at his print shop was all theatre, of course. A few hired men, a couple of false leads, and when Cecil's dogs arrived? Traps in the floor. The men scurried out like rats, leaving behind exactly what I wanted them to find."

Fitzwarren nodded slowly, his gaze calculating. "Effective. But Somer? That couldn't have been so straightforward."

# A Queen's Rebel

"No," Myles admitted, though the glint of pride never left his eyes. "Somer was a challenge, I'll give you that. His household is tightly run, but even the best defenses have cracks. I arranged for workmen—masons, supposedly repairing a wall. In reality, they were planting the items as instructed in the ambassador's chamber. It took longer than I'd hoped, but the results speak for themselves."

"And the last?" Fitzwarren's voice was quieter now, his strokes along the cat's back slowing. "The gift destined for Holland?"

Myles' grin faded slightly, replaced with a look of satisfaction so profound it bordered on arrogance. "Now that... that was art. A masterpiece, if I may say so. Cecil's locked room, near his own office. Infiltrating that space required patience, skill, and a touch of genius."

"Yours, no doubt," Fitzwarren said dryly, though his interest was clear.

"Indeed." Myles stood, pacing to the small window and leaning against the frame. "The coffer was locked, and the Queen's Protestant statement lay within, ready to be sent as a symbol of her unyielding stance. The lock had to be opened without a trace, the contents carefully repacked with a new centrepiece."

"And what was this centrepiece?" Fitzwarren asked, though his tone suggested he already knew the answer.

Myles turned, his face lit with a mischievous glow. "A painting. The Virgin Mary, no less, embossed with gold and studded with jewels. A thing of beauty, really. And utterly damning in its implications."

Fitzwarren let out a low whistle, shaking his head. "You've outdone yourself."

"I aim to please," Myles said with a mock bow. "By the time anyone realises, it will be too late to undo. The Queen's enemies will seize upon it like wolves on a carcass. And you now have your bargaining tool."

"And Cecil will be too preoccupied chasing shadows and tying up loose ends to see what has truly happened. By the time he gets his bearings, the game will already have changed." Fitzwarren regarded Myles for a long moment, his hand stilling on the cat's fur. "You're very pleased with yourself."

"Shouldn't I be?" Myles said, raising his glass in a mock toast. "You wanted the job done. I've delivered, and with flair, if I may say so."

Fitzwarren inclined his head slightly, the corners of his mouth curving upward. "You have, Myles. And I'll humor your theatrics for now. But be careful. Even the cleverest fox risks the hounds if he strays too close to the hunt."

Myles grinned, unbothered by the warning. "Oh, Fitzwarren, I'm no fox. I'm the hunter."

Myles swirled the wine in his goblet, watching the firelight refract through the deep crimson liquid. Finally, his gaze lifted, sharp and curious, to meet Richard's. "So," Myles drawled, his voice tinged with sardonic amusement, "your little game appears to be closing on the final act. Four men tangled in your web already. But tell me, why these particular flies?"

Richard leaned back, his eyes narrowing slightly. "Adams was the first, as planned."

Myles took a slow sip of his wine, savoring the moment before speaking. "Nicholas Adams. A man whose only crime, as far as I can tell, is existing loudly in rooms where no one wants him. Tell me, Richard, what exactly did Adams do to warrant this elaborate undoing? Placing Catholic paraphernalia in a man's home is not the work of a passing grudge."

Richard's lips curved in a faint, humorless smile. "If you must know, it began with a spilled glass of wine."

Myles raised an eyebrow, setting his glass down with deliberate care. "A spilled glass of wine? Remind me never to upset you at dinner."

# A Queen's Rebel

"Not just any wine," Richard said smoothly, leaning forward. "It was spilled over my notes. Notes that were critical to an ongoing negotiation."

"And Adams?" Myles asked.

"He dismissed it with a wave of his hand and that infuriating braying laugh of his. 'Ah, Fitzwarren,' he said, 'you're clever enough to draft it all again, aren't you? Or just get your clerk to do it for you!" Fitzwarren said, imitating Adam's loud accented voice.

"Surely this can't all be about a clumsy gesture and a poor attempt at flattery?" Myles said, his tone dripping with mock shock.

"Not entirely," Richard replied, his voice cooling. "Adams has a history of being insufferable. His speeches in Parliament are a tedious mix of pomposity and ignorance, especially when he pontificates about the unification of Scotland and England—a topic about which he knows precisely nothing."

"Ah," Myles said with mock gravity, "a man guilty of wasting breath and spilling wine. Surely enough to earn him a stay in the Tower."

Richard's smile widened slightly, though there was no warmth in it. "There's more. In his foolish ambition, Adams involved himself in bringing John Knox to England—directly against Her Majesty's orders, I might add. That particular escapade was gifted to me. You do not know what it was like to shepherd that insufferable Scotsman across hostile territory while avoiding threats from every quarter?"

Myles leaned back in his chair, clearly enjoying himself. "So, when you saw a chance to humiliate Adams..."

"I took it," Richard finished, his voice calm but firm. "With a certain amount of relish, I might add. He deserves far worse than humiliation for the trouble he's caused."

Myles shook his head, a smirk—no, a grin—playing on his lips. "Remind me never to ruin your notes, Fitzwarren. Your memory is far too long, and your methods far too effective."

Myles tilted his head, setting his glass down on the table with a deliberate clink. "All right then, Adams I understand—clumsy, insufferable, and a perpetual thorn in your side. But what of Walls? What did he do to deserve the spectacle of a ruined reputation and a possible stay in the Tower?"

Richard's expression darkened slightly, the firelight casting sharp shadows across his features. "Walls," he said slowly, as though testing the weight of the name, "is a sycophant of the highest order, a man whose loyalty bends whichever way the wind carries the promise of power. He is dangerous not because of his intellect—he has none—but because he is a willing tool for cleverer men. And some years ago, he lent himself to a scheme that could have destroyed Elizabeth before she even ascended the throne."

Myles leaned forward, his interest piqued. "Go on."

Richard's fingers drummed lightly against the table as he began. "Before Elizabeth became queen, during her sister Mary's reign, there were factions within England and abroad that sought to unseat Mary Tudor. Some of these factions, surprisingly, had little love for Elizabeth herself but saw her as a convenient figurehead. Walls was part of one such group. Their plan was as ambitious as it was foolish: abduct Elizabeth, smuggle her to Holland, and set her up as a puppet queen of England."

Myles let out a low whistle. "Bold, to say the least."

"Bold, yes. Treasonous, undoubtedly. And entirely against Elizabeth's wishes." Richard's tone hardened. "Elizabeth had no desire to be thrust into a position of rebellion against her sister. She was playing to ensure her survival while Mary's reign ran its course. But Walls and his conspirators thought they knew better. They nearly succeeded, too—Elizabeth was being closely watched, and had it not been for the vigilance of those loyal to her, she might have found herself spirited away to Holland under the guise of liberation."

"And Walls?" Myles asked, his voice low.

"Walls wasn't one of the ringleaders, but he was a willing participant," Richard said. "He provided funding and resources, helped arrange safe houses, and ensured the conspirators had access to information to aid their scheme. When the plot fell apart, Walls was never exposed. He was clever enough to keep his name off any documents and his hands seemingly clean. But I knew."

"Of course you did," Myles said, grinning. "You always do."

Richard ignored the remark, his gaze fixed on the fire. "Walls thought he'd escaped judgment. He returned to court, fawning over Elizabeth like nothing had ever happened. She saw through him, of course, but she let him stay—she thought it better to keep him close, where he could be watched. But I've never forgotten. And now, I've reminded him that past sins have a way of catching up."

Myles chuckled, shaking his head. "So, in a way, you're not just punishing Walls. You're tying up loose ends from the past."

Richard turned his gaze to Myles, a cold glint in his eye. "I'm ensuring that men like Walls understand one simple truth: loyalty isn't optional, and betrayal never goes unanswered."

The fire in the hearth crackled softly, casting flickering shadows across the room. Myles Devereux reclined in his chair, his expression curious but carefully measured. He swirled the wine in his glass, the liquid catching the firelight as he watched Richard Fitzwarren carefully.

Sam Burnell

Richard's face was unreadable, the lines of his jaw set in a way that suggested the conversation was nearing a point he'd rather avoid. Yet Myles, ever one to tread where he shouldn't, tilted his head and asked, "And Somer? Why him?"

The air in the room seemed to shift, the warmth of the fire suddenly feeling oppressive. Richard didn't respond immediately. His gaze, cold and deliberate, locked onto Myles like a hawk assessing its prey. The silence stretched, the weight of it thick enough to stifle the flickering light of the flames.

Myles's easy demeanor faltered for the first time. He leaned forward slightly, setting his glass down with a soft clink against the wood. "Richard," he pressed, his tone quieter now, "what did Somer do to earn your wrath?"

Richard's lips pressed into a thin line, his dark eyes narrowing. When he finally spoke, his voice was low, each word sharp enough to cut. "He betrayed me."

The simplicity of the statement struck like a hammer, and for a moment, even Myles didn't know how to respond. The room seemed to grow colder, the flicker of the fire doing little to temper the icy intensity in Richard's gaze.

"Betrayed you?" Myles echoed carefully. "How?"

Richard's knuckles whitened as his fingers gripped the edge of the table. He leaned forward, the shadows of the fire carving harsh angles into his face. "That," he said, his voice laced with steel, "is none of your concern."

Myles raised his hands slightly in a gesture of surrender, though his sharp eyes didn't waver from Richard's. "Fair enough. But you must admit, for someone like you—someone who plans everything to the finest detail—this betrayal must have been significant."

Richard straightened, the hard lines of his face unmoving. His silence spoke volumes, more damning than any words could be. Myles studied him, the tension in the room palpable.

"I see," Myles said after a moment, his tone deliberately light to cut through the heavy atmosphere. "Well, I can't say I blame you, then. Betrayal is a sin not easily forgiven."

Richard's gaze lingered on Myles, unflinching and unrelenting. "Not forgiven," he said softly, his voice carrying a chilling finality, "and never forgotten."

Myles nodded slowly, leaning back in his chair as though to put more distance between himself and the storm brewing behind Richard's eyes. He picked up his glass again, taking a deliberate sip before remarking, "Remind me never to cross you, Fitzwarren."

Richard didn't respond, his expression remaining as cold and impenetrable as stone. The fire continued to crackle in the hearth, but the warmth it offered seemed now a distant memory.

## CHAPTER THIRTY-ONE

Richard dismounted at the back of the Angel, handing the reins to a stable boy with a brief nod. The familiar scents of roasted meat and ale greeted him as he pushed open the door, stepping into the brightly lit interior. The fire crackled in the hearth, and the low hum of conversation filled the air. True to his word, Jack arrived not long after. He spotted Richard at a corner table, wine already in hand. Crossing the room, he dropped into the chair opposite with a weary sigh.

"Well?" Richard asked, his gaze steady.

"The house is as I left it," Jack said, waving for ale. "Quiet. Catherine is still in her rooms with her women, and I am told it will be another four weeks before the babe arrives." He leaned back, stretching his legs.

"The time will pass soon enough," Richard said, not unkindly.

The room was quiet except for the soft clatter of dice on the table and the occasional pop from the fire in the hearth. A jug of wine sat between Jack and Richard, half-empty, the ruby liquid catching the flickering light as they sipped and talked. Jack leaned back in his chair, rolling a die between his fingers while Richard studied the game board.

"You've come a long way, Jack," Richard said, moving his piece and giving his brother a sidelong glance. "When I first saw you in London, I wasn't sure you'd get out of that bed, let alone hold a sword again."

Jack chuckled, shaking his head. "I had my doubts too. But I couldn't have done it without Sebastian. That man is relentless." He tossed the die onto the table, watching it bounce and settle. "I think I called him a 'meddling monk' when he first arrived."

Richard raised an eyebrow, a faint smirk tugging at his lips. "You did. I remember it vividly."

Jack laughed, raising his cup in mock salute. "He's been a damn good teacher. His skill at arms and his knowledge of training... exceptional, really. I owe him a great deal."

Richard leaned forward, picking up the dice and shaking them idly in his hand. "It should be exceptional, given who he is."

Jack frowned, setting his wine down. "What do you mean, 'who he is'?"

Richard hesitated, his eyes locking with Jack's. He studied his brother for a moment before shaking his head and leaning in closer, lowering his voice. "Sebastian De La Pole. General of the Order of St. John, friend to the Grandmaster himself."

Jack's eyes widened in surprise. "What?" he asked, leaning forward in disbelief.

Richard tossed the dice onto the table, watching them tumble before settling back in his chair. "You've spent the summer being retrained by one of the most decorated and respected military minds in Europe. Sebastian De La Pole commanded the Order's forces until a Saracen blade nearly took his life. Since then, he's been stationed on Malta, overseeing all military training for the Knights of St. John."

Jack shook his head, the pieces slowly clicking into place. "That explains why he's so good. But why would someone like him come all the way to England to help me?"

Richard sipped his wine, his gaze steady. "Because of Emilio. Your Italian friend and his family have a long-standing bond with Sebastian. When Emilio asked for his help, Sebastian agreed—out of respect, loyalty, and perhaps a touch of duty."

Jack exhaled sharply, running a hand through his hair. "And I called him a meddling monk."

Richard laughed, a deep, genuine sound. "To his face, no less."

Jack shook his head, a grin breaking across his face. "I suppose I should feel honored—and grateful."

"You should," Richard agreed, raising his glass.

Jack raised his own glass, meeting his brother's gaze. "To Sebastian," he said, his tone more serious. "And to meddling monks."

Richard clinked his glass against Jack's, the faint chime of glass ringing in the air. "To meddling monks," he echoed, his smile lingering as they drank.

The quiet camaraderie was interrupted by the creak of the door and the sound of boots on the wooden floorboards. Jack and Richard looked up simultaneously, and Jack's face broke into a grin as two familiar figures stepped into the warm light of the room.

"Emilio!" Jack exclaimed, rising from his chair with a genuine smile. "What brings you here?"

Emilio De Nevarra, impeccably dressed, opened his arms theatrically. "I had word from Sebastian that you were back in London and in one piece. How could I resist coming to see for myself?" His eyes sparkled with mischief as he embraced Jack briefly before clapping him on the shoulder. "And look at you! Healthy, hearty, and, dare I say, almost respectable."

Jack chuckled, waving to the empty chairs at their table. "Sit. We've a jug of wine that won't finish itself."

Alphonso, a dark expression on his face, seated himself next to Emilio who settled in with a flourish, his movements fluid and self-assured. He glanced at the half-finished game on the table, raising an eyebrow.

"Dice? Truly, Jack, I expected more refinement," Emilio teased, reaching for the jug of wine and pouring himself a generous glass.

"You're losing," Richard interjected dryly, rolling his dice with practiced ease.

"Details," Jack retorted with a wave of his hand.

# A Queen's Rebel

Emilio leaned forward, his expression softening as he studied Jack. "Truly, Jack, it's good to see you."

The warm glow of the taproom belied the tension weaving its way through the thick haze of ale and smoke from the hearth. Men crowded around tables, their laughter rising and falling in waves as glasses clinked and dice clattered across wood. Amid the chaos, Alphonso sat stiffly, his dark eyes darting toward Emilio, who strummed a lute he had purloined with careless ease, the melody weaving through the noise.

Richard, perched casually on a bench close to Alphonso, tilted his head, his lips curving into a knowing smile. "You've let your master stray," he said quietly, the words heavy with insinuation.

Alphonso's languid gaze turned toward Richard, his expression unreadable at first. After a pause, his eyes narrowed, and he finally replied, "He is not my master."

"True," Richard conceded with a slight nod. "But he is your prince."

The remark struck a nerve. Alphonso's face darkened, his tightly held composure slipping for just a moment. "So why does he embroil himself with peasants?"

"We all have our weaknesses," Richard replied smoothly.

Alphonso's arm shot out in a dramatic gesture toward Emilio, who was now deep in conversation with Jack. "This is no weakness. Why would he debase himself? It is a humiliation."

Richard's smile sharpened as he leaned in closer, lowering his voice. "A distraction, perhaps."

"A distraction," Alphonso repeated, folding his arms and sinking back into his chair.

"Indeed," Richard said with a shrug. "Like hawking."

"To hunt with a hawk is a noble pastime, but this..." Alphonso leaned forward, gesturing toward Emilio with disdain. "This is no noble hunt."

"I'm not sure the hare would agree with you," Richard remarked, his tone dry as parchment.

Alphonso scowled, his lips curling in anger. "A curse on your opinions!"

Richard tilted his head, studying him with an expression that was too calm to be innocent. "Perhaps it's not the distraction that troubles you so much, Alphonso," he said slowly. "Perhaps it's that your prince has slipped his leash and strayed."

Alphonso's sharp intake of breath was the only sign the remark had landed. He straightened in his chair, his face carefully neutral, though the flush rising to his cheeks betrayed him. Richard leaned back, his point made, and let the conversation drift into silence as the tavern crowd pressed Jack for another song and Emilio returned, taking a seat opposite Alphonso once again.

"Go on, Jack!" a voice called from across the room.

Jack ignored the cheers, a glass in one hand and a jug in the other as he made his way toward his brother's table.

"Are you going to disappoint them?" Richard asked as Jack neared the table.

Jack put the jug down with a loud thud. "I'm not in the mood."

"That's never happened before!" Richard teased. Leaning to his right, he called loudly across the room toward the lute player who had reclaimed his instrument from Emilio. *"The Blacksmith's mare?"*

A cheer erupted from the men in the tavern as they recognised the name of the popular song. Grinning, Richard shoved Jack's stool under the table, leaving him no place to sit.

Jack, shaking his head, poured himself a drink from the jug, downed it in one go, and scowled at his brother before returning to the middle of the room. He spoke briefly to the lute player, who nodded.

"Come on, Jack!" someone shouted.

Another voice joined in, "We're waiting!"

"Stop clacking like fishwives, then," Jack retorted, clearing his throat as the room fell into a hushed anticipation.

He began his tale with a slow, unaccompanied rhythm, recounting the story of a blacksmith who repeatedly wagered on the wrong horse until, one fateful day, a vision of a mare with a white blaze like a crescent moon promised him a turn in his luck.

Alphonso muttered loudly in Italian, "Peasant music."

"Silencio!" Emilio's sharp command cut across the table. He turned his focus back to Jack, whose voice carried clearly over the room.

The unaccompanied section of the ballad continued. The blacksmith placed all his money on the mare and watched breathlessly as the race began. Just as the song built to the race's start, the lute issued a slightly out-of-tune flurry of notes. Jack paused, turning to find the lute player had been relieved of his instrument. Emilio now perched on the table behind him, tightening a string.

"I have the measure of it. Continue," Emilio commanded, plucking the string to test the note.

"Not with you making that ghastly noise!" Jack complained.

Another flurry of notes followed, punctuated by a pause. Then Emilio strummed the lute with confidence and said, "Continue."

Shaking his head, Jack relented. "Try to keep up!"

The song resumed, the mare stumbling at the race's start but slowly finding her stride. Emilio's lute followed, its notes tentative at first, mirroring the mare's early steps. As the ballad quickened, so did the pace of the music. The crowd began to bang their ale cups on the tables, providing a steady percussion.

Jack's voice grew stronger, and Emilio's lute matched him note for note. The mare overtook one horse, then another, until she reached the middle of the pack. The tempo quickened further, Emilio's fingers a blur on the strings, drawing cheers and shouts of "Faster! Faster!"

The tavern was alive with energy, the rhythm of the song and the pounding cups creating an intoxicating pulse. Jack clapped in time, laughing as Emilio ended his solo with a flourish, gesturing for Jack to finish the ballad. The room roared with approval, the shared revelry briefly dissolving the tensions simmering beneath the surface.

Over the next hour, the revelry in the taproom grew louder, the shadows deeper, and the air heavier with the scent of spilled wine and sweat. Alphonso moved with calculated ease, slipping between groups of drunken men, his steps unremarkable. Each shift brought him closer to Jack, who was seated at a table near the hearth, his head thrown back in laughter as he played a hand of cards.

Alphonso lingered just behind Jack, his movements deft and precise. A hand disappeared briefly into his doublet, a moment later, Alphonso drifted away, returning to his seat beside Emilio.

At Jack's table, Richard observed everything through the haze of drink and smoke, his posture slouched and his eyes half-lidded. As soon as Alphonso had turned his back, he met Emilio's eyes where he was already rising from his seat to cross the room, and raising his hand, bid him stay. Then with exaggerated clumsiness, he pushed himself up from his bench, staggering slightly as he approached Jack's table.

# A Queen's Rebel

Alphonso arrived back and retook his seat next to Emilio, smiling and feigning ease, his expression carefully schooled. Emilio, however, wasn't fooled. The prince's face was pale with fury, his sharp gaze fixed on Alphonso as though he could burn him to ash with his glare alone. Alphonso avoided his eyes, lifting his own glass to his lips as though nothing had happened.

"Jack!" Richard bellowed, dropping onto the bench beside him with a loud thud. His hand clapped Jack on the shoulder, jostling him mid-laugh. "Winning again, are we? You'll leave these poor bastards without even a groat by the end of the night!"

Jack laughed, shaking his head. "Not this time, I fear. The cards are cursed against me tonight."

Richard reached for the jug of wine, his movements deliberate beneath the veneer of drunken carelessness. As his hand brushed against Jack's glass, he tipped it over with a sweep of his arm, sending the glass and the poisoned wine cascading onto the floor.

"Jack, I'm sorry!" Richard exclaimed, laughing uproariously. "I must be drunker than I thought."

Jack waved him off with a grin. "No harm done."

Richard reached for the jug again, pouring a fresh glass with an exaggerated flourish. "Here, let me make it up to you. A fresh drink for the victor!"

Jack took the new cup with a laugh, lifting it in a mock toast. "You're too kind, Richard."

Across the room, Alphonso's face twisted into a scowl, his jaw tightening as he glared at Richard. Emilio's reaction was more restrained but far more dangerous. His dark eyes burned with fury as he watched Alphonso, his lips pressed into a thin line. He leaned forward slightly, his hands gripping the edge of the table as though holding himself back.

Richard settled back into his seat, his expression as jovial as ever, but his sharp eyes flicked briefly toward Alphonso. Their gazes locked for a fraction of a second, enough to send a clear, unspoken message: *I know.*

As Jack continued to laugh and play, oblivious to the danger he had narrowly escaped, Richard lifted his own glass, his smile never faltering. But inside, he was already calculating his next move. The game had changed, and Alphonso had just made a fatal mistake.

A Queen's Rebel

## CHAPTER THIRTY-TWO

The atmosphere in the taproom thickened as the tension between Emilio and Alphonso became palpable. Emilio, usually so composed, growled low in his throat, his sharp tone cutting across the noise. "Stop where you are," he commanded Alphonso, his voice like the crack of a whip.

Alphonso froze, his scowl deepening as he glared at him. Emilio didn't wait for a response. With a deliberate stride, he crossed the room toward Richard, who was leaning back against the bench, his expression deceptively calm. Emilio leaned in close, his breath warm against Richard's ear, and spoke low enough that only Richard could hear.

"I am leaving," Emilio said tersely, "and I will take Alphonso with me."

Richard turned his head slightly, catching the fury simmering in Emilio's eyes. He understood immediately. Emilio intended to deal with Alphonso in private, and the weight of what that meant settled heavily in Richard's chest. Emilio straightened, spun on his heel, and gestured sharply for Alphonso to follow him. Alphonso hesitated for a fraction of a second, casting a venomous glance at Richard and Jack before falling into step behind Emilio.

Richard waited, his fingers drumming lightly against the table as he watched the two Italians disappear through the heavy door that led to the corridor. Then he turned to Jack, his expression darkening.

"We're leaving," he said, his voice low but urgent and very sober,

Jack frowned, startled. "What? Why? What's going on?"

"No time to explain," Richard snapped, already pulling Jack to his feet. "Just trust me."

Jack hesitated for only a moment before nodding. The tone in Richard's voice left no room for argument. They hurried through the room, weaving through the drunken crowd, and slipped into the dim corridor. The air was cooler here, the light from the few flickering wall sconces barely reaching the shadows that stretched across the stone walls.

Richard moved quickly, his steps purposeful as he led Jack down the corridor. The sound of their boots against the flagstones was muffled by the faint hum of the revelry behind them. It wasn't long before Richard stopped abruptly in front of a closed door to the left. He held up a hand, motioning for silence.

From behind the door came the muffled sound of raised voices. Richard pressed his ear against the wood, straining to make out the words. Emilio's voice was sharp and commanding, while Alphonso's tone was lower, defensive and laced with anger.

Richard glanced back at Jack, his expression grim. Without a word, he pushed the door open, the hinges creaking loudly in the quiet corridor.

The room they entered was stark and dimly lit by a few sputtering candles. The air smelled faintly of smoke and damp stone. At the center of the space stood Emilio and Alphonso, their faces flushed with anger as they faced each other. Emilio's hand was clenched into a fist at his side, his body taut with restrained fury.

"You think I didn't see what you did?" Emilio was saying, his voice low and dangerous. "Do you take me for a fool, Alphonso?"

Alphonso's jaw tightened, his eyes flashing with defiance. "I did what was necessary."

"Necessary?" Emilio's voice rose, echoing in the empty room.

Alphonso opened his mouth to reply, but the sudden intrusion of Richard and Jack stopped him.

# A Queen's Rebel

Both men turned toward the door, their expressions a mixture of shock and fury.

"What is this?" Emilio demanded, his voice sharp as a blade. "Why are you here?"

Richard stepped forward, his gaze sweeping over both men. "Perhaps to stop something far more regrettable than what's already been done," he said coolly.

Jack's hand rested on the hilt of his poniard, his eyes narrowing as he studied Alphonso. "What exactly is going on here?"

Emilio didn't answer immediately, his chest rising and falling with barely contained anger. Finally, he turned back to Alphonso, his voice a harsh whisper. "You've shamed me enough for one night. Speak, if you dare, and explain yourself."

Alphonso's lips parted, but no words came. The weight of everyone's gaze on him seemed to crush whatever defiance he had left. His hands balled into fists, but his shoulders sagged slightly, a hint of defeat creeping into his posture.

Richard's voice cut through the tense silence. "We know what you did, Alphonso. The question is whether Emilio will deal with it... or whether Jack and I should." His tone was deceptively calm, but his eyes burned with cold fire.

The room fell into a charged silence, the flickering candlelight casting long, restless shadows on the walls. The confrontation had reached its peak, and the next move would determine whether blood would be spilled—or secrets would be buried.

Relaxed and arrogant, Alphonso sauntered towards Emilio, closing the gap between them, the smile on his face warm, his eyes fixed on the other man. His body moved with eloquence beneath the fine silks of his clothing, his composure complete.

"I am sorry," Alphonso said, his voice told of a tender and genuine sadness.

Emilio, transfixed for a moment, didn't move.

"It is a pain so hard to bare, my heart, it breaks for you," Alphonso said, he had crossed the room now and stopped only a few steps from Emilio. His eyes, filled with pain, laid on Emilio. "You have been misled, my prince."

"Have I?" Emilio's voice was barely above a whisper, his assessing gaze upon the other man. So close now that he could see the paste smeared to fill the creases that told of a youth now lost and the slight darkening of the Chol, making Alphonso's eyes stand out. Emilio's eyes dropped to his own hands for a moment, running along the scars, some he could remember gaining, most he could not. White traces criss-crossing his hands telling him of his life as a Knight of the Order, of skills hard won, of battles lost, of victories and of pain.

Alphonso's outstretched hand was before him, it hovered in mid-air, bridging the gap between them. The fingers curled invitingly, extended towards him, willing him to place his hand into the offered grasp.

He took the hand, gently and pulled Alphonso closer. His eyes on the pale palm, the perfect nails and the bands of gold that encircled the fingers. Emilio turned it over, the knuckles looked as if they had been hewn from marble such was their perfection, the back of his hand was so unlike his own. Smooth and pale, not raised with sinew and tendon and scarred with healed cuts.

Alphonso slid his fingers between Emilio's slowly and the Knight let him. Emilio closed his eyes and let Alphonso draw him forward half a step.

Jack hauled against the hold Richard had on him.

"Be still, damn you," Richard hissed in his brother's ear, putting every fibre of his strength into staying Jack's advance across the room.

Jack, straining against the hold, wavered as he watched the two men in the centre of the hall.

"Wait," Richard growled in his ear.

# A Queen's Rebel

The word was at the same time a command and a plea. Jack stopped from trying to wrench himself free, suddenly uncertain.

"We are always one," Alphonso spoke the words quietly as he stepped towards Emilio, his face upturned, his eyes fastened upon the knight.

Emilio, his eyes upon Alphonso's face found himself suddenly repelled by the mask before him. The only scars the other man bore were those inflicted by time, and he would not even wear those with pride, they were concealed beneath a cake of paste. Emilio knew his own face was one scarred not only by time, like his hands it bore the tell-tale scars of war. War and so much more.

Closing his eyes for a moment he remembered another injury, the pain of a knife as it sliced through the leather straps of his cuirass. It had continued onward to cut into the skin leaving him with a long thin scar across his ribs. A scar that had saved his life. Without that selfless act he would have been at the bottom of the harbour in Valetta.

"You have always been my true love, come with me," Alphonso said.

The words broke through Emilio's thoughts, souring in his mouth, and the hold he had on the other man's hand tightened involuntarily. Alphonso reading it as an affirmation smiled and pulled Emilio closer.

Emilio, solid, unmoving, met the other man's gaze, when he spoke his voice was calm and devoid of emotion. "Then why do you trade England's secrets against me?"

Alphonso looked puzzled for a moment only. "It was for Gregor."

"Gregor," Emilio echoed the word. There was a moments hesitation then he said. "For what we were, and what we could have been, I would never see you suffer."

Alphonso smiled, his body relaxing and he allowed himself to be drawn a little closer to his deadly companion.

"No!" Jack gasped and Richard tightened his grip on his brother.

If Jack's exclamation may have served as a warning, it came too late.

Alphonso never heard it. Emilio stepped back, said something that the other two men didn't hear, Alphonso's smile broadened as the knife cut through the air, the sharp blade severing his throat. Still smiling, his step faltered, Emilio caught him as he fell, his blood soaking through his clothes as he slowly knelt, bearing the weight of Alphonso as the life left his body.

Emilio held Alphonso close, his eyes staring over the other man's as the life emptied onto the floor around him.

"For the love of God, wait," Richard whispered fighting to hold Jack back.

The sickening noise began as the Italian's body tried to take in gasping breaths through the knife wound, the blood gargling in his throat, a deep wretched cough, feral and desperate wracked his body, and all the time Alphonso preserved the smile upon his face, it remained, as if he had forgotten it was no longer of any use, his alarm was in his eyes, fixed unwaveringly on Emilio's, wide, and terror stricken.

When eventually it was done the silence was infinite. The only movement the dust motes trapped for an eternity in the candle light.

Emilio released his burden and lay him on the floor. The smile still present above another that was a gaping, deep cut across the perfect neck. The eyes, lifeless, still holding the terror of his last few moments were fastened now on the roof beams, a shaft of light, orange and bright cut, like another knife wound across his throat. Emilio laid his hand above where the stilled heart was, and kneeling, bent

# A Queen's Rebel

his head. His words quiet. When he'd finished he rose smoothly from the floor, the knife was still in his right hand and he was covered in blood, it had plumed over his right cheek, soaked his doublet and hose, and ran, sticky and wet over the black leather of his boots.

Richard released his brother, and added a hard push sending him stumbling forwards towards Emilio.

Jack with a certainty he had never known before and a sense of purpose that filled him strode towards Emilio. Emilio, silently watched him, releasing his grip on the hilt of the knife, he let it fall, the point splintering the wood as it landed. Jack's fingers unclipped his own cloak from his shoulder and wordlessly lay it over the fallen man. Emilio watched him remove Alphonso from view but said nothing, he stood still, just as he had risen.

When he was done Jack turned to Emilio, there was no request, no invitation, he simply stepped towards him and wrapped his arms around the other man holding him close. Emilio's arms hung limp at his sides for only a moment before he returned the embrace, his head falling forwards, downturned against Jack's chest.

Behind him, Jack heard the quiet closing of the door and knew his brother had left them.

Richard, his back against the closed door, his eyes closed listened. It took longer than he imagined it would, and despite what had happened he couldn't stop a rising impatience begin to seize him. Opposite him in the corridor, Froggy Tate, arms folded across his chest waited as well.

At last Richard heard the sound of the door closing on the opposite side of the room. Pushing himself away from the wood Richard pointed towards Froggy. "Raise the alarm."

"Are you sure?" Froggy hesitated.

Richard didn't reply, the look on his face was answer enough and Froggy marched off down the corridor.

Opening the door Richard stepped into the death chamber. It was empty of life. Alphonso lay, covered now with Jack's cloak still in the middle of the room.

Sighing. Richard stepped quickly across the room and leaning down flipped the cloak away from the body before descending to his knees next to the corpse.

"I've heard that the soul tarries for a time after death. I can't say I believe it, but on this occasion I do wish it to be so," Richard retrieved the fallen knife, before continuing. "What did you underestimate, I wonder? Was it the depth of Emilio's feelings for you? Were you just so foolish as to believe in your power over him? Or did you underestimate his loyalty to my brother? In either case, what is damned annoying, is that I shall now never know."

Richard dipped a hand in the pond of blood that was beginning to seep away through the gaps in the planking, and daubed it on his doublet, adding some to his face for good measure. "However we can, I think conclude, that in those final moments you at least had time to consider the error. Or even at the last were you too vain to face the truth?"

The door burst open, the scene before them stopping the guards in their tracks for a moment. Richard heard their boot steps faltering on the boards. Haste, after all wasn't needed, he wasn't going to make a bid to escape, or resist, and they could instead savour those first moments of discovery. The brutal scene was theirs alone to enjoy.

## CHAPTER THIRTY-THREE

The blood had dried into stiff patches on Richard's clothes, its dark stains marring the fabric like shadowed warnings. He reclined on the narrow bed, his shirt partially untied. His gaze was fixed on the low, cracked ceiling, his expression unreadable. The clink of keys preceded the groan of the cell door, and Cecil stepped inside, his posture sharp with authority and satisfaction.

"Her Majesty is furious," Cecil announced, his voice smooth and deliberate, the words carrying a sharp edge of triumph. The heavy door slammed shut behind him, sealing them into the damp chamber.

Richard didn't rise. His head turned slightly on the thin pillow, his lips quirking into the faintest of smirks. "Furious, you say? What's piqued her wrath—the crime, the outcome, or the method? Or dare I hope it's all three?"

Cecil chuckled softly, the sound devoid of warmth. "You've overplayed your hand, Fitzwarren. Killing one of the Italian Ambassador's entourage cannot be overlooked. It was clumsy, reckless—a price will be demanded. To strike at him was to strike at Italy itself."

Richard let out a low, humorless laugh. "And yet here you stand, basking in what you think is my downfall. Spare me the sanctimonious lecture, Cecil. We both know you're reveling in this."

Cecil allowed himself a thin smile, stepping closer, his boots echoing against the cold stone floor. "I'll admit," he said, his voice cool, "that the irony is... satisfying. That the instrument of your undoing would be yourself is a twist even I didn't foresee. Congratulations, Richard—you've made my work easier than I ever anticipated. You have presented me with a rare gift."

Richard's eyes, sharp and unyielding, shifted to meet Cecil's. "Not all gifts are what they seem. Your appreciation is noted, though I confess I could live without it.."

Cecil's smile widened, a flicker of genuine amusement flashing across his face. "Not for much longer, I fear." He reached into the leather folder tucked under his arm and pulled out a single sheet of parchment. "I thought you might like to see this."

He laid the paper on the rough-hewn table between them and slid it across with deliberate precision. Richard rose smoothly from the bed, his eyes flicked down to the document, and his lips curved into a faint smile as he lifted it.

"A Bill of Attainder," Richard murmured, his tone dry. "Legislative execution without the tedium of a trial. A masterstroke, Cecil. Efficient and bloodless, at least on your part."

He scanned the text, his finger tracing the carefully penned lines. "Ah, here it is. 'The inheritable quality of the traitor's blood is to be extinguished and blotted out forever.' Such poetry."

"Enough," Cecil snapped, extending his hand to reclaim the document.

But Richard held it aloft, his grip firm. "Patience, Master Secretary. I'm savoring your work. You've gone to such lengths, after all. But tell me, why bother coming here? The ink will hardly dry before Her Majesty affixes her name to this. So, what brings you to the Beauchamp Tower tonight?"

Cecil's smile returned, colder this time. "I wanted to see you humbled, of course. And," he added, leaning forward slightly, "to offer you a chance."

Richard raised an eyebrow, the amusement in his expression flickering into curiosity. "A chance? How benevolent of you."

# A Queen's Rebel

"I could commute your sentence," Cecil said, his voice even, measured. "A simple hanging instead of the full spectacle of a traitor's death. No dragging through the streets, no quartering, no heads mounted on Spikes. Just a quick drop and an end to your misery."

Richard feigned shock, his hand resting theatrically over his chest. "Not the block? I'm wounded by your lack of ceremony."

Cecil's jaw tightened. "The block is too grand an occasion for the likes of you. A noose will suffice."

Richard's gaze sharpened, his amusement fading into something darker. "And what do you want in exchange for this... favour?"

Cecil leaned back slightly, allowing himself the pleasure of control. "Tell me why you killed the Italian. The truth, Richard. No games, no evasions. Give me the reason, and I'll see to it that the end is merciful."

Richard's eyes narrowed, his lips curling into a thoughtful smile. He appeared to weigh the offer, his fingers drumming lightly against the edge of the table. The silence stretched, heavy with tension, as Cecil watched him like a hawk, certain he had finally cornered his prey.

"Well?" Cecil prompted, his tone clipped. "Time is of the essence. Her Majesty's fury remains unchecked, and a murder at court—your murder—would be a fine way to placate it."

Richard leaned back in his chair, exhaling slowly. For the first time, his confident façade seemed to falter, a flicker of something unreadable crossing his face. "I'll need time to consider your offer."

Cecil's eyes gleamed with satisfaction, convinced he had finally glimpsed the cracks in Richard's armor. He nodded, the victory sweet on his tongue. "Consider quickly, Fitzwarren. Your time is running out."

Sam Burnell

Cecil rose and turned on his heel, his cloak sweeping behind him as he strode to the door. The guards opened it without a word, and Cecil paused just long enough to glance back at Richard.

"You've always played a dangerous game," he said, his voice low. "But even you must know when the odds are no longer in your favor."

The door slammed shut, the sound echoing through the chamber. Richard stood motionless for a long moment, his face inscrutable as he stared at the closed door. Then, slowly, his lips curled into a faint, sardonic smile.

"Perhaps the odds have never been better," he murmured to himself, his voice barely above a whisper.

Cecil sat alone in his office, the flickering light of a single candle casting shadows that danced across the walls. The Bill of Attainder lay on the desk before him, a symbol of his triumph over Fitzwarren. The edges of his lips curled faintly as he leaned back in his chair, fingers steepled in thought. That Fitzwarren had brought about his own downfall with such reckless abandon was almost... disappointing. He had expected more cunning, more resistance. It seemed an anticlimactic end for a man as calculated as Richard Fitzwarren.

And yet, a phrase lingered in his mind, unbidden but insistent. *"Not all gifts are what they seem."* Fitzwarren's voice echoed in Cecil's memory, the faintest trace of mockery behind the words. At the time, Cecil had dismissed it as one final act of bravado, Fitzwarren's attempt to retain some semblance of control over his narrative. But now, the phrase wormed its way deeper, stirring an unease that clawed at his composure.

A gift.

His mind stumbled over the words. Not the metaphorical one Fitzwarren had mentioned—his demise—but something else. Something tangible. A cold feeling crawled over Cecil's skin, prickling at the back of his neck. His mind pivoted sharply to the diplomatic gift meant for Spain. It was already packed, ready to be shipped.

He bolted upright, his chair scraping loudly against the floor. The gift—carefully chosen to underscore Elizabeth's Protestant rule—was meant to serve as a message of unity and strength. Fitzwarren had been nowhere near it. Or had he? Cecil's thoughts churned with mounting dread as he replayed recent events, piecing together the implications.

Without a moment's hesitation, he grabbed his cloak and swept from the office, shouting for his guards.

The warehouse was dimly lit by oil lamps, their flickering light casting long shadows across crates and barrels stacked haphazardly. The scent of sawdust and sea brine hung in the air as Cecil strode through the space, his presence cutting through the stillness like a blade. The guards he'd brought flanked him silently, their expressions uneasy as they followed his hurried pace.

"Here," Cecil barked, gesturing to the largest crate in the center. His tone brooked no argument. "Unpack it. Now."

The workers hesitated, their hands fumbling at the edges of the wooden crate. Cecil's icy glare spurred them into action, and soon the sound of crowbars prying nails loose filled the room. The lid came off with a groan, revealing layers of straw and protective cloth.

"Quickly," Cecil snapped, leaning forward as the workers removed the padding piece by piece.

At last, the contents were revealed: the ornate gift intended to underline Elizabeth's power and independence from Rome. At first glance, it appeared untouched—elaborate, gilded, and pristine. But

Cecil's eyes, sharpened by years of scrutiny, caught the faintest glimmer of something hidden at its core.

"Move aside," he ordered, pushing the workers out of his way. His hands trembled slightly as he reached into the crate and pulled away the final layer of cloth.

There it was.

The painting, unmistakably Catholic in its design, its depiction of the Virgin Mary embossed with gold and encrusted with jewels. A cold knot twisted in Cecil's stomach. The gift, meant to proclaim Protestant strength, had been subverted into a weapon of humiliation. To send this would be to invite scandal and questions about Elizabeth.

"Fitzwarren," Cecil hissed, the name escaping his lips like a curse.

He stood there for a moment, the implications crashing over him like a wave. This wasn't just Fitzwarren's doing—this was the culmination of everything: Adams, Walls, Gill, Somer. It had all been Fitzwarren. The tangled web Cecil had thought he controlled had been spun around him by a man he had underestimated.

"What else?" he murmured, his voice tight with fury. "What else has he done?"

The thought sent a fresh surge of rage through him, and he turned sharply on his heel. "Seal this," he barked at the workers. "Not a word to anyone. You, guard this crate. No one touches it without my explicit permission."

Without waiting for acknowledgment, Cecil stormed out, his cloak snapping behind him as he moved with purpose. The journey back to the Tower was a blur, his thoughts churning with questions and bitter realisation that Fitzwarren had left traps that Cecil hadn't even begun to uncover.

# A Queen's Rebel

## CHAPTER THIRTY-FOUR

The Beauchamp Tower loomed dark and foreboding as Cecil approached, his footsteps echoing on the stone floors. The guards opened the cell door without question, and he stepped inside, the candle light casting harsh shadows on Fitzwarren's face.

Richard was seated at the small table, his hands resting lightly on its surface. He didn't rise, didn't flinch at Cecil's arrival. Instead, he offered a faint smile, his expression one of infuriating calm.

"Well, that was quick," Richard remarked, leaning back slightly. "Back so soon, Cecil? Did you forget something?"

Cecil slammed his hands onto the table, leaning in close. "The gift," he snarled, his voice low and venomous. "The painting. You think this game of yours will go unnoticed? You think you can embarrass the Queen and walk away unscathed?"

Richard's smile widened, though his eyes remained cold. "Embarrass? No, no, Master Cecil. It's not embarrassment I'm after. It's enlightenment. You're a clever man—you must see it now."

"Damn you," Cecil spat, his composure cracking. "How many more traps have you set? How many threads am I yet to untangle?"

Richard tilted his head, his gaze sharpening like a hawk's. "Now that," he said softly, "is the right question. But I'm afraid the answer will cost you."

Cecil's fists clenched, his knuckles white. "You think this will save you? That this—this chaos you've wrought—will spare your life?"

Richard leaned forward, his voice dropping to a whisper. "No, Cecil. I don't think it. I know it. Because you can't afford to kill me. I've shown you what I can do, call it an amusement on my part, each step a little

# A Queen's Rebel

higher up the political ladder. Adams, Walls, Somer, By the way has Somer managed to extricate himself from that mess he found himself in?"

"Your vengeance will cost you," Cecil growled.

Richard's smile faded, replaced with a hard, unyielding expression. "No, it will cost you. Something you should have anticipated before you tried to have the Santa Maria sunk or a warrant signed for my execution. Now you'll have to go to the Queen, crawl on your knees, and tell her you were wrong. Tell her that Richard Fitzwarren is loyal, serving her Majesty's best interests, and that you, Cecil, made a grievous mistake when you foolishly sent me to investigate Amy Robsart's death. That, Cecil, will be your penance."

The blood drained from Cecil's face, his lips pressing into a thin line.

"And let us not forget there is something else. The truth about Topcliffe and Amy Robsart is just a breath away from the wrong ears. That was a mistake, Cecil—a fatal one. And now, we're all trapped by the rash actions of a woman scorned."

"That was not my doing," Cecil said.

"I wouldn't have thought it was, it was rash, foolish and badly thought out. Not your style at all. It must have baulked you that it happened, that orders left this court that had not first whispered their way past your ears," Richard said shaking his head. "Of course if it ever needed to be accounted for those orders could never have come from the queen, that I have no doubt, would land on your head."

Richard picked up his doublet from the back of a chair, his expression one of distaste as he discarded the bloodstained garment.

"And the Italian you murdered," Cecil said, his voice icy. "That act cannot be overlooked."

"Oh it can, and you will help. He was a subversive, sent here by Rome to destabilize the Queen's government. He nearly succeeded, but I stopped him. Piece it together yourself! Or must I provide you with every answer?" Richard said coldly. "Welcome to the web, Master Secretary. Shall we see how long you can survive it?

## CHAPTER THIRTY-FIVE

Richard stood at the threshold of the Queen's chambers, the weight of knowledge pressing down on him. Elizabeth sat at her desk, the picture of regal control, though her features betrayed a tautness she rarely allowed others to see. The flickering candlelight accentuated the hollows of her cheeks and the sharpness of her profile, casting shadows that deepened the unspoken divide between them.

She did not acknowledge him immediately, letting the silence grow oppressive, as though daring him to break it. When her gaze finally lifted to meet his, her dark eyes pierced him, their intensity a challenge few would dare to face.

"You know why you are here," Elizabeth said, her tone clipped, almost detached. Yet beneath the veneer, Richard detected the bite of steel, the hint of accusation.

Richard bowed deeply, though it felt like a hollow gesture. "Your Majesty summoned me."

"Cecil," she began, her voice softening ever so slightly at the name, though it held no warmth, "argued on your behalf. He is loyal, perhaps to a fault. He claims you still have value to the crown. Do you?"

Straightening, Richard met her gaze, knowing the peril in doing so. "If Lord Cecil believes so, Your Majesty, I will strive to justify his faith."

Her lips curved into a semblance of a smile, though it was devoid of kindness. "So dutiful. Always so... loyal." She rose with deliberate grace, the folds of her gown whispering against the floor. Though she was slight, her presence filled the chamber, her movements slow and deliberate as she approached him.

"I had the warrant before me," she said, her words cutting through the stillness like a drawn blade. "My quill poised. And I almost signed it. I thought of your questions, your insistence on truths that should remain buried."

"With respect, your Majesty, they were questions I was sent to ask, it was not a task of my choosing," Richard said, although he knew well that the reminder was wasted.

Her eyes locked with his. "I could still sign it."

Richard held himself perfectly still, his features unreadable. "I thank your Majesty for staying her hand."

"It was Cecil's arguments that saved you. He believes you can still serve me. I, however, remain unconvinced," Elizabeth replied cooly. She stopped a breath away from him, her voice dropping to a near-whisper. "Tell me, Richard, did your investigation lead you to a suspect?"

The question hung in the air, a trap set with perfect precision. He knew the truth she spoke of, a truth that burned in his chest like a wound. Amy Robsart had not fallen to her death. She had been murdered—Topcliffe's bloody work, carried out at the Queen's behest. The knowledge clawed at him, its implications as unbearable as they were damning.

Why had she done it? The reasoning seemed both cruel and maddeningly shortsighted. If Elizabeth had sought to free Leicester to wed him, the act had killed that possibility. Amy's death had cast a shadow over Leicester's name, tying him irrevocably to scandal and suspicion. It had rendered any possibility of marriage unthinkable. Had it been impulsive? A fit of jealous rage? Or worse, calculated cruelty—a reminder to her court, to her lover, of the lengths to which she would go to assert her will? The uncertainty gnawed at Richard's faith in her.

"It was an accident, Your Majesty," he said at last, his voice steady despite the tumult within. "A tragic fall. Nothing more."

# A Queen's Rebel

Elizabeth tilted her head, her sharp gaze narrowing as she studied him. "An accident," she repeated, her tone dangerously flat. "Is that what you would have me believe?"

"It is the conclusion my investigation reached," he replied evenly, his expression carefully neutral.

Her lips pressed into a thin line, and she stepped back, her gaze unwavering. "You are thorough, Richard. Perhaps too thorough for your own good. I know you have found the truth, whatever it may be. And yet you speak of an accident. Do you take me for a fool?"

"Never, Your Majesty," he replied swiftly. "I take you for a queen."

Her expression remained inscrutable, though something flickered in her eyes—anger, amusement, or perhaps both. "Very well," she said finally, her voice colder than the stone beneath their feet. "If that is the conclusion you present, I will accept it. For now. But let us not pretend that you and I do not both know the truth."

The dismissal came unspoken but unmistakable. Richard bowed deeply, retreating with measured steps. The air in the corridor outside felt lighter, but the weight in his chest did not lift. He walked away knowing that the woman he had once revered, even admired, was capable of decisions that were not only reckless but dangerously unmoored from reason. Foolish or cruel—he could not decide which was worse.

Elizabeth remained at her desk, her fingers brushing the edge of the warrant she had threatened to sign. She did not pick it up. Instead, she stared into the flames licking at the hearth, their flickering light reflecting in her eyes. The choices she had made, the power she wielded, and the trust she had lost—none of it showed on her face. But in the silence of her chambers, the consequences of her actions loomed as vast and unrelenting as the shadow she cast.

Richard stepped into the dimly lit interior of the Angel, the warm glow of candles casting flickering shadows on the stained wood walls. The raucous noise of patrons enjoying their evening washed over him, but it didn't reach him. His mood was a storm cloud in the room's amber glow, and the weight of his earlier encounter with the queen pressed on him like a vise.

Nonny saw him immediately. She didn't glide toward him as much as she stalked, her sharp gaze locking onto his with the precision of an arrow finding its mark.

"Richard Fitzwarren," she said, her voice low and cutting, though her lips curved into a smile. "You look like the devil himself spat you out."

"Good evening, Nonny," Richard replied, his tone clipped, his eyes dark.

"Good is it?" she said, arching a brow and linking her arm with his, her hold firm.

Richard didn't answer immediately, his hand tracing the edge of the nearest table. "I've had a conversation of some import."

"You forget, I know everything. I know you've come from the court, and I know you are out of favour," Nonny said.

Richard's head snapped toward her, his eyes narrowing, but he didn't deny it.

"Well," Nonny continued, leaning closer, her voice dropping so only he could hear, "what verdict did the queen deliver today? Did she crown you with laurels or cast you to the wolves?"

"She doesn't cast anyone," Richard said, though the words sounded hollow even to his own ears. "She acts as she must."

# A Queen's Rebel

Nonny tilted her head, her lips curving into a knowing smile. "Flesh and blood. Fallible and cruel is a woman. Remind me, was it Plato who said that?"

"Perlinus. She is not *just* a woman," Richard replied sharply, his jaw tightening.

"Oh, but she is," Nonny said, her voice soft but unyielding. "You've been playing hound to her hunter for so long, you forgot to look for the snare."

Richard turned away, his hand clenching into a fist. The anger roiling beneath his skin was a tempest, not easily soothed. "You don't know her, Nonny," he said, his voice low and dangerous.

"No," Nonny said, stepping into his line of sight again, her dark eyes pinning him in place. "But I know you. And I know that look. That cold, furious look of a man who's had his loyalty turned against him once too often."

Richard's silence was answer enough, and Nonny pressed her advantage, her voice softening. "Perhaps it's time you remembered who else holds a claim to you."

His gaze flicked to hers, cold and unyielding. "What do you mean?"

Nonny's smile was slow, her eyes glinting with something like mischief. "You've forgotten, haven't you? If you dig through the rubble of your memory, you'll find it. A vow. A promise. A wife."

Richard's face darkened, his eyes narrowing as if her words were a blow.

"I wonder," Nonny continued lightly, "if your loyalty might be better placed elsewhere. To the woman who shares your name, perhaps?"

Richard didn't answer. His hand clenched and unclenched at his side, his eyes burning into hers with the force of a man torn between fury and reason.

Nonny stepped back, satisfied. "Think on it, mon cher," she said softly.

Sam Burnell

The sun hung low in the sky, its golden light spilling across the rolling fields and dappling the quiet house in a warm, honeyed glow. The air smelled of freshly turned earth, and the faint hum of insects filled the silence. It was a day of peace—a stark contrast to the cold and storms Richard had endured at Cumnor, both within and without. The world here felt untouched by the schemes, betrayals, and bloodshed he had left behind.

Richard's steps slowed as he approached the gate, his hand brushing the weathered wood. Beyond it lay the house he had arranged for Lizbet and the child. The house was not as he remembered it. When last he had seen it dark skies had made the windows look bleak and uninviting, now they glittered in the sunlight, each small pane catching the sunlight, its garden a riot of blooms that swayed gently in the breeze. The house calm a he had not expected.

Richard's hand rested on the gate, fingers curling loosely around it as he paused. He stood there for what felt like an eternity, watching the house. The windows glinted in the sunlight, reflecting the world outside rather than offering a glimpse of what lay within. Did he truly have the right to disturb this peace?

The question hung heavy in his mind. Here was a life untouched by his schemes, untainted by the lies he had woven and the blood he had spilled. His presence, his very shadow, would change everything. Did he dare cross the threshold? Or should he leave them to the tranquility he had worked so hard to secure?

He closed his eyes briefly, his hand tightening on the gate as indecision clawed at him. His instinct was to turn away, to leave before his presence shattered the delicate serenity of this place. He had done enough—hadn't he? Yet, the pull was undeniable, an ache he couldn't quite ignore.

# A Queen's Rebel

Just as he was about to release the gate and step back, a sudden burst of barking shattered the stillness. A dog, large and black, came bounding toward him, its tail erect, ears pricked, barking furiously. Richard instinctively stiffened, his hand tightening on the gate.

"Cease!"

The command came from behind the dog, a voice clear and familiar. Lizbet's voice.

She emerged from the shadow of the house, her skirts gathered in one hand as she hurried after the dog. The moment she saw Richard, she froze mid-step. The world seemed to hold its breath.

Their eyes met, and in that instant, the distance between them vanished. Neither moved, neither spoke. The air between them was charged, heavy with unspoken words and the weight of shared history. Her face, a mixture of surprise and something softer—recognition, perhaps, or understanding—held him captive.

The dog bounded back to her side, nudging her leg, but Lizbet didn't break her gaze. Slowly, hesitantly, Richard pushed the gate open and stepped through.

The faint creak of the gate was the only sound as he crossed the threshold. Lizbet remained still, her breath catching as he stopped a few paces from her. The space between them was nothing compared to the weight of all that had gone unspoken.

The sun cast its warm light over them both, the dog circling Richard briefly before trotting off into the garden. Still, neither of them spoke. Words felt unnecessary, too heavy for a moment so fragile.

Richard's hand twitched at his side, as if reaching for something unseen. Lizbet's lips parted, but no sound emerged.

And then, with a slow, deliberate step, he moved closer. The quiet enveloped them once more, but the silence was no longer oppressive. It was something else entirely—an understanding, a beginning, a fragile truce.

Richard and Lizbet stood only a step apart. His eyes, darker than usual, searched her face, lingering on the faint curve of her lips and the softness in her gaze.

Lizbet's hands tightened around the fabric of her skirts, her breath shallow. She had so many questions, too many emotions warring within her. Anger, relief, confusion—but above all, there was a warmth that refused to be extinguished, one that flared brighter now as she looked into his face.

Richard reached up slowly, his hand hovering in the air before brushing a stray strand of her dark hair away from her cheek. The touch was so light it barely registered, but Lizbet felt it as though it burned. Her eyes fluttered closed for a brief moment, a tremor passing through her as his hand lingered near her face.

"Lizbet," he murmured, her name rough on his lips, as if it carried more weight than he could bear.

She opened her eyes, her gaze locking onto his. "Why are you here, Richard?" she whispered, her voice trembling, not from fear but from the overwhelming intensity of the moment.

"For you," he said simply, the words raw, stripped of his usual layers of guarded cynicism.

A silence followed, but it was no longer empty. Lizbet tilted her head slightly, her eyes searching his face as though trying to decide if she could trust what she saw there. He made no move to close the space between them, waiting, as if afraid that any sudden motion would break the fragile thread tying them together.

It was Lizbet who leaned forward first, hesitantly, her lips parting as she drew in a breath. Richard's hand, still near her cheek, moved to cradle her face, his thumb brushing lightly along her skin. The warmth of his touch sent a shiver down her spine, and she stopped just short of him, her breath mingling with his.

"Lizbet," he whispered again, his voice almost a plea.

She closed the final distance, their lips meeting in a kiss so tentative, so feather-light, it was as if they were afraid to disturb the air around them. His other hand found her waist, steadying her as the kiss deepened just slightly, the barest press of his lips against hers sending a jolt of warmth through her chest.

Lizbet's hands released her skirts and rose to rest against his chest, her fingers curling into the fabric of his doublet. She felt the rapid beat of his heart beneath her palm, and it steadied her, gave her the courage to lean into him fully.

The kiss broke naturally, as soft and unhurried as it had begun. Richard's forehead rested against hers, his hand still cupping her cheek. Neither spoke, their breathing the only sound in the stillness.

In that moment, the chaos of the world beyond the garden seemed to fall away. There was only the warmth of the sun, the scent of lavender, and the quiet promise lingering in the air between them.

For the first time in what felt like an age, he allowed himself to breathe deeply, to let the weight he had carried for so long slip just slightly from his shoulders. The world had always been a battlefield, a place of cunning plans and dangerous games, but here... here was something else entirely. Here was a life that did not demand his vigilance, his sacrifice. Here was a chance.

Richard's eyes returned to Lizbet. She glanced up, catching his gaze, and her lips curved into a soft, uncertain smile. It wasn't the confident smile of a woman accustomed to winning a game; it was something far more vulnerable, far more genuine. It struck him deeply, like an arrow loosed straight into his soul.

Sam Burnell

There was a future here, he realised, one that was yet unwritten. A future that would not be dictated by the ambitions of courts or the machinations of powerful men. It was a future that was fragile, untested, but filled with possibility.

For so long, he had lived in a world where every move was calculated, every word weighed, every decision fraught with consequence. But this... this was something new. A blank page, waiting for a story to unfold.

"Will you stay?" she asked, her voice barely above a whisper.

Richard hesitated, the instinct to guard himself rising unbidden. But then he nodded, a small, almost imperceptible motion. "I think I might."

Her smile widened, a glimmer of hope lighting her eyes. "Good."

As the sun warmed the earth around them, Richard felt something shift within him. The road ahead was unknown, the path unmarked, but for the first time in years, he wasn't afraid of what lay ahead. The future was his to shape, and here, in this quiet, sunlit haven, he felt he might finally find what he had never dared to seek.

A future waiting to be written.

**THE END**

Printed in Great Britain
by Amazon